Heartbreaker

"Who says I was stealing anything?" Adelaide asked.

Clayborn stepped closer, his words low and dark. "I know a thief when I see one." He reached for her, and she held her breath, wondering where he'd touch her. What the leather of his glove would feel like on her skin.

Except he didn't touch her skin. Instead, he said, softly, "Red."

For a moment she didn't understand, and then she felt a tug at her temple, where a lock of her hair had escaped.

Adelaide went hot with his discovery and the sudden realization that he was close and warm and he smelled fresh, like citrus—a scent that did not come with the South Bank.

It was not a scent for Adelaide.

This man was not for her, which made him a wicked temptation, like sweets and silks and purses and pocket watches. Like all of them put together. Too much for a thief to resist.

So she tilted her face up to his and stole him. For a moment. A heartbeat.

Intending to give him back.

By Sarah MacLean

Hell's Belles
BOMBSHELL
HEARTBREAKER

The Bareknuckle Bastards
WICKED AND THE WALLFLOWER
BRAZEN AND THE BEAST
DARING AND THE DUKE

Scandal & Scoundrel
THE ROGUE NOT TAKEN
A SCOT IN THE DARK
THE DAY OF THE DUCHESS

The Rules of Scoundrels
A ROGUE BY ANY OTHER NAME
ONE GOOD EARL DESERVES A LOVER
NO GOOD DUKE GOES UNPUNISHED
NEVER JUDGE A LADY BY HER COVER

Love by Numbers
NINE RULES TO BREAK WHEN ROMANCING A RAKE
TEN WAYS TO BE ADORED WHEN LANDING A LORD
ELEVEN SCANDALS TO START TO WIN
A DUKE'S HEART

THE SEASON

SARAH MacLEAN

HEART BREAKER

A HELL'S BELLES NOVEL

AVONBOOKS

An Imprint of HarperCollinsPublishers

HEARTBREAKER. Copyright © 2022 by Sarah Trabucchi. All rights reserved. Printed in the United States of America. No part of this book may be used or reproduced in any manner whatsoever without written permission except in the case of brief quotations embodied in critical articles and reviews. For information, address HarperCollins Publishers, 195 Broadway, New York, NY 10007.

First Avon Books mass market printing: August 2022
First Avon Books hardcover printing: August 2022

Print Edition ISBN: 978-0-06-305678-7
Digital Edition ISBN: 978-0-06-305588-9

Cover design by Amy Halperin
Cover illustration by Alan Ayers
Cover images © Depositphotos Inc.; azzardo © 123RF.COM
Chapter opener art © Peter Hermes Furian / Shutterstock, Inc.

Avon, Avon & logo, and Avon Books & logo are registered trademarks of HarperCollins Publishers in the United States of America and other countries.

HarperCollins is a registered trademark of HarperCollins Publishers in the United States of America and other countries.

FIRST EDITION

22 23 24 25 26 BVGM 10 9 8 7 6 5 4 3 2 1

For Louisa,
the absolute best

HEART
BREAKER

Adelaide

St. Stephen's Chapel
South Lambeth
October 1834

Storm clouds, they said, brought good luck on a wedding day.

The bleakness of the sky over the marriage vows, they said, would mark the bleakest point of a union. Sheets of rain, they said, would wash away any ill fortune fated for the couple, leaving only the future, filled with good luck.

After all, they said, weddings were the happiest of days—times for blushing brides and fresh-faced grooms and new frocks and families full to the brim with joy at the prospect of doubling in size. What was a bit of rain against the promise of such happiness?

Bad weather, they said, would make the worst of the day and the match.

But what if the weather was not the worst of the day? What of the match then?

That late October morning, as the rain came in sheets, thunder shaking the rafters, Miss Adelaide Trumbull stood at the altar of St. Stephen's Chapel in South Lambeth, the scents of incense and candle wax all around her, in a frock thieved in the dark of night from Mayfair's finest dressmaker, and considered the possibility that *they* were wrong.

There was nothing blushing about Adelaide, the twenty-one-year-old daughter of Alfie Trumbull, a brute with a fist the size of another man's face. Alfie had put that meaty weapon to good work as soon as he'd been big enough to pack a punch, and he'd built himself a small empire, such as it was, on the South Bank, the head of The Bulls, a gang of thugs and thieves named for the man who'd brought them together. Adelaide had learned fast that if she was to survive her father's violent dominion, she would have to earn her keep, and by six years old, she'd been one of the South Bank's finest nippers—with long, slim, quick fingers that could lift a pocket watch or cut a purse, her mark none the wiser.

A princess of thieves.

And when it came time to marry, there was no question that her father would choose the groom—that was the role of kings, was it not? To marry off their daughters for land or power or an army made exponentially larger by the match.

It did not matter that Adelaide was too tall and too plain, or that John Scully had absolutely no interest in her. Oh, he smiled when she came into the room, and he'd been more than willing to sample the wares, which her father had all but insisted she allow, and when he talked, he did so with the easy patter of a man who knew how to catch flies with honey. But he didn't have any interest in catching Adelaide, so she expected that once she was caught, there'd be far less honey than there would be vinegar.

What mattered was that Scully was the leader of The Boys, a smaller, newer gang making waves on the South Bank. More anarchy than organization, The Boys posed a danger to residents, businesses, and the kingdom belonging to Alfie Trumbull—a man who believed strongly in the adage that friends should be kept close and enemies closer.

If that meant sacrificing his daughter to them, so be it.

Adelaide didn't care for her father. And she highly doubted she would care for her new husband. But this was the life into which she was born, and if she was lucky, she would survive marriage to a monster better than her own mother had. Perhaps John Scully would die young.

A wicked crack of thunder sounded, and it occurred to Adelaide that pondering the death of one's groom while before the parson would likely offset the good luck of the torrential rain outside.

A tiny, wild laugh bubbled out of her. No one noticed.

She adjusted her spectacles and touched her fingers to her throat, where the high lace collar of the wedding gown made for another was too tight.

The priest prattled away, his words a run of stuttering gibberish, born of fear of what might come if he failed in following his instructions, no doubt.

Adelaide made out something about Cana of Galilee as she cast a look at the man she was to marry—rocking back and forth on his heels, as though he had somewhere else to be. Her gaze slid past him, to his mother, seated in the first pew—the one hiding the entrance to the underground cellar that held half-dozen cases of weapons waiting for whatever war Alfie waged next. The older woman's gaze was stern, as though they were before the magistrate and not the minister.

Adelaide's attention shifted to the others in the row. Two young women, Scully's sisters, looking as though they might be rendered unconscious from the boredom of the day. Behind them, a row of men. Scully's brothers, one by blood and the rest by fire. Soon to be her brothers, too, she supposed. Hideously brutish, brows low over eyes, heavy enough to shade their noses, broken so many times over that *smashed* was a better term for their state. They, too, fidgeted.

An ordinary bystander might think the movements the result of a collective fear for souls. That a house of God was not their preferred location for a Saturday morning.

But this was no ordinary house of God, and Adelaide was not an ordinary bystander.

The priest continued, finding enough clarity to say something about hellfire, which Adelaide thought a bit much for a wedding, but perhaps he was attempting to turn the assembly to the light.

Good luck to him.

She shifted, just enough to see her father out of the corner of her eye. Just enough to see that he was not watching the ceremony. Instead, he was staring over her head, past the priest, to the stained glass in the windows beyond.

His meaty fingers tapped against his knee. His jaw worked as he chewed the side of his tongue—a tell that Adelaide had learned early meant she should find a way out of the room, and fast. Squinting through her spectacles, she looked to his boots, still caked with muck from the Rookery beyond. There, touching the heel of one, was the wooden handle of the club that was her father's preferred weapon.

And that's when she realized that she wasn't going to be married that day. It was not to be a merger, but a conquest; her father planned to kill her groom.

She snapped her attention back to the priest, instinct taking over. There was a chalice on the altar behind him. Likely made of pewter, though. Not heavy enough. No, she'd be better with the brass candlestick. The short one on the far side of the altar. She'd have to get there first, up two steps. *Were candlesticks holy?* Adelaide lowered her hand to her skirts, annoyance flaring. If she'd known she was going to have to fight, she would have protested this frock. She rolled one shoulder in the too-tight dress.

There was no way she would be able to swing that candlestick hard enough to do damage. And she needed to be able to do damage.

What kind of animals turned a wedding into a turf war?

And more importantly, what were they waiting for?

"If any here assembled . . ."

Adelaide rolled her eyes. Of *course*. No one liked theater like a lifelong criminal, thinking himself a hero.

". . . has reason for these two to not be joined in holy matrimony . . ."

Beside her, Scully shifted, his hand slipping beneath his coat, to where he no doubt had a blade holstered. Her father wasn't the only one out for blood that day.

"Oh, for God's sake," she muttered.

The priest turned censorious eyes on her, as though no bride would *ever* consider speaking up at this moment. ". . . speak now, or forever hold your peace."

For a moment, silence fell, long and heavy, and for a heartbeat, Adelaide wondered if she was wrong.

She held her breath as thunder boomed, filling the church, reverberating off the centuries-old stones.

The war began.

The assembly was on its feet, fists flying, blades unsheathing, a hatpin or two entering the fray, all punctuated by grunts and shrieks.

Adelaide headed for the candlestick, nimble and quick as she'd ever been—as she'd been trained to be since she was four years old. And while she went, aiming for that brass prize, she did the other thing she'd been doing since she was four years old—she picked pockets. She was no fool, and knew that she might well be on her own after this brawl, with nothing but a stolen, too-tight wedding dress and no coin. Years on the street had taught her to plan for the fight and prepare for the flight.

She took three watches—one while ducking an impressive punch—and two purses heavy with coin, and shoved them up the tight sleeves of her gown, on her way toward her goal. Lifting her too-short skirts, she rushed up the steps, past the priest, now tucked behind the altar—the safest place for a man of the cloth to hide while his borrowed chapel became the stage for a bloody battle.

A shout came from behind her, too close—and she looked back to find one of Scully's men reaching for her, red in the face. "Where are you goin', gel?" He grabbed for the back of her gown, and the fabric stuck like skin, refusing him purchase.

Adelaide increased her speed and grabbed the candlestick, immediately turning and using all the force she could muster to knock him back. "Nowhere with you!"

He howled and grabbed her weapon, yanking her toward him in the moment before he lost consciousness, but Adelaide was ready, releasing it as he fell like a tree. She paused for a half second—less—to consider her options, her mind racing. *Did she want this fight?*

Was it hers?

She was saved from having to answer, a hand coming to her shoulder. Before she could turn and fight, she was pulled backward through a door hidden behind the altar.

It closed with a soft *snick*, the sound of the battle beyond fading away, muffled by wood and stone and distance and the infernal rain, pounding high on the lead-cased windows above.

The soot-covered stained glass barely filtered the dim light from the dark sky beyond. Adelaide grasped for the first weapon she could find. Spinning to face the door, she brandished the book . . . and immediately lowered it.

The woman just inside the door smiled. "Decided against walloping me?"

"I don't imagine eternal punishment is easy for those who strike nuns," Adelaide replied.

"Even worse for those who strike nuns with the Holy Bible."

Adelaide returned the book to its place.

The nun moved past her, to the far side of the room, where she retrieved a hamper from a low cupboard. She set it on the table between them, next to the Bible, then stepped back from it.

Adelaide eyed the basket and the woman warily. "You ain't like no nun I've ever known."

"Have you known many nuns?"

She considered the question. She hadn't, but that wasn't the point. She pushed her spectacles up her nose. "Who are you for?"

The woman's brows rose. "Is that not clear?"

"I mean, are you The Bulls or The Boys?"

The nun tilted her head. "I could ask you the same question."

Neither.

Adelaide kept quiet.

"Imagine this, Adelaide Trumbull," the nun said, her blue gaze sharp and full of truth. "What if I were for *you*?"

Adelaide lifted her chin. What if there was a third path? A better one?

Impossible. There were no better paths for girls born in Lambeth. Not even for the princesses born there. Especially not for them.

High above, Adelaide found the face of one of the stained-glass figures and found herself envious of the shrouded woman's position. Unidentifiable. Unseen by all but a very few. Unimportant. Rain pounded on the window, threatening to shatter the already cracked panes of blue glass that made the figure's body.

A scream from beyond penetrated the quiet of the room.

"You need somewhere to put your loot, do you not?" The nun who did not seem so nunnish indicated the hamper once more.

Adelaide met the woman's eyes, the trio of pocket watches heavy and warm against her skin up her sleeve. "What loot?"

The nun lifted a knowing brow.

Adelaide approached the basket, uncertain of what it would reveal, and knowing that whatever it was would change her life. Possibly not for the better.

Though, to be honest, it could not get much worse.

She lifted the lid to reveal a small portrait in a round silver frame. She looked to the woman watching her carefully from across the room. "Me."

"So you know what is within was for you all along."

Adelaide considered the door and what was beyond it. "You knew what he planned," she said. Her father. The battle beyond. The war that would come.

A nod.

"You, and who else?"

A little head tilt. "That comes later."

"How do I know there is a later?"

"How do you know there is a later out there?"

The nun made a fair point.

Adelaide reached into the hamper and extracted a pile of clothing. Trousers. A peaked cap. A shirt and waistcoat and coat. A black umbrella.

"They'll be looking for a bride," the other woman explained, lifting a chin in the direction of the altar, where half of Lambeth's muscle no doubt turned the church stones red. "One in a stolen frock."

Adelaide didn't misunderstand. The clothing was a disguise—one that would never work in the long run, but would absolutely work for the next thirty minutes. For the next thirty yards, once she opened the door and stepped into the rain.

Except . . .

"There's nowhere to go," she said, shaking her head. Princesses didn't leave their kingdoms. Who were they without them?

The nun nodded to the hamper. "Are you sure?"

Adelaide peeked inside the now-empty basket to find a small blue calling card at the bottom, thick and lush—

the finest paper she'd ever seen, inked with a beautiful indigo bell. Though the rectangle was the size of a calling card, there was no name on it. Only that bell, and an address in Mayfair.

The bell, the address, and, when she turned it over, the message.

It is time for you to disappear, Adelaide.
Come and see me.
Duchess

And like that, the third path rolled out before Adelaide, clean and clear. And coveted.

Turned out, they were right.

Rain made luck on a wedding day, after all.

Chapter One

The South Bank
Five years later

There were any number of words London might use to describe Adelaide Frampton.

North of the river, in Hyde Park and on Bond Street and in Mayfair ballrooms, when people spoke of the bespectacled distant cousin to the Duchess of Trevescan, which was rare, they used words like *plain*. If pressed, they might add *tall*. Or perhaps *ordinary*. Certainly *spinster* was not out of the realm of possibility for the twenty-six-year-old woman who had absolutely no hope of prospects, what with her flame red hair always tucked tightly beneath a pristine cap and the way she wore her collars high and *out of fashion*, her frocks *drab*, and her face *common*, without rouge or kohl.

Barely seen, rarely heard, neither titled nor rich, never droll, lacking in charm or extraordinary skill. *Uninteresting. Unassuming. Unremarkable* and therefore *unnoticeable*, allowed into Mayfair thanks only to a faraway bloodline.

South of the river, however, in warehouses and laundries and workhouses, in the rookeries and streets where Adelaide had been raised not Adelaide Frampton but Adelaide Trumbull, she was *legend*. Little girls across

Lambeth would tuck into their beds at night, hungry for hope and the promise of a future, and their mothers and aunts and older sisters would whisper the stories of Addie Trumbull, the greatest nipper the South Bank had ever seen—fingers so fast she'd never once been caught—and a future so bright that she'd fought in the war that had merged The Bulls and The Boys, ensuring her father was king of both before she'd left for a future beyond the coal clouds and the mud puddles and filth of Lambeth.

Addie Trumbull, the story went, *had left a princess and become a queen.*

Remarkable how legends grew without proof, even in places where the soil was salted and the fields lay fallow. Especially in those places.

It did not matter that Addie had never returned. Someone's cousin's friend's sister worked as a maid in the new queen's court, and had seen Addie there. She was married to a good, rich man, and slept on goose down and wore silk frocks and ate off golden plates.

Sleep well, little ones; if you are good and learn early to cut purses and move fast, you, too, might have a future like Addie Trumbull.

Legend. Myth. Luminary.

Unimaginable.

But like all gossip from north of the river, and all stories from south of it, the truth was a little of both and a lot of neither. And because of that, Adelaide remained a mystery in both places, which suited her quite well, as *unnoticeable* and *unimaginable* endowed her equally with the only quality she cared to have—invisibility.

And so, here is the truth: Adelaide Frampton was the greatest thief London never saw.

Her invisibility was on full display on that particular October afternoon in 1839 when, as the autumn sun crept low across the sky, she entered the warehouse that acted as the official headquarters of London's largest gang of muscle for hire, Alfred Trumbull's Bully Boys. The crew had been renamed in the wake of their violent merger on her failed wedding day with a portmanteau devised by her father—a man who knew well how an inexpensive gift could bring bad men to a cause.

It had been five years since Adelaide had seen the inside of the warehouse—five years since she'd left Lambeth and begun a new life across the river—but she remembered the place as though no time had passed at all. It remained full to the brim with the gang's stolen goods—booze and jewels, silks and sterling, and a collection of firearms that should have blown them all up by now, considering the group's notorious lack of sense.

Wearing a high-collared, trim fitting navy coat over a dark shirt and drab skirts, Adelaide made her way through the building. The clothes, along with the unadorned grey cap that hid her hair, were designed for ease of movement during just this kind of activity, ensuring that when she tucked into shadows or ducked behind crates of contraband, she disappeared.

Three separate patrols stayed her passage to the top floor, where her father's office sat empty. Alfie Trumbull took "tea" every afternoon at four o'clock at the Wild Pheasant—a bordello he owned in the shadow of Lambeth Palace. The location of the place, mere yards from where the Archbishop of Canterbury laid his head, was no doubt part of its charm for Alfie, who had always thought himself the highest of beings.

The first patrol had required her to make a quick stop behind the stairs on the ground floor, the second sent her into hiding at the back corner of the warehouse, and the third had nearly caught her as she slipped inside her father's office, sliding between several large barrels of whiskey to wait them out.

Five years, and while the world was changing with wild speed beyond those walls, absolutely nothing was different inside Alfie's dominion. Same patrol schedule. Same hiding places. Same conversations—a bout that had sent a boy to the surgeon the night before but won them a decent amount of blunt.

Adelaide waited for them to lumber off, grateful that her father continued to value brawn over brains when it came to his watchmen. Once they were gone, Adelaide moved to Alfie's workspace and sat, stilling in surprise.

Not everything was the same. Her father had bought himself a desk. One with drawers and locks and a bright shine that Adelaide imagined gave him pride every time he sat behind it.

He wouldn't be happy when he realized his locks were no match for a thief.

Quickly, Adelaide extracted a snuffbox from the deep inside pocket of her coat and pulled a long gold chain from beneath the collar of her shirt. At the end of the chain hung a narrow brass tube, the tip of which she removed before opening the box to reveal the heads of a dozen brass keys. In seconds, she selected the proper one and attached it to the pendant.

Turning her newly created key in the desk lock, she reveled in the clean *thunk* of the steel tumblers within and began her search. She did not find what she was looking for in the first two drawers, nor was it in the deep, locked drawer at the bottom of the heavy desk. Except . . .

She extracted three heavy ledgers from the drawer, deep and well balanced on casters—her father had spared no expense—and set them on the desk, calculating their height before pushing back in the chair and considering the exterior of the drawer itself. A little smile played across her lips. Alfie Trumbull didn't trust his boys after all.

Sliding her fingers over the wood inside, Adelaide found the hidden catch in seconds and threw it to reveal a secret compartment beneath the drawer's false bottom.

"There you are," she whispered, triumph flaring as she lifted a tiny black book, small enough to fit in a gentleman's pocket. She opened it, confirming that it was what she sought: the locations of the eleven caches of munitions The Bully Boys had hidden throughout the city, along with the names of the Boys assigned to each, the schedules of the changings of the guard, and the provenance of each of the weapons within, each meticulously accounted by Alfie Trumbull himself.

Slipping the book into her own pocket, Adelaide moved to restore the drawer to rights before pausing, her gaze falling to the other item in the hidden compartment.

A block of ordinary wood.

With a little frown, she reached for it, lifting the six-inch cube. A lifetime of thieving had taught Adelaide that ordinary things were rarely that—especially when her father kept them in false-bottomed drawers—and so, she did what she often did when something piqued her curiosity.

She took it.

The light was fading fast inside the building, so she worked quickly. Replacing the bottom of the drawer, she returned the ledger books, dismantled her skeleton key, and stood, tucking her snuffbox away and settling the wooden cube into the crook of her arm.

"That doesn't belong to you."

Her heart leapt into her throat as she looked to the doorway, her free hand already sliding inside her skirts to the false pocket at her thigh, headed for the blade she kept there. She preferred to remain invisible and not leave a mess on missions, but she wasn't above taking out this bruiser if she had to.

He was the opposite of invisible, tall and lean, standing in the shadows just inside the office door, peaked cap pulled low over his brow, doing absolutely nothing to hide the sharp lines of his handsome face—a long, straight nose and an angled jaw that appeared to have been honed by the best of bladesmiths.

This was not one of her father's bruisers.

Even if she hadn't been able to hear it in his proper

voice, or see it in the way he held himself, as though it had never occurred to him that he did not belong in a place—even a dark warehouse owned by a hardened criminal . . . even if he didn't look as though he'd spent his youth learning to fence instead of fight . . . it was the nose that gave it away.

He'd never once spent a night hungry. Never once had to brawl for his safety or his supper. Never once had to steal, because he had obviously been born into all he had.

The man was money.

And he was going to get them both caught.

She stood and headed around the side of the desk for the door, refusing to look at him or speak to him, considering her options. She couldn't knife money. But she could certainly serve him a facer if he didn't let her leave the room.

Except, when she got to the door, he stopped her. He didn't touch her—he simply set one hand to the door-jamb and said, "Once again, that does not belong to you."

"And what," she retorted. "It belongs to you?"

He stiffened at the words, as though he was offended that she would deign to reply to him.

Definitely money. With absolutely no claim on this place. And he thought to tell her—Adelaide Frampton, the best thief Lambeth had ever seen—what she could and could not steal? The man should know his betters.

"It does, as a matter of fact."

Surprised, she lifted her gaze to his face, past the rough scruff on his jaw and the low brim of his cap—a meager attempt at a disguise, as Adelaide recognized him instantly. And bit back a groan.

He wasn't just money. He wasn't just *some toff.*

And he most definitely wasn't *handsome.*

The man in front of her was the Duke of Clayborn. The absolute worst of the aristocracy, with a stiff upper lip and a stick up his—

"Oy!"

The shout came from outside the door, where she could see a decent-sized watchman headed their way, beady eyes trained on her.

So much for invisible.

"Dammit, Clayborn," she whispered, her grip tightening on the box. "Of course you would turn up here and see us both killed."

He couldn't conceal the surprise on his face. "You recognize me?"

Of course she did. She'd know this particular duke anywhere. He was impossible not to know. The last time he'd been this close to her, they'd been north of the river in the heart of Mayfair, and he'd given Adelaide a scathing setdown—the kind arrogant, rich, titled men adored delivering with cool disdain to women far below their station. He was lucky she wasn't in the habit of brandishing her blade at dinner.

Though, if anyone could drive her to it, it was this man.

Stern and cold . . . and absolutely rubbish at remaining unnoticed.

"You there! Wot you doin' in Alfie's office!"

Adelaide didn't wait. Instead, she took off, ducking under his arm and flying down the hallway away from the guard.

"Shit, boys! 'Ere's intruders up here!"

"My cue," she said before flying down the stairs to the first floor of the warehouse, calculating that she had less than a minute to get herself lost in the shadows. If she could get herself to the far end of the building, where the large door stood open to the fast-darkening street, she might be able to disappear.

Except she wasn't alone.

The Duke of Clayborn was matching her move for move, light on his feet and faster than she would have thought a man of his size would be, but no less difficult to hide. Which was not her problem.

She tossed him a look. "Get gone, Duke."

"Not a chance."

With an irritated sigh, Adelaide checked behind her as they exited the stairwell, their original pursuer halfway down the stairs from above, and three others coming up from below. Biting back a curse, she headed down a long row of stacked crates, as far as she dared before tucking herself behind one.

He slid in beside her, barely there a moment before he inhaled, clearly planning to speak.

Adelaide covered his mouth with her hand, the scruff of his day-old beard rough-soft against her fingers. Not that she was interested in how he felt against her fingers. If the fire in his blue gaze was any indication, he wasn't interested in that, either. He was annoyed, no doubt, that she was taking charge. Well, he'd have to get used to it if he wanted out of here unscathed.

She shook her head and pointed to beyond the stack of crates, where two of Alfie Trumbull's guards thoroughly searched the passageway. Leaning in, she whispered close to his ear, barely a sound, "Can you fight?"

As she hadn't removed her hand from his lips, he raised a superior brow in reply, his offended answer clear as a bell. *Of course I can fight.*

He likely couldn't fight worth a damn—aristocrats were generally useless—but there wasn't a choice. Adelaide hadn't been caught in sixteen years, and she wasn't about to start now. The men approached.

Releasing him, she shifted silently on the balls of her feet and reached beneath her skirts, slipping her blade from the sheath inside her boot with one hand, clutching the wooden cube in the other. She put a shoulder to the stack of crates that shielded them.

Five yards.

He shifted with her, matching her stance, facing her, his shoulder to the rough-hewn wood.

Two.

The leather of his gloves creaked as his fingers curved

into fists. He'd need them. What they were about to do would bring every guard in the place.

One.

With a prayer that he could, indeed, fight, she nodded once. Twice.

"Now," he mouthed. As one, they pushed, knocking the tower of boxes toward the pair of bruisers that were nearly on top of them.

Twin shouts were punctuated with an ear-splitting crash, but Adelaide didn't stay to look at their handiwork. Instead, she ran, getting nearly as far as the skeleton stairs at the front of the warehouse—the ones that led to the streets outside and freedom.

Clayborn was on her heels, and though she did not look back—no time—she did call back to him, "This is no place for a duke."

"Ideal place for a lady, is it?" he retorted.

She wasn't a lady, but she didn't correct him, telling herself that it was because she was too busy tearing down the stairs. She headed for the door, where two guards were waiting. Without hesitating, she clocked one in the head with the wood block. "I was doing just fine before you turned up." She ducked as the other man swung a ham-sized fist at her head.

She heard it connect with a heavy *thwack*, and something she didn't care for had her turning back to see what had happened.

Clayborn had caught the blow in one large hand. "That wasn't very gentlemanly," he said, all calm, the thug's eyes going wide at the words. "And you're lucky you didn't strike her." He punctuated the words with an excellent facer, dropping the villain to his knees.

Her eyes went wide in surprise as she stared at the unconscious man. "What if he *had* struck me?" When the duke did not reply, she added, "So you *can* fight."

He tossed her another irritated look. "I don't lie."

Of course he took offense to that. Honestly, it was surprising the whole of the South Bank hadn't gone up in flames when the Duke of Clayborn arrived like the angel of judgment.

She'd barely had time to roll her eyes at him before they were off again, out of the warehouse and into the street beyond, Adelaide quickly ducking behind a pile of rubbish and slipping her knife back into the pocket of her skirts, where a scabbard was fastened tight at her thigh.

Clayborn watched her and she ignored the heat that somehow came from his cool gaze. "The Duchess of Trevescan's cousin, are you?"

She hid the surprise that flared when he identified her. For a woman who was practiced at remaining unnoticed and invisible, the Duke of Clayborn's undivided focus proved unnerving, especially since it was clear her secret was out, and he was fully capable of returning to Mayfair and telling the whole of London that she was nothing close to an aristocrat's cousin. Still, Adelaide brazened it through. "What, you don't have remarkable fruit on the family tree?"

He watched her for a moment, and then said, "None so remarkable as you."

Oh. She'd return to those five words at a later time.

But now, Adelaide had somewhere to be. "This is as far as I take you, Duke. They won't come for an aristocrat in daylight, but you'd best hurry if you want to avoid meeting Lambeth's finest."

Before he could reply, she was off, disappeared into the afternoon throngs knowing that if *she* were caught, there would be no quarter.

For Adelaide Frampton, née Trumbull, daylight in Lambeth was cold comfort, as her father and The Bully Boys ran all of the South Bank, and she would find no help anywhere here—not because she didn't have supporters, but because they lacked the strength to go up against London's largest gang of street thugs.

She understood that truth intimately; she'd only gained

the strength to fight The Bully Boys once she'd left the muck of Lambeth, so she didn't blame those who had no means to do the same.

Within minutes, the felled brutes in the warehouse would turn into half a dozen outside, so Adelaide turned north, aiming to disappear into the narrow labyrinthine streets of the South Bank—the maze she'd learned before she'd learned her own name.

Unfortunately, her pursuers had received the same lessons.

She'd made a half-dozen turns before she was trapped, somewhere between St. George's Circus and New Cut. One of Alfie's men stood like a silent, massive sentry on one end, and two more approached, blades out, from behind.

The big one tilted his chin at the cube beneath Adelaide's arm. "You've taken something that don't belong to you, gel."

She touched a hand to her cap, hoping it would keep her from being recognized. Five years away didn't make a new face, and didn't change the color of one's hair. "More than one thing, but who's counting?"

His companion growled.

Adelaide would wager all she had that these two had no idea what she carried. She had no idea herself, and she was surely the cleverest of the assembly.

Before she could say as much, however, the brute behind her spoke. "Set it down, girl, and no one gets hurt."

She definitely wasn't giving it back now. Adelaide extracted her watch, checking the time. Damn. She was going to be late. "I think that if I set this down, someone will absolutely get hurt."

He grinned, showing several missing teeth, no doubt knocked out. "Why not try it and see?"

The trio closed in on her, their lack of hesitation leaving little time for a body to calculate its next move—but Adelaide was no ordinary foe. Within seconds, she knew how hard she would have to swing to knock out Teeth, how long it would take for the others to reach her, and what she'd have to do to bring them down. Angles were measured, force calculated, timing predicted.

She lowered herself to one knee. Set the oak cube to the ground.

"That's it, love," Teeth said, closer now. Her hand moved, searching for the false pocket in her skirts, aiming for the blade strapped to her thigh. And then . . . "Hang on . . ." he said, softly, the tone shifting. No longer full of disdain and loathing.

Now full of something else. Something far more dangerous.

Recognition.

"You're—" he began, but before he could finish the thought, all hell broke loose.

Teeth's attention shot over her head even as Adelaide turned to look at the commotion behind her, the two brutes who'd been heading for her suddenly locked in a battle with the Duke of Clayborn.

Dammit. This was a man who had a home in Mayfair and a seat in Parliament. Did he have nothing better to do than follow her through Lambeth?

Returning to the situation at hand, she reached down for the block of wood at her feet, clasped it in two hands, and brought it up sharply to knock Teeth back. Adelaide was running before he cracked his head against the cobblestones.

A shout sounded behind her.

She shouldn't look. She hadn't asked Clayborn to get involved. She certainly didn't require a protector. This would serve him right.

That, and she had to get out of there before someone else recognized her.

She looked anyway, just in time to see one of The Bully Boys land a heavy blow to the Duke of Clayborn's face.

He came back swinging like his life depended on it.
And it did, she supposed; her father's men were not known
for mercy. The duke held his own, however, landing a
tight jab and another, sending one of his opponents to his
knees before turning to the other, throwing a wicked up-
percut, knocking the man off balance and straight back
into the closest wall, to sink slowly toward the ground.

Adelaide watched until the body slumped over, then
turned her attention to Clayborn. "Impressive."

She could not see his eyes in the afternoon shadows,
but she could feel his gaze on her as he studied her before speaking . . . the words so even and deep one would
never know he'd been in an alleyway brawl moments
earlier. "You're welcome."

Ever the arrogant bastard. Her gaze narrowed on him.
"Was I to have thanked you?"

"Yes." A muscle flickered in his jaw as he stepped over
one of his foes, his movements long and graceful. Not
that Adelaide noticed. At all.

"For what?"

He waved at the ground. "Is it unclear?"

She considered the men writhing at his feet. "Ah, I am
to thank you for your tribute? As though you are a cat
and you've delivered a fat rat to my kitchen door?"

"I thought you might thank me for saving your
pretty—"

Her eyes went wide as he cut himself off. "Why, Your
Grace, were you about to use foul language?"

He scowled at her. "I confess, you tempt me."

She'd like to tempt him.

Now where had that come from?

He extended a hand toward her. "My box, please."

So it was a box. Of course it was. She looked down
at it, turning it over in her hands as she backed toward
the exit to the alleyway, stepping gingerly over the prone
body of her own opponent, putting distance between
them. "What's in it?"

His lips flattened into a thin line and she ignored the way she noticed. "Nothing of import."

"Alfie Trumbull thought it was important enough to steal it."

"Alfie Trumbull thought it was worth enough money to steal it."

Except Alfie didn't like robbery; he didn't think it was worth the risk compared to broader, more lucrative crimes. So whatever was in this box, it *was* worth money. And a great deal of money if her father had risked stealing it from a duke.

Even if it wasn't worth money, it had brought a duke to Lambeth, so whatever was inside was a secret worth having.

As Adelaide had made a life of trading in powerful men's secrets, and was currently very interested in secrets adjacent to this particular powerful man, she wasn't about to give this one up easily. She tossed Clayborn a crooked smile. "Those are the same thing on the South Bank, Duke. But here we play by simple rules. She who finds, keeps."

With that, she ran again, heading from the alleyway at a clip—aiming for the docks.

Of course, he followed. "It's private," he ground out as he kept pace with her, the words tortured from him, as though he resented having to speak them. Which of course he would—this was not a man who would deign to share with someone as common as Adelaide.

"That much is clear, or you wouldn't be skulking about a well-guarded warehouse playing fancy dress." She slid him a look. "You can't possibly have thought you wouldn't be noticed."

He ran a hand over his beard. "Forgive me if I am not as deft at disguise as you." He sent a cool look over her from head to toe, though Adelaide did not feel so cool under his scrutiny. "You thought you could simply walk in there, thieve from the head of one of London's most powerful gangs, and walk out?"

"In fact, I was doing just that until you sent the entire afternoon sideways."

"I was protecting you!" he growled, matching her annoyance with his own.

Something thrummed through her at the words, stern and direct, and she found herself wondering when she'd last encountered a man's protective instincts. In her experience, men left her to her own devices. She wasn't sure how the alternative felt, honestly. Strange. Warm.

Not that she would *ever* admit it. "Really? And how's that gone? Protecting me?"

"Did you fail to notice that I brought down several men big as houses? Or do you require new spectacles?"

Adelaide adjusted the eyewear in question higher upon her nose and made a right turn, then a quick left, sliding into another alleyway. "My eyesight is impeccable." She was tiring. Skirts were heavy and unwieldy—yet another way the world kept women back. One hand fell to her waist, where wide silk ribbons tucked in at her waist.

He followed, keeping pace with ease. "And what—you were going to take on a warehouse full of bruisers after stealing from them?" He nodded to the cube in the crook of her elbow. "Poor choice of weapon."

She had to get away from him. He saw too much. Asked too much. She should give him the box and cut him loose—it was what he wanted, and it wasn't as though she needed it. She'd only taken it because it intrigued her.

The problem was, now that she knew it belonged to him, it intrigued her even more.

Which was as irritating as he was, frankly. She tucked the box under her arm and increased her speed. "A girl must make do in this modern age. So sorry, Duke, but I have somewhere to be, and I do not have time for . . . you."

With a tug, she pulled the final fastening at the waist of her drab, grey skirts, the fabric flying out behind her, revealing a pair of slim navy trousers adorned with a thigh holster for her blade and tall leather boots, releasing her to unencumbered speed.

He made a sound of utter surprise behind her, and she dearly wished she could turn to see the shock on his stern face. Resisting the urge, Adelaide slipped into the narrow gap ahead, grateful for the element of surprise and the additional speed the loss of her skirts had provided . . . she had gained enough ground to topple a pile of barrels and leave her gentleman scoundrel behind.

Not *her* gentleman scoundrel. She wanted nothing to do with him.

His curse followed her—but he did not.

Triumphant, Adelaide burst from the dim light into the late afternoon sun of the Thames hard at work, tide high and packed with boats and people hurrying to and fro to complete their work before dark. She looked upriver, relieved. She'd make her appointment after all.

She slowed her pace, removing her coat and cap and tossing them behind a pile of wood crates, sliding her snuffbox and Alfie's book into her trouser pockets before detaching a peaked cap from where it had been pinned at her waist. Pulling the brim low over her eyes, she lowered her hips and broadened her stride. The woman in the drab dress was gone, replaced by an ordinary dockworker, tall and slim and headed straight for the riverbank, invisible again.

She leapt down from the riverbank onto the nearest barge—heavy and piled high with coal. A shout sounded—surprise from one of the men on the far end of the boat, but Adelaide was already gone, leaping down to the next barge, piled high with sacks of mortar.

There wasn't time for any of this. No time for being chased by Bully Boys. Certainly no time for thinking about sharp, angled jaws and dukes who leapt into the fray.

No time for distracting men who *caused* the fray.

Another leap. Another boat, this one already half

empty of its cargo. There was no traffic like the traffic on the Thames at high tide. No better place to disappear, either. Adelaide had learned that young.

She tucked herself behind a high tower of crates and consulted her watch before looking upriver.

The flat-bottomed barge bobbed and swayed as someone landed on the deck.

Adelaide stilled, slipping her blade from the strap at her thigh and setting her cargo to the ground. *Dammit.* For a lifetime, she'd been able to disappear in a crowd, and suddenly, the skill was gone.

The Duke of Clayborn had somehow ruined it—as though, in seeing her, he'd made it so the rest of the world could, too.

She adjusted her grip on her knife and listened, trying to hear her pursuer's heavy steps over the sounds of the working river.

Peeked around the edge of the crates.

"Dammit," she muttered to herself before narrowing her gaze on him, tall and strong and not remotely worse for wear considering he'd been dockside brawling for the last three quarters of an hour. "You've missed the turn for Westminster, Duke."

"Mmm," he said, the noise low in his throat and rather delicious, if Adelaide were telling the truth. She shouldn't like it. He was the Duke of Clayborn. She'd spent a year not liking him.

He stepped into her hiding place and collected the cube at her feet. "Stealing is a crime."

"Are you going to call the magistrate?"

"No," he said, softly. "But what did you intend to steal?"

He was close enough to touch, and Adelaide knew she should step away from him. Even if he wasn't a duke, it was still daylight and half the Thames could see.

No one on the Thames was watching.

"Who says I was stealing anything?"

There was something about him. About this. Something wild and unfettered and exciting . . . and dangerous. He stepped closer, his words low and dark as he continued, "You don't have to admit it. I know a thief when I see one." He reached for her, and she held her breath, wondering where he'd touch her. What the leather of his glove would feel like on her skin.

Except he didn't touch her skin. Instead, he said, softly, "Red."

For a moment she didn't understand, and then she felt a tug at her temple, where a lock of her hair had escaped. She reached up, knocking his hand away and pushing it behind her ear.

He watched the movements, his gaze unreadable, and Adelaide went hot with his discovery and the sudden realization that he was close and warm and he smelled fresh, like citrus—a scent that did not come with the South Bank.

It was not a scent for Adelaide.

Adelaide Frampton was a woman for working days, and she had a keen understanding of what that meant. Of what she might hope to claim. This man was not for her, which made him a wicked temptation, like sweets and silks and purses and pocket watches. Like all of them put together. Too much for a thief to resist.

So she tilted her face up to his and stole him. For a moment. A heartbeat.

Intending to give him back.

Except it wasn't a heartbeat. Oh, it might have been when he froze, stiffening the moment her lips touched his. He sucked in a breath—her breath—and she wondered if she'd made a mistake. Wondered if he might clasp her by the arms and push her away.

She wouldn't have been surprised. Kissing in full view of London was not for Adelaide Frampton, unnoticeable plain Jane. Nor was it for Addie Trumbull, unimaginable legend.

Except . . .

When he set one hand to her—holding tight to the wooden cube with the other—he didn't push her away. Oh, for a moment she felt the hesitation in his grasp, as though he considered it. But then . . . he took over.

His strong arm came around her back, securing her against him as he lifted a hand to her face, gloved thumb brushing along the line of her jaw, then stroking up over her cheek as he took her in hand, tilting her to gain better access to her mouth.

Suddenly, it seemed very much that he was the thief and she the prize.

And there, on the banks of the River Thames, for all of working London to see, Adelaide let him thieve, giving herself up to this kiss she had started and he had joined—like none she'd ever experienced.

This stern, unyielding man kissed like a practiced and superior scoundrel.

Not that Adelaide complained.

Instead, she pressed closer, one hand coming to his chest, warm and broader than it seemed in the waistcoat and shirtsleeves he wore. She sighed at the feel of his breath. At the heavy scruff of beard that roughened his sharp jawline. At his lips, delivering on the temptation they'd promised.

He took advantage of that sigh, thankfully, stroking his tongue over her open lips, sucking her bottom lip between his own, worrying it with his teeth before soothing it with his tongue and licking into her—just once, like he knew he shouldn't. Like he couldn't resist.

Just as Adelaide knew she shouldn't.

Just as Adelaide couldn't resist.

Daylight be damned; docks be damned; duke be damned.

A bell rang in the distance.

Damn.

She pulled away at the sound, and a growl of displeasure sounded deep in his chest as he chased her lips for a heartbeat, as though her retreat had been a mistake.

It certainly felt like one.

Because suddenly he did not seem so much a duke.

Perhaps it was the sunset—the way the light had gilded the entire river, stealing away reality and leaving nothing but this man, who was somehow far beyond the starched, unpleasant duke. Tall and impossibly handsome and kissed like he never intended to stop.

Which would have been more than fine with her.

Adelaide adjusted her spectacles, knocked askew by their embrace, and wondered if she was going mad, because it was on the tip of her tongue to suggest he not stop, when he said, "I shouldn't have done that."

The light shifted, and reality returned along with the unpleasant confirmation of what Adelaide had always known. That she was Adelaide Frampton, and he was the Duke of Clayborn, and whatever this was . . . it was an enormous mistake. For both of them. One that, if discovered by Mayfair, would ruin more than Adelaide's prospects for dinner invitations.

Luckily, she had a clear path to keeping the man quiet.

She ran her fingertips over his lips, liking the way his eyes closed at the touch, his dark lashes impossibly long. "No," she said softly, almost sad. "You shouldn't have." And then she stepped from his embrace, her hand running along the corded muscles of his forearm to the wooden curiosity in his hands—the one she'd already stolen and was therefore by rights hers.

Taking advantage of his surprise, she reclaimed it and turned for the edge of the barge, the dark, churning waters of the Thames threatening several yards below— even without skirts, the river would take her away.

"What—" His question faded into a harsh shout as she leapt. "No! Adelaide!"

She landed on the deck of the small riverboat as he shouted the last. The broad-shouldered man at the helm of her new conveyance pushed off from the barge with a long pole, putting too much river between the two vessels for anyone to follow her.

Even a man with legs as long as Clayborn's.

She nodded her thanks to the captain of the boat and he tipped his hat in her direction. Neither spoke the other's name. Too many watchful gazes on the river.

And one, in particular, above.

He'd called her Adelaide.

Adelaide dipped under the canopy that shielded the rest of the boat from the world at large. It took all she had to resist looking back. To keep from confirming that he watched.

To feel his keen focus once more.

It was nice to be noticed.

Chapter Two

Adelaide ducked into the dimly lit cabin of the small riverboat that appeared to all the world as though it were going about small riverboat business that afternoon: delivering coal, or grain, or some other bit of ordinary cargo. From the outside, there was no possibility that the tiny vessel would house a single interesting thing, let alone four of them.

As the day had already revealed, however, appearances were deceiving.

Inside, there was no pile of cargo on its way to Richmond. No coal to be delivered to the palatial manor houses east of the city. No packages to be offloaded on the London docks.

Instead, the boat boasted a lavishly appointed room lined with privacy screens to ensure that no one would see the silks and satins that hung on the walls, or impressive furniture and lush pillows that filled the space, making it an ideal conveyance to move silently and unnoticed through the city, without anyone realizing that four of London's most powerful women were within.

Of course, most of London wouldn't acknowledge that the four women in question were powerful to begin with, and the women in question had no intention of correcting them.

Low expectations were far better cover for secrecy.

"Impeccable timing, as always," Adelaide said, extracting the notebook she'd swiped from The Bully Boys from her pockets. She set it on the low table before dropping onto a settee just inside the door to the cabin before accepting a cup of tea from Lady Sesily Calhoun, her friend and confidante—and wife to the captain of the vessel.

"Are you sure about the timing?" Sesily asked with a casual air.

Adelaide drank. "That it was impeccable? I am."

"If one wishes to escape, I suppose it might be," Sesily offered. "But I shall tell you—"

"It did not appear as though you wished to escape, Adelaide." This from Lady Imogen Loveless, her wild black curls fairly trembling with excitement as she leaned forward from her own seat on the other side of the cabin.

They'd seen the kiss. Adelaide drank more tea, considering her reply and finally settling on a tepid, "I don't know what you mean." She returned cup to saucer and leaned forward, making a show of looking at the blue folder on the table, inked with an ornate indigo bell. Opening it, she considered the document within—a full dossier on one Lord John Carrington, coincidentally, the younger brother of one Henry Carrington, Duke of Clayborn, whom Adelaide had just kissed on the dock.

Coincidentally, being the important bit. There was no reason to discuss that kiss with her friends. Ever. It was unrelated to the dossier in her hands.

That, and they would never let her hear the end of her moment of weakness. Which was what it had been. Clearly. Indeed, she was only scanning the dossier to reacquaint herself with Clayborn's brother. She was certainly not looking for information on the Duke.

Why would she want that?

Her heart began to pound, and she willed her tone calm. "What time is it?"

"Time enough to get there," Sesily said, waving away whatever hiding Adelaide had intended to do. "Who was he?"

It didn't seem possible that they didn't recognize him. His day-old scruff did nothing to hide his true identity, and she'd recognized him instantly. *Just as he'd recognized her.* Still, she brazened it through. "Who was whom?"

Her friends did not even pretend to hear the question. Of course they didn't. They saw too much. Understood too much. Such was the work they did, was it not?

"Not a Bully Boy," Imogen said.

Adelaide shuddered. "Definitely not." He'd said he was protecting her.

"Old friend?" Sesily offered.

"Absolutely not," Adelaide said, and that much was true. She and the Duke of Clayborn had shared no more than twenty words on the north side of the river, and during those short, awful moments, she'd vowed never to make a friend of the horrible man. Indeed, she'd spent more than a normal amount of time attempting to uncover the man's secrets so as to hold them against him.

She'd been under the impression that his only secrets weren't his at all, but his brother's, enumerated in the folder in her hand. Adelaide made a show of flipping through the dossier, as though she had not already committed the entire thing to memory. "He was . . . nobody."

The pair blinked at her, blank-faced, before Sesily burst out laughing. "We are to believe that you—Adelaide Frampton—kissed some . . . nobody?"

"For . . . no reason?" Imogen added.

"In broad daylight?" Sesily again.

"It was dusk, actually," Adelaide interjected.

"While waiting for us to collect you?" Imogen replied. "After you'd committed a bit of light crime?"

Adelaide set her teacup down and stood, removing her cap and working at the buttons of the form-fitting waistcoat the group's seamstress had created for her.

Sesily watched her for a moment before adding, ". . . in trousers."

Adelaide adjusted her spectacles. "I'm perfectly well covered."

"Oh, yes, no one would blink at a lady racing around the riverbank in trousers," Sesily teased with a salacious grin. "Especially not when she's kissing handsome men at dusk."

"Why would they?" Adelaide quipped. "You've surely done all of that before."

Sesily's smile broadened, revealing a row of shining white teeth. "Indeed I have. But they expect it from me."

That much was true. Sesily was a renowned scandal—daughter to a recently minted earl and his brash countess and, until several months earlier, unmarried, thirty, rich, beautiful, and with the absolute fearlessness that every woman on her own deserved to claim. Of course, society didn't care for fearless women, so they'd spent years trying to beat Sesily down, calling her Sexily behind her back . . . never realizing that the name simply gave her more freedom. More power.

The other woman did not kiss handsome men at dusk any longer, however. She kissed handsome *man*. Caleb Calhoun, who captained the boat from the deck beyond.

Adelaide leveled her friend with a look. "Would you believe I stood upon that dock, waiting for you to arrive, and wondered, *Now, Adelaide, what would Sesily do?*"

Sesily laughed and retorted, "In that case, you did the absolute right thing."

"If you both are through," came a new voice from the far corner of the cabin, the Duchess of Trevescan, known simply as The Duchess in many of Mayfair's finer circles, as though she was the singular representation of the title—beauty, grace, money, power . . . and a long-absent duke who cared not a bit what his wife did with her days or with his funds, as indicated by the vessel upon which they all traveled at that very moment.

Adelaide turned toward The Duchess, her gaze falling to the newspaper in the other woman's hands, emblazoned with a bold headline that read:

PETTICOAT JUSTICE? OR PRETTY VIGILANTES?

"They still attribute crimes across London to us, I see," Adelaide said. "So all is right with the world." After several years of working beneath the notice of Scotland Yard, the foursome had caused a minor scene at Whitehall one year earlier, drawing the notice of the new Metropolitan Police and, by extension, the papers. Surely there was no one who loved a rumor about ladies causing trouble like a newspaperman.

"Not *crimes* today," Duchess said. "A particular crime."

"Which one?"

"Lord Draven's tumble at the Beaufetheringstone ball." It was a gentle way of referring to the man falling three stories to his death. "Apparently there was a woman seen fleeing the scene," Duchess continued. "As we all know."

Lady Helene, daughter of the Marquess of Havistock, who had *also* been at the scene of the crime that had left one Lord Draven—odious, unpleasant man—dead as a doornail in Lady Beaufetheringstone's prized rosebushes two weeks earlier.

The lady's father hadn't simply *been* at the scene of the crime, however. He'd been the one doing the killing. The rotten man came from an aristocratic family that had built a fortune through the mistreatment of people across the globe. In London alone, he was invested in several private prisons that boasted abominable conditions and a half-dozen factories that "borrowed" their workers from South Bank workhouses, forcing them to labor in unbearable situations. *Workers.* They weren't workers. They were children—vulnerable and forgotten . . . considered disposable by men like Havistock.

Like many others, the Marquess of Havistock had

been on Adelaide's list for years. She'd been waiting for the man to do something that would see him sent away forever, and here it was. While most of the aristocracy happily ignored the truth about how Havistock had built a fortune, they would not be able to stomach the murder of one of their own, by one of their own.

All the group needed was proof—which Lady Helene, Havistock's own daughter, would be able to provide, just as soon as she was liberated from the gilded cage of her father's London home.

Which was where Adelaide and the others came in. "So they think it was us who gave Draven the push." When Duchess nodded, Adelaide added, "And it was you who made sure of it."

"I called upon Mr. and Mrs. West last Tuesday." Duncan West, owner of the *News of London*, and his wife, who knew everyone and everything one might wish knowing in Britain. "It may have slipped that I heard that it was not one woman seen fleeing the scene, but a pack of them."

Sesily raised a brow at that. "Surely we can come up with a better collective than *pack*?" She paused. "Pride? Bevy?"

"A group of ravens is called an unkindness," Imogen offered.

Sesily's brows rose. "Now *that* I can support."

Adelaide laughed, but kept her attention on Duchess. "I picked Havistock's pocket that evening. That's when we got the accounting of his factories." A little book, not unlike the one she'd just lifted in Lambeth, that the marquess rarely let out of his sight, with information on each of his five factories, including worker counts, schedules, funds paid to workhouses for the workers' day labor, and more.

"And there hasn't been a peep of that at Whitehall," Sesily spoke up. "Havistock no doubt decided not to report our minor crime in order to stay clear of the attention of his major one. Honestly, I'm a bit offended. If we mean to be rid of someone, we do it publicly. Not by tossing someone from a balcony."

Adelaide agreed. The group might take joy in punishing men who took joy in punishing those who held less power, but they did what they could to avoid trial for murder.

"Nonetheless," The Duchess continued, "the papers like the story of mysterious women scorned."

Adelaide scoffed. "As though the only way to see the truth of the world is to be scorned by a man."

"As though being scorned makes one mysterious," Sesily added.

"Are we mysterious?" Imogen asked.

"Not if you have anything to say about it, Imogen," Adelaide replied.

Imogen, wild about explosives, smiled broadly. "I like to make an entrance."

"You like to make a *scene*," Duchess said. "Lucky for you, no one ever expects you can actually pull one off." Adelaide couldn't help the little smile that came at the words. No one ever expected women when real damage was done.

No one ever expected women, period.

"The point is," Duchess added, "Havistock is both mad and cunning, and I don't expect him to rest until he discovers who witnessed his murder of Lord Draven. That person—Lady Helene—is in danger. It won't matter she's his daughter; he will absolutely end her if he discovers what she saw. And if he discovers that she's run off . . . he'll stop at nothing to fetch her back."

Adelaide winced at the words, shuddering at what came next. "Or silence her."

The quartet went quiet. They'd spent years fighting the worst of London—those who misused money and power to keep those who were weak under their thumb, and during that time, they'd come up against more men than they could count who would happily disappear their child to keep their power.

Lady Helene knew what her father was capable of and had come to them, following the network of whispers about the mysterious quartet of women who meted out justice to men who were too powerful for the regular channels.

Like dozens of other young women before her who'd witnessed horrific events, Helene had sent word through one trusted servant to another and another and another down the line to the Duchess of Trevescan, who had immediately sprung into action and ensured that the young lady would never have to sleep under her father's roof again.

The Duchess had returned the missive instantly, instructing the lady to be prepared at precisely seven o'clock that evening. Lady Helene was to wait, bag in hand, to be removed from Havistock House.

As a diversionary tactic, Adelaide would meet with the young woman's mother at the same time, ensuring that Lady Helene would have a touch of a lead before the whole of Havistock House came looking for her. Including her terrible father.

Of course, by the time London realized she was missing, the girl would be happily ensconced just under its nose in The Duchess's Mayfair town house, no one in the aristocracy the wiser as she delivered a witness statement to Scotland Yard and had several lovely long luncheons with the man she was to marry, while Duchess, Sesily, Adelaide, and Imogen completed months' worth of work to bring her father to justice.

The whole thing would be sorted in ten days if it all went to plan, which it would. No plan would ever defy Duchess.

"Now. Where are we? Adelaide, I assume your visit to The Bully Boys was a success?"

Adelaide reached for the little book on the table and

tossed it to Duchess, who caught it with ease. "Well done," Duchess said, thumbing through the scribbled notes as Imogen leaned forward to lift the cube from the table while Sesily helped Adelaide with her clothes. "I imagine Alfie Trumbull won't enjoy having lost the location of every weapons cache in twenty miles." She looked up. "No trouble?"

"A few surprises, but nothing I couldn't handle."

Duchess's blue eyes narrowed. "What kind of surprises?"

The Duke of Clayborn was there.

She should say it. It was important. He was not a fool. She had taken his mysterious wooden cube and it would not be long before he was asking questions about her, trying to understand the full scope of her affairs on the South Bank—questions that would put them all, and their work, in danger.

The box would only buy his silence for so long.

But somehow, when Adelaide opened her mouth, all she said was, "Alfie has a new desk—locks and false-bottomed drawers."

"Does he?" Duchess quipped. "If he's not careful, someone might think he's a businessman. Anything else?"

"The Bully Boys gave chase."

The whole room stilled, the only sound Adelaide's waistcoat sliding off, each woman staring at her as though no one inside had ever considered the possibility that Adelaide might be seen. Chased. Caught.

Noticed.

Even Imogen halted her inspection of the wooden box. "What do you mean, *gave chase*?"

Adelaide pretended not to notice her friends' surprise, instead shrugging one lean shoulder. "They saw me. They chased me. I escaped."

More silence. Then Sesily said, "They *saw* you?"

Adelaide yanked her shirt over her head, exchanging it

quickly for the chemise in Sesily's hands. "Yes. It was, as you pointed out, the broad light of day."

"I thought it was dusk?" The Duchess asked, dry as sand.

"But you're . . . *you*," Sesily said, moving to quickly lace a corset over the undergarment. "No one *sees you*, Adelaide."

"Well, today they did," Adelaide replied, disliking the heat that flooded her cheeks at the words. "Today I was . . ." She paused, considering the earlier events. She'd been distracted. By a man. Spoken to him. Accepted his assistance. Enjoyed it, if she was honest. And then she'd done the most un-Adelaide-like thing she could imagine; she'd kissed him. Not thinking of the repercussions. Not thinking at all. She pushed her spectacles high on her nose. "I was . . . not myself."

"I should say not," Imogen said, returning her attention to the wooden cube.

"I told you the appointments were too close together," Duchess said, turning, a mass of silk in her arms. "We could have sent Imogen."

Approaching, The Duchess shook out the black silk, revealing a lush gown. Adelaide removed her spectacles and tossed them to a nearby chair before raising her arms and allowing Sesily and Duchess to pull the frothy garment over her head, speaking through the crinoline and petticoats within. "Imogen would have been noticed."

"Oh, unlike you, moving like the fog?" Imogen retorted.

She had been moving like the fog. It wasn't her fault Clayborn had just *appeared* there. Uninvited. She poked her head out of the neck of the dress. "You would have been noticed when you exploded the place, Imogen."

Imogen Loveless was the kind of woman people noticed because it was impossible not to notice her. She was a whirling dervish—a book that could absolutely be judged by its cover. Short and plump, with a head of riotous black curls and a taste for chemistry experiments that were as likely to save the day as they were to destroy it, Imogen was a friend who was, by turns, exciting and absolutely terrifying.

Suffice to say, she was a delight at parties.

"Explosives can be a useful diversion!" Imogen said, brandishing the box in Adelaide's direction. "What's this?"

Adelaide held out a hand as Sesily began tightening the laces at the back of the gown. "Give it to me."

Imogen's gaze lit up. "What is it?" She relinquished the box to Adelaide, who immediately turned it over, considering the simple oak cube from all angles.

From over her shoulder, Sesily said, "It looks like a child's toy."

And it did. A simple block of wood, six inches square, with no keyholes, no discernible latches or seams, no evidence at all that there was a top or bottom or inside to it. "It's not."

"How do you know?"

Because it belongs to the Duke of Clayborn.

Again, she didn't say it.

"Because Alfie Trumbull has no reason to keep a child's toy in the false bottom of his desk drawer. I would wager all I have that there's something valuable inside it." A safe wager, as secrets belonging to one of the most respected, powerful aristocrats in Mayfair were one of the most valuable currencies in the world. Adelaide liked nothing more than a puzzle, and this one was magnificent. She tumbled the cube over and over in her hands.

"The question is, how does it open?" Imogen asked.

"I don't know," Adelaide said softly. *But she would.*

"Absolutely no way *that* was made by a Bully Boy," Sesily said, the words distant as Adelaide pressed and pulled at the box, to no avail.

"Dammit," she whispered, wincing at the sting in her scalp as Sesily pulled her hair into a wickedly stern coif, seating hairpins as far and tight as they might go. "Ow! Go easy, Sesily."

"I can't help it," the other woman clipped, shoving another pin into Adelaide's unyielding hair. "It was all falling down."

Adelaide's cheeks warmed at the words. At the memory of Clayborn's gaze on the lock that had been loosed from her cap. At the soft relief in his voice when he'd whispered *Red*, as though he'd been waiting a lifetime to know what color her hair was.

"We could explode it!" Imogen offered.

"I think we want to know what's inside such a curious container," Duchess said, returning Adelaide's eyeglasses. "Something important enough that The Bully Boys thought it worthy of hiding."

"Worthy of stealing to begin with," Adelaide said, the words urgent and eager. "Which is why I'm going to get it open." She wanted to open the thing. And then she wanted to march into Clayborn's Mayfair town house and show off her skill. She imagined she'd shock him again, just as she had with that kiss.

That kiss.

The one he'd thought was a mistake, she reminded herself before looking up again to discover that all three of her friends were watching her. "Out of curiosity," she added, though none of the three looked convinced.

"Well," Duchess said, coming forward, passing Adelaide a new set of gloves, waiting for her to pull them on before following the movements with a button hook. "We shall return to the mystery of the wooden cube when we are done with our current performance, ladies, which I like to call *Protecting Lady Helene from Her Odious Father, and Keeping Her Safe Until We Can Deliver Him to Scotland Yard*."

"It's not the drollest of titles," Sesily remarked.

"Agreed," Adelaide replied. "It doesn't exactly trip from the tongue."

"Though I *am* looking forward to the bit where I flummox Tommy," Imogen said, happily.

Adelaide grinned as Duchess worked on her gloves. "I don't imagine the detective inspector would take kindly to you calling him Tommy, Imogen."

"Nonsense," Imogen retorted. "We're good friends now. I'm thinking of having him round for dinner."

Sesily spoke around a tea cake she'd found. "You blew up his jail, Im."

"And think of the way he shall regale others with that story! It was practically a gift."

"Be that as it may," Duchess said through a laugh, "I do hope we can take care of this particular . . . problem . . . without attracting the attention of *Tommy* . . . or those others."

Imogen grinned. "I shall do my best."

"Right, then. We move quickly. Adelaide off the boat, Helene on." Duchess looked to Adelaide. "There is already a carriage on its way to remove you from the house when your meeting is through. Remember, we don't want to ruin the boy. We simply want her to fuss."

Adelaide nodded as Sesily settled a black hat upon her head, hiding away every errant flame of Adelaide's red hair that might lack control or reveal too much. "We've done it a dozen times before."

There was movement at the entrance of the cabin, where Sesily's husband filled the doorway. Sesily turned, and Adelaide saw something she could not understand in the tall man's gaze. "Caleb?"

"We're here," he said, quietly.

Sesily moved to him like a magnet, as though she had no other choice than to match with him when he was in the room, tucking herself into his arms in greeting. Though Adelaide had seen these exact movements a hundred times over the last year since the two were married, that evening, she wondered at it.

Wondered what it would be like to experience it—just once, to feel as though one had another half. A pair.

What. Nonsense.

She shook herself from the reverie. There was no time for wondering.

Straightening her shoulders, she lifted the folder from the table. When she left this cabin, she would no longer be Adelaide Frampton, lightest fingers in London.

She would be someone else entirely—more valuable to the women of London society than diamonds or silks or even the latest gossip. More dangerous to the men, too.

"But—" Caleb said, his low voice carrying through the space.

Everyone looked to him.

"The girl . . . she's not here."

Chapter Three

Henry Carrington, sixth Duke of Clayborn, did not enjoy being summoned.

In his thirty-six years on this earth, he'd discovered that there were few good things that came from the experience.

When he was ten, he'd been summoned home from Eton to Sussex for the birth of his younger brother, Jack, and the subsequent death of their mother, four days later. When he was seventeen, he'd been summoned back to the estate to discover that his father had died, and he had been made duke.

After that, the summonses came more frequently—bringing him home for any number of reasons. At twenty, it was a drought that threatened the crops. At twenty-two, it was a bout of strangles that lay waste to the stables at Clayborn Manor. At twenty-three, twenty-five, and twenty-nine, he'd been summoned to Jack's school to deal with Young Master Carrington's errant ways (impossible).

Society enjoyed summoning him, as well—after all, it was not every day a duke turned up at a ball/luncheon/dinner/musicale/country dance/tea. Neither was it every day that a duke was born the way Clayborn had been—imbued from the womb with a sense of unflagging responsibility, which he bore with a classic stiff upper lip. Stern, well-bred, and impeccably mannered.

Thankfully, now that he was regarded as a respected peer of the realm and was one of the few active members of the House of Lords actually attempting to serve the people and Her Majesty, few dared summon him.

Apparently, no one had apprised the Marchioness of Havistock of that fact. The aging aristocratic lady, married to a despicable man who deserved an early grave, had flatly summoned Clayborn for seven o'clock that evening, which explained why the duke was in a particular mood upon his arrival at the elaborate manor house situated east of the city on the banks of the River Thames.

His mood had nothing to do with the bruise that bloomed in his freshly shaved cheek, nor did it have anything to do with the fact that, not two hours earlier, he'd lost hold of his stolen goods. It certainly had nothing to do with the intriguing thief who'd taken them.

Miss Adelaide Frampton, who had marched past him as he'd stood outside Alfred Trumbull's heavily guarded, highly protected headquarters, wondering how he would get inside and retrieve his puzzle box. The lady had had no difficulty in making such a plan—walking directly into the warehouse, picking the lock on a well-secured desk drawer, and stealing the only thing that held any value to him . . . without being noticed.

How the wide world did not notice Adelaide Frampton the moment she entered a room, he would never understand.

The entirety of London thought her a quiet, unassuming miss—an unfortunate leaf on the familial branch of the Duchess of Trevescan, one of the aristocracy's most powerful figures. In the past five years, Clayborn had heard a dozen stories about Adelaide's past. She was a poor country mouse, arrived with nothing but the clothes on her back. A vicar's daughter, orphaned too young. The Duchess's childhood companion—barely a cousin. More like a servant's child.

The stories were myriad and short, and always told

with a slight twinge of surprise and disdain, as though it were unfathomable that anyone would actually *wish* to know about Adelaide Frampton.

The stories were also bollocks, which he'd known for a year—one need only look at Adelaide Frampton to know it. In the year since he'd discovered her, Clayborn had seen her pickpocket a half-dozen aristocrats in full view of all of London and dress down an earl who'd landed soon thereafter in Newgate—a monstrous man who had been born into power and privilege and had never had a woman stand up to him.

If Clayborn were a man who wagered, he would have placed his entire fortune on the likelihood that Adelaide had more than a small amount to do with that particular arrest.

That afternoon, he'd watched her lift his own belongings from the warehouse of the South Bank's notorious gang. If he hadn't been so concerned about her safety, he would have been impressed.

The Duke of Clayborn was a man who understood circumstances of birth, and there was no way on earth Adelaide Frampton was a vicar's daughter, a country lass, or the cousin to a duchess.

How it was that no one on either side of the Thames seemed to notice her was a puzzle for the ages. Clayborn couldn't help but notice her. He noticed her constantly. In ballrooms, when she turned up with her odd friends, and at dinner parties, when she was the quietest one in the room, and on her morning walks through Hyde Park. He'd been able to pick Adelaide Frampton from a crowd for years. Christ, he'd been unable not to.

The point was, since then, he'd noticed her freely. Which he didn't much care for, as the woman never seemed to notice him.

Irritating, that.

She'd noticed him that afternoon. Spoken to him. Sparred with him. Stolen from him.

Kissed him.

And . . . to add insult to injury, she had his puzzle box.

He was going to have to get it back from her. Hell, he'd be searching for her right now if he weren't here, in the foyer of Havistock House . . . summoned.

But the notice had been clear.

Clayborn—

> *We must discuss your brother.*
> *I shall see you at seven o'clock.*

> *Olivia, Lady Havistock*

Clayborn had been expecting this particular summons for several months, as Jack had fallen, as he described it, *utterly and irrevocably in love with the Lady Helene.* As though he were in a Shakespearean comedy and been shot with an arrow by a man with a donkey head.

Clayborn tilted his head.

It was something like that; he'd always been better at maths.

The point was, Jack was in love, and Lady Helene seemed somehow willing to suffer his wide-eyed affection. As Clayborn hadn't seen Jack drink or gamble or even smoke in the last several months, he was inclined to support a marriage between the two.

Though thirty-six years of receiving summonses made him think that the Marchioness of Havistock might have a different opinion on the situation.

He followed a liveried servant through the halls of the manor house to a richly appointed sitting room, complete with a small, elaborately carved desk that had clearly been chosen for appearance rather than purpose. Nevertheless, the Marchioness of Havistock sat behind it, as though holding court—an affect that was underscored by her impressive beauty. Despite what could not have been an easy marriage to a vile husband, or the production of six children with the same, the marchioness had somehow avoided the weathering that came for others' pale skin, her face devoid of all but the most graceful signs of age.

"Clayborn," she said as he entered the room, the name clipped, as though she was in a terrible rush and he was putting her out. "Good of you to come."

Wishing he could be anywhere but there, Clayborn knew the part he was to play, crossing the room and giving a short bow over the marchioness's hand. A better gentleman would have told her he'd been happy to receive her summons, but the bow was as much as Clayborn could muster.

"I read about your . . . *display* in Lords last week," she said, disdain dripping from every word as she referenced his losing his temper before the assembly as he attempted to move them to compassion for literally anyone but themselves. "What a good Samaritan you are, speaking on . . . what was it? Labor of some kind?"

"Child labor," he replied, cold as ice. The kind of labor her husband used without hesitation or conscience. The kind of labor that made the marquess enough money that he'd hired a gang of thieves to destroy Clayborn's future on the floor of Parliament.

Of course, now, the stolen item, and the information within, was in the hands of another, far more interesting, thief—one with whom he'd much prefer negotiating.

"Ah, yes," the marchioness went on, waving a hand as though the entire topic was beyond her grasp. "You know Havistock never speaks to me about the things you *men* debate."

"Child labor should not be a thing only *men* debate."

Clayborn turned at the words, and that's when he noticed that a woman sat nearby in lush, cascading skirts of black silk, wrist-length gloves, pristinely polished boots, a small hat and a half veil.

He froze in all too familiar shock, his gaze tracing

over her, registering her straight spine, the trim tuck of her waist beneath her corset, the freckled skin of her breast above the gown, the long column of her neck, her angled jaw and full lips—lips he knew intimately as of that afternoon.

Lips belonging to Adelaide Frampton. Lips attached to the rest of Adelaide Frampton's body.

If he were another man, his brows might have risen in surprise. But he was the Duke of Clayborn, and surprise was never for public revelation.

What in hell was she doing here?

She didn't move, and he couldn't read her enormous, brown eyes hidden behind her short veil. He would have done anything to see those expressive eyes. It was a clever disguise—one that shielded the spectacles that would so easily reveal her identity. Still, he had the wild instinct to rip the silly black hat from her head and loose the hair that she usually kept tightly moored. The fiery, red hair he'd discovered that afternoon.

It was a decidedly un-Clayborn-like instinct.

Much like all the others she summoned from him.

"It should not be a debate at all," she continued, as he ignored the wild pounding of his heart. *"A scourge. A thing we should banish to the darkness of the past and lock away."* She paused. "Is that not what you said in your speech last week, Your Grace?"

"It is," he agreed. How did she know?

"You are wrong, of course."

The marchioness sucked in a shocked breath as Clayborn's brows rose. It was not an assessment he heard often. "Do tell me how."

"When we banish sins to the past, we must not lock them away. We must keep them close so that their memory reminds us never to allow them back to the light."

How could anyone fail to notice her?

"Well, I am not certain that we should call this a sin. My husband tells me that the children are well rewarded by the work. It keeps them from developing a taste for idleness."

It was a disgusting argument, one Havistock had made a dozen times during debate in the House of Lords. Clayborn held his tongue rather than deliver a scathing setdown to the woman behind the desk, who was as odious as her husband, it seemed.

Adelaide Frampton had no such hesitation. "Truly, hearing such an argument in a home built for idleness with funds earned via the work of those children and others around the world is . . ." She paused, and he imagined she searched for a word she might use in polite company. ". . . a journey."

The marchioness's eyes nearly rolled from her head. "Madam. You *overstep*."

A retort sprang to Clayborn's lips—words commanding the marchioness to watch her tone. To know her betters.

Before he could speak, however, Miss Frampton said, "We have not been introduced."

Silence fell as the marchioness collected herself and spoke. "I suppose you would not know each other."

Why not? Adelaide Frampton was regularly at balls and dinners, dances and musicales.

Before he could point it out, the marchioness continued, "Men do work their very hardest to avoid the messy bits of life, do they not?"

Clayborn assumed the question was rhetorical.

"This, dear boy," the marchioness pressed on, "is the Matchbreaker."

Another surprise to hide.

Generally, Clayborn did his level best to remain outside the gossip and discussion of society. Oh, he attended balls and turned up at his club and showed his face at the races, but that was for politics and propriety, not pleasure. Even so, one would have to be birthed beneath a rock not to have heard of the Matchbreaker.

Hired by the women in society to check the pedigree

of the men who wished to marry their daughters. The Matchbreaker was whispered about throughout Mayfair, any time a society jewel was courted by a less than ideal gentleman. *Poor girl*, they would whisper behind their fans, *someone should summon the Matchbreaker*.

And when she was summoned, usually to confirm an already existing suspicion, she knew everything— childhood fears, schoolboy foibles, adult flaws. Full accounting of debts. Webs of friendships and business acquaintances. Mistresses. Illegitimate offspring. Incurable vice.

There was no secret the Matchbreaker could not uncover. She was a legend to the women of Mayfair . . . and enemy to many of its men.

And no one knew her name. At least, no one admitted to knowing it, despite the unmarried men of London being willing to do virtually anything to get it. The true identity of the Matchbreaker was the best-kept secret of their counterparts in skirts, until that moment, when the Duke of Clayborn discovered her identity.

A sizzle of excitement coursed through him at the knowledge that, suddenly, the field that stretched between him and Miss Adelaide Frampton was once more level. She thought herself disguised, never imagining that he had watched her long enough to turn a veil into a day-old beard—barely any disguise at all.

Showing none of his thoughts, Clayborn turned in the little chair, keenly aware that the legs were as fragile as matchsticks, to consider the woman in black. "The Matchbreaker?" he asked, willing his tone slow and even, despite nearly a dozen questions immediately on his tongue. "Is that a formal designation? A post from the queen?"

Lady Havistock chuckled. Adelaide did not, and Clayborn marveled at her even, cool demeanor. "I believe you're about to discover just how important it is, Duke."

He leaned back in his chair, not replying, not liking

how unmoved she was by his presence. She'd been well moved earlier; why was she so even-keeled now?

Adelaide reached down to her feet where a small bag sat, barely large enough to fit a piece of paper, and extracted a blue file, inked on the front with a large indigo bell.

Clayborn's heart began to pound. "What is that?"

"This," she said, the words measured and careful, as she set the file to her lap, laying one gloved hand, clad in magnificent lace as dark as midnight, atop it, "is your brother's file."

Clayborn shot forward. "And in it?"

Pink lips curved beneath her veil. "Everything."

What did she know?

Had she opened the box? This quickly? No. She'd barely had enough time to change disguises—it was impossible to imagine that she'd found the trick to the puzzle box. That she'd understood what was inside.

And yet, even without his stolen property, the idea that such a dossier would exist—something that might haunt Jack for the rest of his years—and that such a thing would be in the hands of Adelaide Frampton and whomever else she worked with—was . . . unnerving, to say the least. What was in it? About Jack? About *him*? And who would commission such a dossier?

The answer was clear: the Marquess of Havistock. His own father's once friend, then sworn enemy. The man who would stoop to anything to destroy Clayborn, including, apparently, ruining his brother's chances with the woman he loved.

The man who'd hired Alfie Trumbull to steal his puzzle box, now in Adelaide Frampton's hands.

Not for long.

She opened the folder. "John, your younger brother by ten years."

Dammit. Jack was foolish but he wasn't evil, and he would bear the heirs to the line. He didn't deserve whatever this was—especially if it was a message designed to silence Clayborn himself. In the Marquess's hands, it would be used to silence Clayborn in Parliament. To stop his work to end child labor. To keep Havistock's coffers filled with gold made on the backs of those who could not stand for themselves.

Let them come for him. But she would not ruin Jack. Not if Clayborn had anything to say about it.

He ran a thumb along the edge of his index finger, the only movement he allowed himself, as he resisted the urge to move closer. To crane his neck. He ignored the scatter-shot of his pounding heart. *What did she know?*

"I'm sure you meant to refer to him as Lord Carrington."

Her lips flattened at the cool correction. "Is his nose as straight as yours?"

What?

Before he could ask, she continued, casually, "Hard to believe it would be, considering the company he keeps."

"I knew it!" Lady Havistock interjected. "A scoundrel!"

As though the woman weren't married to something far worse.

Clayborn did not have to speak the thought, as Adelaide was there first. "It's not as though most men in Mayfair don't deserve the descriptor, but yes. It seems this Carrington man—"

"*Lord* Carrington," he corrected, leveling Adelaide with all the cool disdain he could muster. Did she know what she played at? What a weapon her dossier might be?

She couldn't. He'd watched her with the aristocracy for the last year. For longer. He'd witnessed the loathing in her eyes when she watched them from the edges of ballrooms. He'd once watched her pick Havistock's pocket. She couldn't possibly be in league with the man.

What then?

She stayed quiet for a moment, and he found himself perversely pleased that he'd unsettled her. "*Lord Carrington,*" she began again, "like so many toffs before him, is quite skilled at amassing enormous amounts of debt in extremely short amounts of time."

Had she forgotten that she was standing in a home owned by a toff? That there was another toff in the room? And not just any toff. A *duke*.

Clayborn bit back an instinctive noise of disgust. He was not the kind of man who lorded his title over others. He certainly never used it to impress. He'd spent his whole life attempting to live up to the damn thing. To deserve it. But this woman had tied him in knots with her black gown and her straight spine and that flame red hair that even now he wished to release and that pretty blue folder that threatened him with all the secrets she might know.

Secrets she already had in her possession, because he'd kissed her instead of taking his box and walking away. *That kiss.*

It had been a mistake. Obviously. The Duke of Clayborn did not make a habit of kissing women on cargo barges. Certainly not women like this, threatening his future in a dozen different ways.

"What kind of debt?" the marchioness asked, not at all offended by Miss Frampton's clear disdain for the aristocracy.

"The ordinary kind." The list came calm and relentless and unsurprising—all things Clayborn knew about his brother. "He's a habitual gambler, having lost thousands of pounds to several casinos around London." She looked to Clayborn. "Lucky for him, he retains access to them because the duke is known to clear Lord Carrington's debts at regular intervals."

It was all true. Jack was young, rich and without purpose. At least, he had been. Clayborn leaned back in his chair and watched her. "My brother hasn't set foot in a gaming hell in three months."

"Carrington likes drink."

"He's given it up."

Her lips pressed into a straight line. "And women."

At twenty-six years old, yes, his brother had done his fair share of carousing. "Again, he packed it in."

"When?"

"Three months ago."

Clayborn imagined her gaze shot daggers at him. "I assume we are to believe that is when he stopped drinking, as well?"

"In fact, it is."

There was a pause as she watched him, and he resisted the urge to rip the veil from her eyes. "Why? What happened three months ago?"

He did not hesitate. "He fell in love."

Her lips slackened for a moment beneath her veil, and she repeated, "Love."

"Quite," he said, as though it were enough.

"Well that's sweet, but irrelevant to my report on this proposed match." She set one gloved hand over the other on her file and returned her attention to the marchioness, who sat like stone, the only sign that she had heard the litany of items the tight grip of her fingers as she clenched her hands together.

After a long moment, the older woman said, "Go on, then. Is it your opinion that he will harm her?"

Adelaide hesitated and Clayborn clenched his teeth, anger thrumming through him. His brother was many things, and could be an absolute idiot at times, but he would *never* raise a hand to someone weaker than he. "He will *not*," he bit out. "My brother is a changed man. He loves Lady Helene, which you would know if you had attempted to produce one of your files with more than a handful of records from gaming hells. He would *never* harm her."

A beat of silence, and then she said, "Spoken like a man who has never considered the woman's lot in marriage." The words were a straight shot of disdain, and the temperature in the room seemed to rise harshly in their wake. "A woman cannot eat love. Cannot wear it. Cannot live in it."

"It's almost difficult to believe they call you the Matchbreaker."

"It's almost difficult to believe you're a grown man," she retorted. "As believing in love is for fairy tales and children."

His brows rose.

Who in hell did this woman think she was?

Dismissing him, she turned back to the marchioness. "In my opinion, my lady, the man's worst trait is his poor judgment, which could well impact Lady Helene's happiness in the future. I am less concerned with his inability to remain out of debt—"

"I am quite concerned about the *debt*!" The marchioness shrieked the word, as though it was a crime akin to murder. As though it came with a death sentence.

And for moneyed people, it did come with exactly that—especially when the debtor in question was to marry their daughter. Forget about love—no one ever expected titled daughters to love their husbands. Marriage, to them, was a business proposition. The merging of families. As though two great nations were joining forces.

"Oh for—" Clayborn began, barely biting off a rude remark. "Even if I was not keenly aware of the amount and location of every penny of my brother's finances, I might remind you that Jack is my heir, and I have no trouble paying my debts."

"Oh, please," Lady Havistock said, suddenly full of all the steel that came with a matchmaking mother. "He shan't be your heir for long. You're soon to realize that you're getting too old to catch a young bride who will actually want you, and you'll snatch up the first pretty face you see."

Well. Clayborn certainly could have done without the *too old* remark. He had no intention of snatching up any kind of face, pretty or otherwise, but he did not say so.

Not even when Adelaide Frampton decided to offer her opinion. "The lady makes an excellent point, Duke. It's a surprise I've not compiled a dossier on *you*, what with your unflagging belief in love . . . surely there's some poor woman out there willing to win your heart?"

"I've spent the better part of my time on earth dodging women looking to win my heart, as a matter of fact." Silence fell in the wake of the words—words that made him sound like an absolute horse's ass—and for the first time in his life, the Duke of Clayborn felt himself heat with . . . Christ, was that *embarrassment*?

He refused to look at her, this infuriating woman who had tied him in knots twice that day. Not even when she said, in a voice dry as sand, "Truly, it's almost difficult to believe you succeeded."

He stood from his chair. He had to leave this house. And this woman. "Lady Havistock," he began, "if you summoned me here to press me into service—to end my brother's courtship of your daughter with whatever information this woman has collected in her *dossier*—I assure you, you have wasted both of our time.

"My brother is twenty-six years old, and whatever his failures or successes, he is more than a collection of accusations on a sheet of paper. I refuse to play this game of secrets and lies. Should they decide to marry, Lady Helene and Jack have the full blessing and support of the Dukedom."

"Really, Clayborn—you would throw my daughter to the wolves?"

In a feat of immense strength, he refrained from pointing out that Lady Havistock and Adelaide Frampton were far closer to wolves than was his brother, who wanted no more than to marry the woman he loved.

Instead, he ignored the question and turned to leave, making it only three steps before a cool voice stopped him. "Since you insist that your brother has been impeccably behaved for three months, Your Grace, perhaps you can explain why, two weeks ago, he threw his lot in with a group of men in the South Bank who have not a care in the world when it comes to recklessness?"

She meant The Bully Boys. Men the Marquess of Havistock himself consorted with, Clayborn wanted to add. Yes, The Bully Boys ran the third-rate casinos that Jack frequented at his lowest point, but they were also thugs for hire, lacking all code, and willing to do anything for a price.

The Bully Boys, whom they'd battled together, shoulder-to-shoulder, that very afternoon.

He turned back. "You're wrong. Jack hasn't been near the South Bank in months." She did not reply, and his jaw clenched painfully. "Tell me, then."

She looked to her folder. "Thirteen days ago, your brother took a night of bouts in an underground fight ring."

"*What?* Why?"

"For the same reason most do, I assume. Money." She considered the dossier. "He's fought seven times since, and . . . won six. Impressive."

Impossible. He'd have noticed the remnants of a bare-knuckle fight on him. When was the last time he'd seen Jack? Longer than two weeks.

Still, Clayborn shook his head. "Your information is incorrect. If my brother were in trouble, he would come to me."

"Your Grace," the Matchbreaker said, the words cold as ice. "I think you'll find this particular audience will go much more smoothly if you accept that my information is never incorrect."

It's time for you to stand on your own, Jack.

His own words, whispering through him. The words he'd spoken, cool and paternal, three months prior. *If you wish to marry the girl, you must prove you can care for her.* Lady Helene, small and fresh-faced, looking barely out of pinafores in her first season out.

They'd stood outside a South Bank casino, where

Jack had once more lost his monthly allowance to the promise of making an easy fortune. *This is the last debt I pay.*

What if there had been trouble, and Jack had not come to him?

Whatever he'd said—however he'd played the firm older brother—Clayborn would have intervened, because that was what firstborn sons did. Even as he made stupid decisions for stupid reasons, Jack was his responsibility. In his care.

Just as he always had been.

But in that moment, he knew the truth. Adelaide Frampton's information was not incorrect. Something had gone wrong. Jack had needed help. Instead of turning to his brother, he'd turned to The Bully Boys. And they'd taken their fee. They knew Jack and his weaknesses. And they were not afraid to exploit them. Nor would they hesitate to exploit Clayborn's. They knew he was the line to Jack's funds, and were willing to do anything to keep that line open.

Including taking a commission to steal his secrets, secrets that were now in the possession of this woman, who made a career of revealing powerful men's secrets to the world.

He had to get that box back. Along with that file on her lap, which included God knew what.

And he had to get to Jack.

"Sir, I appreciate that your brother's new hobby might come as a shock, but the difference between three months ago and two weeks ago is—"

She stopped short, the air fairly crackling around her. She looked to the notes in her folder once more, before turning to look at him. Clayborn's breath held in his chest. What else did she know? Where was the additional shoe to drop? And who would own it when it did?

"Do you know the whereabouts of your brother right now?"

"I do not."

"I don't believe you," she said, summoning a little shocked gasp from the marchioness.

"I do not lie." The second time he'd said it to her that day.

"But in this, you are not telling the whole truth, are you?"

How did she know?

"I've heard enough," the marchioness interrupted, standing to her full nonexistent height. "I don't particularly care about the rogue's whereabouts. He shall never come near my Helene again. In fact, I shall happily share this information far and wide. The young ladies of the *ton* must know the truth. It would be one thing if he were a duke and she were made duchess by the match. But a *second* son? One who spends his evenings fighting like a dog?" She turned to Clayborn. "I can barely think of it and you allow this . . . this *stain* upon your name?"

Clayborn bit his tongue, resisting the urge to point out the irony that a woman married to the Marquess of Havistock would consider debt and illegal fighting a stain while turning a blind eye to her husband's disgusting, avaricious, myriad crimes.

"My brother loves your daughter, Lady Havistock. And she loves him, as well."

"Love!" The marchioness spat the word. "That man sold my Helene a false bill of goods, Clayborn. There's no question about it. She's a girl with a head on her shoulders, and she would *never* marry your ne'er-do-well brother knowing any of this. Not now, not *ever*!"

The vow grew louder and louder until Lady Havistock's final words echoed throughout the room, pinging off mahogany and gilt, beneath the disdainful gaze of the Havistock ancestors. She stood and swooped to the door of the room, yanking it open to shout a demand through the house. "Someone fetch Helene. Immediately."

Clayborn sighed. There was no way *this* would end well. Leave it to these women to ruin his day. "I assure you,

Lady Havistock, whatever has happened between my brother and your daughter, she has been an active, willing participant."

It was the wrong thing to say. "I do not care for that insinuation. Were I a man, I would call you out." She turned to her Matchbreaker. "I hope you do not mind staying a bit longer, madam. I should like Helene to hear about this from you, directly."

Clayborn's hands fisted together behind his back. "There is a problem with that plan, my lady."

Adelaide Frampton looked to him, and he found himself once more willing to do any number of things to see her eyes. To know her thoughts.

The marchioness's eyes narrowed. "What problem?"

A knock sounded at the door, and the servant who had shown Clayborn into the room stepped quietly inside, a folded piece of parchment in his gloved hand. "Ma'am," he said softly, dipping his head in deference.

"What is it?" The marchioness had clearly had enough.

The servant's throat worked, but he did not speak.

Clayborn's pulse pounded in his ears.

"What is that?" the marchioness said, her words high and tight once more. As though she already knew what it was.

She was saved from reading it, however, as Adelaide Frampton stood from her chair and said what they all knew to be the truth. "I would wager it is a note from your daughter, apprising you of her plans."

The marchioness turned shocked eyes on her Matchbreaker. "What plans?"

She did know everything.

"Duke?" Miss Frampton asked, standing, the sound of her silken skirts falling into place like gunshot in the shocked silence that punctuated her words.

For a moment, he was distracted by those skirts. By her tall, lithe form—a form he knew intimately from not three hours earlier, when it had been pressed tight against his chest. By the soft scent of her—thyme and fresh rain and secrets—forevermore the scent he would associate with trouble.

"Where is my daughter?!" It took all he had not to wince at the marchioness's shriek.

How did she know?

Adelaide replied, as though he'd asked the question aloud, "Have you not yet realized, Your Grace? I know everything."

The sheer arrogance of the words should not have intrigued him. Should not have tempted him. His brother was on the run with an unmarried lady in tow, and Clayborn would have to tidy up the mess as soon as possible.

He did not have time to notice this woman who had upended his day, and likely more than that. With a sigh, he reached into his pocket and extracted his watch before answering the marchioness. "If all is well, she is on her way to Nottingham."

Something shifted in Adelaide's posture. Softened. Released. Like relief.

She hadn't known; but now she did.

And she was relieved that the lady was gone. *Why?*

"Why in hell would she be there?" Adelaide and Clayborn turned in surprise to look at the marchioness, who had just used language deeply unbecoming a marchioness.

"Because they are eloping," Adelaide answered.

"Eloping!" The marchioness squealed her anguish. "To where?"

"I assume they are headed where all couples head when they are looking to marry quickly."

"Gretna Green?" Lady Havistock was wailing now.

"Gretna Green," Clayborn confirmed, suddenly feeling he could regain control of the situation.

"Unoriginal, but effective," Miss Frampton replied. "Unless, of course, you've someone on hand who is willing to follow."

Lady Havistock clung to the words and turned on Adelaide. "You! I have paid you handsomely to break this match, and break it you shall!"

"I shall ready my carriage immediately, my lady." An even nod and a small smile punctuated the words, as though she'd been planning just that the whole time.

What was she up to?

The woman had a file on his brother, was in possession of Clayborn's family secret, and had plans to leave the city with both. Which would happen over his decaying corpse. There was no way she was going alone.

"Can you do it?" Lady Havistock asked, skeptical.

Oh, Adelaide would not like that.

"My lady, I've followed eleven couples to the border in my time as the Matchbreaker, and I've never had a match elude me," Miss Frampton said, an unmistakable thread of annoyance in her tone as she returned the dossier to her case before standing and facing the marchioness across the desk. "I don't intend to start now. I'll have your daughter back to London in ten days' time. Your work, at this point, is to ensure that no one is aware that she has left."

Lady Havistock nodded, looking relieved. "Helene is visiting friends in the country."

Adelaide's full lips curved. "How lovely for her."

She crossed to him, at the door, her gaze shielded by the webbing of her veil. *Rip it off.* Her hat disguising the brilliant red of her hair. *Loose it.* Her lips, pink and soft, tasting like sunlight and rain. *Kiss them.* Tall enough that it wouldn't be difficult to do just that.

"I've never seen such a straight nose," she said.

His brow furrowed in surprise and confusion at the words. What did she care about his nose?

Before he could ask, she answered, simply, "Hard to believe some people get through life without breaking them."

She was silent for a moment, as though sizing him up,

and then she stepped closer, and his breath caught in his chest at the nearness, inappropriate in any room considering they were strangers.

Not entirely strangers, though.

As though he'd willed it, the woman lifted a hand and reached for a tender spot high on the ridge of his cheek.

Lady Havistock let out a little gasp. Even she, who hadn't hesitated to summon him to her home, would never have dreamed to touch him. It simply was not done. No one had told Adelaide Frampton such a thing, apparently, because she touched him.

No. Not quite. But there, in the space between her glove and his skin, the heat of her was electric. The threat of her touch more powerful than the thing itself.

It took him longer than it should have to realize that she was hovering over the graze he'd taken earlier in the day. The punch that had half landed, delivered by one of The Bully Boys in the alleyway between the warehouse and the south bank of the Thames.

His breath caught in his throat.

"You ought to have someone look at that." The words were far too soft considering their location. Far too private. A straight shot of pleasure from this woman who was ever more maddening.

With a nod to Lady Havistock, she pushed past him, the scent of her, the heat of her, the slide of her lingering against him, long enough to tie his tongue. At the door, she looked over her shoulder. "I suppose you intend to follow?"

He cleared his throat, the only indication of the inappropriate way he responded to her. *Follow whom?*

His brother. Lady Helene. Gretna Green. *Her.* "I do."

"Fair enough." In the shadow of that infernal veil, she smiled. Why did he like it so much? "It shall be a race then."

Chapter Four

That evening, after the sun set over the rooftops of Covent Garden, Adelaide readied her carriage for the drive to Scotland. It was not the first time she'd done such a thing in the dead of night. Not the first time she'd headed north to stop a misguided match. Not the first time she would do it alone, with only a coachman in tow—carriages moved faster with fewer passengers, and Adelaide was adept at going unseen.

It was, however, the first time she was excited for it.

It shall be a race, then.

The look on the Duke of Clayborn's face when she'd said it, like he'd been waiting a lifetime for such a challenge, had been enough to set her heart pounding.

The duke was the kind of man who absolutely relished going head-to-head with women like Adelaide Frampton. His superior snobbery made him deeply unpleasant—how many times had he referenced his title that evening?

He could make a body feel unwelcome with nothing but a cool glance, which Adelaide knew firsthand, as she had been on the receiving end of more than a few of *those* for the past year. From a distance, of course. The Duke of Clayborn wouldn't deign to get near her.

Not in public at least.

Or rather, not in Mayfair public.

South Bank public was different, apparently. In South

Bank public, he got so near to her that he kissed her. Not that she gave any additional thought to the kiss. It was absolutely forgettable.

As was the feel of his arms, like steel around her. The roughness of his beard against her skin. The low rumble of pleasure that came from deep in his chest.

Forgettable. All of it.

Wasn't that what he'd said when it was over?

No . . . he'd said something far worse. He'd said it was a *mistake*.

Ignoring the wash of heat that filled her at the embarrassing memory, Adelaide added extra carriage wheels and a hamper of food and drink to the inside of the vehicle, carefully balancing the weight as she ticked off the items required for her preparations, working quickly and efficiently, eager to get on the road.

Inside her pocket, a list of stables with strong horses.

Eager to win.

A map of inns friendly to women traveling alone. Her carpetbag, complete with clothing, medicinal supplies, and Clayborn's unopenable box.

It had been barely six hours since he'd inserted himself into her life with his alleyway brawling and his turning up at Havistock House and his insistence that he follow her to Scotland, and his *my brother loves the lady*. As though it mattered.

And his long, lanky body and his unnecessarily tempting kisses.

Which she had already forgotten.

Adelaide cleared her throat and checked the rear hatch of the carriage, carefully confirming that she had all she needed for her journey. It was a lesson left over from her childhood, learning to cut purses.

Speed ain't worth a damn if you ain't made a plan.
Her father's words, punctuated with a twist of her wrist, punishing her for taking two shots at the strings of his purse as she practiced.

Taking the extra time here, in the alleyway behind her apartments, would prevent her losing it on the race north.

She expected she'd need every minute if she was going to beat Clayborn to Helene and Jack, wherever they were. He did not strike her as the kind of man who took competition lightly. Which worked well for Adelaide, as she was not the kind of woman who lost.

She'd be lying if she said she wasn't half thrilled by his rising to her challenge. It had been a long time since she'd felt she'd met her match in battle. There was nothing like this battle—racing to find a girl who was in danger. To protect her from those who would harm her. To ensure that she could make a future for herself, free and without compromise.

What a gift for a woman in the world.

Satisfied with her work, Adelaide straightened and closed the hatch.

"So, the girl is off to Gretna Green."

She turned to discover the Duchess of Trevescan approaching from the rear door of the tavern that abutted the alleyway—the tavern above which Adelaide kept rooms.

Adelaide palmed her skirts. "Like so many before her—choosing the hope of security over the promise of it."

"You think she marries the boy only to escape the father?"

"I think any woman with a brain in her head who chooses a hasty wedding over freedom is doing it for a reason." Adelaide tightened a cinch on one of the matched greys she'd selected for the first leg of the journey before heading to the front of the carriage to check bridles and halters.

"So cynical."

Adelaide cut her friend a look. "Since when do you believe in love?"

Long married to a duke who never left his estate in the Scilly Isles, the Duchess of Trevescan was more merry widow than she was duchess, delighting in what had to be the best of all marriages—one that included an absentee husband. Instead, Duchess spent her days diminishing the duke's vast fortune, living in his vast home, and growing her vast network of informants—all in service to a higher good: destroying the worst of London's men.

"Oh, I believe in it," Duchess said, approaching. "I believe it's an absolute mess, which leads me to *also* believe the girl loves him, as the plan went entirely sideways." She set a hand to the nose of one of the horses, lowering her voice to please the animal. "I suppose we can't really blame her. If he's charming and handsome."

"Is he?" Adelaide moved to the side of the carriage.

"Charming?"

Adelaide inspected a carriage wheel she'd inspected twice before. "Handsome."

One of the duchess's brows rose in a perfect high arch. "I think he must be if he looks anything like his brother. Clayborn might be insufferable, but he's not the worst thing I've ever laid eyes on."

Adelaide was grateful for the darkness and the way it hid her flush. "I have not noticed."

Silence fell and she crouched, peering into the inky blackness beneath the carriage, as though there were something very important within, feeling suddenly as though she'd said the exact wrong thing.

Duchess gave a little laugh. "You absolutely have noticed, Adelaide."

She sighed and stood, facing her friend. "The man is arrogant and superior. He's awful, and I shall enjoy absolutely demolishing him on the race north."

Something lit in Duchess's gaze. "You're out for blood."

"He deserves a proper setdown. He lacks anything to recommend him—he is pompous, stiff, stern, unpleasant . . . pompous."

"You said pompous twice."

"Because he is twice as pompous as any other peer," she replied. "But the point is, all of that flatly diminishes any value found in his handsome face or his decidedly *un*ducal lips."

The Duchess's brows rose. "Unducal lips?"

Adelaide waved a hand. "You know what I mean."

The Duchess tilted her head. "It has been many years since I have been in contact with ducal lips, so I shall have to take your word on it."

Adelaide ignored the teasing in her friend's tone, and the lingering silence as Duchess watched her curiously, no doubt considering her next words.

Leaning against the carriage, she settled on changing the topic, for which Adelaide was immensely grateful. "So, if you had to wager, what is the girl up to?"

"Idiocy," Adelaide said without hesitation.

Duchess laughed. "Fair enough. But map it out for me."

"Two weeks ago, Helene witnesses her father kill a peer."

"That we know."

"She tells us, but we're not the only people she tells."

Duchess nodded, understanding. "The fiancé."

"Who, instead of asking his powerful, arrogant, ir-ritating, *pompous*, angel-of-judgment brother for help, decides to take matters into his own hands, and—"

"—we shall come back to *angel of judgment*," Duch-ess interjected.

They absolutely would not. "—and returns to Alfie Trumbull's fight ring to make some quick blunt, and get the girl out of town."

"They're not eloping," Duchess added, understanding. "Or, rather, they're eloping, but they're on the run. Chased by the Matchbreaker, the Duke of Clayborn, and . . . if their luck runs out, her monster of a father."

"A butcher, a baker, and a candlestick maker." Ad-elaide paused. "I, of course, am the candlestick maker. Very clever indeed."

Duchess's laugh heralded the opening of the rear door to the tavern, releasing the quiet roar of the teeming masses within, and revealing the tavern owner herself. Maggie O'Tiernen dropped an empty cask and let the door close behind her as she approached. When she spoke, her voice was lush and deep, rich with the sound of the Galway coast of her youth. "Alright, girls?"

Adelaide smiled. Only Maggie would address a duchess and a thief as such, even as she found them in the alleyway behind her tavern, clearly up to something.

A Black woman who'd left Ireland for London the moment she was able, Maggie had come with the clothes on her back to build a new life, where she could live freely as a woman, embodying her true self. Knowing, as she did, what the world could do to those who wished to live authentically, she'd built a safe haven here, in the dark corners of Covent Garden—a tavern known only as The Place. The rules were simple: if you were a woman, and you could find it, The Place would have you, however you came, whomever you loved.

The Place was no different than the palace that rose not a mile to the west; in both locations, women reigned.

If you asked Adelaide, however, she'd be the first to tell you she'd take Maggie's over Victoria's any day, because at Maggie's, every woman could be a queen. Adelaide could still remember her first time inside The Place— the first time she'd felt home in the weeks following her escape from the South Bank.

Maggie had seen her fear, her uncertainty. Adelaide's panic that she might have to return and face the wrath of her father and the censure of the world she'd tried to escape. They'd become fast friends—two women born into a life that had not been for them. Destined for more. Within a week, Adelaide was living in the rooms above the tavern, working for Duchess, a part of a new, vibrant world she'd never imagined.

"Makin' plans?" Maggie asked.

"Always," Adelaide replied.

Maggie lifted a chin in the direction of Duchess. "It's usually you making them, no?"

The other woman inclined her head. "Not tonight. Tonight, it's Adelaide outlining the battle."

Battle. That word again. The promise of the formidable opponent she'd face along the way. Her pulse sped, readying her for what was to come.

"Seen the papers this week, Duchess?" Maggie asked.

A ghost of a smile flickered over Duchess's face. "I have, in fact."

Maggie laughed, the sound warm and deep. "I should have guessed you'd be happy with it."

"With what?" Adelaide asked. "Some of us don't have the luxury of lying about and reading the papers, you know."

"Poor babe," Maggie teased. "The *News* has gossip from Scotland Yard."

Adelaide turned to Duchess. "What gossip?"

The other woman made a show of brushing an invisible speck from her sleeve. "It's important to note that it's simply gossip. Rubbish alongside an account of Lord Draven's demise." She slid Maggie a look. "Which we had *nothing* to do with."

Maggie nodded. "I didn't think so. It lacked your finesse."

Adelaide wasn't a fool. She knew as well as anyone that gossip was never entirely false; certainly not when reported by the *News*. "Tell me."

"Sources from inside Scotland Yard have revealed that Detective Inspector Peck has a name for the group that staged an explosion therein last year."

The group. That *had* been them. Adelaide grinned. "*Allegedly* staged."

The Duchess dipped her head in agreement. "Quite right. Allegedly. Absolutely anything in that jail could have spontaneously combusted."

"Go on, then. What is he calling this *group*?"

Maggie and The Duchess wore matching grins. Ear to ear. "Hell's Belles."

Adelaide couldn't stop the delighted laugh that bubbled out of her at the moniker. "That's—" She shook her head. "It's—"

"Perfect, isn't it?" Maggie laughed, big and bold.

"Does Imogen know?"

Duchess nodded. "She just told me she was going to pay Detective Inspector Peck a visit to praise him for his creativity."

Adelaide laughed at the idea—the last time Imogen and Thomas Peck had been in close proximity, an explosion had rocked Scotland Yard. "I can't imagine Peck will let her anywhere near the place now." She paused. "Hell's Belles. Perfect."

And then, as though summoned by the name, a bell sounded in the darkness, from high above. A watch on the roof, signaling something was amiss.

The trio stilled, nothing but the cool October wind whipping around them.

Duchess's gaze fell to the opening of the alleyway, over Adelaide's shoulder. "Warm night."

"Unseasonably so," Maggie added, moving shoulder to shoulder with Duchess, her hand sliding into her skirts, to the blade Adelaide knew was hidden within.

Adelaide slowly lowered herself into a crouch, heading for her own blade, tucked into her boot. Before she could get to it, however, Duchess said, loud and bright, as though they were anywhere but in a Covent Garden back alley in the dead of night, "Your Grace! What a delightful surprise."

Adelaide froze, then spun around.

Sure enough, the Duke of Clayborn approached, the light from the swinging lanterns on the back of the carriage lighting the blue eyes in his handsome face.

What in hell? Why was he there?

Not that she would ever give him the satisfaction of her surprise. Instead, she pushed her spectacles higher on her nose and leveled him with a cool look. "A bit far from Mayfair, aren't you, Duke?" She paused, then added, "Oh, but after the places you've been today, why wouldn't you try the Garden on for size?"

"I've seen a fair bit of the city, I'll admit," Clayborn said, stopping a few yards away, the shadows of the alleyway painting over the harsh lines of his aristocratic face. His gaze took in the scene—the trio of women in a dark alley behind a legendary tavern.

"Ladies," he said, offering a little, gentlemanly bow, as though they were in a ballroom and not a back alley. "Going on a journey, Miss Frampton?"

He knew.

She lifted her chin in his direction. "North."

"How interesting. I'm headed in that direction as well." He knew precisely where she was going. Which meant her veil had not hidden her in the slightest at Havistock House, and he'd known from the start who she was.

She should have been shocked at the revelation. Angry. At least frustrated. But instead, she found herself . . . excited by it.

A worthy opponent.

And a dangerous one, as he knew the true identity of the Matchbreaker—a piece of information that half of London would pay dearly to learn. She'd have to deal with that, eventually. But the box tucked into the bag in her carriage was enough to ensure his silence for now. Even arrogant dukes understood information was currency, and revelation required retribution in kind.

"I'll say, Duke," she said, "I did not expect that you would know where to find me."

"I think you'd be surprised by how much I know about you."

"Well," Maggie said, low beneath her breath.

Indeed.

"Adelaide Frampton, a Duchess's cousin"—he looked to the Duchess in question—"with rooms above The Place."

"Which place?" Maggie asked—her favorite question.

One side of his mouth lifted in amusement. "Your place, if I had to guess, Miss O'Tiernen."

Maggie lifted her chin. "You've the better of me, Duke."

"Maggie, meet the Duke of Clayborn," Adelaide said.

"Charmed," Maggie said when he offered a bow in her direction.

"Don't be so sure," Adelaide said, adding, "I don't care for people knowing my secrets, Duke . . . and you've learned too many of them too quickly."

He approached, movements long and easy, different than they'd been that afternoon. This was not the same man, of course. He was not on his back foot any longer. Now, he was leading the charge. "The feeling is mutual. I don't care for the secrets you have, either."

"And what secrets are those?" Duchess asked, too casual.

Clayborn's attention flickered to the other woman before he repeated, "I don't care for people knowing my secrets."

"Don't worry, Duchess; I shall tell you later," Adelaide said, not looking away from him.

Clayborn's gaze went stormy as the Duchess said, "Mmm," as though she expected nothing less. And she did. The woman made a business of collecting information on London's most powerful men. She'd be particularly interested in the fact that Adelaide believed the Duke of Clayborn was the owner of the box she'd thieved that morning.

Though why The Bully Boys would be in possession of such an odd thing, Adelaide had not yet divined. She considered him in the darkness—nothing like the type of man who spent time with The Bully Boys. Too straight. Too pristine. In the year since she'd begun noticing him, she'd never seen him looking anything but a duke. At least, not until that afternoon. Bearded and throwing punches like a docklands prizefighter and kissing like one, too.

He shouldn't care to find her. Shouldn't think of her at all. And still, he said, "You've something that belongs to me."

The box. She tilted her head in his direction. "And what is that?"

His gaze glittered in the lamplight, irritated with her. This man who did not lie would either have to reveal the existence of his stolen property, or lie. And he did not like it.

Good. She did not like him much, either.

"Your dossier."

Duchess made a little sound in the back of her throat at the words, even as Adelaide gave a little triumphant laugh. "There's absolutely nothing about that file that belongs to you."

"It is information about *my* family."

"Ah, but haven't you heard? She that finds, keeps." His gaze narrowed at the echo of her words from earlier in the day. She made for her carriage and tossed another bomb. "Even when the item was previously owned by *a duke*."

A hit. The barest flinch at the emphasis on his title, as though he was ashamed of the way he'd wielded it like a weapon earlier in the day.

"You cannot think I will simply allow you to keep it," he said, moving toward her, stopping only when Maggie and Duchess stepped between them.

All toffs were exactly the same. "There's no *allowing* about it. It's mine now."

A muscle twitched in his cheek. "How much do you want for it?"

"What makes you think I would sell it to you?"

"This is your job, is it not? Collecting this information and delivering it to the highest bidder? You don't match-break out of the goodness of your heart—if you did, you wouldn't set foot in Havistock House, as Lord and Lady Havistock exemplify the worst of the aristocracy, don't you think? So much for saving the women of the world."

He meant to insult; it did not work.

Few ever noticed the true strategy of the Matchbreaker. On the surface, she seemed to choose her clients without thought—available for all circumstances, all scandals being equal. But scandals were not equal, and neither were the homes she accessed. Instead, she chose the scandals most impacting the *ton*'s most powerful families, led by powerful men with too much to lose. Through her work, she could access a network of wives and daughters and sisters, who always knew more than men imagined, and often wished to share it, to atone for the ultimate sin . . . connection to a bad man.

The Belles were there to help them atone. And to bring the worst of those men down.

The Marquess of Havistock was one of the worst of the worst—unkind to his family, cruel to the world, and a murderer to boot. Adelaide would delight in the man's demise.

"It is not for sale." She paused. "Especially not to you."

A beat, as he checked his irritation. "You said you wished to race me."

She did not blink at the change of topic. "I did. And I daresay I am already the frontrunner."

"If I win, you return it."

"I only compete with worthy opponents."

"What's that mean?"

"Prove yourself, and we'll see." He waited for her to continue. "Win the first leg."

Satisfaction crossed his face. Arrogant man. "Done. Name the location."

Maggie laughed then, already connecting the dots. Or

the posting inns, as the case might be. They shared a look before Adelaide returned her attention to the duke. "Where's the challenge in that?"

The Duchess of Trevescan watched Clayborn over Adelaide's shoulder. "Wicked bruise you've got there, Clayborn," she said, her attention moving from his face to Adelaide's as she asked, "Where'd it come from?"

Adelaide raised a brow. "Are you surprised someone wanted to knock the toff back?"

Maggie coughed to cover her laugh and Duchess smiled. "I don't know a single duke who doesn't deserve a knocking back, come to think of it."

"Yes, well . . . this one got his today." *While fighting alongside her.*

Adelaide ignored the thought and the sliver of guilt that came with it, instead making a show of looking over her shoulder at him, noting that his cool gaze revealed nothing of his reaction to her words. She didn't like that. It made her want to rattle him. She met his eyes—startlingly blue in the dim light. "I'd best be going, Duke. Your brother isn't going to find himself."

She turned her back on him, nodding to the driving block, where Marcus, the coachman who would drive the first leg of the journey, keeping her from watchful London eyes, was already seated, ready for distance and speed. When they changed horses, Marcus would return to the city, and she'd be alone in a fast, light carriage . . . unbeatable.

Still, Clayborn watched her.

"Until tomorrow, then," he said.

"I shan't hold my breath."

He rocked back on his heels, sliding his hands in his pockets, and suddenly, for a moment, the man from the docks was returned. Casual, graceful, and tempting.

No. Dukes were not tempting. Certainly not this one.

Not even when he said softly, "We'll see."

Not even when he turned away and made his way back

down the alleyway, fading into the darkness, making her feel, wildly, as though she was the one who was left behind.

After a long moment, Maggie's low whistle sounded. "I wouldn't mind that man stowing away in *my* carriage."

Adelaide scowled and Duchess laughed, the sound punctuated by the roar of distant chatter and laughter from inside the tavern beyond. "I'll say this," Duchess added, wry. "Those lips . . . they're not like any ducal lips I've ever seen. It's no wonder you were kissing them in broad daylight this afternoon, Adelaide."

Adelaide's cheeks flamed. Dammit. She should have known they'd sort it out. Adelaide cut her friend a look. "Did you two come out here for a reason?"

"In fact, we did," Duchess said, turning serious. "You've riled The Bully Boys, Adelaide. You were seen and you escaped, and Alfie doesn't like being made a fool of. Danny is already sniffing around. Looking for you."

Adelaide curled a lip. Danny Stoke was Alfie Trumbull's right hand—sent to sort out dirty business important enough that it required a modicum of finesse. He was Adelaide's age, and the boy Alfie regularly referred to as the child he'd never had.

Which had never bothered Adelaide, as she'd regularly wished she had also been the child her father never had.

Danny's appearance wasn't a surprise. She knew she'd been recognized as she'd fled the warehouse—Clayborn's fault. And Alfie wouldn't be able to stand even a whisper of his long-lost daughter—already whispered about in Lambeth—returning to steal from him.

"Alfie is lookin' to punish me," she said, letting the South Bank edge into her words.

Maggie nodded, her dark eyes serious. "Askin' questions, at least."

"It won't be asking for long, though, will it?" The Bully Boys weren't known for tact or gentility. They moved with brute force, and The Place had suffered before.

"They'll have to come armed to the teeth if they want to take us on here again," Duchess said. The Place was heavily protected by several layers of security both inside and outside the tavern. Not even The Bully Boys would be stupid enough to come for it. "But they don't want all of us tonight."

Adelaide looked to the closed door of the tavern. "Just me."

Still, she'd die before putting these women or those inside The Place in danger. If The Bully Boys had information on her, it was her battle. Alone. She looked to her friends, these women who years ago had given her a new path, a fresh start. "What of you? If they think you're hiding me . . ."

Both chins lifted in challenge.

"Let them come," Maggie said.

Duchess came forward, taking Adelaide by the shoulders. "We'll send word. Keep to the safe places. The ones where the walls listen for us." A vast network of taverns and inns on post roads throughout Britain, managed by one of their crew, Mithra Singh, a Punjabi brewmistress with a skill for ale making and secrets. "And stay alert."

As she'd been her whole life.

Adelaide cursed harshly, knowing they were right and hating it all the same. With no choice, she turned to the carriage. She nodded up to Marcus, who put a hand to his brim in acknowledgment as she made for the dark cabin.

Duchess followed her, staying the door before Adelaide could close it behind her. "Ten days isn't long." When Adelaide did not reply, the woman who prided herself on always being one step ahead pressed on, her tone dry, with a hint of amusement. "I'm almost sorry I'm not joining you, Adelaide. I'd dearly like to watch this game play out."

"It's not a game," Adelaide said sharply. "A girl is

alone, possibly pursued by her murdering father, with nothing but a useless aristocrat to keep her safe, and I'm in the wind." She bit her tongue before adding, *With the Duke of Clayborn.*

"You shall find her, as you always do," Duchess said simply. "You'll find her, see her back safely, and we'll see her safe afterward. If she loves the boy, she can have him eventually. But right now—"

"—we've other plans," Adelaide finished. Ruining an aristocrat. Exposing him for a murderer. Meting out justice.

"That shall all be the easy bit."

Adelaide's brows rose. "Then what's the difficult bit?"

Duchess and Maggie shared a grin before Maggie replied, "The game with the duke."

The answer thrummed through her. "There won't be any game with the duke."

"Of course there will be," Duchess said. "And if I know you, being in the wind with that duke chasing you, it will turn out to be your favorite game."

Adelaide didn't care what that duke did. And still, she asked, "What game is that?"

"Cat and mouse."

Maggie laughed from beyond the door of the carriage, her rich voice carrying through the darkness. "Who is the cat and who is the mouse?"

"Look at her: Adelaide Frampton, a solitary genius with a wicked sense of justice and a talent for stealing." Duchess smiled that smile that meant everything was going according to plan. "Obviously, she's the cat."

Chapter Five

Clayborn made his way into the Hawk and Hedgehog posting inn the next night, covered in mud and full of frustration.

The tavern was warm and filled with chatter as he pushed inside, squeezing past a customer on his way out, into the cold rainstorm beyond. It took Clayborn a moment to register the way the volume of the room quieted, as his eyes adjusted to the bright interior, awash in golden light.

He'd attracted the attention of most of the people within—a wide cross section of travelers and locals. A group of women in workaday frocks laughing at a far-off table. A pair of young bucks standing at the bar, muddy boots making a mess of the scuffed oak floor. A round-faced, dark-skinned farmer as big as a house, with a buxom beauty pressed to his side. And behind the bar, a plump tavern mistress with gleaming black hair, porcelain skin, and a mouth turned up like a bow. He met her dark, hooded eyes, noting her amused recognition, as though she knew something he did not.

Or, rather, as though she knew what he did not wish her to know.

He'd lost Adelaide.

He knew he shouldn't think of her in such an informal way. He was a duke, after all, and she was a woman he barely knew, no matter how much thinking of her made him imagine differently. And Lord knew he'd been thinking of her for the last twenty-four hours.

He'd thought of her as he left London behind, dawn breaking in the east, certain that he would catch up with her larger, heavier carriage within hours. He'd thought of her as the skies had opened and he'd pulled his cap low over his brow, hunching his shoulders and refusing to find shelter. The thoughts had bounced from irritation to frustration before lingering on a catalogue of her features. Her keen brown eyes, glittering with knowledge behind those wire-rimmed spectacles. Her pert chin, lifted in defiant challenge. Her cheeks, bright with October's evening chill . . . or more? They'd been pink when he'd kissed her, too. Pink as her lips.

His thoughts had lingered on those lips for longer than they should have, as his matched horses had raced north. As he'd begun his search, hours into the journey, for any sign of their owner.

Adelaide Frampton had disappeared.

There'd been no sign of her at the Tipped Pheasant in Hanslope.

None at the Cock and Canary in Wilton.

There'd been four drunken louts in Shawell at the Singing Stone Inn, too deep in their cups to be any help.

So, by the time he'd arrived in the drive of the Hawk and Hedgehog, Clayborn was ready for a meal, a bath, and a bed in which to sleep off his irritation that she had, as promised, outrun him. He'd never be able to boast of his driving skills again.

And now, to make matters worse, an entire taproom's worth of people watched him.

Clayborn stiffened, shoulders and spine straightening as he attempted not to notice the room noticing him. He was a duke, after all. People noticed him more often than not, but they usually did it with admiration.

This group instead stared at him as though he were a curiosity—a lumbering creature stepped from Mary

Shelley's novel. The siren song of warm food and sleep was more powerful than the urge to retreat, however, so he approached the proprietress of the tavern.

"Good evening, traveler." She waved to a spot at the end of the bar. "Ale? Food?"

Clayborn nodded in the direction of the tapped cask behind the bar. "Thank you."

"'Course," she said, turning to pull a pint, setting it on the shining mahogany before him. "Your Grace."

He met her eyes. "You've the better of me."

She grinned. "Your carriage carries a ducal crest—you should be careful of that, you know . . . you're a highwaywoman's prize." Before he could query the word, she added, "Though if I'm being honest, even looking like the road tossed you through the doors, you reek of title."

Apparently, title did not carry much weight in the Hawk and Hedgehog. "Should I apologize?"

"Don't see why you would," she said matter-of-factly. "Ain't your fault how you were born."

The words echoed through him, true and somehow impossible to believe, but he had no reason to discuss it with this woman, no matter how welcoming she seemed. "I'd like a room, please. And a bath. And a meal."

She smiled, a big broad grin, as though he'd said something wildly entertaining. "Lord knows dukes' money spends as well as anyone else's."

Clayborn knew a prompt when he heard one, and reached into his pocket, prepared to pay whatever additional tax this shrewd businesswoman would add to find room for an aristocrat that evening.

Except his pocket was empty, save for a three-inch slit in the fabric. His purse was gone.

He looked up into the twinkling eyes of the tavern mistress, suspicion flaring even before she tilted her head. "Problem, Your Grace?"

She knew exactly what the problem was. "I don't suppose you'll extend credit."

She made a show of sucking in a breath. "In my experience, the rich ones never pay their debts."

Snickers spread through the room, though when he looked around the space to confront them, their audience appeared deep in its own business. Bollocks. He'd never met a group of people more in his business.

Clayborn swallowed a curse as a voice spoke at his shoulder. "I shall cover the duke, Gwen."

He grew hot at the words.

He hadn't lost her.

Triumph sizzled through him, even as he knew it was silly to feel it. It wasn't as though she was priceless treasure, dammit. And still, he turned toward her as though she were just that, doing his best to remind himself that Adelaide Frampton was a troublesome, contrary, unruly woman, and a thief as well.

She looked as though she'd been riding as long as he had, her rich green traveling dress beneath a dark cloak damp with the rain, the hem of her skirts caked with mud. Her cheeks were red with the cold air of the night beyond as she lifted one hand to remove her spectacles and clean them of the fog that had appeared on them when she entered the warm pub. The only thing that remained impeccable was the one thing he wished to see unraveled—her hair, tightly hidden beneath her cap, the copper shine that had tempted him on the docks tucked out of view.

She should have looked a mess—unkempt and wayward, in need of a looking glass and a washbasin. After all, in all his time knowing Adelaide Frampton—watching Adelaide Frampton in Mayfair ballrooms and on South Bank barges, he'd never seen her out of control.

She should have looked all wrong.

Instead, she looked extremely right. She looked like she belonged here, in this tavern full of thieves.

It didn't help that she was smiling at him, as though she held a lifetime of secrets. Which of course she did, because no matter her outward appearance, Adelaide Frampton remained one step ahead of everyone, all the time.

Not him, though. Not then. "I won."

She took her time, returning her spectacles to her nose before tilting her head. "Did you?"

"It was a race. And you just arrived."

"Did I?"

He didn't like the way it seemed as though she was humoring him. "You weren't here when I entered."

"Wasn't I?" she asked.

"I would have noticed you." Something shifted in her eyes, the bright, teasing warmth in them going dark and rich, making him want to explore it.

"Mmm," she said, her smile turning secret as she turned to the owner of the establishment. She pushed her hood back, letting it fall to her shoulders, drawing his attention to her cap once more. To what it hid. "What's he owe you?"

"The ale," Gwen said, lifting her chin in the direction of the pint glass. "And a meal."

Adelaide nodded and extracted a purse from beneath her cloak.

Clayborn immediately protested. "No. I can't take money from—" The words stopped as he watched her open the leather pouch. The *familiar* leather pouch. Her long, nimble fingers dipped inside to extract a pound note.

"That should cover it. And the same for me."

It should cover meals and pints for the entire place, but that wasn't the point. "You pickpocketed me."

She turned to look at him. "That's quite an accusation."

"And that's no kind of denial, you thief. That's my purse."

"Are you sure?" Her full lips quirked as she tested the weight of the coin within. "It certainly feels like it's mine."

His gaze narrowed on her. "She that finds, keeps?"

"Fast learner," she said before sliding his purse across the smooth mahogany toward him. "I grew bored while I was waiting for you to arrive."

"That's an excuse?" he asked, ignoring the pleasure that came with the knowledge that she was waiting for him. He didn't care if she waited for him or not. All that mattered was that she didn't find Jack and Helene first.

Nevertheless, when Adelaide lifted a shoulder in a tiny shrug, he found he liked it more than he should. And then she said, "Idle hands and all that," and he liked that *far* more than he should, as it made him consider any number of ways she might keep those idle hands busy other than picking his pockets.

He cleared his throat. There was obviously something in the air in this roadside tavern that made it difficult for him to recall that he did not get along with Adelaide Frampton. He lifted his purse, sliding it into the pocket she hadn't ruined. "I didn't feel you."

"Of course you didn't," she said, the words full of offense. "There was a time I was the best nipper in London."

"I beg your pardon," he said. "I wasn't aware of your place as cutpurse royalty."

"Deference would not be out of line."

"What if I buy you a meal instead?"

"Another time, I'm afraid, as I have already paid for *your* meal." She pushed past him, the scent of her, thyme and fresh rain, lingering as she crossed to a table in a far corner of the room.

He shouldn't follow.

He should sit alone and eat his supper and retire to his room to rise early and get ahead of her. But *should* was no longer applicable for the Duke of Clayborn. Not when *must* had taken over. Not when *need* was pulling him along behind her, a dog on a lead.

She slid into a chair on the far side of the table, leaving

him with his back to the room, the heat of dozens of curious eyes unmistakable.

"Dukes are a rare sighting in these parts," Adelaide said.

"Are we so obvious?"

She laughed, and the warm, full sound affected him like physical touch. He shifted in his seat as she said, "You cannot think you blend."

"I can indeed think that."

Another laugh, this one brighter. "In your lifetime, you have not blended."

"I blended perfectly well yesterday afternoon."

She cut him a disbelieving look. "You did not."

"Why not?"

She enumerated the reasons on her fingers. "You walk like a duke. You talk like a duke. You dress like a duke."

"I did not dress like a duke! I was wearing shirtsleeves and a greatcoat, workaday boots and a cap. I did not shave!"

She cut him a look. "And even your day-old beard was perfect. Soft and oiled and exactly the way a duke's beard would be if he'd ever let anyone besides his valet see it."

He couldn't help raising a brow at that. "Soft, was it?"

She blushed. *Triumph.* "I couldn't help but notice when I was making sure you stayed quiet. You couldn't even *hide* like an ordinary person."

"Ah," he said, still enjoying the moment.

Her gaze tracked over his face. "Your beard grows quickly."

He ran a hand over his cheek, where a day's worth of scruff had grown. "I shave twice a day."

They fell silent for a moment, locked in a stare before realizing simultaneously that they should not be discussing the rate of his beard growth. Gwen returned, two heaping platters of food in hand. Setting them on the table, she looked from him to Adelaide. "He's forgiven you, I see?"

Adelaide smiled and adjusted her spectacles, a pretty dimple flashing in her cheek. How had he missed that before now? "He enjoys a challenge."

The tavern mistress laughed. "Well, he's certainly got one with you lot."

Clayborn looked to Gwen. "Lot?"

The woman ignored the question and tucked a hand into the pocket of her apron, extracting a small square of paper and passing it to Adelaide. "Came to the kitchen door not five minutes ago."

"Hmm," Adelaide said, sliding a finger beneath the wax seal. "It's late."

As Adelaide read the message, Clayborn leaned forward. Before he could decipher any of the words, her long fingers refolded the paper and slipped it into the folds of her skirts. "Thank you, Gwen. It looks as though I will stay the night after all."

She hadn't been planning to spend the night? "It's raining sheets out there," he said, surprise in his words. "Surely you weren't intending to drive in it."

Adelaide looked to him. "If your brother was intending to drive in it, I was, yes. But Lord Carrington and Lady Helene have made camp at an inn two hours' ride up the road. In this weather, that's closer to four hours, which means I"—she finally looked to the pile of food in front of her—"can gorge myself on Gwen's steak and ale pie, roll up to bed, and make up the time tomorrow."

"Aye, ye can." Gwen laughed and waved to a dark-haired boy nearby. "I'll have Wei bring your bags up."

"I shall pay for my room, if you'll have it, Miss Gwen," he said to the proprietress before leveling Adelaide with a cool look. "Now that I have my money returned."

Gwen turned instantly serious. "I'm afraid we're out of rooms, Duke."

Clayborn's brows snapped together. "You had one not five minutes ago when I entered . . ."

"Aye, but you didn't have any money then. So I gave it away."

He looked around the room, taking in the collection of faces—unchanged from when he'd arrived. "To whom?"

Silence fell, understanding coming heavy and quick. He looked to Adelaide, who looked like the cat that got the cream. "Early bird and all that."

"I should take offense to you comparing my rooms to worms, Adelaide Frampton," Gwen said before looking back to Clayborn. "There's a warm loft in the stable if you'd like."

"Not a single room available," he said, turning to Adelaide. "Imagine that."

She shrugged and lifted a fork, tucking into the flaky pastry of the pie in front of her. "One room available, as a matter of fact. The last room. My room."

Not just the last room. The last bed.

Her bed.

Where she'd be sleeping without him. While he slept . . .

"The stables, then, Duke?" Gwen asked, and Clayborn had the distinct impression that he was part of a game—*Toy With the Duke.* He didn't like that.

Nor did he like the way Adelaide Frampton watched him, as though she expected him to make a fuss. As though she expected him to play the part, too pristine and perfect for a night of discomfort. "The stables will be fine," he said, enjoying the surprise that flared in her eyes at his reply.

"Excellent. I shall add it to your bill."

"I shall pay a premium for the hay, I imagine."

Gwen offered a bawdy wink. "Soft as goose down, I vow it."

"Only the best for the duke's smooth skin," Adelaide said, her lips curving in a little wry smile.

He shouldn't have let her tease him. Shouldn't have let her

draw his gaze to skin of a different kind, a pretty, peachy expanse above the line of her traveling dress. Shouldn't have let her words hint at how smooth it would feel.

The door to the tavern opened behind him, letting in the cold from the wind and rain beyond, reminding him that the roads would make a late-night journey to another inn interminable. The hayloft of the Hawk and Hedgehog was better than nothing.

"I'm sure it will be fine, Gwen. Thank you."

Gwen laughed, big and bright, clapped him on the shoulder and looked to Adelaide. "Not the worst duke I've ever had in here, I'd say."

Adelaide raised a brow in his direction. "Give him time."

With another chuckle, Gwen disappeared in the direction of the bar and Adelaide lifted her fork, stabbing one round potato and popping it into her mouth. She watched as he dug into his own food, tracking his movements for long moments before he grew uncomfortable under her gaze.

He set down his fork. "What is it?"

"Why are you chasing your brother and Lady Helene?"

The question was a surprise—the kind that came so quickly and unexpectedly that it summoned the truth. "Because my brother deserves happiness."

She waited for more. "As simple as that?"

"Does it have to be more complicated?"

"I don't know," she said. "I don't have a brother."

"No one to teach you to climb a tree?"

"There weren't many trees where I grew up," she said, softly, and he wondered at the words.

"Not the Duchess's cousin, and not a faraway vicar's daughter, then?"

She smiled. "A poor example of a vicar's daughter, indeed, if one considers yesterday."

"If one considers yesterday, I'd imagine you were raised on the South Bank."

She returned to her food, taking her time to compose the perfect bite on her fork. Was he right? Had she been raised there? It seemed impossible that anything else could be true—with the way she'd weaved in and out of the alleyways, like the place had been mapped on her skin.

Chewing thoughtfully, she finally replied, "I didn't have a brother, or trees, but I had plenty of rooftops, and even more children willing to show off their skills in climbing them. Rooftops and trees aren't so different, after all. They both come with a better view."

A vision flashed—Adelaide Frampton on a London rooftop, the sun setting on the horizon, turning her red hair into pure flame. And then, unbidden, the vision shifted, and Clayborn was there, reaching for her. Pulling her close. Claiming her full lower lip with a soft bite before licking into her mouth. He went instantly hard at the image, one he knew would be bested by reality.

Not that he would ever find out. He cleared his throat, willing the sinful thoughts away. She deserved better than kisses on docks. Than fantasies in roadside taverns. Than what he could offer her. Now was not the time to imagine Adelaide Frampton naked on a rooftop.

"But did you?" she asked.

He blinked. Cleared his throat again. "I beg your pardon?"

Her brows lifted in what might have been a knowing smile. "Teach your brother to climb trees."

"Ah. No." He paused. "In fact, Jack fell out of a tree when he was eight and broke his arm."

"And where were you?"

He'd been inside. Studying. Wanting to impress their father who had, by then, been dead for a year. Wanting, even then, to make sure he lived up to the legacy.

Instead, he'd missed Jack falling from the tree. Missed helping him to the house. "I didn't even know he'd done it until after he'd seen the doctor." Jack had returned with his arm in a cast, brave smile on his face, ready for whatever reckless adventure came next. He hadn't been disappointed in the slightest. But Clayborn had been.

"I should have . . ." He paused, looking to her as she chewed a bit of steak thoughtfully, watching him with those enormous brown eyes that even behind her eyeglasses seemed to see everything and somehow judge nothing—and he found he couldn't stop himself. "I should have paid closer attention. I should have taken better care of him."

"You were . . . what, eighteen?" she said, and he immediately looked to her, shocked by her knowledge before he remembered that she would of course know it. It would have been in her dossier. A basic fact of Jack's. Of their family.

What else did she know?

Before he could ask, she added, "Barely a man yourself."

"Man enough to hold the title. Run the estate," he said, hearing the cool edge in his words. Knowing it was unpleasant. Maybe that was why he said the rest. "Man enough that I should have taken better care of him." He paused. "Then and now."

Christ. Where had that come from?

Something flashed in her eyes. Something understanding. Something like pity. Dammit. He didn't want *that*.

Don't say anything, he willed her, silently.

No such luck. "He deserves happiness." She repeated his words, and he nodded, before she added, "So you follow him, and you try to keep me from revealing his secrets."

"There are no secrets in that folder that should stop his wedding," Clayborn said. "Nothing that prevents him from a strong, sure future as Lady Helene's husband."

"Because he is your heir."

He nodded. "Because he is my heir."

She speared another potato and waved it in his direction as she asked, "What makes you so sure that you won't marry and have one of those on your own?"

I won't allow it.

He was saved from having to find a different answer when Gwen returned, this time friendlier, her hand stroking over Clayborn's shoulders as though he were anything but a duke. "Oh, I've a tavern full tonight. The rain's brought everyone in lookin' for heat. Chatty, too—so many questions."

He stiffened at the familiarity and looked up at the tavern mistress, her hip tucking tight to his shoulder. Before he could insist on propriety, she set her back to the rest of the room and leaned down, making a show of wiping the mahogany tabletop. "Can't blame them. Warm in here, ain't it, Adelaide?"

It wasn't warm. Not at all.

Adelaide's attention flickered away from him—had he ever been studied so carefully?—sliding over his shoulder to the door. Something shifted in her deep brown gaze, impossible to notice for the rest of the room. Only noticeable to him because he had a terrible habit of noticing this woman.

"What kind of questions?" It sounded casual, but wasn't.

"People lookin' for rooms. Wonderin' if I've got space in the stables." The look she gave Adelaide was meaningful enough to draw Clayborn's question. "Same questions you were asking."

Adelaide's gaze tracked away again, brown eyes keen behind her spectacles, tracking the taproom before settling somewhere behind him, in the direction of the bar.

He made to turn, to see what had stolen her attention, but she reached for him, her hand coming to his on the table, staying his movement. His attention snapped to her touch, his breath going shallow at the feel of her fingers, soft and warm. A wild impulse urged him to lift her hand and kiss it. Run his tongue over her knuckles. *More*.

He shifted in his seat, stopping the fantasy from running away from him. Up the stairs to a quiet room and a soft bed. A pillow decorated with the flame of her hair.

"Clayborn," she whispered, urging his attention. He gave it to her as she released him and pulled her hood up, the heavy brim of it shading her face. "Join me in my room?"

What in hell? The sound in the pub went discordant, fizzing about in his head. He'd misunderstood her, surely.

Even Gwen looked shocked by the offer. *"What?"*

"Don't tell Duchess." Adelaide was already moving, rising from the table, Clayborn's manners pulling him up alongside her.

The other woman gaped for a moment, then, "To the grave, obviously."

"What does the Duchess have to do with anything?" he asked.

"She likes secrets."

This invitation was worthy of a secret. A night in her room. Alone. Just the two of them. The noise was back, clouding his thoughts. But the desire . . . that had not left.

Nevertheless, he started to resist. "I could not—It would be—"

"Improper," Gwen finished for him, and he was simultaneously grateful for the word and irritated.

"Yes. That."

Adelaide stood, shaking out her skirts. "Have you ever known me to worry about propriety, Gwen? It shall be too warm in the stables, and the duke requires a decent night's rest if he's to keep up with me."

Clayborn would wager his entire fortune that it was not warm in the stables. Not with the wicked chill that pervaded this full tavern every time the door opened.

"Ahh," Gwen said as though she'd been silly not to think of it herself. "Quite right. Far too warm for sensitive aristocrats."

"I'm not sensitive," he said.

"Nonsense. All aristocrats are sensitive." Adelaide turned to the other woman, her gaze firm. "You'll take care of his carriage?"

Gwen was already moving for the bar, where the boy she'd called Wei stood, ready for his next instructions. Clayborn looked to Adelaide. "What's wrong with my carriage? It's a new barouche."

"Mmm, and handsome," she said, lifting his plate from the table and shoving it into his hands. "Made for speed in town, not strength out here. And emblazoned with a ducal seal."

"Of course it is," he said. "It is owned by a duke."

She raised a brow. "Should I kneel in reverence?"

He bit his tongue at the teasing words. At the image they summoned—wildly inappropriate. Not to mention unwelcome, considering her sharp tongue.

Don't think of her tongue.

"Dukes don't sleep in haylofts. You shall share my room. And we shall retire *now*." He did not follow as she lifted her own plate and made for the rear stairway. When she noticed, she turned back, the hood of her cloak hiding her eyes as she prompted, "Your Grace?"

The title shook him free. He straightened his spine. Something had changed, and she was hiding it from him. He considered the tavern, finding nothing amiss. A newcomer had taken a seat at the bar, back to them. The farmer and his beauty were growing more indecent by the moment. The trio of young women in the corner were laughing and shouting for ale.

She shook her head, looking to Gwen. "It's too warm down here."

Gwen nodded. "You know how fires are, impossible to keep a place comfortable."

"It's not at all warm in here," he said, feeling as though he was in a stage performance without his lines.

"That is how people sometimes feel when they are extremely warm," Adelaide said, spinning away from the table. "They mistake it for cold."

"That's the opposite of what happens," he said. "People mistake cold for heat. Take their clothes off and die of exposure."

"The man's talking of removing his clothes, Adelaide. You'd best get him upstairs before he offends the whole place," Gwen interjected.

That was an impossibility, he was sure. Although he shouldn't be discussing clothing within earshot of women. It simply wasn't done.

None of this was done, come to think of it.

He froze. No matter what games he played, he remained the Duke of Clayborn. Which meant that when something was not done, it was not done *by him*.

Adelaide barely turned, her face shadowed by the edge of her hood. *Hidden.* From what? From *whom*? Someday, he'd have a chance to look at this woman in full daylight, without barriers between them, and ask her questions she would answer.

"Now, Duke."

He blinked, unaccustomed to receiving orders. "Now?"

"Now," she said softly, before she was gone, disappearing into the crowd, toward the stairs leading up to the rooms of the inn.

He shouldn't be doing any of this.

Shouldn't be eating with her, or conversing with her, or following her from inn to inn.

And he *certainly* shouldn't be following her across a taproom, to a staircase that would take him up to private rooms.

Room. A single, private room. *And bed.*

But that damn vision was back. That bed. Adelaide in it with her hair spread out in silken waves. And it was difficult to refuse an opportunity to see it made real. Certainly, he *would* refuse it. Just as soon as he found the words.

Just as soon as he was through imagining it.

Except there were more people in the tavern than he'd initially thought, and she had already disappeared, expecting him to follow.

No, came a whisper at the back of his mind. *Not disappeared.*

Fled.

Which meant someone was chasing her. Someone other than himself.

And he couldn't have that.

Chapter Six

When they reached the top of the rear stairs of the Hawk and Hedgehog, Adelaide told herself her heart was pounding because of the possibility of discovery below.

Alfie Trumbull hadn't built one of the largest criminal gangs in London without knowing a thing or two about tracking people outside the city. If a peer was looking for a less than savory solution to a problem, The Bully Boys would handle it—for a hefty price.

Watching her father build his empire had inspired Adelaide to bring the idea of a network of safe taverns to Duchess and the Belles. Now, more than twenty called the Duchess of Trevescan a patron, and were serviced by Mithra Singh and her crew of brewers and messengers.

The man asking questions below—whether he worked for Alfie or not—had unsettled Gwen, and when she'd mentioned they were asking the same questions Adelaide had, the message was clear. The man in the tavern was hunting Helene and Jack, just as Adelaide was. What he did not have was Adelaide's network of scouts, and the knowledge that the pair were two hours north.

Adelaide, on the other hand, now knew that she and Clayborn weren't simply racing each other to Gretna; they were racing Havistock's hired men. Any tracker worth his salt would know that Helene came packaged with John Carrington, brother to the Duke of Clayborn.

And so Clayborn had to stay out of sight, too, lest the men chasing Helene sniff him out.

That, and if he were found with her, it would be too easy to connect her to the Matchbreaker.

Honestly, aristocrats made everything more difficult.

Especially aristocrats like the Duke of Clayborn, who drew all attention with his broad shoulders and the way he carried himself—as though the entire world would bend to his will if he ordered it.

Gwen would feed the scout, water him, and tell him the truth—that there hadn't been a free room at this particular inn since the morning, and she'd seen no couple come through, hurrying to Gretna Green. In the stables, the seal on the duke's carriage had already been muddied, ensuring that no one would notice it in the dark.

Good Lord. The man couldn't even travel discreetly.

And he thought he could *blend*.

Her heart again, thumping in her chest as she reached the top of the stairs and turned toward her room, tucked away from the rest of the guests. This time, Adelaide told herself, it was likely due to exertion. She hadn't eaten much that day, and she was tired from the drive.

It most definitely was not her companion.

Nor was it the fact that, when the door closed behind them with a quiet *snick*, they were completely alone, with no fear of being discovered.

At first glance, the room appeared ordinary, ready for any passing traveler who happened by. But as in all inns supported by Duchess, there was little ordinary about it, directly above the posting inn's dining room, complete with a large window that offered a clear view of the drive.

The room, like twenty others in taverns across Britain, was never offered to passing travelers, unless that traveler arrived with the introduction of The Duchess herself . . . or the traveler was one of Duchess's trusted lieutenants.

Adelaide could have arrived long after the Duke of Clayborn darkened the door of the Hawk and Hedgehog, and he still would have been left to the stables.

As he should have been that night.

Alone, she would have stayed in the taproom, invisible. And even if she were noticed, she had no doubt that she could hide—stay to the safe places, trust that tavern owners deep into Scotland would happily throw anything that came for her—even The Bully Boys—off her scent, keeping her unseen.

The Duke of Clayborn could not hide, however. He was a stallion in a herd of sheep. The moment he was noticed, anyone looking for Lady Helene would know they were on the right path, which would make everything else more difficult, and so Adelaide had no choice. She had to keep him close.

That was the only reason she'd invited him up.

Inside the room, she removed her cloak, hanging it on a hook on the far wall, taking the plate from his hand as he moved to do the same. After setting the food on a nearby table, she turned to find him standing back to the door. "Are you not hungry?"

"No."

She shrugged one shoulder and lifted a roasted parsnip from her plate. Biting into the delicious vegetable, she chewed for a bit. "I would have thought you'd prefer privacy for a meal."

"Not like this. Not with you."

She was a mistake.

Adelaide tried not to be offended by the words. "By all means, then, Duke. You may return to the taproom." He remained silent and unmoving, and she added, "I, for one, am going to eat. It's been a long day—longer even, for you. I suggest you do the same."

Lifting her plate, she perched on the bench at the window behind the table, looking through the rain-streaked glass to the drive, empty of stable boys and travelers.

They'd be lucky if the roads were passable in the morning. "If you think to insult me with your lack of companionship, I assure you, it is not possible. I have made a lifetime of eating alone, and on the fly."

And with that, she returned to her pie and took an enormous bite, wondering if the duke had ever seen a woman eat outside of a formal dining room before that evening.

"Why?"

She swallowed the delicious food and spoke to her plate. "It speaks!"

"Shelley again," he grumbled.

She did look at him then, curious. "Again?"

"Why have you made a lifetime of eating alone?"

Adelaide did not like the tone of the question. She might have been alright with it if it had had some kind of pity in it, as though he thought less of her for it. That might have activated her pride and preservation. She wouldn't have blinked if it had been full of distaste, as though being alone were a failing. But instead, it was without judgment at all. Just . . . a question.

And it activated something that Adelaide loathed.

Shame.

"I don't mind it," she said.

"Alright."

"I don't," she insisted, as though she had something to prove. "I am used to doing things alone. I prefer it, honestly."

He was watching her carefully, and though she searched for it, she could not find judgment in his attention.

She shrugged and forked another bite of pie. "Eating alone is preferable to sharing a meal before being cast out in the cold. Alone, there is no transaction. You never fear you will not measure up."

A long silence fell—long enough for Adelaide to grow embarrassed, so she busied herself with her food. After what seemed like an eternity, he came off the wall and crossed the room, joining her, taking several bites in silence before he said, "I find it difficult to believe anyone would think you do not measure up."

The heat of embarrassment turned to heat of a different kind. "You have to say that. It is my room or the stables for you."

When he smiled, she liked it too much. Enough to stop whatever this was in its tracks. "At any rate, I have plenty of meals with other people. With friends. I've been to dinners with you, even. Though you likely do not remember."

"Of course I remember." *That* was a different tone altogether. Affront. Irritation. Offense.

"I—" she started and stopped. "I am surprised. You were not exactly polite to me."

"Miss Frampton," he said, and she couldn't help her scoff at the formality, considering they were in a bedchamber at a posting inn miles from anywhere. Formality had rather flown out the window. "I stopped you from making yourself a powerful enemy—Lord Coleford was a dangerous man."

She laughed. "You think I did not know that?"

"I know you knew it. I have always suspected you are the reason he will spend the rest of his days in Newgate."

"The man murdered *several* of his wives. *That* is why he will spend the rest of his days in Newgate."

"Thanks to you and your . . . What do you call yourselves?"

She hesitated, not liking the way he noticed her. She wasn't used to it. "I don't know—to whom are you referring?"

"I've seen you," he said. "That night, at the dinner, there were only three of you. Lady Imogen was not there. But often, there are four of you. And then, last night, it occurred to me there might be more."

There were more. Duchess. Imogen. Sesily. Maggie.

The others. "My friends." Scotland Yard called them the Hell's Belles. The papers had any number of names for them. The gossamer gang. Crinoline chaos. Muslin mayhem.

"They aren't like any friends I've ever met," he said. "They seem like more. The kind of friends who can end an earl on a whim."

"It wasn't a whim," she said, knowing she shouldn't get close to acknowledging his theory. Knowing she risked more than was reasonable—more than herself.

"No, I don't imagine it was. I imagine it was well planned. Quietly," he said. "No pretty parliamentary speeches necessary."

"Quiet until we must be loud enough to make change," she agreed. She met his gaze. "Loud enough for you, though."

This man, who saw everything. Who noticed everything.

Who noticed her.

"Your secret is safe with me," he said, something like admiration in his eyes, and she believed him. Even though she shouldn't.

He was dangerous.

"I'm not sure I understand the full scope of it, anyway."

"It is friendship," she said, firmly. Adelaide had never spoken to anyone about her friends, and she shouldn't want to. Shouldn't want him to understand. Still . . . "They were the first people to make me feel . . . not alone. I barely suit with them—I'm not titled like Duchess, not rich like Sesily, not . . . well . . . no one is really like Imogen."

"Lady Imogen is rather like a helter-skelter."

"She's quite brilliant." She smiled, thinking of her madcap friend.

"One does not preclude the other," he said, and there was a half smile in his own voice.

Resisting the urge to say more, Adelaide cleared her throat and adjusted her spectacles. "I don't know what you think you've noticed."

A secret smile played across his lips. "I've noticed that when powerful men fall, you're often nearby."

Of course he had. "Does that not worry you? You are a powerful man."

He watched her for a moment before answering. "I am not worried. But I think that if I were, I would have good reason to be, as matchbreaking is not the most dangerous thing you do, by far, Miss Frampton." He added, "Though you are currently racing across Britain, alone, to do just that."

"Not alone," she said without thinking. When the words were out, she flushed, dipping her head and taking another bite of food, knowing that he watched her carefully. Ignoring the enjoyment that threatened under his scrutiny.

"Shall I tell you what else I think?" he said, continuing when she nodded. "I don't think you are chasing them to matchbreak. My brother might be an ass at times, and he could certainly be called stupid at others, but he would never hurt Helene." He did move, then, as though his certainty propelled him toward her. "And I think you know it."

She swallowed her surprise. "What would make you think that?"

One of his dark brows rose. "I pay attention, Adelaide Frampton. And when you heard my brother and Lady Helene were headed from London to Gretna, you weren't shocked and you weren't angry and you weren't fearful. You were *relieved*."

He was right. She had been.

And he'd noticed.

"Someday, I hope you'll find your way to telling me why," he finished. "But I am not asking you to feed that hope now. Nor am I asking you for money or power or revenge. Instead, I am asking if you would let me eat dinner with you. So neither of us is alone."

And in two days of thinking that the man was dangerous, that was the moment he became most terrifying—when he offered her something she could not resist. Companionship.

They ate together, the sounds of the taproom below a distant hum in the space. Adelaide watched him from the corner of her eye until she could not stay quiet any longer. "At Havistock House, you called John your heir."

He met her gaze, his eyes like a clear blue day. "Jack is my heir."

"Because you have no plans to marry."

"Correct."

"Why not?"

It was the question he'd avoided answering downstairs. Clayborn sat back in his chair and watched her for a moment. "Are you offering?"

"What? No. What?" He couldn't really believe she would—

"Adelaide," he said, with an amused smile that she hated and liked too much. "I jest, but thank you for putting me directly back into my place with a wicked blow to my pride."

"I didn't mean that you weren't marriageable," she rushed to say.

"Thank you."

"I mean, you're a *duke*."

He nodded. "I am."

"A duke who believes in love . . . or so you say." Which made him the closest thing Adelaide had ever seen to a mythological creature.

"I believe my brother is in love with Lady Helene, yes."

"And that is enough?"

"As the lady loves him back, I shall do all in my power to ensure that they live happily ever after." He said it with a firm certainty, as though it were a simple fact.

It was the kindest thing she'd ever heard anyone say,

and perhaps that was why she asked, "Why do you believe in it?"

He returned to his food, speaking to his plate. "Because I have witnessed it."

The honesty in the confession summoned her reply. It was the only explanation for her asking, "And you do not wish it for yourself?"

Silence fell between them, heavy with something Adelaide could not identify. Something that made her hot with discomfort, as though she had overstepped. Which of course she had. Whether or not the Duke of Clayborn wished for love was absolutely not her concern.

"Well," she said, when it became clear he was not going to answer. "I'm sure any number of pristine, perfect misses would happily marry you and produce an absolute gaggle of heirs."

"I should prefer to remain out of the Matchbreaker's sights."

The slight tease in his words released her from her nerves, back to normal. Whatever *normal* was when she was with him. "Is there something I should know about you, Henry Carrington, Duke of Clayborn, impeccably educated, wildly erudite, handsome enough to send the young ladies of Mayfair to their smelling salts, and a proper hero for the common people?"

His brows shot together. "Don't call me that."

"Handsome?"

"A hero." There was distaste in the words.

"The newspapers call you that," she said. "They love your pretty words. You're to change the world, they say."

"A worthy goal, no?"

"Absolutely," she allowed. "But you can't do it from Parliament."

"You don't care for politics."

"I am a woman alive in the world, Your Grace. My existence is politics, whether I care for it to be or not. It is not the politics, but the politicians."

He nodded. "You do not think we can make change."

"I think large groups of powerful men have little reason to make change." She paused. "Though I daresay your speeches are pretty."

And they were. Once, she'd been in the gallery at the House of Lords when he'd spoken on child labor, on those born without silver spoons and titles, and he'd nearly sent her to her feet with his righteous anger. She'd recognized it, akin to her own.

Not that she would admit it.

"Pretty," he said, "but not enough."

She shrugged one shoulder and forked another bite of pie. "Why talk when there is action to be taken?"

"I confess to feeling that way myself on most days." He leaned back in his chair. "Then your file contains plenty about me, after all."

"I don't need a file to know about you," she scoffed. "I simply need a subscription to the *News*."

"And if you were hired to matchbreak me? That would be enough?"

Who would wish to matchbreak you? Another bite, needing the moment to tamp down the immediate response. Chewed thoughtfully. Swallowed. "Everyone has secrets. Even heroes."

Something flashed in his dark gaze. Something that sent triumph coursing through Adelaide, because you could take the girl out of South Lambeth, but you couldn't take the thief out of the girl. And the Duke of Clayborn was hiding something. A secret.

"Why did you offer to share this room with me?"

She couldn't tell him the truth. He did not seem the kind of man who would stand for fleeing an enemy when he might fight. Indeed, she'd seen him fight men stronger and stouter than he, and without hesitation.

That, and the single scout searching for a girl who was safe in the arms of her love two hours up the road in a rainstorm was not the reason she'd invited him here.

I should have taken better care of him. That story—the way Clayborn shouldered the burden of his brother. Responsible. Thoughtful. Decent. There'd been something noble there that Adelaide had liked. Something honest.

But he wasn't *all* honest. He did have a secret, and it was dear enough to have been stolen by Alfie Trumbull and chased by the duke himself.

Setting her plate on the table, Adelaide crossed to her carpetbag, on a low bench at the end of the bed. Aware of Clayborn's intense focus, she opened it and searched within, until she found what she was looking for.

Turning toward him, she set his brother's file on the table. On top, she placed the oak cube, before lifting her plate. Resuming her seat, she took another bite of pie and watched him resist the urge to race for his prize.

He found her eyes. "You brought it back to me."

She tilted her head. "Perhaps."

Suspicion flooded his face. "For a price."

"The sheer goodness of my heart is not a possibility?"

He gave a little huff of air. Not enough to be a laugh, but enough for her to wonder what his laugh would sound like. "Not even a bit."

She pointed her fork in the direction of the cube. "Open it, and the dossier is yours."

The humor disappeared from his gaze immediately. "No."

Her brows shot up. "Interesting. So whatever is inside . . . it is more precious than your brother's file?" *Fascinating.*

He hesitated at that, clearly loathing that he had given her more information than he'd intended, simply by refusing her request. "What is inside is *private.*"

The second time he'd used the word to describe the contents of the cube. She set down her plate and lifted the box, inspecting it, allowing satisfaction into her words. "And it *can* be opened."

"Yes." The word was pulled from him, as though by force.

She turned the box over and over in her hands, searching for something. "Then there must be a key."

He watched her for a long time, until he was unable to remain at a distance. Crossing to sit across from her, he asked, "Would you like a hint?"

"I know better than to think you'll give me one for free."

He inclined his head. "What's the fun in that?"

"There isn't any." This, she understood. A trade. "What then? Name your price."

"Answer my questions."

That could be extremely costly. Still, she brazened on. "That's it?"

"Yes. For each question you answer truthfully, I shall give you a hint to open the box. And when you open it, I get everything. What's inside and what's in the dossier."

She tilted her head. "And what do I get?"

"The satisfaction of knowing how to open it."

Desire thrummed through Adelaide at the smug answer, delivered as though there was no doubt in the man's mind that he'd offered her a prize beyond measure.

He couldn't possibly be serious, unless the questions would be the kind she would not answer truthfully. But Adelaide had gone before the magistrate on more than one occasion in her short life, and knew well how to spin a yarn. "How many questions?"

"As many as you need."

She nodded. "Go on, then."

"How do you know where my brother is?"

"Right now?"

"Yes."

"How do you *not* know? You knew they were eloping."

He nodded. "I did, but for barely any time before you

did. A hastily written note, received in the moments before I was summoned to Havistock House."

She nodded. It made sense. Helene and Jack had left quickly, and if the scout downstairs was any indication, just in time to escape her father's hunt.

In exchange for Clayborn's truth, she offered a bit of her own. "Couples on their way to Gretna Green are rarely smart about their choices. They regularly choose speed over security, and they barely ever cover their tracks—the downfall of entitlement." She could have stopped there, but added, "Your brother and Lady Helene had a half-dozen possible choices for the night. The Matchbreaker has a far-reaching network that puts eyes in every one of them. They aren't difficult to track. We'll catch them tomorrow."

"We?" he asked.

She bit her tongue. "*I* will catch them. You'll catch up eventually, I'm sure."

The corner of his mouth twitched, which was the only reason she noticed his mouth at all. It had nothing to do with the dim light and the warm fire and the fact that they were in a bedchamber together. Nor the constant memory of how those lips felt on hers when she'd kissed them.

I shouldn't have done that.

She urged herself to remember his words after he'd kissed her. She'd been a mistake.

He lifted his chin in the direction of the box. "If you apply pressure to two opposite corners, you'll be able to rotate an exterior panel."

A wave of excitement crashed through her as she tumbled the oak cube over and over, rushing to follow instructions. After a failed first attempt, she found the corners that activated the puzzle and—*twist*. She looked to him. "Amazing."

She could feel his attention on her, more focused than before. "Mmm." It wasn't the first time he'd rumbled like

that, a cross between agreement and something else . . .
something like *approval*.

She shouldn't like it.

There were too many things about this man she
shouldn't like.

And still, she couldn't seem to stop herself.

"Did you make this?"

"No."

"What next?" she asked, her fingers chasing over the
box, looking for new trips, for switches or buttons. And
there, where it had not been before, was a tiny notch.
Barely noticeable. She gave a little sound of delight and
inspected it. Pressing, pulling.

An idea sparked. She lifted her fork.

"No." The word was firm. Insistent. Not to be dis-
obeyed.

Her attention flew to him, and she stilled. "No?"

"No," he said, as though it was enough.

She set it down. "So . . . what?"

"Another question."

"Or I keep working at it."

He nodded. "Or you keep working at it. But I don't
expect you'll have much time with it now that I know
where it is, and we are locked together for the evening."

The words sizzled through her. She did not look to the
bed, despite the way it beckoned.

He leaned back, crossing his arms over his chest.
"Shall I ask another question? Speed things along?"

She nodded. Just one more. One more, and she'd stop
this game, which was getting more and more dangerous.
"I am an open book."

"No, Adelaide." Her name. He'd said her name.
"You're nothing like an open book. Now tell me, what
happened downstairs?"

She didn't flinch. Instead she leveled him with a cool
look. "What's in the box?"

He hesitated—he couldn't possibly be thinking of answering, and still, for a moment she thought he might. "Nothing that would send you racing from the room."

"I don't know what you mean," she said. "And I didn't race."

He tutted his disapproval. "I don't give hints for falsehoods. Something in that taproom unnerved you, Adelaide Frampton. And you don't seem the kind of woman who startles easily. What was it?"

She shook her head, she couldn't tell him. Couldn't trust him. What Helene had seen—what she still faced—she could not trust he would not get in the way of Adelaide reaching her. Protecting her. "There was nothing."

He was out of his chair like a shot, returning to his place at the door, his back to her for a long moment before he asked, "Are you in danger?"

Of course he asked that. "No."

He looked over his shoulder. "Will you be?"

"Yesterday we dispatched a half-dozen Bully Boys together, Your Grace. I believe I might be in danger again someday, yes."

He gave a frustrated sigh at the bold answer, tacit acceptance that she was not going to tell him the full scope of the situation. He turned and set his back to the door, crossing his arms over his chest. "So, you are simply chaos."

Something warmed inside her at the description—one no one had ever used with her.

"And to think," he went on, "you imagine yourself unnoticeable."

"How did you find me here?"

"I thought I was asking the questions."

She set the box to the table once more. "It's my turn. How did you find me tonight?"

"I searched three other inns first. It was bloody cold and bloody wet."

She tilted her head. "And if I hadn't been here? Would you have given up?"

"No, Adelaide," he said, "I wouldn't have given up."

The answer unsettled her. She shook her head as though she could clear the sensation. Erase the truth of the words. "For your box and your brother."

"Mmm." A half agreement. Like a word on parchment, washed out in the rain.

"And how did you know to find me in Covent Garden? At The Place?" She avoided calling it her rooms. He didn't need to know she lived there. She didn't want him to know she lived there, alone in the two-room flat, only the roar of the tavern for company.

"You think you are the only one with access to information?"

She narrowed her gaze on him. "I don't like my information being shared without permission."

He raised a brow in the direction of the dossier on the table. The information on his brother, shared with Lady Havistock. "How odd. The rest of us enjoy it quite a bit."

She didn't pretend to misunderstand. "The information I share is to be used against people who deserve it."

"My brother does not deserve it."

"No, he does not."

She surprised them both with the quick answer. "When did you realize that?"

"Yesterday, at Havistock House." When she'd realized Jack, Lord Carrington, had turned to bareknuckle fighting for The Bully Boys to keep Lady Helene safe. A decent man doing his best to protect the woman he loved.

Decent, like his brother.

"Yet you chase them, still. To break this match."

Not for that reason. "Yes."

"Why?"

Because a terrible man was after an innocent girl. And the Belles needed to keep her safe. And the Matchbreaker was the best tool in their arsenal. But those were secrets that were not hers to tell. The best she could do was, "Because your brother is not the most important piece of this."

His body stiffened and his lips pressed together, his arms crossed over his chest like armor as he leaned against the door.

"And so we are to be at odds."

She lifted her chin, ignoring the way the simple words, devoid of anger and full of truth, felt. "It is neither the first nor last time I will be at odds with powerful men." She should have left it there. There was no more for him to know. Except she added, "I have spent a lifetime at odds with powerful men."

She waited for him to argue. To tell her that his brother was different. That he was different. That they were to be trusted. To press her for more. It was a play she knew well.

When he finally spoke, however, it was with a new script. "Not tonight."

Her brow furrowed. "What?"

"Tomorrow, we begin again. Tonight, we are not at odds."

Impossible. "Why not?"

"Because we are here, in this room, together. And whatever unnerved you downstairs. Whoever unnerved you. Tonight . . . they shall have to come through me."

If she'd been given a dozen guesses as to what he would say, that wouldn't have been on the list. And she could not deny how much she liked the promise in the words, a promise that no one had ever made to her before.

To protect her. For no other reason than because he could.

Pleasure bloomed in her breast, unbidden. Unwelcome. Who was this man? What was this game? "I am no damsel in distress."

"I do not disagree. I've seen the blade you keep strapped to your thigh."

The weapon in question grew heavy in its holster. "And still you stand sentry, as though I am."

Another long silence, long enough for Adelaide to wonder if they were through for the night. To rise and head for her bag once more, eager to busy herself beneath his watchful gaze.

"My father liked puzzles."

Four words, like a revelation. A gift from the Duke of Clayborn, who even when he spoke of love, revealed nothing of himself.

She stilled, looking to him. "He made the box."

He did not have to reply. She was right, and it explained a number of things, not the least of which was why the Duke of Clayborn had ventured into South Lambeth in shirtsleeves. Whatever was inside the box held value beyond riches. It was as he had said—private.

"I like puzzles as well," he added, and she nodded again. He came off the wall. "It's why I followed you from the warehouse. To the docks. To Covent Garden. Why I followed you to this inn at the edge of the earth."

"We're a day's ride from London."

"But the rules here are different, aren't they?" The words were a quiet rumble as he drew closer. "We might as well be on the other side of the planet." She was beginning to regret urging him from his place by the door, his movements, smooth and sure, setting her heart pounding, heavy and quick, a mere change in his proximity enough to send her spinning. It was nonsense, of course.

Except then he was there, standing in front of her, tall and toned—not like any aristocrat she'd ever seen before. Aristocrats were supposed to come in small, narrow, pasty packages. They were supposed to scare and cower and complain. No one had apprised the Duke of Clayborn of such a thing.

She lifted her chin and tried very hard not to reveal the way her insides were tumbling about. "Are you still hungry?"

"I am." He did not stop at the table, however. He went round the edge of it. Until he was close to her, his trousers threatening to brush up against her skirts.

She stood.

Food. Food she could do. "The roasted veg is quite—"

"I noticed." He cut her off. And did not move.

She was vibrating. Was she vibrating?

"Your meal grows cold."

"I like puzzles," he replied.

She gave him a little smile. "You cannot eat a puzzle."

One side of his mouth lifted in a wry smile. "Mmm."

The sound sent something heavy and hot deep within her. She sucked in a breath.

He heard it, one dark brow rising in a perfect arch. "I promised to give you clues about the box if you told me the truth . . . and I think that breath . . . it might be the most truthful you've been tonight." And then he lifted his hand, reaching for her. Tempting her.

She stilled, waiting for his touch, her breath gone shallow and uneven in her chest.

"What was it you said downstairs?" he asked, low and deep. "It's warm in here?"

The words were a code downstairs. Adelaide had a feeling they were a code here, as well. But a different code. One she did not understand.

"That much is true," he continued. "You are flushed." His fingers touched her cheek, setting fire to her skin. "Here." He ran them along her jaw, down the line of her throat, to the gold chain that hung, always, around her neck, then low—lower, until it disappeared beneath the fabric of her dress. He lingered there, and she wondered if he would lift the chain, pull the pendant from where it lay like a secret against her skin.

When his touch moved again, tracing the chain once

more, back to the base of her neck, she closed her eyes, keenly aware of the way her heart raced.

"This . . ." He painted a little circle on her skin there, where her pulse throbbed, betraying her. "This is the most truthful you've been."

Her eyes flew open, meeting his, already watching. Waiting for her to look at him. Glittering with knowledge of what he did to her. *Dammit.*

He lifted his hand, removing his touch. *Dammit. Dammit.*

"The box does not have a key," he said softly. "If you force it, it will lock. There will be no way of accessing the information within. But you sensed that already."

She nodded, barely listening. Wondering what he would do if she grabbed his hand and returned it to her skin. "You could break it open," she said, barely recognizing her own voice, gone breathless. "A hammer would do the job."

"You could," he replied. Was he closer now? At her ear? The words a caress? "But then it would be destroyed. And that is *unacceptable.*"

Adelaide shuddered at the word, spoken with firm certainty and a thread of darkness, as though he would not allow such a thing.

They hovered in silence, Clayborn finally breaking it as he took a step back and looked away, to the food. "Apologies. I should not have . . ."

When he trailed off, Adelaide said, "It was not—"

She did not have to find the words to finish her own sentence, because he cut in. "It was unacceptable."

How could one word spoken twice in mere seconds carry such different meanings?

"I should not have touched you tonight."

But she'd wanted it.

"I should certainly not have kissed you yesterday."

She clenched her teeth and slid away, putting distance

between them, hating the apology. She made a show of inspecting the contents of her carpetbag. "There is no reason to apologize for yesterday."

He gave a little huff of humorless laughter. "That's the most severe of my infractions."

"I don't know why," she said. "You did not kiss me."

"What?" He could not keep his surprise hidden. She liked that.

"You did not kiss me."

"I did." Insistence.

"You did not."

"Miss Frampton—" She *hated* that he called her that. "I assure you I did. I was there."

She looked to him then, and at another time, she might have enjoyed his surprise. Not then, though. "No. I kissed you. That's quite a different thing altogether. Therefore, you needn't apologize."

He let out a harsh sound. "You—"

"You needn't dwell on your mistake, is my point, Your Grace." She cut him off, waving at the bed, and continued, quickly and with a practiced lack of emotion. "Now. I am tired, and tomorrow will be a long day catching your brother and Lady Helene. Would you prefer to sleep in the bed or the chair?"

Another sound, this one as though he was being strangled.

She looked to him again, brows raised in question.

"The chair," he said.

Of course he chose the chair. Such a gentleman, apologizing for being kissed and for touching her and being generally difficult to tolerate. "Then if you do not mind, would you exit the room so I might . . ." She waved a hand at the bed.

He immediately spun to face the door, putting his back to her. "Of course. Excuse me. Yes. Of course." He took a few steps toward the door and then stopped, as though a hound reaching the end of a lead. He looked back. "Only, if I leave . . ."

"Yes?"

"You're not safe here."

Adelaide could not help her little laugh.

He scowled. "You think that amusing?"

"I think it amusing that you think me unable to keep myself safe." As though she hadn't learned early to be her own savior.

His brow furrowed. Without a reply, he left, closing the door. Adelaide turned to the washbasin in the corner, telling herself it was all for the best. The apology. The way he'd clearly been horrified by the kiss on the docks. By touching her. He was a duke, after all, and she a thief born on the wrong side of the river.

Everything else was disguise.

She fetched soap and tooth powder from her bag, removed her spectacles and made quick work of her ablutions before stripping to her chemise. Crossing the room, she fetched the dossier from where it lay, but left a candle burning on the table, shadows dancing across the smooth surface of the puzzle box.

Returning the file to her bag, she told herself he could have his secrets. She wasn't in the market for them.

It was a lie, of course. Every moment she spent with the Duke of Clayborn, she wished to know more of him. Which was dangerous, indeed, because knowing made for liking. And liking made for wanting.

And the Duke of Clayborn was not for Adelaide Frampton.

She woke in the morning to find the oak cube remained on the table, next to the snuffed candle. Across the room, the Duke of Clayborn slept in the chair . . . which he'd moved to block the door.

They shall have to come through me.

Adelaide ignored the tightness in her chest at the memory and the image of him, relaxed, in shirtsleeves, a wedge of somehow sun-kissed skin beneath a woolen blanket he'd found somewhere. She dressed silently—years of practice making it possible—marveling that he'd left his secrets on the table. That he'd trusted her.

A mistake. A thief was born to steal, was she not?

She was gone before he woke, his treasure in hand.

Chapter Seven

The Duke of Clayborn was in a foul mood.

He hunched his shoulders beneath his greatcoat, pulled the brim of his hat low over his brow, tightened his grip on the reins, and cursed into the biting wind that felt more like December than October should.

It was not the weather that had put him in his mood, however.

Nor was it the backbreaking ride in the carriage, bouncing and rocking, wheels groaning as the road grew less and less smooth and the afternoon sun began to set.

No, he'd been in this mood—cursing the weather and roads and vehicles and an overhanging oak branch that had nearly removed his head and a broken wheel that had set him back a full hour while he replaced it—since he'd woken that morning, gnarled into the most uncomfortable position a body could find in sleep, in a hard chair, in a cold room, at the Hawk and Hedgehog.

Truthfully, his mood might have survived the crick in his neck.

Except, Adelaide had disappeared.

It was impossible, or at least he'd thought it had been when he'd set the chair to the door as she'd slept. By the time he'd entered the room, she'd been in bed, all but a single candle extinguished, lighting his way as he made himself as comfortable as one could with a small blanket, a waning fire, and an uncomfortable chair.

When he'd extinguished the light and tried to sleep himself, it had been nearly impossible, knowing that he should not be sharing a room with an unmarried lady.

In the darkness, he told himself it was all in service to their race. Adelaide not being able to leave without waking him had been an added bonus. He'd keep pace with her from the start on their second day's journey—having eyes on her from daybreak would ensure he would not lose her again.

It was only half true. There was another reason to share her room. To station himself like a sentry by the door. He wished to keep her safe.

He'd chased sleep for hours, doing his best to remain gentlemanly. To avoid thinking of her, warm and soft in the room's only bed. To avoid wondering whether she'd removed her dress before climbing into bed. Whether she'd taken down her red hair. Whether it spread across the sheets as he'd imagined before, when he absolutely shouldn't have.

He'd made a list of all the things he shouldn't wonder, and the activity had done nothing to deliver rest. The clock in the hallway outside had marked eleven. Then midnight.

When one chimed, he gave in, finally allowing himself to listen to the smooth, even rhythm of her slumber. To count those breaths like sheep, sure he'd wake before her.

Instead, he'd woken without her.

He hadn't liked it.

He cursed again, leaning into the ride, pushing the horses farther up the road, grateful that there'd been a fast, strong set waiting for him when he'd stopped to change the team—the only good thing that had happened that day, considering he was behind in his race to catch Adelaide, and he had no indication of how far she would push her own horses in her pursuit of his brother.

Clayborn had done all he could to catch her, coming

out of the chair in which he'd slept instantly. It hadn't
taken him long to discover two things—first, the room
had a secret exit, a door perfectly hidden in the tapestry
of elaborate wallpaper on one side of the bed, which led
to a set of back stairs that exited directly to the stables.
He should have expected it—Adelaide Frampton would
never allow herself to be trapped, when she could be
free.

And second, she'd taken his box with her.

He leaned forward and gave the horses an encouraging
yah!, hoping they'd find themselves motivated to close
the distance she'd left.

She'd left.

He'd trusted her with the box, telling himself as he
sat in the darkness that he'd hear her if she came for it.
No. That was nonsense. What he'd told himself was that
she'd stay, and the box, in her hands or in his, would
remain with him.

But Adelaide Frampton was a thief first and everything else second . . . and she'd slipped away under cloak
of night, just before dawn, according to the stable boy
he'd terrified with ducal interrogation at half six in the
morning.

He wasn't far behind, and a strong set of horses could
make all the difference.

But Clayborn knew better than to underestimate Adelaide, and as the sun set and the cold began to bite, and
he was reminded that his horses would soon tire, Clayborn lost control of his thoughts—the ones he'd promised himself he would hold at bay.

It started innocuously. A whisper of logic. Her horses
would tire too, would they not?

She, too, would have to stop.

She, too, would be tempted by warm food. And a
soft bed—

That was his mistake, allowing himself to think of
her in a soft bed. To remember the other bits of her

that were soft. Her breath as she slept. The skin of her cheek when he'd touched her the night before. The flutter of her pulse when he'd found it, rapid and tempting. Her lips.

And all the other bits that he had not yet explored. An onslaught of fantasy crashed over him, long limbs and flushed breasts and the skin at her back as she arched toward him. The sigh he teased from her. That flame red hair that he still hadn't seen, but that he'd touched . . . soft as silk and pure temptation.

Softness faded, replaced by thoughts of the firm grip of her hands in his hair, the bite of her teeth at his shoulder. The demands she might deliver.

He groaned, cursing his frustration as he rounded a curve in the road, willing himself to think of anything but her—the pounding of hooves, the rattle of the brougham's wheels, the creak of the springs in the cold.

Finding the straightaway once more, his gaze narrowed into the distance, and he wondered if he'd summoned her with his thoughts. Because there, one hundred yards ahead, was a carriage, moving at a clip, to be sure. But slow enough that he could catch it.

Catch her.

And it was her. He knew it without question.

As though she'd summoned him to her.

Triumph came, hot and rewarding, and he gave his team full rein, spurring them forward with a single goal—to close the distance. The woman wanted a race? He'd give it to her. And when he won . . . *he'd claim his prize.*

One hundred yards became fifty, then twenty-five. He pulled away, putting distance between them on the road as he prepared to come alongside her. He made to shout—to announce his presence so she was not unsettled by his arrival, but before he could, she turned and looked over her shoulder, unsurprised.

She'd known he was there.

Her brows rose and she shouted, "Come to give me the race I was promised, have you?"

Pleasure thrummed through him at the words, at the taunt in them. The challenge. "I could have given it earlier if you hadn't snuck off!"

She flashed him a grin, lighter than any he'd seen from her before. Fresh and honest and beautiful enough to set his heart pounding. "I couldn't bear wake you, Duke . . . you looked so comfortable!"

He turned back to the road at the words, checking the path of the horses as he hid his own smile and shouted, "Tonight, I intend to win the available bed!"

She tossed him a look. "A real race, then! To the next inn!"

His gaze slid over her, the gleam in her eyes visible even behind her spectacles, the pink in her cheeks, her wide smile like a gift. Her gloved hands gripping taut reins, she wore a coat, but the wind from the ride had blown the skirt of it wide over her driving dress, a rich green the color of spring, fabric molded to her torso and legs.

It occurred to him that he'd race her wherever she wished to go. Ignoring the thought, he called out to his team, urging them to go faster. Eager to win . . . not just for the prize, or the ability to boast of it, but to show her he could.

To win the race . . . and her admiration.

She was not going to give it to him easily. Good; he wanted the game. When was the last time he'd had one? Had he ever had one?

She came forward on the box, leaned into the reins, her coat billowing out behind her, skirts molding to her strong thighs. He was nearly even with her now, unable to stop himself from checking on her in a constant back and forth—the road, her carriage, the road again.

Ahead, a tree leaned into their path, a leafy branch particularly low on Adelaide's side. They both saw it, and he shouted at her to watch herself.

He didn't need to. She sat back on the block, leaning over to duck, easily clearing it, and came up smiling, smooth as a Roman charioteer. She adjusted her eyeglasses and flashed him a smile, her arrogant pride clear and absolutely perfect.

He could watch this woman race carriages forever.

The thought had barely crossed his mind when a gust of wind blew across the road, cold and brisk and harsh enough to lift the hat from her head. She reached for it with an "Oh!" but it was already gone, whipped off into the brush at the side of the road, chased by her laugh, rich and beautiful.

For a heartbeat, instinct took over, and he made to slow his horses—to stop and fetch it. To return it to her like a prize at a tourney. He meant to stop. Meant to be a gentleman.

Except the hat wasn't all the wind claimed.

Her hair had come loose, a wild cloud of silk and fire.

And he forgot everything, because he could not look away from it, finally free, billowing around her in a gravity-defying squall, long and lush and vibrant and so much more beautiful than he'd imagined.

This woman, whom he'd noticed from the moment they met, was now impossible to ignore.

Which was why he missed the dip in the road.

"Clayborn!" she shouted, looking to him, concern behind her wire-rimmed spectacles. "The road!"

It was too late. He hit the uneven patch—sunken from weather and wear—before he could do anything to stop it, even as he reacted, fast and capable, pulling hard on the reins, coming to his feet on the block, he knew it was too little and too late. The carriage tilted, the shift punctuated with a mighty crack. A stutter in the already wildly bouncing ride. And then the tilt went farther, more dangerous. He didn't have a choice.

Confirming Adelaide's carriage was not in the path of whatever was to happen to his own, he released the reins and jumped.

Following the momentum of the leap, he tucked and rolled and tried his damnedest not to break anything, but when he came to a stop in a ditch on the side of the fast-darkening road, the breath knocked from his lungs, he was fairly certain he was not in one piece.

Nevertheless, the groan of metal, punctuated by the crash of wood and glass and the wild sounds of two rightfully terrified horses trying to drag an overturned carriage had him rolling immediately to his feet, testing legs and arms and finding himself luckier than he deserved.

Somehow, however, there was little joy in the revelation. His carriage was wrecked, his horses panicked, and his body bruised.

Not to mention his pride.

"Clayborn!" He winced at the words when Adelaide appeared, having stopped her own carriage to check on him. "Are you all right?"

"I'm fine." Approaching the wreck, he waved her back, not wanting to face her as he moved to calm the horses, unhitching the animals as quickly as possible and discovering, miraculously, that they were unharmed.

"You're not fine!" she said. "You could have been *killed*."

"I wasn't, though," he said, working for calm as he led the horses to a nearby tree before returning to crouch by the carriage and consider the tangled mess of the vehicle, turned on its side, halfway in a ditch on the side of the road.

"When you jumped—" she went on, coming to stand near him, unaware of the way his jaw tightened at her words. Of the hot embarrassment that flooded him. "God, I thought you were—" She cut herself off, something caught in her throat.

He looked up at her. *Was she worried about him?*

"I thought you had—"

He didn't like what he saw in her eyes. "Adelaide," he said, firmly. "Look at me." She did, staring down at him, and he held her pretty brown gaze for a moment before saying, "I am here."

She nodded as he climbed into the wreckage to rescue his bags. It took longer than he would have liked, having to pick apart the detritus—so much for the brougham being the best conveyance for a modern gentleman, as the salesman had promised him. It had fallen apart like a child's toy.

"What happened?" she asked, and he stilled at the words.

You happened.

I couldn't look away from you.

Even then he stared at her, failing to learn his lesson.

"It appears you won the race," he said. "Why not press on and claim your winnings?"

A room of her own. A soft bed.

No. He wouldn't think of her in beds any longer.

"What? I am not leaving you."

He ignored her as he continued his search, willing her to do as he asked. Finding his bag at long last, he climbed back out of the mess. "I do not require you to linger."

Her brows furrowed, the fast waning light casting her skin in an orange glow. "You absolutely require me to linger. Who else is going to get you to the nearest inn?" She paused. "Who else is going to get you to your brother?"

"So now we are a team?" he said.

A pause, and then she said, "Perhaps, but I shall drive. You can't be trusted."

He stiffened at the teasing. "That accident had nothing to do with my skill on the box."

"No?"

"No."

"What, then?"

"I was distracted." It was all he would allow himself to say.

"By what?"

By your hair. "By your hat."

Something flashed in her eyes. "By . . . my hat."

"Indeed. You lost it." Christ. He sounded idiotic.

"I lost my hat and you crashed your carriage."

"It's a brougham," he clarified, hoping he'd change the topic and instead simply sounding pompous.

"Is that relevant to my hat?" Were her lips twitching?

"I see nothing amusing about this situation, Miss Frampton." Her lips were definitely twitching. He scowled. "I'm saying you should go—" he began, turning away from her before he revealed entirely too many thoughts.

He stopped when he looked to the horses, only to discover that they'd been collected by two men, one white, one Black, both broad as houses, who seemed fully disinterested in Clayborn's presence. "Oy!" he shouted, pushing Adelaide to the side of the wreckage before dropping his bag and heading for them. "Leave off!"

They didn't pause.

Fucking hell. His entire body ached, and he was going to have to fight these men.

"Clayborn—" Adelaide began just as a woman's voice sounded from the shadows.

"I wouldn't do that if I were you." He turned to find a tiny woman coming out of the brush, dark eyes twinkling and a bright smile on her brown face. In one hand, she held a pretty silver pistol, gleaming like fire in the setting sun.

"What in hell?" He moved immediately back toward

Adelaide, putting himself between her and the weapon. First she crashed his carriage, now she was going to get him killed.

The woman with the pistol didn't hesitate. "A surprise, am I not?"

He blinked. "Who are you?"

"That isn't important. What's important is that *you* are the Duke of Clayborn, and you've taken a bit of a header, haven't you?"

His brows shot together. "How do you know who I am?"

"Your crest is on the outside of—" She waved a hand in the direction of his former conveyance. "You really ought to have better wheels for these roads, Your Grace." Before he could reply to the dry words, she added, "Didn't you tell him that, Addie?"

Of course she knew Adelaide. They likely had a weekly whist game during which they discussed which of the great houses in Surrey had the most easily nicked silver.

"To be honest, I didn't," Adelaide replied as though they were all at tea. "We are in competition."

The newcomer smiled. "Well, good news. It looks like you've won. Now, Duke, you seem a decent fellow, and Adelaide hasn't done you in, which means you likely *are* a decent fellow—they're rare. So what say I take that bag and those horses and whatever blunt you've got in your purse, and leave you to it?"

His brows rose. "Highwayman. Of course."

She tutted her disapproval. "Highway*woman*, if you don't mind." She waved the pistol in his direction. "Empty your pockets, please."

He spread his hands wide. "And if I told you your friend fleeced me last night? Stole my purse right out from under me?"

"She'd know you were lying," Adelaide said at his shoulder. "I didn't take his money. At least, not all of it."

"Goin' soft, eh?"

Clayborn cut Adelaide a look and gave her his best ducal censure. "I take it you work with these fine people?"

The highwaywoman snickered. "Doesn't sound like he thinks we're fine."

"Oh, I wouldn't take it personally, he doesn't think most people are fine," Adelaide said casually before nodding at the pistol in the smaller woman's hand. "Though the weapon likely doesn't help your cause."

"You say it like you don't carry as deadly a weapon on you."

He looked to Adelaide. "Don't tell me you've a pistol as well."

She shook her head, but did not look at him, instead considering the wreckage. "I don't like guns. They're too often more trouble than they're worth. Lucia, meet the Duke of Clayborn. Clayborn, meet Lucia." She waved a hand in the direction of the two brutes who were now walking Clayborn's horses toward them. "And Tobias and Rufus."

The men tipped their hats in reply, as though everything going on were polite and aboveboard.

"Ach," the highwaywoman scoffed. "It's just for show. We weren't out for blood. We were simply doing our part."

"And what part is that?"

Lucia turned a bright smile on him. "Redistribution of wealth."

Of course.

She lifted the bag in the air. "This one is locked, which tells me there's something worth thieving inside."

"There probably is," Adelaide retorted. "Dukes don't travel light."

"Wot say, Duke?" Lucia played along. "Is it a gold bar or something within?" She looked to Adelaide. "No chance you've your keys with you?"

"Of course I have my keys with me," Adelaide said. "But this one ain't for thieving, Lucia."

Lucia raised a brow. "Under Duchess's protection?"

Adelaide lifted a noncommittal shoulder.

A second brow matched the first. "Under *your* protection?"

Clayborn had had quite enough of being spoken about as though he weren't there. And certainly not like this, as though he were a child requiring a governess. "I require absolutely no one's *protection*."

"Are you sure?" Lucia asked. "My boys could easily rob you blind."

"I am perfectly able to fight," Clayborn said, ignoring the ache in his shoulder from where he'd taken the impact from the leap off the carriage. "I boxed for six years at school."

"You don't say?" Lucia tilted her head. "Six years of school boxing?"

Adelaide's lips twitched. "And such a straight nose to show for it!"

Clayborn slid her a look. "Perhaps I've a straight nose because I didn't make a habit of losing."

"More like no one was willing to let fly with a duke, but whatever gives you comfort at night, Your Grace." Before he could say more, Adelaide looked to Lucia and tipped her head at the carriage. "Can't be repaired, can it?"

"It's matchsticks and metal at this point. That's what your duke gets for coming this far north with a ride made for Hyde Park."

"Not my duke," Adelaide retorted.

It was true, but he didn't like how quickly she said it, as though she couldn't wait to be rid of him.

Her gaze flickered away, and she moved around to inspect the back side of the wreck, crouching down, reaching a hand into the broken slats, searching for something.

"At odds again, are we?"

She didn't look to him. "Aren't we always?"

He supposed they were. But there were moments—

last night, today as they'd raced, on the docks as they'd kissed—when it seemed there was another path. "And yet, you remain with me instead of leaving me to . . . whatever this is."

"A little gratitude wouldn't be out of line, Your Grace, considering what Lucia and her boys would have done to you."

She turned to smile as the brutes neared. The enormous men smiled back, as though they were all at a holiday fair, and not lingering about a carriage on the side of the road.

Clayborn clenched his teeth at the ease among the trio. He didn't want her smiling at other people. He wanted her smiling at *him*, dammit.

It didn't matter that the last time she'd done it, he'd been so dazzled he'd flipped a carriage.

No. It did matter. The woman was mayhem.

Clayborn pulled himself straight and looked down his nose at her. "I do not require your protection, Miss Frampton."

Everything stilled at the words. Tobias and Rufus froze. Lucia looked up from where she was rummaging through another bag, this one unlocked.

"Of course you don't. You were perfectly fine out here with your brougham tumbled into a ditch," Adelaide said, extracting a lantern from within the wreckage.

Dammit, he could have done that.

She shoved it into his hands. "Let me be clear, Duke. On the list of people I am interested in protecting, you are at the very bottom. But the absolute last thing I need is Lady Havistock telling half the world that the Matchbreaker is the reason the Duke of Clayborn lies dead in a ditch. It would be extremely bad for business."

"And here I was thinking you'd miss me if I were gone," he retorted, reaching into his pocket to fetch a match and light the lantern.

"I'm sorry to disappoint you." The words were full of frustration, and something else that he did not like.

Once more, he felt like an ass. "Adelaide."

She looked away. "Next time you decide to race someone across Britain, you should choose better wheels."

Silence fell between them, heavy and uncomfortable, and Clayborn had never been more grateful for a highwayman—highway*woman*—than when Lucia interjected, "You should know, Duke, your brother passed through here about six hours ago. Had a pretty girl with him, and they were gazing at each other like there was nothing else in the world for them." She cut Clayborn a firm look. "He's better looking than you."

"He's a decade younger than me."

"It's probably the broken nose," Adelaide added.

Lucia turned away, considering the dark road that turned to inky night outside the pool of light from the carriage.

Clayborn slid Adelaide a look. "Never fear. Between The Bully Boys and my luck when I am near you, I expect my nose to be broken in no time."

Lucia held up a hand. "Shush."

He shushed and heard the sound in the distance.

"Single rider," Lucia said softly, not looking away from the darkness. "Coming at a clip. Best hide your toff."

"Not my toff," Adelaide said quietly, already moving, pulling him to crouch low behind the wreckage and reaching for the blade in her boot.

Every ounce of Clayborn resisted her. "I don't need hiding."

"Out here, with your carriage in tatters, you don't need finding, either," Adelaide said with another tug. He allowed her to pull him down next to her, ignoring the pain from the crash in his side as he slipped his hand into his pocket, extracting a blade, which gleamed sharp and wicked in the light.

"Impressive," she said quietly.

"I should be insulted. Did you think yourself the only one who carries a blade?"

She was staring through the wreckage, close enough to touch. If she turned to look at him, she'd be close enough to do more than touch. When she replied, it was barely a sound. "Pretty enough, Duke . . . but can you use it?"

He clenched his jaw but did not reply as the rider came into view, slowing to take in the wrecked carriage.

Tobias and Rufus came around to the front, placing themselves between the vehicle and Lucia, massive guards. Clayborn stiffened, hating that he was hiding like a child. He might be an aristocrat, but he did not require protection. He protected, dammit.

He made to stand, to head round and face the rider. But, as he came into view—a tall white man in his late twenties, cloak heavy on his shoulders, cap low on his brow—everything changed. Adelaide turned to stone beside Clayborn, her soft gasp summoning all his notice.

She recognized the man. And she didn't like him.

Which made Clayborn absolutely despise him.

He stared at the man, memorizing his weasely face as he touched his cap on his high mount. "Bad luck."

None of the trio moved as Lucia's reply rang out. "Or good, if you're us."

The rider laughed, too loud, and inspected the carriage, his gaze narrowed directly at the place where they hid. He couldn't see them, Clayborn knew, but Adelaide's hand tightened into a fist on her thigh.

He didn't like that, either. Without thinking, he reached for her, settling his hand over hers. Feeling the tremor there. Nerves.

He *really* didn't like that.

Lacing his fingers through hers, he held her tightly, wishing they were not wearing gloves, watching her. Waiting for her to look at him. She didn't, but her grip tightened, and he was grateful for that tiny movement—

for the infinitesimal proof that she trusted him . . . at least more than she trusted the newcomer.

"None of you look like a duke," the man pointed out.

Clayborn gritted his teeth. He'd recognized the crest.

"Nonetheless, they that find, keep," Lucia said, bold and bright. "This loot is ours; carry on."

A pause, while the rider considered his next move— madness, considering Rufus and Tobias were big as houses. Still, it seemed the whole of the assembly held their breath.

Finally, he rode off, and Clayborn waited for Adelaide to release her breath before he did the same. When she stood, he followed, the urge to keep her safe screaming through him.

"Adelaide."

She shook her head, hearing the question he wanted to ask before it could form. Her reply was soft steel. "No."

Lucia came around the edge of the carriage before he could ask for the man's name. Insist on it. "Let Rufus take you to the Hen," the highwaywoman said.

Adelaide adjusted her spectacles. "That's not necessary. My carriage isn't five minutes from here."

Lucia looked as though she had something to say, her gaze tracking to Clayborn and down to their hands, where their fingers remained intertwined.

Until Adelaide dropped his like it burned, and he wanted to curse. The whole night was getting away from him.

Lucia looked to him again. "And Lord Six-Years-at-School-Boxing is your body man?"

"When was the last time I needed a body man?"

The other woman gave a little laugh. "You don't have your girls with you tonight, Adelaide Frampton." She lifted a chin at Clayborn. "He might be your best bet."

He resisted the urge to enumerate The Bully Boys he'd dropped three days earlier. "How much to disappear this carriage?"

Lucia considered him for a moment. "And the crest?"

"Especially the crest."

She smiled broadly. "Five quid for the carriage. Another ten for the crest."

A fortune. "I suppose I'm getting the best of service."

"The very best, Your Grace."

He reached into his pocket to pay Lucia. "I'm taking the horses. And my bag."

She handed the bag off happily. "What do I want with a sack of cravats and a pot of shaving soap, anyway?"

He turned to Adelaide. "How far to the inn?" He was sure she'd knew precisely where their race ended. Was sure, too, that the people there would welcome her with open arms.

"Thirty minutes."

He nodded, holding back a groan. He needed a bath and a bed and possibly a needle and thread after the leap he'd taken. He did not want another hour on these roads. But he wasn't about to give these four the satisfaction of acknowledging his weakness.

"I assume it is rife with people well paid by the Duchess of Trevescan and full of secret passageways for your escape?" At least she had the grace to look chagrined. "Excellent. I shall be right at home. Not to mention *prepared* for whatever is to come."

Having had enough of whatever this madness was, he turned back to Lucia with a quick nod. "It was a pleasure meeting you, Miss Lucia."

Her brows rose with an amused smile. "Any friend of Adelaide . . ."

"He's not my friend," she protested.

"Absolutely not," Clayborn agreed. "We are at odds."

"There, you see?"

"I'm simply the man she came back to save when she could have disappeared into the night and won the day."

Her jaw dropped, and if he weren't in pain, he might have enjoyed it more. "That's not—"

Filing the memory away for later consideration, he hefted his bag over his shoulder, and looked to the men at a distance. "And you two. Thank you for not stealing my horses."

Tobias tipped his cap.

That sorted, Clayborn looked to Adelaide. "Your carriage, if you will, Miss Frampton."

There was a beat while everyone realized that the Duke of Clayborn had taken control.

"I'll say this—" Lucia began.

"I wish you wouldn't," Adelaide cut her off.

"—he might be the first duke I've ever liked."

Chapter Eight

Thirty minutes later, they entered the Hungry Hen to discover a tavern full of people and another lady barkeep. Mary Bright wasn't quite as openly friendly as Gwen, but she poured a long pint, made a lovely bed, and happily held messages for Adelaide and others as they made their way north to the border. Messages like the one she set on the bar when Adelaide and Clayborn arrived.

Mary was a new addition to the Hell's Belles network, having only recently inherited the management of the Hungry Hen from her aunt, a longtime contact of Duchess. But she was quick to leap into action when Adelaide introduced herself, heading off to fetch the key to the Belles' reserved room.

The drive had been silent, Adelaide playing over the events of the afternoon, the pleasure of their race, the terror of watching Clayborn's carriage disintegrate in the road.

Not because he might have died, of course. He could do whatever he wished. She wasn't warming to this handsome man who was less and less the straitlaced aristocrat she'd thought him to be, negotiating with highwaywomen and sleeping in chairs by the door to feed a wild instinct to keep her safe.

His hand in hers, his fingers laced through her own.

Had that ever happened to her before? Had she ever felt so protected?

Of course not, and it was fine. She was perfectly capable of protecting herself. It was *he* who required protection, anyway. Why, if she hadn't been there, he would have been robbed by Lucia and her men, or worse, at the hands of Danny Stoke, Alfie Trumbull's trusted lieutenant, who'd been looking for her the night she'd stolen from The Bully Boys' warehouse, still looking for her, here.

Which meant The Bully Boys were involved, and she had to stay out of sight.

She was slightly surprised that Alfie sent Danny outside of London to find her. Adelaide didn't make a habit of leaving the city, and when she was there, she wasn't impossible to find. But being hunted here, two days north of the city, meant one of two things: either she'd stolen something extremely valuable, or Alfie Trumbull was angry.

With the way Danny had looked at that coach—the way his gaze had traveled over the Duke of Clayborn's crest, like a hungry fox at a henhouse—she had a feeling it was both. And while most of The Bully Boys were hired guns with little between their ears, Danny was different. Danny was her father's right hand for a reason. He knew what he was doing, and he was far closer than she liked.

She pushed the thought away, sliding her finger beneath the wax seal and reading the brief message within, amazed, as always. Mere mortals required rest but Duchess employed a vast network of messengers who appeared to need no such thing. When combined with Mithra Singh's vast network of taverns and posting inns, there was nowhere on the island of Britain that the Belles could not access within forty-eight hours.

Adelaide closed the message. Helene and Jack were safe. For now.

"My brother, I assume?"

"An hour north," she said. "Even with your detour to a roadside ditch, we're not far behind."

"They had a six-hour start on us," he said. "Why are they moving so slowly?"

"Couples headed to Gretna have a tendency to linger if they believe there is time to do so."

"Why? Wouldn't they want to get it done?"

She met his gaze, heat flaring in her cheeks. "They want to get . . . other things done, as well."

His eyes went wide with understanding. "Ah."

She adjusted her spectacles. "We should change horses and go, once we've had food and a rest."

Clayborn's lips flattened into a thin line. "You still intend to break the match? Leave the girl unmarried and ruined?"

"I intend to return Lady Helene to London." Adelaide did her best to avoid the question.

"To her unpleasant parents' home? When she might return to that of her loving husband?"

If all went well with the Belles' plan, Helene and Lord Carrington would live out their days in romantic bliss, with her father deep in the bowels of Newgate Prison. But if Helene was lost, so, too was the plan. "To London."

He let out a sigh. "At some point, you are going to have to tell me what you are up to." It was impossible. She couldn't tell him anything without revealing *everything*. Havistock's murder. The threat to Helene and Jack. The Belles' plan.

When she did not reply, he made a sound deep in his chest—pure frustration. A growl that ceded absolutely no ground.

She looked to him, his face light in the glowing candlelight of the tavern, and winced. "You're . . ." She hesitated, reaching for him, stopping just before she touched him. There was a scratch high on his right cheek. A scrape along his left jaw. His hair was in disarray.

"A mess?" he offered.

She nodded and said, softly, "You lost your hat, as well."

He ran a hand through his dark hair, his gaze tracking

over her own, which she'd hastily repinned when they'd left the scene of his accident. Something flashed in his eyes—something half dangerous and half exciting—and Adelaide forced herself to look away. Clearing her throat, she considered the room, cataloguing each occupant, searching for Danny.

Danny, who she knew, without question, was searching for *her*, wherever he was.

"He's not here," Clayborn said, the words low and harsh, his blue gaze serious and urgent. "You think I would not have looked? You think I would have let us linger if he were here? You needn't look so surprised, Adelaide. I would never let him near you." He paused, then added, soft and firm, "Has no one ever kept you safe before?"

She was saved from having to answer when Mary returned with the key to the Belles' room.

Clayborn leaned over the bar in an entirely unducal manner. Was he *charming* the other woman? The barmaid tittered from her side of the scarred mahogany before making a pretty show of looking at the reservation book.

Resisting the urge to scowl at the pretty tableau the pair made, Adelaide leaned in as Mary said, "I'm afraid we've no free room for the evening, sir."

"Nothing at all, you say?" He leaned further over, his gaze tracking the notes in the book. "Hmm." And then, before she could suggest he find a bale of hay in the stables, he turned to Adelaide and shot her a smile warm enough to raise the temperature in the room.

Warm enough that when he reached a welcoming hand toward her, she forgot that she shouldn't catch it. Shouldn't let him tug her closer.

Definitely shouldn't let him say, "That's alright. I shall simply have to share with my wife."

Adelaide's eyes shot wide at the words. "Your *what*?"

"Only one room," he said, the words liquid and doting.

"Again, would you believe it?" She ignored the thrill that tumbled through her as he grinned and lifted her hand—the hand that had betrayed her!—to his lips and brushed a kiss over her knuckles.

She absolutely did not like that.

But she did not pull away when he did it a second time, for some reason, and turned that smile back to Mary. "Newlyweds. We're still getting comfortable with the descriptors. Would you send food and a bath to our room?"

"*Our* room?" Who did this man think he was? Last night had been a special case.

"Quite," he said, patting down his pockets, fire and irritation flaring in his gaze. "And lucky, I'll say, as it seems my purse is gone once more."

"Lucia," she said with a wicked smile. He deserved that.

He raised a brow. "Your kindred spirit."

"Light fingers make heavy pockets," she replied, simply. "It's honest work."

"Is it?" He paused. "Her men, Tobias and Rufus—are they—"

"Her men," Adelaide said, simply. Clayborn's brows rose in surprise. "Though if you ask me, that is more men than a body requires."

"Seems Lucia feels differently," he said dryly.

Adelaide had never heard Lucia complain, that much was true.

"Mary!" Adelaide was saved from the conversation by a too-big, too-loud brute shouting from across the room for the tavern mistress, who started in a way Adelaide knew too well, her spine going straight and her chin dipping to hide the loss of her smile. "Bring me anowwer drink!"

The man didn't need another drink. Adelaide was certain of that, even as storm clouds crossed the other woman's face and she made to do as she was bid. Adelaide had seen this particular play before; going up against the lout did not end prettily for Mary, nor for any traveler who wasn't rich and powerful and male.

She reached for Mary's arm, staying her movement and meeting her eyes. A lifetime of conversation passed between them before the other woman pulled away and crossed to the drunk.

"Who're they?" the man asked, loud enough for the query to carry across the room, but it was impossible to hear Mary's quiet response. "Stop talkin' to the toff. You ain't expensive enough for him."

His laugh was overloud—the kind men laughed when they wanted attention, and not amusement. Adelaide stiffened, her fingers itching to find a blade. To give the man a warning.

"If you're to take him on, you'll need a second," Clayborn whispered at her elbow, his words sharp as steel.

She didn't move her attention from the man at the end of the bar. She couldn't make out his tone, but she didn't have to. The way Mary's shoulders drooped a touch, as though she could somehow make herself small—invisible—was enough. Anger flared. "Are you offering?"

"Depends. Are we trying to avoid notice?"

Her heart rate increased. "I'm rarely noticed."

He made a little disbelieving sound.

She looked to him. "What's that supposed to mean?"

"Someday, Adelaide Frampton, you are going to realize that you are absolutely impossible to miss."

Before she could respond to that, the man across the bar chucked Mary beneath her chin—an action that could have been playful if it didn't feel like such a threat. Clayborn stiffened, a fist forming on the bar.

Adelaide set a hand to his sleeve, feeling the tight muscled cord of his arm. "Not now."

"Why not?" He looked to her, and she liked the fire in his eyes, as though the idea of doing nothing was anathema to him.

"Because there are other ways to deal with men like this," she said. "Ways that are quiet. And effective." Ways that would send this man into the night and see him never darken the door of the Hungry Hen again. Because they couldn't afford the kind of notice they were about to receive, with half the place already looking and the other half turning to do so.

"Oy!" The shout came from across the bar. The enormous man was scowling at them—at Clayborn, who came to his full height then, because how could he not?

"I also know ways that are effective, Miss Frampton."

Before she could reply, the drunk continued. "Wot are you lookin' at, toff?"

"Dammit, Clayborn," Adelaide muttered beneath her breath. They had to get upstairs. Quickly. "Say nothing."

For a moment, she wasn't certain he'd heard her. And then, raising his voice, he said precisely that, in the most superior tone Adelaide had ever heard.

"Nothing."

The brute across the room didn't mistake the insult, coming to his feet, fists balled like boulders.

"Dammit, Clayborn!"

"Outside!" Mary shouted, pointing at the drunk. "I'm tired of your shite, Billy."

"Outside then," came the reply as Billy started pushing people out of the way to reach Clayborn.

Adelaide did her own pushing then, trying to get Clayborn to the door. If they hurried, they might get to the carriage before the horses were unhitched.

But Clayborn had turned to stone. Immovable.

Adelaide looked to him, riveted by the man who advanced. "You can't fight him."

"I wish you would stop that," he said, in a voice filled with calm.

"Stop what?" Dammit. She was going to need her blade. She reached into her pocket, searching for the opening within, for the blade strapped to her thigh.

"Stop insisting that I'm no good in a bout."

The enormous man drew closer, and Clayborn wasn't even watching. Adelaide protested, "Six years of fighting at school isn't—"

"Stand back," he interrupted.

She blinked at the cool instruction. "You can't think to—"

"Over there, by the stairs."

"Deliver me from men and their insistence on fighting without sense." She shook her head, her gaze tracking his opponent. "No. We have to go."

"For once, you'll listen to me, you absolute harridan. By the stairs. Now."

The command was sharp and unyielding, and somehow, though she'd never understand why, Adelaide followed it, backing away.

Just as he knew she would, as he did not wait for her to follow his command, instead turning to face the foe already reaching for him.

The brute never had a chance.

Clayborn's fist flew with uncanny speed, straight into the larger man's face, dropping him like a sack of flour, directly to the floor.

"That will do!" Mary shouted, sounding half delighted and half relieved.

"Oh, my!" Adelaide whispered, feeling wholly something else altogether.

Clayborn looked to Mary, eyes wide behind the counter as Billy's compatriots came to fetch their fallen man and take him from the tavern. "It is none of my business, but this man should not be allowed to frequent your place, miss." Mary blinked, but before she could reply, he turned to Adelaide. "Now. What are your ways?"

When she did not immediately answer, Clayborn added loud enough for the whole room to hear, "My wife and I are not to be disturbed."

And then he was heading directly for Adelaide, his countenance stern and unyielding. Her heart began to pound as he closed the distance between them, and she fairly vibrated as she held her ground, refusing to back away from his advance.

Not wanting to.

When he reached her, he leaned in, close enough to touch her. To do more.

To kiss her.

She lifted a chin. "Only six years?"

One dark brow rose. "At school."

Where'd he learn the rest?

"Impressive," she said, meaning it. Wanting to say more.

"Upstairs. Now."

"Why did you call me that?" She didn't move, even as every muscle in her body screamed to follow the order. "Your wife?"

"What would you have preferred? Foe? Adversary? Nemesis?"

"All more accurate," she said.

He sighed. "Perhaps I was looking for the quickest way to protect you."

"I don't need protection," she said instantly. She'd been protecting herself for years. Others, too.

He didn't disagree, but his lips pressed into a thin line. "A path of least resistance, then."

"Resistance to what?"

"Resistance to me. I've no interest in battling you right now."

And that's when she realized there was something wrong. Her focus narrowed on him, the way he stood, straight and proud . . . and leaning just barely to the left. Not enough for anyone to notice, truthfully, but Adelaide wasn't just anyone . . . and neither was this man. She should have noticed earlier, when he tossed his bag into the rear of her carriage and climbed onto the block, his movements stiffer than they'd ever been.

She should have noticed when his jaw clenched tight in the final minutes of their journey. Or when he hefted his bag and walked into the Hungry Hen, his shoulders hunched a touch more than they should be.

Not that any of it had stopped him from putting a man into the ground.

Her brow furrowed. "What is it?"

He looked to her. "Nothing of consequence. A leap from a moving carriage and some bruised knuckles can make a body wish for a warm bath and an amicable companion is all."

Her gaze flickered to the scrape high on his cheek. He turned away instinctively, not wanting her to see it. Not wanting to show her even a hint of weakness.

"I'm perfectly amicable."

"Yes, that's exactly how I would describe you," he said, humor in his tone, letting her take his hand. Letting her lift his fist and run a thumb gently over his knuckles, raw from laying the brute out.

When he sucked in a breath at the touch—pain?—something else?—she spoke, her words barely a whisper. "Up, then."

Up, to her room. To the bath. To food. To rest.

To the two of them, alone.

She led the way.

The room was at the rear of the inn, overlooking the stables and far from the noise of the tavern below. In the time it had taken Clayborn to bring chaos to the taproom, food and scalding bathwater had been delivered, and when the door was closed and locked, they were left alone with nothing but the steam rising from the water.

He inspected the tidy room, small and unassuming, with the exception of a massive oil painting on one wall, nearly as tall as a person, depicting a collection of six women, each clad in diaphanous white accented with gold, and each holding a blade and shield. "Why am I not surprised you were assigned the room in which goddesses watch over you?"

"Shield-maidens," she corrected him.

He turned questioning eyes on her.

She made for her bag, itching to keep busy—not wanting to consider how the events below had changed the way she thought of the duke, who no longer seemed so ducal. "They decided which warriors lived and which died on the battlefield." Moving quickly, she fetched a vial of oil and added several drops to the hot bath, stirring the water to release the rich scent of rosemary into the air.

She did her best to keep her back to him even as he watched from his place by the door, pressed to the wall. She didn't want to look at him. Didn't want to think about what came next.

"What is it?" The question was quiet, like the room, but still it scraped over her skin like a touch.

She returned the oil to her bag. "Bay and rosemary essence. And willow bark. It will help with the pain."

"So you have decided I shall live," he said.

He didn't deny there was pain, and she admired that. "For another battle, no doubt," she said. "You should get in. Before the water cools."

He grunted and she moved to the window, looking out on the darkness below, the light from the candle reflecting in the glass. "There is no screen," she said softly. "I shan't look."

He didn't seem to mind, and Adelaide was consumed with the sound of his undressing—the slide of wool and cotton a slow, sinful temptation in the silent room. She heard him step into the water. His muffled groan. A deep inhale. A long exhale.

Her skin grew tight, hot and uncomfortable over muscle and bone, and it took all she had not to turn and look at him. This man who came from a world so different from her own—it seemed impossible that they were in the same universe, let alone the same building . . . let alone the same room. While he bathed.

He was too much for looking at.

Like jewels or silk or fur in a shop window. Too costly. *Steal him.*

"Thank you. For the bath."

Adelaide stiffened at the words, rummaging through her bag for nothing. "Of course," she replied into the dark brocade.

"Adelaide," he said softly.

"You shouldn't call me that," she said, because she felt she should.

"You're right. Miss Frampton." Dammit. She didn't like that he agreed.

"On the other hand," her traitorous tongue added, "if we are to play at being married . . ." Silence fell as she trailed off, and she willed the heat from her cheeks in the interminable stretch.

"Many married couples use titles."

She wrinkled her nose. "How romantic."

"I would not have thought you were interested in the romantic."

"I'm not," she leapt to say. "But you must agree, given names are the literal least one should expect from the person who is to be our partner in all things—tying cravats and folding trousers and whatnot."

He gave a little laugh. "Are we speaking of a wife or a valet?"

"Are they very different?"

"I suppose that depends on whether the marriage is romantic or not." His blue eyes glittered in the candlelight. "Adelaide."

He said it like he was testing its flavor.

How did it taste? Why did she care?

"If we play at it, we might as well play at the romantic version."

She stilled at the suggestion, another offering. Another thing she could thieve. But in all the time that Adelaide Frampton, quick-fingered pickpocket and legendary thief, had operated on either side of the Thames, she'd never been so unnerved by what might happen if she committed the crime.

"Look at me." Another command.

Her heart thundered in her chest. Knowing that if she took the chance tonight, if she stole tonight, it might be her only opportunity. Knowing, too, that the punishment might be worse than any she'd suffered before.

Eager for something to keep distance between them, she reached into the bag, collecting his box from within. Only then, with the oak shield in hand, did she face him.

As a rule, Adelaide did not find aristocrats attractive. She didn't like all their smooth, straight edges and impeccable clothes. Didn't like the way their hair never slid out of place and their white gloves were never marked. Didn't like the fact that they never laughed too loud and were never caught unaware by a sneeze and never slurped their soup. Aristocrats, in Adelaide's view, spent far too much time trying for perfection when it was imperfection that made for a life well lived.

And the Duke of Clayborn was perfection personified. Usually.

Except then, in the bath, his hair out of place and his cheeks red with the marks of his carriage tumble and the damp heat rising from the water, with a bruise blooming on his shoulder where he'd taken a hit, and his right hand, flexing absently on the rim of the copper bathtub, as though he could release the sting of the blow he'd landed below . . . nothing about him was perfect.

Oh, his jaw was sharp and his nose was straight and if he opened that beautiful mouth—for it was empirically beautiful—she knew that he'd speak with the even, smooth tone of a lifetime in the best houses and the best schools. The kind of man Adelaide never found attractive. The kind of man who was not for her.

But there, in a bathtub in a tiny room above the taproom of the Hungry Hen somewhere in Lancashire, his blue eyes on hers, full of heat she didn't dare consider, the Duke of Clayborn looked . . . rough. Wild. Free.

Like he could be hers.

Adelaide sucked in a breath, but did not speak. What could she say?

I want you.

She was saved from speaking when his gaze moved to the box in a slow slide that sent a sizzle of heat through her. "Are you returning it?"

Tightening her grip on the cube she said, "As your wife, does it not belong to me already?"

One side of his mouth twitched. "Go on then, have you worked out the solution?"

Grateful for the distraction, Adelaide looked down at the box. She turned the bottom. Pressed the corners as he'd shown her the night before, and then returned the base again, popping a small square in the side of the cube, a button of sorts that, when pressed, revealed a narrow cylinder no more than an inch long.

She met his gaze, pleasure thrumming through her to discover the outright surprise and—even better— admiration there. She held the cylinder aloft. "The solution?"

He shook his head. "No, but a step in the right direction. I am impressed."

She dipped her head. "Thank you."

"I should be unnerved by the speed with which you have advanced."

She offered him a wry smile. "You would not be the first to hesitate at my advances."

He did not laugh. "I assure you, Adelaide, if you were to make advances, I would not hesitate."

Oh, no, this was dangerous.

Do it. Advance.

She couldn't. No good would come of following her desires with this man. Instead, she cleared her throat and waved the cylinder. "What is it?"

He shook his head, and she knew before he spoke that he was about to invoke the rules. "Did you like our race?"

Dangerous. She hedged. "I haven't thought much about it."

It was a lie. She'd loved the race. Could still feel the way her heart pounded when she'd realized he'd found her. Caught her.

His gaze narrowed, just barely, just fast enough for her to know he knew what she played at. "You liked it."

She pretended to inspect the little tool. "Are you looking for praise for your carriage leaping and tavern brawling?"

"I was good at dockside brawling, as well, was I not?"

He had been. *Too good.*

Her gaze narrowed on his. "What kind of duke is good at brawling?"

"Tell me you liked it when I found you. When we raced."

Truth for truth. What stupid rules.

When she did not reply, he set both hands to the edge of the bath and said, "Fair enough," and before Adelaide could do a thing to stop him, he stood. Without shame.

Dear God.

Had she been prepared, she might not have looked. She might have turned away, avoided noticing the rivers of water sluicing down his body, over the ridges and angles of his muscles—muscles no aristocrat should have. She might have missed cataloguing the bruises along his torso—not just from the leap from his carriage, but remnants of the bout on the docks. The one he'd fought for her. To keep her from falling into the hands of The Bully Boys, just as he'd intended to keep her from Danny earlier, and then, from Billy, downstairs.

Bruises were not new to Adelaide. She'd spent a lifetime looking at them. Tending them. They were the way of the world on the South Bank.

So why did she itch to touch his bruises? To heal them?

Why did they feel like they belonged to her?

Why did she like it?

And why did she *dislike* it so much when he reached for a towel and wrapped it about his hips, hiding the rest of him, the shadowed private places that she'd been unable to catalogue.

He stepped from the bath, the sound of the water interrupting her thoughts and summoning her attention from where his large, muscled hands tucked one corner of linen tightly against the corded sinew of his hip. Good lord he was handsome.

"Thank you."

Her gaze flew to his, and he clarified, though not without a mysterious smile, as though he could read her thoughts. "For the bath. The oil—you were right. It helped."

She waved off his words. "It was nothing. What wives do for husbands, no?"

What on earth? Where had that come from?

"I wouldn't know. Likely not all wives."

She looked to him then. "Only the fake ones."

He laughed, and she liked it more than she cared to admit. "Puts the entire institution of marriage to shame."

"Such as it is," she intoned, immediately regretting the words when he looked to her, sharp and curious.

"You don't care for the institution of marriage?"

She shrugged. "I am the Matchbreaker."

"Why?" When her brow furrowed, he added, "Why do it?"

She thought for a long moment, and then said, "At the beginning, I did it because someone did it for me."

"You were to be married."

"I was to be married *off*," she corrected. "My father's only daughter—a peace offering to a business rival."

His brows shot together, and when he spoke it was with a low, threatening growl. "What happened?"

She was lost to the memory for a bit. "It was all very ordinary—no different than it has been for countless others. I was born a girl, and so my value was in marriage. In being traded for money or power or peace. I knew what was expected, and I prepared for it. I donned my wedding dress and walked alone to St. Stephen's in the rain."

"Alone." He whispered a curse. "St. Stephen's," he said. "Where is that?"

She didn't want to tell him. Didn't want this to end just yet.

He nodded, seeming to understand. No judgment. "Go on."

"The groom stood with me, and it was all perfectly ordinary. Perfectly normal. The parson began and . . ."

"And?" he prodded.

She shook her head. "Before the ceremony could end, a new path was offered to me."

"The Duchess of Trevescan."

He noticed so much. So much more than anyone else ever had. Adelaide nodded. "She helped me escape."

"And the wedding?"

She didn't misunderstand the question. He wished to know if she was married. "It didn't take."

"Thank God for that." She liked the relief in his voice. Like he would have asked for an Act of Parliament himself if her answer were any different.

She nodded. "After that, I knew that this was the work I wanted to do. Ending bad matches. Offering women new paths. Reminding them that marriage to a bad man is not better than a lifetime without one. Ensuring that they enter their matches with wide eyes and, hopefully, full hearts."

"Full hearts," he repeated.

She nodded. "I do not pretend that every match is a love match, but when you marry, wouldn't you like a bride who comes to you with hope for it?"

In her lifetime, Adelaide had never imagined having such a conversation with a half-nude man. Let alone a half-nude *duke*. She would do well to remember that bit. Dukes and men were vastly different flavors.

He hesitated, and she wondered at the pause. What it meant. Instead of asking, she said, "It is the least we should expect."

"A full heart," he said, tasting the words on his tongue. "That sounds like you believe in love to me."

She pushed her spectacles up on her nose. "You would know."

"Mmm," he replied. "So you do believe in it."

"I believe in it," she said, and it was the truth. A year ago, she might have said differently. But she'd seen Sesily fall wildly in love—seen the lengths to which her friend would go to protect the man who was now her husband. Seen the sacrifice and the sorrow and the immense joy. But that was Sesily—who had never once in her life taken no for an answer.

Adelaide was not Sesily. "I also believe it is not for everyone."

He watched her for a long moment, and she wondered what he was thinking—all the replies he tossed out before settling on, "I agree."

He did?

"It is not for you, either?" Why had she asked that? She didn't care.

"It is not," he said, as if he'd given the question a great deal of thought. "I have no intention of marrying."

She lingered over the words, the memory they summoned of his declaration that his brother was his heir. "You do not intend to marry," she said. "But that is not the same as not intending to love."

He shook his head. "Neither are in my cards."

"What nonsense," she said, unable to keep the judgment from her tone.

Surprise flashed in his eyes. "Is it?"

"It is. You're a decent man, rich, powerful, and aristocratic, and with a single purpose, if we're being honest."

"It seems we are," he said, crossing his arms over his bare chest. "Go on."

"You're essentially required by law to marry. Preferably someone with an understanding of your rich, powerful, aristocratic world, who will then provide you with rich, powerful, aristocratic heirs."

Someone the absolute other end of the world from a girl who'd spent her childhood picking pockets of wealthy toffs who'd lost their way on the South Bank. Someone who would never find herself in a dark room above a roadside tavern in casual conversation with a half-nude man. *Duke*.

She left that bit out.

"Jack and Helene will deliver me rich, powerful, aristocratic heirs," he said, leaning on the edge of the tub. "And now you know why I am so committed to seeing him married."

"For *your* heirs?" She felt as though she were under water. He might marry and have his own heirs, and yet he left the work to his brother.

She looked down at the box in her hands. *What secrets did this man keep?*

"For his own heirs. For his own love match. Which has always been the plan."

"What of your plan? What of your love match? With your perfect wife?"

There was absolutely no sadness in his eyes when he said, "There is no love match for me." He hesitated, and then added, "And if she does not come with rosemary oil for my wounds, I think she will not be so perfect." It should have been a joke. It honestly started as though he meant it to be. On the surface, the words were perfectly cordial, full of ordinary, gentlemanly gratitude.

But they turned soft and low, and when he added, "Thank you, Adelaide," they sounded not gentlemanly at all.

They tugged her toward him, even though they shouldn't. "You're welcome."

He kept speaking, his voice low and filled with promise. "Tonight, we play at marriage, and I vote for the kind that comes with given names. It seems not worth playing at all if the only perk is someone to fold my trousers."

"You are not wearing trousers."

His eyes darkened and he straightened, closing the distance between them. "You're very perceptive."

"It is a well-honed skill," she said distractedly as he advanced. Still half nude. Mostly nude, if she were the kind of person who was particular about such things.

"If we were married, I would call you Adelaide, and it would not be a scandal."

If they were married, she wouldn't be so warm. So tempted. She wouldn't be moving toward him. Closer, closer, until there was nowhere left to go. Until she could smell the rosemary oil on him.

Close enough to feel the heat of his bath. To touch him.

"I would call you Adelaide, and you would call me . . ." His words were so low, they were a rumble in his chest. She felt them like a touch on her skin. Like a promise.

Don't finish it. Don't say it.

"Henry." Close enough to savor the taste of his given name—forbidden—on her tongue.

Close enough to see the way his eyes darkened, the centers of them blowing wide.

Close enough to like it as his hand came to her cheek, as he tilted her face up to his and kissed her.

Which she liked even more.

Chapter Nine

There were at least a half-dozen reasons why kissing her was a bad idea.

First, this was not a leisurely holiday. They were on a quest to find Jack and Helene, and they should be preparing for a change of horses, not lingering in shared rooms in posting inns.

Second, Adelaide was a tremendous thief—which the regular collection of society idiots seemed not to have noticed—but he had noticed, and, as she was currently in possession of the most important thing he owned, kissing should be out of the question.

Third, though she did not appear to be lying to him, she was most definitely holding back enormous amounts of information relating to their quest. For that alone, he should not kiss her.

And the most important reason? Adelaide Frampton deserved a man who would kiss her, love her, and marry her. And Henry was not that man.

But in that moment, as candles and firelight cast long, dancing shadows around the room, and the aches—in his shoulder . . . at his side . . . on his cheek—waned in the fragrance of her rosemary magic and the memory of her long, lovely fingers circling the water to slowly brew her elixir, he didn't think of any of those reasons.

Instead, he thought that Adelaide Frampton was wearing too many clothes.

And then she gasped, a soft little sigh that opened her to his kiss, and he wasn't thinking at all. He was pulling her closer, and the box she'd been holding dropped to the carpet with a soft *thunk* that he might have cared about if not for the wild temptation of her mouth, wide and soft and so *pretty*.

When he returned to thinking, he would remind himself of all the reasons kissing her was a bad idea.

But now, those pretty lips parted and Henry deepened the kiss, aligning his mouth to hers and sliding his tongue along her full bottom lip, savoring the taste of her, sweet and sinful, as she leaned into him, sliding her hands over his broad shoulders, wrapping her arms about his neck, and pressing herself close.

Yes. With a groan of approval, he deepened the kiss, stroking his tongue over hers once, twice, before she broke the caress and tilted her face to the ceiling, baring the long pale column of her throat to him . . . an offering.

He took it. Knowing he shouldn't. Knowing a gentleman wouldn't.

Knowing he wasn't a gentleman.

She sucked in a breath when he pressed kisses along her neck to her ear, where he whispered her name again, "Adelaide," loving the taste of it on his tongue. The way speaking it made him feel like a thief, undeserving of the familiarity. She loved it, too, in the way her fingers slid into his hair and tightened, the sting of her grip driving him forward.

He answered the bite of her touch with a bite of his own, taking the soft lobe of her ear between his teeth, worrying the skin there until she shivered her pleasure.

He couldn't stop his smile. "You like that."

"Mmm," she said, and the sound, low and rich, was nearly his undoing. He was hard and hot and the only thing that kept him from lifting her in his arms and taking her immediately to bed was the desire to undo her in turn.

"What else do you like, Adelaide Frampton?"

Her eyes flew open at the question, her pupils wide with pleasure . . . and something else. As though she wasn't sure of the answer. As though she was afraid of it.

He pulled back, his thumb stroking across her cheek, something unexpected tightening in his chest as he waited for her to answer. He would have waited forever.

She whispered, "I don't know."

He leaned in and pressed a soft kiss to the corner of her lips, lingering there, marveling at her soft skin. "That was the truth. Shall I tell you the next step to opening the box?"

She gave a little laugh, her fingertips coming to rest on the bare skin of his arms. "Please don't think less of me if I tell you I do not care about the box right now."

He would have laughed if he hadn't been so damn grateful for her answer. And still, he trod lightly, afraid he might scare her off. "A different game, then."

She pulled back, her big brown eyes full of curiosity and nerves, and something tightened in his chest, unexpected and important. He released her instantly, enjoying the way her hands came to his forearms, gripping him tightly. Maybe for balance. He hoped to keep her close.

He turned from her even as she let out a little, questioning sound, and made quick work of finding his trousers—trading his towel for them before facing her once more. He worked the buttons on his falls as she watched, her gaze greedy and welcome on his still bare skin.

"Are you—" she started, then stopped, considering the next word. "Through?"

Christ, no. "Not unless you wish to be," he said, retracing his steps to her. Slowly.

She shook her head instantly. "I do not."

Good. "I only thought you might enjoy the game more if it was not so . . . urgent."

Her attention was back on his body, lingering at his hands at the waist of his trousers. She swallowed. "Trousers make it less urgent?"

He gave a little, humorless huff of laughter, the hard length of him protesting the garment in question. "They help."

That little sound again—the one that suggested she was considering the information and had not yet made up her mind how to proceed.

Proceed, Adelaide, he willed.

Her gaze lingered over his torso. "You've a wicked bruise. More than one."

He didn't take his attention from her. "They're fine."

"They're not," she said. "You might have broken something."

"I haven't." Even if he had, he wouldn't have admitted it. Wouldn't have risked her stopping before they began.

"How would you know?" she asked, and the question had a bit of wildness in it. She was frustrated. Unsettled. Uncertain. Out of control. She didn't like that, which Henry understood.

"Adelaide," he assured her. "I shall mend."

She met his gaze. "You're sure?"

"No dead duke on your hands today, love."

She gave a little laugh at that, and he warmed at the sound, before going hot at her next words. "Then I think you should tell me about your game."

Yes. "We discover what you like."

Her eyes went wide as saucers. "What I like?"

The squeak in the words was more appealing than it should be. "Is it so foreign a concept?"

"No," she replied, the word dragged out so he didn't quite believe it. "But . . . no one has ever . . . that is . . . I've never really . . . I don't . . ."

"Miss Frampton," he teased. "Imagine my surprise that it is possible to render you speechless."

Her brows shot together. "I am not speechless."

Henry reached for her then, the mad, mad world beyond the room fading away as he slipped one hand around the back of her neck, his thumb settling to the line of her jaw and tilting her face up to his as he closed the distance between them. "Then I must do a better job of it."

The chit opened her mouth to argue and he stole the words from her in a slow, sinful kiss that had them both breathing heavily when it ended. "The fact that no one has ever asked you what you like is an unforgivable wrong. I intend to see it righted."

"I thought you didn't like kissing me."

He froze. He'd surely misheard. "What?" Her gaze flickered away, past his shoulder. He leaned into her view. "No. Don't do that. What did you say?"

"You . . ." She hesitated, and he forced himself to be patient. "You said I wasn't worth kissing."

What in . . . "When did I say that?"

"Last night."

"I most certainly did *not*." He was affronted by the very idea.

"Well, you apologized for it." He watched her as those beautiful brown eyes turned downward, between them. To his chest. Christ, the woman had lashes that would wreck a man.

Not that Henry had ever given much thought to eyelashes.

Back to the matter at hand, however. "I apologized because it wasn't gentlemanly," he said. "It wasn't the time. You were being chased, and I took advantage of you."

She looked to him. "You didn't take advantage of me."

"I assure you, I did."

"No," she said. "I kissed you."

"And I kissed you back."

"Because . . . you wanted to."

He nodded. "Very much."

She gave a little, secret smile at that, one he liked very

much. Even more when she said softly, "Good. I know I'm quite plain, but . . ."

There were a dozen things he wished to say in reply. But he started with the most important. "Adelaide . . . who ever told you that you were plain?"

She started at the question and shook her head. "Everyone. No one. No one has ever had to. I know what is beautiful and what is not and . . . I have other attributes." He was having trouble finding the words to simultaneously tell her she was wrong and also not have her leave him in that room forever, and she must have taken his pause as encouragement to enumerate her attributes. "I am strong and I am quick and I am clever . . ."

"You are all of those things," he allowed. "But you are also . . ." He paused, searching for the proper description. ". . . Christ, there is nothing plain about you. You are . . . *magnificent.*"

She blushed at the word, dipping her head, and he knew she did not believe him, which left him deeply frustrated. He cupped her face in his hands and said, firmly, "I told you—I do not lie."

She searched his gaze for a long moment. "And you think I am worth kissing."

He let out a little disbelieving laugh. "I assure you, Adelaide; there are few things more valuable than kissing you." He stroked the soft skin of her cheek. How was it that she was so soft? "Right now . . . I'm not certain there's anything more valuable than kissing you." He waited for her to look at him and said, "Shall I prove it?"

"Please," she whispered, and he grew impossibly harder at the soft word—a wicked temptation that made him resolve to hear it again and again that night.

He began with a kiss, slow and deep, until she sighed and leaned into him, her lovely long fingers tracking up his bare chest, leaving fire in their wake as he lifted her, carrying her to the chair and settling her on his lap. She gasped at the movement, as he lingered at her sweet, full bottom lip for a moment. A little bite. Delicious. When he released her and met her delighted eyes, he said, "What of this? Do you like this?"

Another little smile, which he kissed quickly from her lips before she said, "I do." Her long fingers slid over his skin, barely there. "But are you not cold?"

"Christ. No." He was on fire. Scorched by her. He licked at the place where her neck and shoulder met, where the gold chain she kept hidden in her bodice lay hot against her soft skin, shielding her pulse, strong and fast. Satisfaction thrummed through him at the proof of her response. "And neither are you."

"No, I am . . . on fire."

"Mmm. That, *I* like." He growled his pleasure and tilted her chin up. "But this game is about what *you* like." He pressed his lips to the underside of her jaw, loving the way she shivered in his arms and sank her fingers into his hair.

"This," she whispered. "I like this."

He rewarded the confession with a long, lush stroke over her back, pulling her tighter to him before sliding one hand around to the edge of her breast.

They both froze, Henry using all he had to wait for her approval.

Her fingers tightened in his hair and she looked down at him with that secret smile once more—not so secret any longer. Not so demure. A woman who suddenly knew precisely what she wanted. "I think—"

He let his thumb move, a slow slide along the outer swell of her breast.

She gasped, her hand finding his. Holding it firm. Pressing it tight.

"What do you think?" He growled, unable to stop himself. Christ, he wanted this woman.

"I think . . ." The words trailed off, and he thought he might lose his mind.

And then she moved, her grip tightening. Moving his hand. Using it. Using him.

Putting him where she wanted him.

Where he wanted to be.

"Here?" He barely recognized the word that came out low and broken as his fingertips teased over her breast, finding the tight, pebbled nipple beneath her bodice. Worrying it until she squirmed in his lap, and they both were gasping. "Do you like this?"

"Yes," she answered. "Yes, I like it."

He rewarded her with a kiss. "What else would you like?"

"I want . . ." He hung on the silence after the words. Whatever she wanted, he'd give it to her.

And then she stood up, dammit.

He reached for her. "Where are—"

But before he could finish the question, she was working at the tie of her skirts, magically, magnificently untying something and unbuttoning something else and they were gone, leaving her in nothing but the bodice of the dress and a pair of fitted trousers in a lush green silk. She climbed back onto his lap, as though she'd done it a hundred times before, and he said, "I find myself immensely grateful to your dressmaker."

She laughed, her knees tucking into the chair beside his hips as she sat back on his thighs.

He gripped her hips and pulled her closer, stealing another kiss, leaning down and tracing the line of her bodice with his tongue, sliding his hands up over the long line of her torso until her hands found his once more, moving them to capture her breasts, to test the delicious weight of them.

Her beautiful eyes slid open. "More."

"More, what?" he teased.

"More, please."

It wasn't what he expected, but good God, it was what

he wanted. It made him desperate to give her anything, everything she asked for in that breathlessly needy voice. He found the front lace of her bodice. Worked the ties until they barely kept her covered. Grasped the edge of the garment, the backs of his fingers stilling against the hot skin of her breasts. Torturing them both.

"Henry," she gasped, and his given name was almost enough to send him over the edge.

Almost.

"Ask again."

She looked to him. "Please."

"Mmm," he growled, and gave her what she wanted. What they both ached for, pulling her bodice down and finding her nipple with his mouth, soothing the straining tip with soft licks and lingering sucks, reveling in the whispers she couldn't keep from him.

"God, yes, *please.*"

And every time she said that word—that delicious, decadent word—every time she asked for him, he sucked again, licked again, gave her what she wished, until she was panting her pleasure, her nails in his shoulders as she rocked on his lap, the heat of her a gift and a punishment against his straining cock.

Releasing her, he yanked the half-tied bodice up, over her head, wanting to touch her, to gain access to more of her skin. She lifted her arms and let him, and he held them there, in one hand, high above her head, tangled in the fabric and ties, while the other stroked down over her skin, testing its heat, marveling at its smooth perfection.

"Look at you," he said softly, turning her toward the firelight, reveling in the swells and curves of her. He set a finger to the heavy pendant he'd finally revealed, a brass cylinder between her breasts. He looked up at her. "Full of secrets."

"I shall trade them for yours."

He almost agreed. But he had other plans that evening. "You are beautiful."

She shook her head. "You make me think I could be."

She was wrong, of course, and he set about proving it, kissing and licking and sucking his way across her body, stroking over the dip at her waist, the soft skin of her side, the pretty swell of her belly.

And she let him, stretching long in his grip, sighing her pleasure when he licked at the underside of her breast, squirming when he teased her. She was so responsive, he forgot everything beyond that room in the long minutes she let him explore her.

He felt the scar before he saw it, a two-inch-long raised line at the bottom of her ribs on her left side.

He didn't mean to linger on it. Indeed, as soon as he realized what he'd found, he told himself to leave it. To ignore it. It was old and healed and not his business.

Maybe he could have, if she hadn't flinched, as though his touch had brought back a memory. Someone had hurt her. And though the scar might have healed, she was not through with the pain.

Henry released her from the binds, tossing the bodice across the room as she wrapped one arm over the mark. *Who hurt you? How? When?* He bit back the questions and the insistence that she give him a name. He did not need to ask to know that she would not like it.

And he wanted her to like it.

He wanted her to like *him*.

The shock of the thought had him looking at her again, capturing those eyes that saw everything—that followed every path, calculated every risk. He knew enough of Adelaide Frampton to know that she spent her days facing risk. And he did not want to be risk. He wanted to be all reward.

He met her eyes. "Adelaide?"

"Yes." An answer to a question he had not yet asked.

"Take down your hair."

She did not hesitate, reaching up to pull pins from their tight moorings. There were a dozen of them, maybe more, and it was not a quick process. But Henry reveled in every slow, lingering second of it, loving the way errant curls began to tumble down over her shoulders, teasing her curves, wrapping themselves around her breasts, and then . . .

There was so much of it, wild and free like a cloud of fire. He cursed, low and wicked, reaching for it, sliding his fingers through it, reveling in its soft, silky texture.

"This," he growled. "Christ, Adelaide, this hair was nearly the death of me today . . . and I think it might be again."

He picked up a long, red lock and used it to paint circles around her nipple, his cock hard as steel as she writhed against him, giving herself over to him. When he couldn't keep his mouth from her any longer, he leaned forward to scrape his teeth across the straining pink peak before soothing it with the flat of his tongue. She cried out, and he released her, backing away again.

"I like that," she said. "All of it."

"I know."

She gave a little laugh and reached for him—her touch a gift—leaning down to kiss him, her glorious hair falling around them like a curtain. "You are exceedingly arrogant."

She made him so. Made him want to crow to the wide world. "You say that as though I don't have cause to be."

A pretty red brow arched high in challenge. "You're also exceedingly certain of yourself."

In answer, he moved, lifting her, turning her, reversing their positions and setting her to the chair as he fell to his knees in front of her. A tiny sound of delight came from her as he leaned in and kissed her. Her fingers tangled in his hair as she met him. Matched him.

He tugged at her hips, pulling her down the chair, to the edge of it, as she stroked over his chest and torso to the edge of his trousers, where it was her turn to grasp fabric. To tug closer.

She opened her thighs and Henry thought he might lose himself then, at the look of her, bare to the waist, gazing up at him with delight and desire and that bold, beautiful assessment that made him want to show her all the best parts of him.

"Shall I tell you what I would like?" he asked.

"Please."

That word again. It would be his undoing. "I would like you naked."

Her eyes widened in surprise. "I—you would?"

"Very much," he said, his hands falling to the fastening of her trousers. "And in this particular case, the trousers are not helping."

She gave a little giggle, but the sound seemed to startle her, and one hand flew to her mouth as though she wished to keep it in.

He hated that, that she kept her pleasure bottled, and vowed that he would do all he could to show her the kind of pleasure that would not be contained as he worked at the buttons, loosening the green silk. "Someday, I would like to spend an hour or two watching you in these. But tonight—" Finished with the buttons, he tugged at the waist, loving the way she lifted her hips and let him strip her bare.

He sucked in a breath at her laid out before him, the firelight casting shadows over her naked body, over the swell of her breasts, the muscles of her torso, the scar at her rib, the angles at her hips, and the thatch of auburn curls between her long thighs, muscled and strong from a lifetime of work.

She was like nothing he'd ever seen before.

A gift from the damn gods.

He sat back on his heels and rubbed a hand over his mouth, distracted by the sight of her, long and beautiful.

He didn't realize how long he'd been looking at her until she moved beneath his gaze, to cover herself. And only then, when he realized what she was about, did he move as well, capturing her hands and threading his fingers through hers. "No."

She blushed, and somehow the riot of red across her cheeks made her even prettier. Made him even luckier.

"I—" She searched for words. Settled on, "Say something."

A dozen things came instantly to mind. He could have told her she was beautiful. That she fascinated him. That he wanted to know every inch of her. He could have told her that he'd never been as hard as he was, that he'd never wanted someone quite as much as he wanted her and that he certainly hadn't ever wanted someone in quite this way—in the urgent, eager way that made him think he'd gone just a little mad.

But he didn't want to frighten her. And he wanted her to believe him.

To trust him.

So, instead of saying any of the wild, unexpected things that rioted through him at her words, Henry pressed a kiss to the soft skin above their entwined hands and painted a slow, leisurely circle there, until her breath came harsh and ragged and her fingers were once more in his hair.

And only then did he say, "Shall we see what else you like?"

Chapter Ten

She'd done this before. Not much, but a girl born as she was learned quickly not to prize virginity. She'd been engaged to be married, and there'd been a few boys when she was young and angry. Once or twice it had even been pleasant.

Of course, she knew that other women found the act more than pleasant—a year witnessing Sesily and Caleb's habit of disappearing and returning wrinkled and mussed and glowing had proven it—but Adelaide had never really imagined it could be *good*.

And then the Duke of Clayborn had taken a bath in front of her. And he'd called her Adelaide and he'd singed her with his touch and he'd kissed her in a dozen places where no one had ever kissed her before, and suddenly that act that had always been fast and fumbling and at best *fine* . . . seemed as though it might be . . . well . . . extremely *good*.

And then he'd stripped her bare and looked at her as though he were hungry, and she'd gone hot and heavy and more willing than she'd ever been, and not just from his touch—though that was magnificent—but because he so clearly wanted her.

He didn't want her skills as a thief, or access to the power around her, or the vast amounts of information she had on the men of London.

He wanted *her*.

And Adelaide liked that more than everything else.

Because she wanted him, too.

He pulled her even further down the chair, sliding his big hands along her thighs, coaxing her open. She let him, marveling at the sensation—she'd never been so warm or heavy, never felt so needy before. She couldn't resist reaching for him, letting her fingers slide over his chest and torso, exploring the muscles she'd admired earlier. She lingered over a bruise blossoming on his side. "You are hurt."

He caught her hand, pressing the palm flat to his hot skin. "This helps."

She liked that, too. Liked the way his muscles tightened beneath her touch as she traced over him, lower, to the place where his skin met his trousers.

They both hesitated then, and a burst of delight exploded in Adelaide's chest—a heady sense of exploration. She reveled in the low hiss of pleasure that came as she explored the hard length of him—straining against the fabric of his trousers.

"Show me," she whispered, ready for what came next. Eager for it.

He shook his head. "You first." And he opened her thighs, moving between them to hold her wide, exposed and hot and bare for him.

She held her breath as he stared down over her, his gaze stern and focused, as though he memorized the sight of her. Seconds seemed to stretch into an eternity, until she couldn't bear it any longer and moved to cover herself.

He caught her hands before she could, setting them to the arms of the chair as he kissed her once, rough and wild. Before she could return the caress he was gone, moving to lick over the soft skin of her shoulder, to graze his teeth along the swell of her breast, to gently suck at first one nipple and then the other, until she didn't care that she was bare to him—she only cared that he make good on the endless waves of pleasure he promised.

She lifted her hips, empty and aching and *wanting*.

As though she'd spoken aloud, he trailed his lips lower, sitting back on his heels, spreading her wide and open until she could feel his gaze on her core. "You like this, too, don't you, love?"

Another cant of her hips. Another gasp.

She gasped his name. "Henry . . ."

The bastard laughed, the sound low and full of praise. "Soon," he whispered, turning the promise to the soft skin of the inside of her thigh. Pressing a line of kisses there.

He was clearly doing it to torture her—it couldn't possibly be for him. She didn't fool herself into thinking that men enjoyed all the bits beyond the actual event. And though she was enjoying this more than she'd enjoyed anything ever, she found herself more than willing to get to the actual event herself. "You can—" She stopped, uncertain of how to say it. "What I mean is—" Another false start. "That is—"

His tongue swirled in a circle, higher up her thigh, sending pleasure sizzling through her. She took a deep breath. "I have done this before."

Henry slowly lifted his mouth, and looked up at her from his place at her feet, on his knees. *Oh, my.* She liked that. He was broad and handsome and his lips, which had given her such pleasure, were set in a small, curious curve that sent heat crawling over her cheeks, especially when he said simply, "I have, as well."

She closed her eyes. That much was clear. With the way she felt, Adelaide imagined he was in high demand behind potted ferns in Mayfair ballrooms. Likely by women who were less embarrassed by this particular scenario. "What I mean—"

He turned to her thigh again. Kissed again. Higher. Closer to where she ached.

Dear God. "You don't have to—"

More kisses. Higher still.

She squirmed, and he set one heavy hand to her stomach, staying her movement. But he did not stop, delivering another kiss—this one to the opposite thigh. A little lick. A suck.

She exhaled on a little sigh. "You can simply . . . do it."

This time, when he looked at her, there was something new in his cerulean gaze. Something that cut through the desire. Something wild. "Do what?"

She looked to the ceiling, wishing she could vanish into the shadows above. "I—"

"No," he said, his thumb stroking over her skin his only movement. "Tell me. Do what?"

For a moment, she considered what a lady would say. And then she realized there was absolutely no situation in which a lady would say anything even approximating the answer to his question. So she settled on the words she'd heard her whole life. What she knew he wanted. "You can simply . . . fuck me."

The air came out of him in a *whoosh.*

She closed her eyes. She'd been too crass. Dammit. He was going to stop.

Except he didn't. Instead, he said, "Hmm," as though he hadn't considered that as a possibility, and moved, his hands sliding down to her thighs and opening them wide. "Thank you for the suggestion."

"You're . . . welcome," she said, the words coming uneasy, as his thumbs circled over skin that had never been touched with such lingering purpose.

"Tell me, can I do this? Touch you like this?"

"Y-yes."

"Do you like it?"

"I—yes." Very much.

He moved, stroking up, over her skin. "And can I kiss you here?"

A kiss at the seam of her thigh, where it met her torso. How did that feel so good? "Yes."

"You like that?"

"Yes."

"Hmm." That sound. It shouldn't do things to her. It wasn't even a word, and still it made her ache. "And would you mind if I . . ." He trailed off and blew a long stream of air over her core.

"I—oh—no . . ." she panted.

"You like that."

It wasn't a question, but she answered anyway. *"Yes."*

"Good," he said, the word feeling like praise. Making her warmer. Wetter.

A soft rumble came from his throat. "Mmm . . . You like that, too, don't you, Adelaide? When I tell you how good you are? How much you please me when you talk about your pleasure."

"Yes," she whispered.

"Good girl," he said, the words sending a sizzle of pleasure through her.

And then he rewarded her honesty with a long, slow lick that set her entirely on fire. She cried out at the pleasure, at the way he lingered at the top of her pussy, and when he lifted his head, she was panting and her body was no longer hers, her hips lifting toward him, her fingers itching to capture his hair and return him to his position.

He knew it, too, the gleam in his knowing gaze an arrogant promise. "I have no intention of *simply fucking* you, Adelaide. There is nothing simple about what I intend to do to you. There is nothing simple about the ways I intend to touch you. About the ways I intend to kiss you." God, his fingers were there, at her core, sliding one finger through the soft curls that shielded her, parting her folds. "And when I do . . . there will be nothing simple about that, either."

She was vibrating with excitement, the feel of the silken promise on the most private part of her. She'd never wanted anything as much as she wanted him.

And then he said, "But I'm not going to fuck you tonight, love."

"You aren't?"

He wasn't?

"No," he said to her core, stroking over the wet heat of her, two fingers now, up and down in slow, excruciating movements that made her want to scream and cry and laugh. He pushed them inside her heat, giving her a taste of what she wanted. A hint of what it would be like to be full of him, strong and deep.

A pause, and then, "Well, maybe a little fucking."

How was it that the accent honed in Mayfair and Eton and Oxford and the House of Lords made the curse sound even more filthy? She couldn't help herself. She moved against him, urging him deeper. "Yes. Please."

"Is this what you need?"

She closed her eyes at the soft caress and let out a low moan of pleasure. "Hmm." That sound, low and rich, and full of discovery. And then he added his thumb, circling, searching, finding the places that made her gasp and sigh, and the whole time, talking. "You're so wet here. So soft." He pressed a kiss to the inside of her thigh. Whispered, "So sweet."

He worked a tight circle where pleasure pooled and she cried out. "There!"

"You like that, too." His reply was so arrogant that she would have happily kicked him if he weren't the instrument of her undoing.

"Don't stop," she panted.

He didn't. But he did ask, "Are you sure?"

"God, yes."

He moved faster, circling tighter, and she lifted herself again, riding his touch, knowing that later—much later—she'd be embarrassed of her wantonness. Of the spectacle she made with her desire. But right now, she did not care. Right now, all she wanted was his touch on her.

All she wanted was him.

"So pretty," he whispered. "So perfect."

She wasn't, she knew. But in that moment, she believed him. "Please don't stop."

She tensed as her climax rushed toward her, just as his fingers thrust deep, deeper, matching the rhythm of her hips, the staccato sound of her breath, harsh and desperate.

So desperate. It wasn't enough. "Henry . . ."

She didn't have to say more. To ask for more. He already knew. "Hmm." That noise she was coming to revel in—the one that said he was thinking about all the wicked things he might do with her.

And before Adelaide could think of those wicked things, he was doing them, settling his mouth to the place just above his fingers, where she ached for him, wringing a curse from her.

Sliding her fingers into his hair, she pressed against him, his growl of approval making her wild, making her beg for more even as he gave her exactly what she wanted, his mouth like a gift. Like paradise.

His tongue licked over her, exploring the dark, wet, heat of her in every fathomable way—when long, firm strokes had her panting, he slowed to delicious torture that made her curse and thrust and ache and plead, and then, draping her thighs over his shoulders, spreading his large hands over her bottom, lifting her close, speeding up, dancing over her until her eyes flew open and she stared down her body to meet the blue fire in his gaze. Smug, satisfied, sinful fire.

"That's it." He spoke to the core of her, the vibration making her tremble, her fingers tightening in his hair. "Take it."

She'd never done anything like this, but she wanted

it. Wanted to follow his directions. And so she did as he told her, holding him tight to her, where his tongue worked in glorious rhythm, back and forth, again and again as she rocked against him, gasping, holding back her screams, chasing that glorious pleasure that was just out of reach.

"Please," she whispered to him. To the universe. "I can't . . . please."

And then, the whole world was moving. No—she was moving. *He* was moving, releasing her—no. *No.* What was he doing? Why was he stopping?

She clung to him as he lifted her from the chair. "What—"

"You'll like it better, beautiful."

Beautiful. What a lovely word. What a lovely name.

Before she could correct him, either in her head or aloud, she was falling backward to the bed, and he was following her down, pressing her thighs wide to the counterpane. Pressing a little kiss to the aching nub at her core. Giving it a little suck, drawing a tiny cry from her. "Better, yes?"

She met his eyes, glittering with pleasure. "No. Worse."

A slight furrow of his brow. "Worse?"

She nodded, not understanding what had come over her. "You stopped."

"Ah," he said, understanding dawning. "Terrible, that."

That hint of a smile was back, and she stroked her thumb over the corner of his handsome mouth. "I like that."

He nipped at the flesh of her thumb, running his tongue over it until she shivered in his arms. "My mouth? I could tell."

She gave a little laugh. "No. Your smile. It's so rare. It feels precious."

It disappeared and she regretted her words instantly.

"Shall I tell you what is rare and precious?"

The heat of the question was undeniable. "Please."

"This," he said, stroking over her again, setting her instantly on fire once more as he found the place where every nerve in her body seemed to end. He circled it once, twice, and spoke to it. "Soft and wet . . ." She made a little noise and rocked her hips against him. "And so responsive." He leaned in and licked her, licking over the bud he'd been tempting. Stopped again. "You taste like summer. Like heat and heaven . . . and sin." Another suck. Another long lick, rubbing over her until she grabbed his hair. "And when you ride me . . ." She closed her eyes at the words, so filthy in his grand voice. "It makes me want you to ride me in every way. Until you've come."

Before she could answer, as the words spread hot fire through her, he pressed her wide with two fingers and leaned in, licking and sucking, stroking in hard, firm, tight circles, giving her no quarter. She didn't have to tell him not to stop now—he wasn't going to. Didn't have to tell him what she liked—he knew. Somehow, he knew her body better than she did now, and when it trembled against him, out of her control, it remained in his—his hands dominating it, controlling it, stroking over her skin, soothing it, leaving pleasure and praise everywhere he touched.

Adelaide cried his name and a dozen other nonsensical things as he devoured her, unrelentingly, until she flew apart, and came, shattering beneath his caress, and the urgent, coaxing, delicious sounds he growled at her core. And when she'd come, hard and fast, he stayed there, his tongue flat against her as she quivered against him, lacking breath and restraint, everything disappeared but him and his touch, returning her to earth.

And then Henry climbed up her body, tucking himself between her legs, pressing his hard length where she needed his touch, knowing somehow that she still ached for him, the rough fabric of his trousers the only thing keeping him from being inside her. He rolled his hips against her, slow and sinful. "You beautiful thing. Touch like fire. Hair like fire. Threatening to burn me up," he whispered. "Where have you been?"

Nowhere. The word whispered through her, and she bit her lip to stop herself from speaking it, even though—in that moment, as he pressed himself along her body, capturing her cheek in one hand and licking into her mouth in a devastating, deep kiss that tasted of her pleasure and somehow of his—she felt as though she'd been remade.

A different Adelaide. One she did not know. One fashioned by pleasure.

One who was not on her own.

And in the realization, Adelaide was consumed simultaneously by fear and by something far worse. Something like hope. Something that made her wonder what it would be to believe him when he ended the kiss and caught her face in both palms, staring down at her as though she were something to be looked at. Something to notice. Something to treasure.

As though there was more between them than this moment. This place. This night.

Which there wasn't.

She was Adelaide Frampton, baseborn thief from the wrong side of the river, more comfortable in dark alleys than in gilded ballrooms. And he was a damn duke.

Get your head on right, gel. The voice that whispered came with the clipped accent of the South Bank—the one she had worked so hard to hide in the last few years.

She resolved to listen, reaching for him, pulling him close for a kiss of her own, claiming him in the hopes that she might regain control of herself. Of the situation. Of whatever was to come. Telling herself that the straight shot of pleasure she got when he gave himself over to her was about that—control—and not about the joy that came with knowing she could affect him as he had her.

She had to get control of the situation. And there was one certain way she could do that.

Adelaide kissed across his cheek, over the rough stubble of his day-long beard, and whispered, "Are you sure?"

He stroked over her bare breast, his thumb circling her nipple until it tightened into a stiff bud. "Sure about what?"

"That you won't take me tonight?"

He stilled, setting his hands to the bed and pushing himself up to look at her, searching her gaze, deep and searing. As though he could see it all—her uncertainty, her desire for control. As though he knew the request was about more than pleasure—about gaining power. "No, love. Not tonight." She didn't like what she saw there, in his blue eyes. Something that might have been disappointment but seemed more like understanding, as though he heard her thoughts and was already a dozen moves ahead in this game they played.

It made her want to hide.

She pushed at his chest, and he rolled to his back. Disappointment coursed through her. It was over—which should not have disappointed. It was expected, was it not? She knew there was nothing more for Adelaide Frampton and the Duke of Clayborn—nothing but this quiet room at the back of the Hungry Hen. Nothing but this night.

Was it wrong that she'd hoped the night would not end quite so quickly?

He interrupted her thoughts by pulling her to him, wrapping his long, sinewy arms around her, and tucking her against his side. And though she meant to resist—to pull away and wrap herself in fabric and hide from him until morning—she couldn't find the will for it. Not when he was so warm and firm and welcome. Not when his fingertips stroked over her shoulder, painting it with his touch.

Not when he turned and pressed a kiss to her temple, holding her so close she could hear his heart beneath her ear.

They lay in silence for long moments, the tavern quiet below, the world forgotten outside. Adelaide wondered at the feel of him and the way she had come apart in his arms, and the way this place, this night, this man somehow felt out of time, as though they were not in competition to get to his brother, to save Lady Helene, to evade her father and his men. As though she were not Adelaide Frampton, girl from the streets, and he were not the Duke of Clayborn.

As though they had a future.

As though they had all the time in the world, when they didn't.

When they only had that night.

Less than a night, when he whispered, "I should—"

He stopped, but she finished the sentence in a dozen ways. *I should not have done that. I should never have kissed you. Should never have followed you. Should never have thrown my lot in with you.*

I should leave.

"Henry," she whispered to his chest at long last, her fingers playing over the dark hair there. She couldn't look at him. Couldn't risk the embarrassment of his refusal—embarrassment that already threatened. That had been there, at the edge of her consciousness all evening—the embarrassment that came of being a woman alone, taking up too much space. Asking for too much. "Sleep with me."

When his fingers stilled on her shoulder, the embarrassment became a living thing, pacing its cage, licking its chops, as though it had been waiting for this exact moment to attack. Silly Adelaide, baseborn girl from the wrong side of the river, propositioning a *duke*.

He would refuse the request, of course, and return to his role as responsible, proper gentleman. Move back to the chair—the one where she had come apart for him—set it by the door, and contort himself uncomfortably into sleep. And she would be left to the bed—to be devoured whole.

But somehow, even in the face of that embarrassment, Adelaide could not resist adding to the request—a quiet, winsome, "I would like it."

And he answered with a low, pained, "Adelaide."

She squeezed her eyes shut. *Awful. Absolute horror.*

She should move. Leave him before he left her. Get in her carriage and head for Lady Helene, who was that very moment in bed with a man who wished never to leave her.

But before Adelaide could do just that, his palm went flat on her skin, warm and heavy, pulling her tight to him as he pulled the coverlet on the bed up over them. Answering her request.

They were silent for a long time, hearts slowing, breath coming less harshly, and Adelaide knew she should close her eyes and try to sleep. She absolutely should not speak to this man—this man who wielded pretty words like temptation. She shouldn't get used to conversation with him.

She shouldn't get used to anything about him.

"Tell me a story."

She lifted her head. "What kind of story?"

He raised a brow. "A lewd one."

She grinned. "There was a duke in a roadside inn once."

His laugh was a low rumble from his warm chest. "I like that one."

"Me, too," she agreed, leaning up to kiss him, slow and soft.

When the kiss stopped, she sighed, and he said, "Tell me about your first kiss."

She hesitated. A girl born in the heart of Lambeth lost her innocence young—even if her father was a king there. Perhaps *because* her father was a king there. Innocence was for girls from Mayfair. Not for girls like her.

"Are you looking for a comparison?"

She'd never seen anyone look so arrogant. "I think I can top it."

She had no doubt about that. But she stacked her hands on his chest and set her chin atop them. "Jamie Buck lived down the road. His father worked for mine."

"Ah. The girl in the tower."

There was no tower, but Adelaide didn't tell him that. She couldn't change where she'd come from, and it would do them both well to remember that hers had been a very different world than his.

Except she didn't want him to think about that. Not right now. Now she wanted him to know the girl she'd once been, and so she told him more than he needed to know.

Ridiculous.

"I like Westminster Bridge." Surprise flashed on his handsome face at the change in topic. "I know it's odd, but I do. I suppose I could simply like bridges—and I do like bridges, generally—but there's something about that one. There's a poem about it; Wordsworth, I think? About looking at the City from it. *The City now doth, like a garment, wear the beauty of the morning.* Do you know that one?"

"I don't," he said, and she feared she'd gone too far in her storytelling—there was nothing interesting about poems written about bridges. "But I'd like to see you wearing the beauty of the morning."

The words tumbled through her, making her pulse race, and it occurred to her that there might, in fact, be something fascinating about poems written about bridges, after all. "That's sweet."

"You are sweet," he replied, his eyes still firmly

closed. "Go on. What does Westminster have to do with Jamie Buck?"

"There is a turret about halfway across that gives you a glorious look at the Houses of Parliament. You'd think the whole bridge would provide such a thing, but it's not true. It's a particular turret, fourth from the Westminster side, at the perfect angle, where you can see directly into the little rooms in Parliament, and if you are there at precisely the right moment, it feels like . . . magic," she said simply, wishing she could explain it more clearly. "I would linger in that little turret for hours, wishing . . ." She trailed off.

"Wishing what?"

She should have known he wouldn't let her stop. "Wishing there were someone there, with me," she said softly. "I was alone a great deal of the time. I didn't dislike it, mind you—but my father . . . he scared people, and boys especially. And those he did not scare were willing to do anything to gain access to him—including pretend to be friends with his daughter."

His eyes were open now, watching her as though he didn't wish to miss a single word, and she worried her lip, feeling embarrassed and strange, like she shouldn't give parts of herself away to this man, who was so different from her—so far beyond her—that when he left she'd have no hope of getting them back.

"I used to stand in the turret and wish for a friend," she admitted softly. "For something beyond the world I had—someone who didn't feign interest in me because they feared my father, or wished access to him. Someone who did not see me as a path to something greater. I wanted someone who might be . . . a partner. Who would like me for me. Who would *love* me for me, I suppose."

He tightened his grip on her. "Go on."

She swallowed, suddenly wishing there was distance between them. "One afternoon . . . I was fourteen? Maybe fifteen? . . . and there, in my turret. Jamie walked by, with a group of other boys—clearly set out for trouble. But he saw me first." She closed her eyes. "He *heard* me first."

"What were you saying?"

She immediately regretted telling him the story, but was too far down the road to stop. "Please keep in mind that I was a young girl with a head full of dreams. I am no longer this impressionable."

"I am already disappointed to hear it."

The laughter helped with the embarrassment. Barely. "I was talking to myself."

"About what?"

"Well, not really myself, I suppose. I was talking to someone else. Someone who was not there. Pretending I had the partner I'd been dreaming of. And Jamie Buck *heard* it. He laughed and laughed . . ."

Henry's eyes narrowed. "And?"

"And he threatened to tell everyone. Which now seems so silly—who would care? But at the time, it was a terrifying proposition. He knew my . . ." She hesitated, not wanting to reveal her past in this moment, when they were quiet and he was close.

It was only a matter of time before he would know everything. But Adelaide was ever the thief, and now, she looked to steal time.

"My father would have loathed it," she said. "He would have made certain I never visited that turret again. Jamie said he'd keep my secret if I kissed him."

Henry sucked in a breath, and her gaze flew to his to find fury in his eyes. "You were fourteen. This would have been, what, eleven years ago?"

She nodded.

"I might have been there. I might have been in Parliament. I might have been walking by at that exact moment. I could have tossed young Jamie right off the damn turret."

She grinned at that. "That does seem a bit overmuch."

A growl sounded deep in his chest. "I am not amused, Adelaide."

"Does it help to know that he was encouraged by a half-dozen boys who were watching from round the corner?"

"It does *not*." He looked positively furious, and she confessed she rather liked it.

"Does it help to hear that he kissed like a codfish and smelled like pickled herring? Two facts I made sure the wide world heard?"

"Well. I was going to suggest you divulge young Jamie's current address, but I don't imagine he was able to escape that particular review for a good amount of time." He paused. "Still, I intend to take you to that turret and kiss you like you deserve."

He wouldn't, but it was a lovely thought. She put a hand to his cheek, testing the roughness of his beard, reveling in the angle of his jaw and the way he inhaled at her touch. "Bridge or no, Your Grace, you are a far more memorable kiss than that one."

He proved it then, long and lush and delicious, filling her with the feel and taste and breath of him. And when he was done, he pressed soft kisses along her jaw and whispered *beautiful* at her ear, and she couldn't stop herself from whispering the words that had been turning around and around in her mind, a puzzle she could not solve.

"Why won't you marry?"

His touch stuttered over the skin of her shoulder, but he did not reply.

She squeezed her eyes closed, grateful that he could not see her in the darkness. "I should not have asked. It is not my business."

He pressed a kiss to her temple. "Marriage should come with a full heart. Isn't that what you said?"

She nodded. "Yes."

"I agree. It should come with every bit that is promised. Family and hope and a lifetime of being seen. *True love*, they call it. I think because it is the most honest a person ever is." He paused, staring up at the ceiling. "I cannot love like that."

She wanted to scream in protest. If anyone deserved love, it was this man—noble beyond words. Honest to a fault. Instead, she said softly, "Why not?"

He took a deep breath, and she reveled in the rich, warm sound beneath her ear. "Because, someday, she might discover something about me that she does not care for, and then where would we be? Me, out of my head with love, and her, desperate to be rid of me."

She understood instantly. "Secrets."

"I have seen what losing love does to a person. I don't want it."

What could it be? What could this remarkable man really be hiding?

His chest rose and fell beneath her ear. "My brother plans to marry a lovely woman, though. Indeed, I would wager they will be married by the week's end, and well on their way to producing heirs to my title."

She lifted her head and met his eyes, offering him a soft smile. "You forget that I rarely fail when I set myself a task."

"Then our race continues," he said, the words soft, without challenge.

"A race no more—we are down a carriage."

"And so, you have won. And tomorrow? Will I wake to an empty room, a wrecked carriage, and a missing purse? Do you think Mary will give me work?"

"It's possible. You'd make an excellent bruiser to keep the peace."

"Six years of boxing at school," he said, dryly.

She laughed again, setting her cheek to his chest. "I believe there is room in my carriage for you," she said, knowing she shouldn't be so happy to offer it. Knowing that every moment they were together was a moment that threatened the life she'd so carefully built for herself.

His hand slid over her shoulder, and he rumbled beneath her ear. "You are willing to share with me?"

Perhaps it was the quiet of the room. The warmth of the bed. The roughness of his beard as he pressed a kiss to the top of her head. But the question did not seem to be about carriages anymore. Not that it would matter, as Adelaide had a feeling the answer would be the same. "Yes. I would like that."

"Mmm." That delicious sound, warm and wonderful. "Must we go tonight?"

They should.

But Jack and Helene were safe in their room an hour north, under the watchful eye of the Duchess's scout. And an hour was not so far. Adelaide and Clayborn could leave early. Catch them by lunchtime. See them to Gretna. Keep them safe there and back.

Stay away from London for a bit longer. Hidden from view.

Together.

"I suppose we could wait," she said, softly, knowing she was thieving time. Knowing it was a risk.

He tightened his arm around her in approval, tucking her close to him, running the tips of his fingers over her shoulder, back and forth in time to his slow, rhythmic heartbeat. She let her thoughts wander from Jack and Helene and the Belles and the Matchbreaker and Alfie Trumbull and Havistock . . . and finally, to Henry. And his secrets.

To the idea that he wouldn't marry—that he would simply . . . languish. That he would be alone . . . Something flared deep in her at the idea. It shouldn't have bothered her. She was alone, was she not? Had been for a lifetime and expected to be for a lifetime more.

But the idea of him alone . . . of them both alone . . .

There was something there. Something . . . free.
What had he done to her?

"If you do not marry," she whispered. His fingers stuttered over her skin as hers began a slow track over his chest, playing in the dark hair there. "If you find a girl who has no plans for it. Who knows what she likes . . ."

Somehow, in the darkness, his plans for his future stretched out before them . . . Adelaide saw something more. Something like possibility.

"I am listening." His hand went flat on her shoulder, pressing her into his warmth.

She breathed him in. "Marriage isn't the only path."

"Shall I let her take me to mistress?"

The question was low and dark and injected with more humor than Adelaide wished. *Maybe.* Maybe there was a middle way? An arrangement with her? One in which she continued her work, remained in her world, and simply . . . added nights like this? With him?

They would have to be discreet, of course. He was one of the most recognizable faces in Parliament. A brilliant orator. A cunning mind. A powerful voice.

But Adelaide had made a lifetime of going unnoticed. What if they could find a way to repeat this night? Why not take it?

They lay in silence, the low rumble of the tavern below having given way to quiet so impossibly still that she could now hear nothing but her heart. Or was it his, beating in a steady rhythm beneath her ear, slowing as the rise and fall of his chest grew heavy and even, and he fell asleep, holding her in his arms.

Adelaide was still for an age—minutes, maybe hours—marveling at the feel of his body against hers. Of his warm skin and the rich scent of sun-warmed leather that mixed with the rosemary from his bath. She'd never noticed a man's scent before. Never reveled in her mark on it.

Never felt the keen pleasure that came with the knowledge that he was, for however fleeting a moment, hers.

Never wondered if there might be a way to keep it close. To hold it tight.

It was the wildness of the experience—the absolute madness of it—that made her whisper to the darkness, "Mine."

It was certainly madness that the word gave her even more pleasure aloud than in her thoughts. Pleasure and triumph and a bone-deep something that she knew better than to name, knowing instinctively that if she inspected it . . . if she put words to it . . . she'd never be able to forget it.

But . . . what if?

For the first time, Adelaide allowed herself to consider the possibility that she did not need to forget the Duke of Clayborn, in all his untouchable aristocratic divinity. That perhaps there was a way forward for them— unconventional and limited, but a path they could tread . . . together.

Mistress, he'd said. A jest.

A word that she'd never considered before, because women like Adelaide were not made for mistressing. She was not pretty enough or droll enough or sultry enough to summon men to her bed. But why not another word? If he would have her? Why not *companion*? Why not *secret keeper*?

Why not *partner*?

She caught her breath as the thoughts took shape. Adelaide Frampton, who had spent a lifetime alone, facing down pain and danger and loneliness, who had made a place for herself in the world as a woman with a wicked sense of justice, and a willingness to do anything to mete it out—found herself undone in those moments, in the dark . . . by *hope*.

Foreign and unnerving, the feeling twisted, becoming

something more familiar. Easier to ignore. Fear. Who was she if she allowed herself to hope for another?

If she allowed herself to put a name to him? A face?

If she stole it? For herself?

The answers were for another day. But that night, for once, Adelaide allowed herself a taste of what it would be to sleep, safe and wanted, in a lover's arms.

Chapter Eleven

Henry woke to a noise beyond the door.

The room was full of the deep dark that came with the heaviest part of night, the candles having long since burned out, the fire down to glowing embers in the hearth. He'd fallen asleep with Adelaide in his arms, warm and soft and relaxed for the first time since they'd met. The scent of her surrounding him, fresh like rain, the weight and heat of her pressed against him, her fingers playing over his chest in smooth, lush circles, making him want to buy the Hungry Hen and never leave it.

Making him want to keep her there, in that bed, until she shared every one of her secrets.

Making him want to tell her all of his.

Which was madness, of course.

Wasn't it?

She'd offered him a future.

He'd known since he was fourteen that he would not marry. That he would do best not to tumble into love like other men. He'd built himself a cool, unwavering identity—one that did not recommend him to women. Or anyone else, for that matter. Once others realized that the dukedom was not accessible, they moved on, as there was little reward in staying.

But somehow, this woman had found her way in with her touch and her kiss and the little glimpses of her that she gifted him, like treasure. A good thing, too—for if she hadn't gifted them, he might have stolen them, with how well he liked them. Bits of her life, her world, her mind. Her kisses.

And then, last night, after he held her in his arms and told her that marriage was not his future, how he feared loving another more than she could love him, she had not asked for his secrets.

Instead, she'd offered a new path.

To be his mistress.

Of course, it was impossible. He'd watched Adelaide Frampton for long enough to know there were no half measures for her. She deserved a man who could give her everything. Marriage. A home—a damned palace if she wanted it. Children to fill it with laughter. Honesty. A life without secrets.

She deserved that full heart.

But there, in the depths of night, in that dark inn at what felt like the end of the earth, if he closed his eyes, he might believe it could be him.

Even as he knew he shouldn't, he tightened his arm around her, pulling her closer. His hand coursed over the soft skin of her back, pausing when it found a raised mark. The hint of another scar. Longer than the one at her side.

What had the world done to this woman? Anger threaded through him, hot and impatient, chased by a heady desire to find those who had wronged her and to destroy them. To avenge her. To protect her.

I don't need protection, she'd said downstairs, after he'd gone for the brute. Called her his wife.

And she didn't. Not all the time. He'd seen her do plenty of protecting herself. He'd seen her go head-to-head with aristocrats and bruisers alike. Christ, he'd seen her leap onto a moving boat, as though a drop into the Thames wouldn't take the life of anyone who had the misfortune to suffer it.

She didn't need protection. And still, he needed to protect her.

The thought clarified in the darkness, and the door to the room splintered open, slamming back into the wall with the force of a heavy boot.

And then, there was no *needing* to protect her; there was only doing it.

Adelaide shot up from her slumber, the bedclothes falling to her waist, and Henry shouted, "Stay!" even as he was out of the bed, already reaching for his blade.

"Oh, there's no way I'm doing that," she said as he stepped up onto the bed and crossing it, leaping down at its foot to face the intruders, putting himself between them and her.

In the lantern light from the hallway beyond, Henry could make out two of them, one tall and slim, the other big and broad and stinking of ale—recognizable by his slow lumber. It was the brute from below. "Ah, Billy," Henry said as he came forward. "You should have stayed gone."

"I won't be bested by a toff, I won't," Billy said, his ham-sized fists raised in the shadows. "And it just so happens that this here man needed my 'elp bringing you down to size."

Henry looked to the other man, standing back, in the shadows . . . and recognized him. The rider from the road. Who had slowed. Leered like a proper predator, as though he'd known what he was hunting . . . and had found it.

Good of him to make it easy for Henry to take him out, too.

A flint struck behind them and a candle flared to life. Billy's eyes went wide as he looked to Adelaide, his meaty lips curving in a disgusting smile. "I didn't expect the view, I'll say. Yer *wife* don't look like much when she's wearin' clothes."

And that was all Henry needed to hear. "It is clear

you *didn't* learn your lesson," he said with cold certainty. "The one where you treat women with respect."

Billy looked to him. "I'll treat 'em with respect when they ain't bare-assed. Turns out even a lady can look a whore."

And when he turned his leering gaze back on Adelaide, Henry's mind went blank, and he knocked Billy back with a sharp, wicked blow. The other man cried out, stumbling in the wake of it, but Henry gave him no quarter. "You—don't—look—at her," he said, cold fury in the words, each one punctuated with another jab, another advance. "You don't *think* of her."

He delivered a final blow and the brute went down again, out cold. Before Clayborn could consider his handiwork, however, something rattled on the bedside table behind him. A candlestick, a pitcher of water, he'd never know. Whatever it was, he didn't like it, and when he spun around to face it without hesitation, he knew why.

He'd made a mistake. While he'd been exacting his vengeance on a man too prideful and genuinely too stupid to be of real danger, the other man—the silent one, the one he would soon discover was far more dangerous—had gone for Adelaide.

And instead of screaming for help as one would expect, she faced him, tall and straight-spined, as though she were a warrior in full armor and not draped in a bedsheet that threatened to tumble to the floor.

She was naked. He'd stripped her bare and taken her to bed, ignoring the fact that he'd made them an enemy below. Ignoring the fact that a handful of hours earlier, he'd leapt from a fast-moving carriage, an action that had left him worse for wear.

They should have dressed before they slept, but he'd wanted to feel her skin against his, all while believing that he could keep her safe from whatever might come their way. And in his selfishness—in his hubris—he'd put her in danger.

He lunged toward them, but stilled when he took in the whole scene.

Draped in nothing but a bedsheet, looking for all the world like a goddess, Adelaide held a sharp silver blade to her would-be attacker's neck.

When she spoke, it was with the calm ease of someone who had certainly threatened a throat cutting before. "Don't come any closer, Duke. I wouldn't want my hand to slip."

He stilled, considering the situation. "I haven't decided how I feel about your hand slipping, honestly. I should have taken care of him on the road."

She didn't look to him—*good girl, stay focused on your enemy*—but she did smile at the other man. "The duke suggests I kill you, Danny. What do you think about that?"

The man called Danny answered with ease, as though he didn't have a blade to his throat. "You ain't never had it in you, Addie."

And there, in the familiarity of the diminutive, Henry realized the two did not just recognize each other; they had a history.

He stayed rigid, watching the play of emotions over her face. Frustration. Disappointment. Anger. And something else. Something like shame. Henry clenched a fist at his side, barely feeling the sting of the welts there for his rage at the man for making Adelaide feel anything like shame.

Danny, several inches taller and easily two stone heavier than she, spread his arms wide and lifted his chin, baring his neck boldly, as though they were downstairs drinking ale, rather than here in the dark, with a blade to his throat. "It don't matter what you call yourself now that you run with Mayfair, you'll always be Lambeth, Addie Trumbull." He leveled Clayborn with a combative stare. "Even when yer tuppin' a duke." He grinned. "But maybe he likes it down in the gutter like toffs often do."

That was when Henry decided he was going to destroy this man.

"Alright, Danny, so you found me. Now what?"

She knew she was being chased? Why in hell was she being chased? And by this . . . lizard?

The man smiled. "Alfie wants to talk to you. He ain't happy you walked into his joint and took what weren't yours."

She nodded. "I've suffered Alfie's punishments before."

He tilted his head in Clayborn's direction. "Now 'im . . . I weren't expectin' *him*. There's a price on his head. Imagine my surprise when the duke's carriage turns up wrecked on the road as I'm on my way to fetch you, Addie? The duke, who's travelin' with the Matchbreaker? Now, that's a lucky day, I'd say." He sniffed. "'Course, it's the duke's own fault for ridin' with a seal on the door like a real ponce. And a set of wheels made for money and not muscle." He tsked. "Not the smartest of choices, Addie. Your da won't be happy."

Her da?

"Who's got money on the duke?" Adelaide asked.

"Havistock don't like loose ends, and is payin' handsome for a few dead bodies." He sniffed. "I intend to deliver 'em."

Havistock. Henry knew Havistock wanted him ruined, but, "Why does Havistock want me dead?"

Danny shrugged, but didn't even look at him. "Don't matter to us—money spends for good reasons and bad."

"Alfie took a job killing a duke?"

The man cut her an arrogant look. "Alfie takes whatever jobs I tell him to take now."

"Well, you ought to send him direct to Bedlam for takin' this one," she said, her tone gone full South London. "Killin' a duke will 'ave you swingin' from a rope faster than you can gut a man, Dan-o."

"I'll take my chances. Now my only question is

this—do I return you to your da, as requested, only a bit worse for wear, or do I bring you back to London as the Matchbreaker? There are enough rich bastards lookin' to see you dead that we could sell tickets and set ourselves up for life."

She sucked in a breath at the words, and Clayborn stiffened at the harshness in the sound. The concern in it. Her secret—the one he knew because he seemed to be the only person in London who could not miss Adelaide Frampton's light—out, and in the wrong hands.

While he considered what it would take to keep her enemy silent, Adelaide said, "So, what, you think I'll pay for your silence?"

"I think you haven't got a choice," the man replied. "But let's be honest—you can't pay me near what the rest of Mayfair will pay to get revenge for the way you've ruined them already. Not even if your girls empty their coffers." He looked to Clayborn again. "Not even if your duke tosses in a coin or two. Mayfair hates you that much."

"Is that supposed to sting?" she asked.

He grinned. "It ain't supposed to feel good, kitten."

She pressed the tip of her blade deeper, and a droplet of blood trickled down the side of his neck. When he inhaled sharply and the grin fell from his face, she said, "I think you'll find it takes more than the collective opinion of mediocre men to upset me, Danny."

"You're still a bitch, ain't you?"

Before Clayborn could tear him to shreds for the insult, the man condemned himself to hell, catching her blade hand in his, yanking it around to her back and using his strength and speed to pull Adelaide close, running his filthy hands over her body, grinning his mouthful of rotten teeth at her.

Henry went wild.

"Get your hands off her," he growled, the words coming from a place he rarely acknowledged—somewhere out of control. They both turned to the sound, and the intruder moved with lightning speed, the moon gleaming off his blade.

Adelaide sucked in a breath as it kissed her neck and Henry stopped instantly, vibrating with frustrated fury.

"Now ain't that divertin'," said the man, his eyes gleaming with perverse delight. "Look at how quickly he stopped. Like a child's toy run out of string." He slid a hand over Adelaide's torso, fisting the bedsheet in one filthy hand. "I always wondered if you were any good in the sheets. Looks like you're good enough."

Henry growled, low and dangerous. "Let her go."

"No, I don't think I will," the man said. "You see—I was wondering how it was that we were going to collect you. It ain't every day you get a chance to catch a duke, you know." The blade tightened against Adelaide's throat and she closed her eyes. "But here you are, willing to do anything to keep our Addie safe, ain't you?"

That *our* was another infraction for which this man would pay. Henry was keeping track.

"You will pay for every second you touch her," Henry said, the words raw with furious control. She was still and unmoved, her face revealing nothing of her thoughts. But there, in her eyes as she met his—there was something he didn't like.

"Aww . . . it weren't nothing," Danny said. "We go back, don't we, gel? Painted with the soot of the South Bank. No hard feelings, right, Addie?"

"No more than usual," she hissed.

"I'd almost think he cared for you. But that can't be right—no one cares for you. You ain't nobody. Ain't nothin'. Not even your da cared when you left. He just turned the whole thing over to me."

Adelaide stilled at the words, barely, but enough for Clayborn to notice, and hate it. He moved, heading directly for the pair, prepared to knock away the blade and do whatever necessary to free her. To keep her safe.

Except Billy had woken up.

Before Henry could reach her, the drunken lout felled him, tackling him with a lack of finesse matched only by his lack of sense. Using the momentum of the attack, Clayborn spun as he landed on the ground to meet his previous foe. "Goddammit, Billy. You're an automaton."

"Is that someone who's going to cut you to ribbons?" Billy asked, aiming his massive fist at Henry's face.

"No, as a matter of fact," he said, twisting away at the last moment, as Billy set his fist into the floorboards. Henry rolled to get up, but his opponent recovered, catching him by the waist, taking him to the ground, and landing several strong blows before he got the upper hand, reversing their positions and dispatching Billy with ease once more.

"I'll say this for you, Addie. You've found yourself a pretty fighter. He does it dirty, too. No Queensberry rules for him."

"Six years at school," Henry said, coming to his feet, slower than before.

"What school?" Danny asked.

"The one that ensured that you'd better have a plan to kill me, because after the threats you've delivered to her, if you leave me alive, I will not rest until I have made your life pure hell."

"Such threats!" Danny said. "Everything's perfectly normal. I'm just havin' a chat with our Adelaide."

My Adelaide. The words crashed through Henry, loud enough that he had to clench his teeth to keep from bellowing them into the darkness. *Mine.*

"I'll come with you," she said.

The room stilled. The entirety of Britain stilled. And Henry could not stop his roar of outrage. "What?"

"I'm listening," said Danny.

"I'll come with you. You bring me to my father, you reveal me as the Matchbreaker, whatever you like."

One of Billy's blows had clearly been harder than Henry had noticed. "Over my decaying corpse."

"No worries, Duke. That's likely how it will be," Danny replied.

"Adelaide. What is this play?" Henry asked.

She shook her head, meeting his gaze, her beautiful brown eyes clear. Full of the truth. "No play. I go with Danny. He takes me back to London. On one condition . . ." She paused. "You leave Havistock's money on the table. You leave Lady Helene headed for Gretna with her man. You leave Clayborn here."

Helene? What was happening?

"Fucking hell, Adelaide," he said. "He'll have to kill me to get me to stay here if you leave with him."

"That can be arranged," Danny replied.

She shook her head. "You need to get to Jack and Helene. You need to keep her safe." Even through his fury, the words penetrated, a new piece of the puzzle. Keep *her* safe. Not Adelaide, Helene. *Safe from what?*

Danny seemed to consider it for a moment—long enough that Clayborn thought he'd go mad from fury that she'd do this—that she wouldn't trust him to take care of it. To get them out of this.

And then the villain said, "Nah. No deal. Pretty words, though." He feigned brushing a tear from his eye. "Little Addie, fallin' for Mayfair just like you always did, standin' on that bridge you liked so much and starin' at Parliament like it might cough up a different life for you."

The moment he released her, Clayborn would rip the man's throat out.

Danny tutted dramatically. "And this is the best you can do, innit? Left us all behind on the South Bank, and you ended up a workin' girl anyway. Duke or no, all men are the same in the dark, ain't they?"

And then she retorted, the broad accent of the South

Bank in her voice. "Don't be so sure, Danny—some know what to do in it."

The insult landed, and Danny let out a cruel laugh, turning her to face him. Henry moved in the heartbeat of the shift, until the blade returned to her throat. Tighter now. A drop of blood formed on her skin.

He bit back a shout.

"Still a bitch," Danny said. "You know, it will be good to take you with me. Teach you a lesson I should have taught you years ago. You always thought you were better than me."

"I *was* better than you. I just forgot how much." He gripped her tighter. "There are things I did not forget, however." Before he could reply, she spat directly into his face, then lifted one long, lithe leg and drove her knee directly into Danny's groin. No quarter.

Good girl.

Clayborn was moving even as she grasped Danny's head while he doubled over in pain and put her knee into his nose.

The man screamed and fell like a tree.

Adelaide was already turning. "We have to go." She crossed the room, lifting his box from where it had tumbled to the floor the night before, tossing it into her bag. "Now. We have to get to Helene."

"Adelaide," Danny called after her from his position, curled in on himself on the floor. She turned back. "Your girls can't protect you everywhere." There was no mistaking the threat in his words. "And your duke ain't going to protect you much longer, either. Will he? Boys from Mayfair don't end up with girls from the South Bank."

Without a moment's thought, Clayborn stepped over Billy and headed for Danny.

"No," Adelaide said, reaching a hand out to him. "No." He ignored her.

"Henry," she said. "There's no *time*."

There would be time for this. He would make time for this. He would *stop* time for this. He leaned over and lifted the other man by the shirtfront, staring down into his eyes, barely open. "You tell her *da*"—he spat the word into the other man's face—"and anyone else who asks, that Adelaide Frampton is under the protection of the Duke of Clayborn—and that anyone who comes near her shall face me." ·

A heavy silence fell in the room. One second passed. Two. And then Adelaide said softly, in a way that indicated that he had done the exact wrong thing: "Clayborn."

"Oooh," the ass crowed. *"Protection."* Henry resisted the wince that came at the emphasis. At the realization of what the word could mean. That Adelaide might be paid for her company. And then Danny turned back to Adelaide and said, "You must be better in the sheets than I expected."

Fuck this man.

With no hesitation, Henry knocked him out cold.

"I don't believe I shall ever tire of watching you do that," Adelaide said, pulling several long ribbons out of her skirts from the day before and extending them to him. "Take these."

"Clever," he said, looking down at the brightly colored ribbons. "Remind me never to disdain haberdashery."

She flashed him a quick smile, there then gone. "If we must follow the rules of proper dress, we might as well use them to our advantage."

Efficiently, Henry bound and gagged the pair, stripping them of their weapons, Adelaide watching through the spectacles she now wore, dressing with quiet efficiency.

When he was done, he went to her, pulling her close and tilting her face up to his, staring deep into her eyes. "Are you alright? Did he hurt you?"

She pressed a hand to his. "No. I am well." She lifted a chin in the direction of the villains' blades in his free hand. "We should take their shoes, too."

extracted a snuffbox from her skirts. "I'm impressed. at one was far more difficult than this."

He watched her carefully as she selected an item from e box and affixed it to the cylinder. She'd made a skel- on key. Brilliant. "Do you have passageways in every an in Britain?"

"I'm sorry, Duke," she said, one half of her pretty mouth lifting in a smile that didn't quite meet her eyes. "I don't have time to play with your puzzle box right now."

He let her have the jest. Let her keep her secrets.

She was magnificent.

"It lets out in the stables," she whispered. "If we're lucky, we'll be out before they wake."

Her carriage was already hitched when they got to the stables, Mary standing beside it. She nodded her thanks to the woman. "Send word to Lucia. We need one of the boys to make a delivery. And tell her I need her. She'll know where to find me."

The young woman nodded, sending a nervous look at Clayborn. "Did Billy—"

"Billy knifed a duke, and is lucky to be alive," Adelaide said.

"And if I wish for him to be alive somewhere other than here?"

"Then send him along with the other. His cargo is paid, and you'll never see him again. We must go—this place isn't safe," she said as she opened the door and tossed her bag into the vehicle, indicating that he should enter. "Get in, Duke. We don't have time for dallying."

Henry shook his head. "I'm riding up top, with you."

"No. You need to lie flat."

"And you need someone to protect you."

"And you will do that how, bleed upon them?"

He turned from her and made to climb up, embarrassed by his weakness. By the way his muscles seemed no longer under his control. When he finally got there, she leaned over him, gazing deep into his eyes, her own

His brow furrowed. "Their shoes?"

She dipped her head in chagrin. "Old habits."

"What kind of habits require stealing an opponent's footwear?"

"The kind that make it harder for the opponent to chase you down. And ensure that you've got a new pair of shoes if you need them."

For all the doubt and uncertainty Henry had experienced over his lifetime, he'd never worried about shoes. The words, a harsh reminder of the world where Adelaide had grown, made him feel like he deserved every ache and sting and pain that he'd collected that evening.

And there were many of them.

He lifted a hand to his nose, aching from the bout. "I think you might have gotten what you desired."

Her lips flattened with concern. "What is that?"

"I wager my nose is broken."

She came close to inspect it, turning to the tub where a towel had been forgotten after his bath, which felt like it had taken place weeks ago. Dipping a bit of the fabric into the now-cool water, she dabbed at the blood on his face, and he winced.

"You've a wicked bruise blooming," she said softly. "More than one."

He nodded. "My face will finally have character."

Her smile was as soft as her touch. As her teasing. "At last, something worth looking at."

"You're going to tell me about Havistock," he said. "There's more going on here than an outraged father trying to stop an unsuitable wedding."

She hesitated.

Trust me, Adelaide. Trust me to help.

He didn't say it, knowing she wouldn't listen.

She met his eyes, searching long enough that he hoped she would find what she was looking for. The truth. That he was an ally. Finally, she nodded. "When we're safe."

It would have to be enough, he told himself as he

searched her in return, needing to make sure she was un-harmed. He did not have to search far. "You're bleeding."

She put a hand to her neck. "A scratch."

He took the towel from her. Repeated her movements. Cleaned the spot where the knife had punctured skin. "I want to tear him apart again. For every drop of blood."

She shook her head. "Not tonight." She was right. Though he did his best not to show it, the battle had taken a toll on his already bruised body. "We're going to do him one worse," she added.

His brows rose. "What's that?"

"We're sending him back to The Bully Boys . . . hogtied to take his punishment for losing. No one pun-ishes a thug for a loss like one of their own."

"I should like to try," he said before swaying and catching himself on the rim of the bathtub, hoping she did not notice.

She noticed. Of course she did. "Clayborn?"

The title, back on her tongue. He wanted to tell her to call him Henry, as the moonlight streamed through the window, casting silver shadows over the skin she swiftly covered. Had she always been so beautiful?

Always.

He sucked in a breath, ignoring the sharp pain that flashed in his side. He needed a bed. A decent sleep. There wasn't time for that—they had to get to Helene and Jack.

"You should have been wearing clothes. Then he wouldn't have been able to hurt you."

She moved toward him, his shirt in hand, her brow furrowed. "Would you believe I didn't have time to lace a corset when the criminals broke down the door?" She pressed the ball of fabric to his chest, and he rocked back at the touch.

"What is—" The end of the question caught in her throat as she directed her attention down over his body, her hands following her concerned gaze in the darkness.

"Adelaide, as much as I enjoy your—"

"Oh, do shut up," she interrupted him.

"I beg your pardon—" *Pain.* His hand f[...] his side. "Christ!"

"Shit." Her exclamation was more colo[...] need a doctor." She looked up at him. "Can yo[...]

"Of course I can!" he insisted, offended. "Bu[...] fectly fine. I don't need a doctor." He looked [...] discover a neat slice in his side. "Billy must have [...] one."

"Even a broken clock . . ." she retorted, but he read[...] worry in her eyes.

"I shall be fine. It's a scratch."

"It's not a scratch," she said. "I've seen scratches and I've seen knife wounds and I've seen what comes of both of them and you need care." She collected both their bags and moved to pass him, heading for the far side of the room. "You need a surgeon," she repeated to herself more than to him, "and we need to get as far from this place as possible."

He snatched his bag from her grip. He would be dead before he let her carry his bag. "Or what?"

"Or Danny will regain consciousness and join us once more," she said, nodding in the direction of the already once-splintered door.

"Danny," he repeated, not liking the thread of anger that coursed through him. "You know him."

She didn't reply, moving with speed to the paint-ing he'd noticed when he entered. What had she called them? The shield-maidens. She gripped the frame and pulled the painting off the wall.

No. Not off the wall.

She pulled it open, revealing another door.

"Another passageway," he said, meeting her gaze. "It took me twenty minutes to find the last one."

Her brows rose at the words as she pulled the chain from her bodice, unscrewing the brass pendant even as pools of brown velvet, full of concern. "We've got to get you somewhere safe."

"He knew you. Danny."

She didn't reply, pulling a carriage blanket over him.

He grabbed her hand. Held it firmly. "He knew you. He knows your father."

She looked to him for a long moment. "Everyone knows my father."

He shook his head. "I don't."

She smiled, but there was no amusement in the expression. "Are you sure about that?"

His brows furrowed, and a wave of weakness crashed over him. *Dammit.* If he hadn't been stabbed, he could think. He could put it together. Who she was. Who her father was. *Danny had said something. Why couldn't he remember?* "I think I might . . ." He gave the seat his full weight, leaning his head back against the carriage behind them. "Shit."

She was already around the other side of the vehicle, pulling herself up beside him. "Duke?"

"Don't call me that," he said, which was a ridiculous thing to say, but suddenly it felt important. He closed his eyes. "Last night you called me Henry."

She sighed and gave him what he wanted, her words soft and sweet in the darkness, almost as though she liked them. Almost as though she liked *him*. "Alright, Henry. We have to get you somewhere safe."

But he was already unconscious, and could not hear her.

Chapter Twelve

Five miles from the Hungry Hen, down several short lanes, two of which tracked back toward the inn, there was a long drive tucked behind a collection of fence and brush that made it impossible to find if a body wasn't looking for it.

Adelaide was looking for it.

She urged the horses up the drive to the small cottage at the top of the hill—a cottage that sat empty most of the year, except on nights like this, when an emergency forced one of the Duchess of Trevescan's vast network of contacts to seek safety.

Adelaide drove as quickly as she dared, using only one hand for the reins.

With her other hand, she applied pressure to the wound in Henry's side, trying not to think about the remarkable amount of blood—blood that soaked through the length of linen she'd stolen from the inn and coated her hand. To keep them both from giving up, she did the only other thing she could think to do—she talked to him.

She began with ridicule and exasperation, having been born in a world that prized this response above all others when faced with extraordinary events. "This is what happens when you learn to fight at some school for rich boys with nothing to do, toff," she groused as they exited the drive of the Hungry Hen, leaning over his unconscious body to make sure they were not followed.

"Six years at Eton is nothing compared to a drunken lout with a dull wit and a sharp blade. Of course you're out cold. Nothing else can be expected." She paused, and added, "Though I will admit I remain impressed with the force of your facers."

Threatening did not work, either; he did not respond to "If you don't wake up, I ought to just tip you out of the carriage and let you fend for yourself." Nor to "I have neither the time nor the patience for whatever you're about to bring to my doorstep, Your Grace. What I do have is a team of women more than willing to help me disappear you."

She tried coaxing him awake. "Come on, Clayborn. If you wake I'll let you ask all your questions. I'll tell you all the answers. I'll give you the file—let you see all we know about your brother. About you." She left out the realization that they knew far less about him than they should, considering how well he lurked outside warehouses and took down brutes. Instead, she tried a different tack. "I'll let you win the race. Let the lovebirds get wed. Just wake up."

And when none of the other strategies worked, she settled on pleading as they trundled up the rise to the cottage, a simple litany of words that might have been prayer if praying were a thing Adelaide did. She'd never found a deity willing to listen to her, so she prayed to things that were not deities. She begged the carriage not to throw a wheel and pleaded with the horses to move more quickly. And she prayed the house would be well stocked with supplies.

But mainly, she prayed to him, she supposed. To him to keep breathing. "Please don't die," she whispered again and again. "You promised me you wouldn't die. *Please.*"

It shouldn't have felt so weighty, that request. She'd seen plenty of people die in her young life—a girl didn't grow where and how she had without knowing the face of death. But somehow, the idea that *Henry* might die . . .

It shouldn't have stuck in her throat and stung her eyes. Shouldn't have been full of such panic. Such worry.

Please don't die.

And then, on the heels of the silent thought.

I like you too much.

She sucked in a breath—knowing the words were silly and selfish. Frivolous. Irrelevant. He would live or he would die, and her feelings about him were irrelevant.

He wasn't for liking. Not for her. Especially not now that he knew she wasn't Miss Adelaide Frampton, cousin to the Duchess of Trevescan with a hobby for petty larceny, but instead Addie, daughter to one of the worst criminals in London, raised in the gangs of the South Bank.

She'd do well to remember that—to cloak herself in the truth of it and protect herself from whatever was to come with this man. Emotions were a luxury Adelaide could not afford, so she pushed disappointment and anger and frustration and shame and no small amount of fear aside, focusing, instead, on the house as it came into full, shadowed view, close enough now to loom darker than the darkness around them. No one was inside.

She drew the horses to a stop out of view of anyone who might decide to look up the hill as they rode past, and leapt down with a "Don't move."

When she returned a few minutes later, having lit several lanterns within, hanging one on the west side of the house, in the center upstairs window, Henry hadn't moved.

He was still as death.

So she did the only thing she could think to do. She released the pressure on his wound, then reapplied it, hard. Fast. Enough to wake him with the pain. He groaned at the sting, reaching for it, his hand covering hers. He looked to her, confusion clearing almost instantly . . . almost. Slower than it should in a mind as quick as his.

"We must get you inside," she whispered, unable to keep the plea and the worry from her voice. Maybe when they got inside he would slumber again. If he was unconscious when she packed and stitched his wound, it would be better for them both.

He peered around the darkness. "Where are we?"

"Somewhere safe."

"Are there others here?"

"No."

He didn't like that. "Then you aren't safe. Not if I can't fight." He tried to stand, but hissed in pain, one hand going straight to his side.

"I can hold my own. And Danny is taken care of."

Anger flooded his gaze. "Stop calling him that."

"That's his name."

"I hate that you know it."

Of course he did. Adelaide Frampton was not an aristocrat—everyone knew that—but the idea that she might be acquainted with actual criminals . . . It was the first brick of her reputation to fall. How many more would there be? "I'm afraid I am bound to disappoint you, then, Duke." She injected the words with false bravado as she caught him under the arm. "You need to focus on staying alive; everything else can wait until you're sewn up."

He looked down at her. "Who will do that?"

She tossed him a bright, false smile. "It's all part of the service I provide."

"Can you sew?"

"You don't believe I have been properly trained in the domestic arts?"

"I have trouble believing that you made time for needlepoint while you were training to be the world's best pickpocket."

She'd learned on knife wounds much like his, as a matter of fact, but she refrained from telling him that. Instead, she said, "I'm afraid, Duke, that picking *your* pocket does not require much training."

He shook his head. "I'm not talking about mine. I saw you pick Havistock's pocket at the Beaufetheringstone ball."

Surprise coursed through her. "You did?"

"I did," he said, wincing as she pointed to the wide slab of wood at the center of the kitchen. "I hope it was a great deal of money."

It had been a list of factories the marquess owned and in which he was attempting to entice others' investment, despite the places being filled with children who worked for scraps and too often didn't survive the harsh conditions. Adelaide had plans for the factories.

She shook her head, her mind spinning, which was likely why she told him, "It wasn't money, and you weren't supposed to notice me. He didn't. I must not have been fast enough."

"You were like lightning," he said, wincing again as he leaned back onto the table. "I simply have practice noticing you."

She ignored the warmth that spread through her at the confession.

But it was difficult to ignore the words that chased it. The words that spilled out of her mouth. "Don't die."

"I won't." He lifted a hand to her cheek, but his fingers barely grazed her skin before they fell back to the table. His eyes slid closed as he added, "You promised me answers to all my questions."

Of course he'd heard her in the carriage. Dammit.

She started to turn away, to fetch the things she would need to work on his wound. But he used the last of his strength to grab her hand and meet her eyes, his gaze clear and firm. "Adelaide."

"Yes?"

"Who will protect you if someone comes?"

That unfamiliar warmth again. "I've spent years protecting myself, Duke. Don't worry."

His dark brows knit together. "You shouldn't have to."

She forced a smile. "You've a massive gash in your side and you're threatening to bleed to death on a kitchen workbench, Your Grace. Now is not the time for courtly love."

"When this is over . . ." His words were thinning. Becoming more reedy as he slipped into sleep.

"Tell me," she said, suddenly desperate to keep him awake. With her.

She wasn't ready to lose him.

"I should have taken better care of you," he said, barely, the admission making her chest tight as she stood over him, considering the constellation of wounds he bore for her. The bruises from fighting for her. The scrapes from his carriage accident as he chased after her. The scratches on his shoulder where she'd clawed her pleasure into him.

Before she could find the words to tell him he had cared better for her than anyone had ever done before, he said, "When I wake . . . I will take better care of you."

She sucked in a breath, resisting the words, more tempting than she'd ever admit. Adelaide knew the truth, after all. When this was over, they'd never see each other again.

Chapter Thirteen

While he slept, Adelaide fetched boiling water and linens and supplies and stoked the fire in the kitchen hearth. She had just begun cutting his bloody shirt free of his torso when a knock sounded and the door opened, revealing Lucia.

"I see I did not miss the good part," Lucia remarked, stepping inside, her gaze on Henry's supine body as Adelaide pushed his shirt to the side, revealing a wide, muscular chest.

Adelaide threw her friend a look. "He's unconscious."

"But not yet dead, and neither am I," Lucia quipped, moving forward to soak a long length of linen in the basin of hot water Adelaide had placed next to Henry. She wrung it out and offered it to Adelaide. "And neither are you."

She wasn't. Even as she told herself she was simply cleaning him, making it easier to see the place where Billy's knife had landed in his side—the gash across his torso where the tip of the blade had slipped and slid until it found purchase in skin—Adelaide could not ignore the ridges and valleys of his body.

"Did you hear from Mary?" Adelaide asked Lucia.

The other woman nodded. "Your deliveries are already on their way to London. I hope you know what you're doing sending Danny back to your father."

"Any hesitation I might have had about my father's

ability and willingness to mete out a fine punishment has been calmed by the knowledge that he sent Danny north to find and fetch me back to London for a similar fate. Alfie doesn't like losing. And he really doesn't like it when his Boys are the reason for it." She placed a cool cloth on Henry's brow. "Thank you for your help."

Lucia waved away the words. "What is the use of having Rufus and Tobias if I cannot watch them toss grown men about?" She pointed to the spot where a fast blossoming bruise spread. "Your man's broken at least one rib. And his nose."

"I noticed," Adelaide said, hating the bumps and cuts and bruises across his body, each one her fault.

"I imagine you did," Lucia said in a knowing tone.

Adelaide told herself that noticing the broken rib was why she noticed the rest—the muscles and sinew. And only then, she'd noticed because dukes were not to have such bodies—they should come soft and pale and unworked for their lifetimes of idyll.

"Doesn't look like only school fighting to me." Lucia voiced what Adelaide was thinking.

"I hadn't noticed," she said.

Lucia snorted her disbelief. "You can admit it, Adelaide. It's just the two of us, and I'm here to help you save the toff. Which is no small disappointment, I'll tell you. I expect a certain amount of softness for aristos from Sesily and Imogen and Duchess, considering they've standing invitations to Almack's or whatnot—"

"No one cares about Almack's anymore," Adelaide said, rinsing the bloody linen.

Lucia's dark brows rose high. "Honestly. It pains me to hear that you know that. What happened to solidarity among thieves?"

Adelaide smiled at the other woman. "Did I not hang the lantern in the window and summon you here?"

"To save a toff, not to rob one," Lucia said, lifting the

bottle of high-proof alcohol that Adelaide had brought with the rest of the medicinal items. "You really want him saved?"

"I really do," she replied. Adelaide said, swallowing the knot of emotion that rose at the words, "He never should have thrown his lot in with me."

And she should have known better than to ask him for more.

Lucia tutted at Adelaide's words. "I wager that if he were awake, he'd tell me this has been the best week of his life. Let's make it even better, shall we?"

She leaned in and shouted into Henry's ear, "Wake up, Duke!"

His brow furrowed.

"Not unconscious!" Lucia announced as Adelaide pushed her irrational relief to the back of her mind. "I suppose that if we're not going to fleece him, it's time to wake him up!" She held the bottle high and looked to Adelaide for permission.

Granted.

The bottle tipped, dousing him in the clear liquid.

With a wild curse, he shot up, coming to a seated position on the table, his hand moving instantly to his side, where the sting of the liquor was no doubt excruciating. Adelaide caught his hand before he could touch it. "No. Don't touch."

"You don't touch!" he roared. "What in hell?"

"What did I tell you? Definitely not dead!" Lucia said happily, and he swung around to look at her.

"The highwaywoman. Of course." He scowled in Lucia's direction. "You've already taken my money; are you here for my blood as well?"

"It's decided." Lucia looked to Adelaide. "I like this duke."

"Henry, please—" Adelaide said. "You need to lie back—"

"You're still bleeding," he said, the words like a lash. Back to Lucia. "She's bleeding."

"It's nothing," Adelaide attempted to interject.

"She's bleeding from the *neck*," he clarified.

"Yes, I noticed," Lucia said. "And you're bleeding from the side. What a pair."

"She needs attention. Now. Before whatever the two of you were going to do to me."

Lucia turned an amused look on Adelaide. "You know this man is half gone for you, right?"

"He's not—"

"She's *bleeding*." He looked to Lucia. "She needs sewing up."

"She doesn't need sewing," Lucia said, as though she were speaking to a child. "It's a scratch."

"It's a *neck wound*."

"Hear me, Duke. If I thought for one moment that Adelaide was in danger, you can wager all the money in that purse you can't seem to keep in your possession that I would see her healed before anyone touched you. But she is fine, and there's a better than fair chance that you won't survive the night, so do shut up and let us get on with it, will you?"

Silence fell in the wake of Lucia's announcement, and Adelaide would have laughed at the Duke of Clayborn's shocked face if she weren't so concerned about the unpleasant chances Lucia had pointed out.

He sniffed the air. "You doused me in rotgut."

Adelaide tilted her head with a little smile. "Some believe it helps keep a wound clean."

"Do you?"

"I do. Be glad of it, for there are others who think urine does the trick, too." Before he could reply, Adelaide pressed him to his back once more. "Don't worry. I'm a dream with a needle and thread. Before we had Jane, I used to sew our clothes."

He lay down. "I am not clothing."

"But think of the embroidery you'll wake with," she retorted, forcing herself to sound light, as though she were not terrified of what was to come.

He reached for her then, his thumb rough on her cheek. "You're bleeding."

"It's a scratch."

"I want it gone when I wake."

She smiled at the arrogant directive. "You can't will it away. This isn't Parliament. You cannot orate at it."

"Do whatever you want to me," he said. "But you are more important."

She swallowed. It was not even remotely true, and yet this man . . . this magnificent man. "You are the one who must wake, Duke. You've a world to change."

"You're already changing it," he said quietly. "You first."

"Oh, I do like him," Lucia said softly.

He didn't look away from her, but he replied to Lucia. "Her first."

"Henry," Adelaide said, catching his hand and holding it tightly, letting herself pretend, for just a heartbeat, that there was more between them than a few stolen kisses and a night of pleasure. That there might be hope for the future they'd whispered about in the darkness.

She looked to his wicked wound, still seeping with blood. Lucia poured liquid from a small brown bottle onto a clean length of cloth, and extended it to her.

Taking it, Adelaide returned her attention to his beautiful blue eyes. "You asked who would protect me earlier." Even the memory of the question warmed her— what a strange, wonderful thing to have someone worry about her.

"I will." His gaze tracked over her face, his thumb stroking over her cheek again. "You're so beautiful."

Her heart pounded in her chest. This *man*.

"Tonight, let me protect *you*."

He didn't like that, she could tell. But before he let her know how much, Lucia spoke up, meeting Adelaide's eyes across the table. "Time."

There wasn't much of it. They had to move quickly.

Without hesitating, Adelaide leaned down and placed a quick kiss on his mouth. His hand came to the back of her head, fist clenching in her hair. She broke the kiss and whispered, "See you soon," then placed the cloth in her hand over his nose and mouth, and knocked him out.

"Remarkable, that stuff," Lucia said. "Imogen has really changed the way we do business, hasn't she?"

Adelaide looked down at the cloth, doused in something Imogen called chloric ether. Harmless and extremely helpful when it came to felling villains. Or, in this case, dukes who required sewing up. "It helps to have a genius in the crew," Adelaide acknowledged.

"I wager your duke won't agree," Lucia said with a pretty laugh. "He'll be furious when he wakes up."

"He's not my duke," she said immediately, because of course she did. But he was hers, in that moment. He was hers to fret over. Hers to keep safe.

"Ah, so we are calling him your Henry now?" Adelaide gave a half smile at her friend's jest. "Addie," Lucia added softly. "People survive stabbings."

Adelaide didn't look away from his sleeping face, bruised and battered and somehow still impossibly beautiful. "Not all of them."

Fever could come quick. And it often never left.

There was a long silence while she worked, putting a row of neat stitches into Clayborn's side. When she was done, she clipped the thread and packed the wound, spreading it with honey before they worked together to bandage it and the rib he'd broken. When they were through, her gaze tracked over his still face, the even rise and fall of his bruised chest, his long arms.

Finally, she looked to Lucia. "Thank you."

The other woman raised a brow. "For what?"

She shook her head. "For . . ." *For being here.* "For being a friend."

Lucia's dark eyes saw more than Adelaide wished, but she did not ask the myriad questions that flashed in her pretty face. Didn't wonder at the way Adelaide gripped the duke's hand. Instead, she said, "He was so furious that you took a blade to the neck; it would not surprise me if he woke up strictly to ensure you were mended."

Adelaide gave a little laugh, swallowing around the thick knot in her throat.

Lucia bustled about for a moment before sliding a look to Adelaide and saying, "And the girl? What of her?"

Lady Helene, whom Adelaide should be tracking even now. Who needed the Belles' protection more than ever, if her horrid father had hired The Bully Boys to bring her home. "She's close enough to the border—with Danny headed back to London, I expect she and Jack will get there tomorrow. And marry." She looked to Henry, unconscious. "For love."

Jack, whom Henry loved beyond measure. Jack, whom Adelaide must keep safe if Henry could not.

"Happy news in the midst of an absolute mess." Lucia paused. "But they have to be told they cannot return to London, or they go to the wolves a matched set."

A new son-in-law would not stop Havistock from silencing Helene. Instead, he was another concern for the marquess, already on the list of heads he was hoping someone would claim for him, if Danny was to be believed. Lucia was right. Adelaide should leave Henry there. Should stick to the plan. Get to Helene and Jack and use the Belles' vast network to tunnel the newlyweds to safety.

Staying was madness. It would change nothing. She had done all she could, and now they had nothing to do but wait. Rosemary oil could not help Henry now. Staring into his face, blooming with bruises and a newly broken nose, she told herself to leave.

"I need help."

Lucia's brows rose. "Adelaide Frampton, asking for help? You *must* love the man."

Love. Was that what this was? This panicked need to see him safe, along with the people he cared for? This unmooring at the idea that he might not wake? At the idea that she might not speak to him again?

Surely not. This was awful.

Pushing the thoughts aside, she looked to her friend. "I need messages sent to Helene and Jack. And to Duchess."

She didn't have to look to know that Lucia's brows rose in surprise, but she was grateful when the other woman said, quietly, "Done."

Adelaide nodded, riveted to his stillness before she whispered, "What do I do now?"

"You let Tobias carry him to bed."

"And?"

A shrug. "Pray?"

Adelaide huffed a single, wild laugh. "I tried that on the drive here. I am not very good at it."

"Luckily, it is a skill that does not require finesse."

The highwaywoman turned away to fetch the man who stood sentry outside the door—protecting the woman he loved inside—and Adelaide stood watch over Henry, riveted to his chest and the way it rose and fell, evenly, if a touch too quickly.

Focusing on his bruised and battered body and the now too pale look of him.

Hating the way watching him restricted the breath in her chest, as worry and frustration and nerves coursed through her.

She'd spent a lifetime running from this feeling. From the way it made her weak. Vulnerable. Out of control.

But there, alone in that kitchen, surrounded by the silence of the English countryside and the flickering light of a few dozen candles and him, filling the space even in slumber, she could no longer run.

She was out of control.

Doing the only thing she could think to do.

Saying *please*.

Chapter Fourteen

The Duke of Clayborn rarely slept for more than six hours at a time.

Oh, he told his valet that he was a man who did not require more than a few hours' sleep. He woke early for morning rides and worked late into the evening, and he simply lived a life that neither required nor had space for languishing in bed.

It was a fine tale, but a false one.

Henry did not sleep, because he dreamed. He dreamed in full, vivid color, with loud sounds and intense smells— the kind of dreams that left a man drained and exhausted when he woke. And sometimes, they left him wishing for something beyond his stern, serious existence.

So he had trained himself to go to bed late and wake early.

But that night, as he lay in that strange bed in that strange house on the top of the hill in the depths of Lancashire, Henry dreamed.

That night, and the next, and the next, as the fever took hold, raging through him, the dreams came wild and vivid and inescapable.

Ominous shadows. Men lurking at the edge of his vision, disappearing every time he tried to see them more clearly. Secrets.

A woman, hair like fire. Eyes like velvet. His name on her lips like the cool water on his brow.

Sometimes, she was joined by another. They made a pair—bright-eyed highwaywomen on tall, stolen horses, stopping carriages to collect more members of their merry band. And the one with the fire in her hair wore enormous skirts that tied round her waist with long, brightly colored ribbons. She twirled and twirled while they waited for the next carriage, the skirts going wide, expanding until he could touch them from where he watched, miles away. But just as his fingers brushed soft silk, she disappeared.

A broken carriage. A boy in a tree.

The flame-haired woman again, this time laughing as she leapt from the edge of a dock into the cool blue lake at his country estate, breaking the water like a mirror. Wait. Was it the country estate? No. It was the Thames, those brightly colored skirts spread out around her as she floated away, her laugh on the wind as he chased her, terrified that he would lose her to the current. To the muck. Terrified he wouldn't be able to keep her safe.

He couldn't catch her; she didn't want to be caught.

But he chased her down the bank, first on the docks and then on the boats and then onto the water itself, then into it, frustration in his chest as he tried to shout for her, but somehow couldn't find her name. He was desperate to get to her, knowing that this chase, however long it took, however it ended, was all he had.

And then, when he caught her, by chance, by the tip of one long, golden ribbon, she turned to him, the ribbon coming loose, a bright, ornate key at the end of it.

He tucked it in his pocket, close to his heart, keeping it warm, as she had done, and they floated, the water cool on his heated skin, her fingers stroking down his arm, tangling in his own.

"Henry," she whispered.

Stillness.

The water was still, a mirror once more. Repaired.

The dream was over, but he could not wake.

It had been four nights since they'd packed the wound and he'd fallen asleep. Four nights of watching him writhe on the bed. The fever had come mere hours later, Adelaide sleeping fitfully in the chair at the side of his bed, waking to spoon broth down his throat and change his bandages and spread salve on his wounds.

On the third morning, they stood watching him as he twisted and turned and kicked freshly washed blankets from his body, and Lucia had voiced the concern Adelaide was too afraid to contemplate.

Or, at least, she voiced half of the concern, sounding more serious than Adelaide had ever heard her. "If it doesn't break soon . . ."

Adelaide's throat closed in the heavy silence that trailed after the words, the place behind her nose stinging with frustrated knowledge. "I know," she said, barely recognizing her voice, exhausted from worry and lack of sleep and the constant repetition of his name—the only word she spoke, because she didn't know what else to say.

She asked Lucia to track Helene and Jack—to make sure they'd found their way to Gretna and were somewhere safe. She might not be able to keep Henry safe, but she could damn well find his brother. Her friend left, tucked beneath Tobias's heavy arm, promising to do what she could, and Adelaide returned to Henry, finding different words now. More desperate ones.

Don't die.

Not now . . . not just as I've found you.

He'd promised he'd wake up, hadn't he? He'd said it. *I will take better care of you.* He'd said it like she was precious. Not just a woman to be traded for partnership, or a thief to be used for business, or a quiet watchman in a ballroom full of awful toffs collecting information worth more than money. Not just a girl from the South Bank dreaming of a duke.

He said it as though she was worthy of care simply because she *was*.

And she wanted it to be true as she watched over him, pleading with the universe to let him live. She imagined that he would make good on that promise. That he would stand with her. Protect her.

Be with her, instead of the two of them being alone. Make their fantasies real.

What would that be like?

Impossible.

Still, Adelaide spent the long, interminable days watching over Henry, telling him stories, willing him to wake, willing him to heal—this impossibly strong, impossibly powerful man who now seemed impossibly quiet.

At first, it seemed that she could calm him with a touch. With a cool cloth and a gentle whisper. She told him a thousand stories in those days—things she hadn't thought about in years. About the cat she'd had as a child, the one she'd hidden from her father, because he thought pets made children soft. About the time she'd stolen hair ribbons from a haberdashery in Croydon. The time she'd snuck into a Drury Lane theater and found herself in the wings of the stage.

She stopped short of telling him the worst bits. The secrets.

But she bargained with the universe and whatever gods might be watching, and when that did not work, she bargained with Henry, promising she'd tell him everything he asked if only he'd wake.

The dreams had stopped soon after that, and Adelaide did not know whether to take it as a good sign or not.

He stopped thrashing and groaning, falling into something that all the world would recognize as slumber, and Adelaide imagined that some would think it a boon. But she hated the silent stillness to which he had succumbed. Hated that his breathing was even and he no longer moved. Hated that he no longer turned toward her when she whispered his name. That he no longer turned away when she pressed a too-cool cloth to his too-warm brow.

Hated other things, too. That she hadn't thanked him for taking a blade for her. For fighting for her. For letting the brute break his nose and one of his ribs.

That she hadn't thanked him for the night he'd held her in his arms and made her feel pleasure like nothing she'd ever experienced.

That he wouldn't wake up, so she might be able to do those things. To have more of them. To have more of him.

She watched him, still as death—terrible phrase, that—until she couldn't anymore. Until she had to move, finding a pot of salve in her bag and tending the bruises and scrapes he'd collected for her.

His nose. His cheek. His ribs. The painful-looking bruise on his thigh. The wicked scrape at his shoulder. The raw knuckles he'd earned when he'd gone mad to keep her safe.

She cursed harshly in the quiet room. He'd been in her company less than a week, and this was what she had done to him. This was her world, and it threatened this good and decent man every step of the way.

The heat at his brow scorched like flame. How long could a body survive a fever? The question threw her from her seat, across the room to rinse another length of linen, a final effort.

He didn't move.

"Henry," she whispered, filling the word with all the fear and sorrow she would never speak aloud. There was nothing left to say, except "Please."

She was tired.

And so, with another soft whisper of his name, she folded herself in the chair, set her cheek to the counterpane, and with her fingers threaded tight through his, slept.

Chapter Fifteen

When he opened his eyes, the room was aflame, and he imagined for a heartbeat that it was another dream, this one featuring nothing but her shining, beautiful curls wrapping themselves around him like fire.

He lay there for a long moment, cataloguing the space—the wood beams on the ceiling and the white plaster walls and the window on the far side that looked to the east, where the sun rose, chasing the night from the land.

It was cold, the fire in the hearth having died sometime in the night, and he turned toward it, an ache waking in his neck, as though he hadn't moved in days. Had he moved in days? It had been night when he'd last been conscious, just before Adelaide had taken a needle to his side. Just before she had knocked him out with a concoction no doubt designed by one of her crew. They would have words about that.

He shifted, testing the place where he'd been stabbed. New, but not fresh.

Slowly, he tracked the state of his body, the sting at his side, the ache in his neck. The simultaneous sense of exhaustion and rest, as though he'd been unconscious for both a moment and an age.

The hand in his.

Her hand in his.

He looked down the bed, over the coverlet, and the

aches and pains faded away, his breath catching in his chest. Adelaide was there, hunched over in a chair, her cheek on the edge of the bed, facing him, asleep.

Asleep, and holding his hand, her fingers tangled in his, as though she was keeping him there, tethered to that bed. To that room. To the earth.

To her.

And in that moment, a wild thought raced through him. Maybe she *had* kept him there.

Maybe Adelaide Frampton, by sheer force of her will, had kept him alive.

He tightened his fingers, knowing he shouldn't. Knowing he should let her sleep, but wanting her to open her eyes more than he'd ever wanted anything before. "Adelaide," he whispered. His first word, like a new beginning.

Her eyes snapped open, wide and beautiful and instantly alert, even without her spectacles. Shock flared in them, and a tiny furrow formed between her brows, as though she could not quite believe what she saw, and he couldn't help the way it pleased him—the idea that she might be happy he was awake.

She shot up, pulling her hand from his, and he resisted the urge to chase it, to claim it once more. To touch her again.

"Adelaide—" he said again, softly, as though he might scare her if he spoke above a whisper.

She sucked in a breath at the word, her spine going straight. And then—

Tears. Her beautiful brown eyes filled with tears, and he couldn't help himself then, reaching for her, saying her name again.

He sat up, ignoring the sting of his wound, the ache in his ribs that didn't matter. Not as long as she was crying.

"You shouldn't—" She started to tell him not to move, but stopped, shaking her head, going silent for a long moment, one hand—that hand that had been his mere moments earlier—fisted and pressed tight to her mouth as she looked at him, tears spilling over. "I thought—"

His throat tightened as she struggled with the words. He set a hand to his chest, where the worst of all his aches flared, the one that came with her pain. "Love . . . no. Don't cry."

"I thought you would—" She paused for a moment, then added urgently, as she wiped away her tears, "I'm not crying."

"Of course not," he said, watching the tears she was powerless to stop, wanting to pull her close and hold her tight and do battle with whatever it was that had summoned them.

It was him, though. He had summoned them.

Because she liked him.

Not that she would confess it. She was babbling, trying to explain them. "I'm not—" She stopped and started again. "This isn't—"

He nodded. "I know."

"I'm only *relieved*, you see." She brushed a tear away. And another. And gave a little wild laugh that made him want to do the same.

"Of course," he said. "You didn't want a dead duke on your hands."

Another laugh, this one richer. The kind of laugh that made a man wish he could summon it every day. For a long time. "Exactly," she agreed. "You're not a bad sort of duke. You shouldn't die."

And while he did not like the tears, he liked the sentiment a great deal. "Not a bad sort of duke," he repeated. "High praise indeed from you, Miss Frampton."

He moved to stand, ignoring his body's protests.

She shot forward. "Be careful, you'll hurt yourself." She reached for him, not hesitating, her cool fingers sliding over his skin to help him, as though he were hers to touch.

Which he was, with pleasure.

She did not seem so certain however, and she let him go

too quickly, pulling away as though she'd been burned. "I'm sorry," she said softly. "I shouldn't be so—"

He cut her off, not wanting her to finish the sentence. Not when she absolutely *should*. Not when he wanted her to. Anytime she wished. For as long as she wished. "Why were you here?"

She blinked. "Here? At the house?"

"Here, in this room. Is there nowhere for you to have slept more comfortably?"

Her lips formed a little O, and for a moment he thought she might not answer him. And then, simply, "You were here. In this room."

Pleasure bloomed in his chest. She didn't want to leave him. *Good.* He cast a glance at the bed, wide enough for two. "With only this bed?" She nodded and he raised a brow at her. "There is a shocking lack of beds in this country."

She gave a little, watery laugh. "Shall I draft a letter of complaint?"

There. The tears she shed for him were gone, at least. Christ, the way they'd made him feel, both full of rage and full of pride—it was primitive.

"No need," he said. "I have been looking for a new parliamentary issue, and I think this is something the whole of Britain will support."

"Additional beds?" Her eyes sparkled, playful, and he tilted his head to watch her, to delight in her, as much a balm as an open window or a hot bath or a bit of tooth powder would be in that moment.

"Now that I think on it, I am quite happy with the number of beds we've encountered during our journey." He paused. "How long have I been in this particular one?"

"Today is day five," she answered.

"My God, really?"

"We thought you might not . . ." She inhaled deeply before the tears could come again. "Well. You did. So it doesn't matter."

"And have you been sleeping here, in this chair, for four nights?" He hated that.

She nodded. "You might have woken. You might have needed me."

"Did I? Need you?"

He knew the answer instantly. Could recall the dreams, the way he followed her, the way he ached for her. The way he ached for her here, too. In reality. Even now, after four days of unconsciousness and a half-dozen pains that were more than a little uncomfortable, the way he ached for her—the need clawing at him—was the worst of them all.

"You might have," she repeated, taking a step back as though to put distance between them. "And so I stayed here."

"Only one chair," he whispered, finally, finally letting himself reach for her. Catching her by the hand—the same one that he'd been holding when he woke. Like it was home.

She let him take it. "It's a small room."

"And a large bed."

She swallowed. "Henry, you were unconscious."

"Mmm," he said. "I am not unconscious now, however, and I don't like your tears. Let me hold you. Let me chase them away."

"I did not cry," she insisted even as, miraculously, she let him pull her closer, letting him wrap his arms around her and breathe her in, fresh rain and rosemary.

"You took care of me," he whispered to the top of her head. "Just as you promised."

She inhaled deeply and relaxed in his arms, going soft and languid. His poor girl was exhausted, which was perhaps why she admitted, "I was scared."

The words shouldn't have run riot through him, and still they did, on that twin course of pleasure and pain—that she had feared for his life and also that he had been the source of her worry. "I am sorry," he said to her fiery curls, tied back but cascading past her shoulders. "I am sorry that I was not with you. But I am here now. Christ. Five days—" he said softly. "They've made it to Gretna."

"Likely," Adelaide replied. "They are being followed by others now."

His brows rose. "Our others? Or Havistock's others?"

She flashed a small secret smile. "Our others. Though I am surprised you claim us."

"If I am allowed," he said. "I've never had a crew."

With a serious nod she said, "You may try mine on for size."

They stood there, wrapped in each other, in the certainty that something had happened between them— something that could not be changed. Whatever Miss Frampton and the Duke of Clayborn had been five days earlier was not what they were in that moment.

Henry marveled at the revelation, at the shift.

At the promise of what it might mean.

There was a wide world of worry beyond these walls. Jack and Helene and The Bully Boys and Havistock and Adelaide's gang of women—there were dangers around every corner. But there, in that room, the sun rose and chased it all away, leaving only the two of them.

For a little longer.

She shifted in his arms, pulling away to fetch her spectacles, cheeks blazing. He understood immediately—his strong, brilliant, solitary Adelaide, who needed nothing but her wits, had liked being held.

Which worked out very well, as there was nothing Henry liked so well as holding her.

Still, he resisted the temptation to pull her close again. To return to the bed with her in tow. He might not have the strength to make love to her, but he certainly had enough of it to hold her for a while.

She tucked an errant lock of hair behind one of her ears, blazing red, and the knowledge that whatever she was thinking had made her blush to her ears made Henry rethink his assessment of his strength for all sorts of things.

He wondered where else she blushed.

Vowed to find out.

Too soon, however, Adelaide regained her composure, and it was clear she had other plans. Turning away, she arranged the small table next to the washbasin and, with a mumbled excuse about food and fresh water, hurried out of the room, leaving him to his ablutions.

As he washed, he considered his wounds—unwrapping the bandage around his torso, revealing the deep scratch across his belly ending with two inches of stitches at his side. Billy's handiwork, he assumed, along with most of the yellowing bruises he could see peppered across his ribs.

Without a mirror, he could not see the rest—but his face was tight with what could only be healing wounds, and he'd most definitely taken a facer in the fight.

It was embarrassing, really. All he could hope was that he'd done a fair amount of damage himself.

She returned with a tray, entering with quiet purpose that he suspected she employed to remain unnoticed. Impossible. Refusing to waste precious moments that could be spent noticing her, he took his time drying his face and chest—he'd been bare to the waist in bed—and watched as she busied herself around the room, doing her best not to look at him, poking at the fire in the hearth, pouring water into a glass, straightening his pillows and sheets, and turning down the bed carefully.

When that task was complete, she straightened, her back to him, and he found he was no longer amenable to not seeing her face.

"Thank you," he said.

She did not turn. "You're welcome."

"Adelaide?"

Her spine could not get straighter. "Yes?"

"Am I so hideous that you cannot stomach looking at me?"

She spun toward him instantly. "What?"

Before he could reply, her eyes went wide, taking in the whole of him. "You unwrapped your bandages!"

She was across the room instantly, her hands on him even as she snatched up clean rolls of linen to repair the work he'd destroyed. "If I'd known this was all it took," he said, softly, unable to look away from her, "I would have taken the bandages off immediately upon waking."

"You can't simply . . . take them off. You've a broken rib."

He nodded. "More than one, I think."

There was a minuscule pause in her ministrations as the words settled. "That doesn't seem like something a toff would know."

"Perhaps I'm not like other toffs."

She slid a look up at him. "You forget, Duke, I've spent a great deal of time in ballrooms with you."

"Watching me?" he said.

She returned her attention to his bandages. "Lift."

"Your ears are turning red, Adelaide."

Her head snapped up. "What?" One hand went to the tip of one of those perfect ears. "I don't know what that means."

"In card games, I believe that's called a tell."

She looked away. "Tell me why you know about broken ribs."

"Admit you watched me in ballrooms."

"I watch everyone in ballrooms," she replied.

"Yes, but I'm asking about me, specifically."

"I would not take it as a compliment," Adelaide said. "I spent a fair amount of time watching you and imagining what it would be like to take you down."

"Mmm," he said. "And look where we've landed—you nursing me back to health."

She couldn't hide her smile. "A task that would be made easier if you did not remove your bandages."

"Ah, but then how would I ensure you would touch me?"

He expected her to blush and bluster. He did not expect her to look up at him through her pretty dark lashes like an absolute goddess and say, "You could try asking nicely." He exhaled harshly at the words, loving them almost as much as he loved the wicked smile on her lips when she realized how she'd impacted him. "Sit, please."

He did as he was told, lowering himself to the edge of the bed, and refusing to lie down. "To confirm, you do watch me in ballrooms."

She rolled her eyes, dropping into the chair in front of him. "Yes. Fine. I watch you."

Why did that make him want to crow with pride?

"Now tell me why you know about broken ribs," she added.

"Is everything with you a trade? I answer one question, you answer the next?"

"Information is the most valuable commodity there is, Your Grace. It brings power and safety and a secure future."

"You have all those things."

She shook her head. "No woman ever really has those things. At best, she has approximations of them."

"Adelaide Frampton, I promise you this—as long as I breathe, I shall keep you safe and secure." Her eyes flew to his, surprise and something like heat in them. He smiled. "You and your gang of women bring the power yourselves."

Her pretty lips went slack.

Good. Let her sit with that while he answered her question. "I told you that I fought for six years at school. What I did not tell you was that I did not fight *in* school."

"What does that mean?"

"It means I was an angry boy of fourteen, looking for somewhere to put my fist that wasn't my father's face."

Her brows rose, but she did not speak.

"Would you believe I was not the only boy at Eton who was interested in finding such a location?"

She gave a little laugh. "I would, indeed. Though I would argue you would have all done the globe a great service if you'd found the courage to deliver facers to the men of the aristocracy."

He matched her smile with his own. "My father wasn't a bad man. He was good. And kind."

"So, what, you were simply fourteen and angry?"

"That's more than enough reason for many fourteen-year-old boys, but no . . . He had kept a secret from me." He met her gaze. "Do you know it?"

She shook her head. "I do not."

He believed her. "But you wish to."

"Of course I wish to."

Why? Because information was currency? Or because she wanted to keep his secrets with hers?

"But more importantly," she added, unaware of his thoughts, "would you tell me?"

Maybe. But not then. "No."

She smiled. "I have no difficulty imagining that you think this secret was big enough to send you on a six-year underground fighting ring spree. Tell me the rest of the story."

"I was furious. I enjoyed putting my fists into other boys' faces in order to make the anger less . . ."

"Angry?" she helped.

He nodded. "While we certainly didn't fight with all the gentlemen's rules of boxing, we had a fairly decent set of rules that kept bruises from faces—"

"And noses from breaking?"

"And that," he said, enjoying her more than he should. "How does my nose look, by the way?"

She made a show of adjusting her spectacles and peering at it. "Like it hurts."

It did, but he'd never admit it. "I'll tell you this—Billy had a damn fine right cross."

"Don't fret, Duke. You did alright."

In the wake of the words, Henry recalled the battle, which came in little snippets and then all at once, with a full accounting of what had happened. "What happened to him? Danny?"

She met his gaze, and he recognized the flash of shame there—wanted it gone. Banished forever. She shook her head. "I sent him back to Lambeth."

She wasn't ready to trust him, and Henry wanted to snarl in frustration. He'd clung to every secret, every bit of information. Patchworked it together. But there still wasn't enough.

Who was Adelaide Frampton?

Not Frampton.

The words whispered through him as he replayed the scene in his mind, turning it over and over, trying to recall every moment. Every word.

You'll always be Lambeth, Addie Trumbull. Clayborn's gaze went wide, things coming together. Trumbull, like Alfie Trumbull.

Suddenly, everything began to make sense.

Alfie Trumbull was the leader of The Bully Boys. And Adelaide—

The stories she told. The wedding for partnership. The boys on the bridge. Her father, the king. Her comfort in that South Bank warehouse, on those docks battling those South Bank bruisers, sparring with that Lambeth thug.

She wasn't simply the Matchbreaker, hunted by criminals hired by Mayfair monsters. She was daughter of the king of The Bully Boys, a South Bank princess, left to her own devices when she'd escaped her father. *How had he simply let her leave?* If she was Henry's, he'd do all he could to keep her. To prize her. To love her.

And Alfie Trumbull had done the opposite. He'd let her go, then sent *Danny* to fetch her back for punishment.

Danny. The man had been so familiar with her. There'd been something there. "Who is he to you?"

Her throat worked, and he willed her to speak, holding back what he suspected. What he knew.

Trust me.

"He is my father's right hand."

He waited for a long moment, wanting to ask a thousand questions. Finally, he let it go. "Is there a mirror?"

She shook her head. "I don't think it's a good idea."

His brows rose. "That bad, is it?"

She smiled. "You shall mend."

"Show me."

While she considered the request, Adelaide worried the edge of her lower lip, and Henry resisted the urge to lean in and kiss her. Finally, she nodded, turning away to her bag, and after a lengthy search within, produced a pocket mirror, smaller than his palm.

It reflected well enough, however, and he grimaced at the wicked bruising where Billy had landed a decent blow. "Christ. That's hideous."

"Shh," she said, and he found he liked the little laugh in her words.

He matched her smile. "All I can hope is that he looks worse than I do."

"Oh, I'm sure he does," she said. "Do not fret. In no time, the ladies of London will titter and swoon to see the stern Duke of Clayborn returned with a handsome bump in his nose."

He lowered the looking glass, keenly aware of how fully unhandsome the bruising was. "Is that what women dream of? Broken bones?"

"It's not the broken bone. It's the idea that you might have gotten it—" She stopped as quickly as she'd started.

He tilted his head. "Go on."

She shook her head.

He extended the mirror to her, and when she reached for it, pulled her close, to stand between his thighs. "Tell me. Tell me the secret ways of women."

She laughed at the words, and reached out to push a lock of his hair behind his ear, almost absently, as though she didn't even know she was doing it. The soft stroke of her fingertips along his temple set fire coursing through him, aching for that stroke in other places.

"It's just . . . we wonder where the nose was broken. Under which circumstances. Were you hero of the play? Or villain? And if you were hero . . . were you fighting for another?"

The last question faded away, until it was more breath than sound.

He met her eyes. "I was."

She nodded. "That break . . . it's . . ."

Her hands were on his shoulders now, soft and warm, her touch a lick of temptation. She wasn't moving, but God, he wanted her to. "What is it, Adelaide?"

"It's not hideous," she said. "It's not. It's . . ."

He would give his entire fortune for her to finish that sentence. He ran his hands over her sides, tracing over her curves, memorizing the feel of her. The shape of her. The way her breath came ragged in her chest like it betrayed her. "Tell me."

"It's mine."

Yes. He was hers.

He would soon sort out how to make her his, but this was a start.

She was close now, and he was wrapped in the scent of her—the mint of her breath and that beautiful, rich rosemary that he knew now was the product of her caretaking.

"You touched me," he said softly, his lips so close to hers, testing both their sanity.

Her fingers flexed on his shoulders. "Yes."

"I was at your mercy."

Her eyes found his, the dark centers of them blown out with excitement and something he identified instantly—desire. "You were."

"You noticed the places I needed you. You rubbed salve on my wounds and placed cool cloths on my brow."

She nodded, the movement shaky and perfect.

"Tell me, Adelaide Frampton, who has noticed me in ballrooms for years . . . did you notice me then? Here? The parts that were not harmed?"

She closed her eyes, and triumph consumed him. She did not wish to admit the truth—the taboo of it.

He wanted every word.

"Tell me," he commanded.

"I noticed."

He nodded. "Good. And did you want to touch?"

"Yes." He swore harshly at the confession and her eyes flew open. "I'm . . . sorry."

"No." The word came harsh and firm. "Don't apologize for it. Don't ever apologize for wanting to touch me. You may touch me whenever you like. Wherever you like. It is only that I find myself in a strange predicament."

"How?"

He pulled her close and set his forehead to hers, breathing her in. Letting her fill him up. "Somehow . . . I am jealous."

"Of whom?"

"Of myself, because I do not remember it."

She let out a little relieved laugh. "You will require additional salve soon enough, Your Grace. And I hope very much you will be conscious for it."

The words—the promise in them—made him instantly hard. Apparently, he'd had plenty of rest. It would take more than a knife to the side and a few broken ribs for him to stop wanting this beautiful woman in his arms. In his bed. In his life. "Adelaide?"

"Yes." Christ. She would be his undoing. The word should have been a curious reply. Should have been punctuated with a question mark. But instead, it came out breathless and aching, and when it reached him, it was full of all the things he wanted to do to her.

How was he to resist kissing her? He licked into her mouth, sucking on the full, pretty swell of her bottom lip until she whimpered her pleasure. Good. He wanted her aching. Christ, she was sweet and soft and warm, and the way she leaned into him, her fingers sliding into his hair as her tongue met his . . . She was perfect.

The kiss went on and on, until temptation had them both gasping for air, and Henry released her for a heartbeat, ready to pull her down and have his way with her. He couldn't look away from her, her hooded eyes, her pink cheeks, her mouth, full with the raw pleasure of their kiss. And there, faint on her skin, the scrape of five days of beard.

He stroked a thumb over her skin, hating the marks on her. "I hurt you."

She shook her head, her hands coming to his face, her nails scratching over his beard. "I don't even feel it."

"You will," he said, leaning in for another kiss, this one soft and lingering and as gentle as he could make it. Not enough. "And so, first things first."

That furrow was back, and he couldn't stop himself from leaning up to kiss it smooth. "I require a shave."

Chapter Sixteen

Adelaide was known for steady nerves.

She had been trained as a pickpocket and tested on the streets of London, and she was notoriously unflappable, which made her an ideal partner in criminal enterprise and information gathering.

But that morning, as Henry sat on the edge of the bed, newly conscious and impossibly handsome, smiling at her and teasing her and asking her questions that set her aflame with a heady combination of embarrassment and desire, she was unsteady.

Unsteady, and grateful for the way he caught her and pulled her close and gave her something to cling to—his firm, warm flesh. His soft hair. Those lips she'd once thought were unyielding but now, as he kissed her, were a tempting reminder that he was alive, and not simply alive, but *hers* for whatever time they had left—until the world returned and he remembered that Adelaide was an imposter, playing at being a part of his world. Born and bred on the South Bank—no kind of woman for the impeccable Duke of Clayborn.

But today, here, in the middle of nowhere, as the sun rose over the countryside, she let herself imagine what it might be if they were a different kind of people—the kind who lived in a little house on a hill, surrounded by farmland, where they woke with the dawn and spent their days with each other—full of each other.

What was the harm in imagining such a thing? Just for a moment.

Just until the world returned, and she realized that he could not soothe all the places he'd marked her—because he had marked too many that could not be seen, and would never return to the way they were.

She would think on that later, and it would consume her. But for now, she willed herself steady, holding the mirror for him as he shaved, watching his quick, economical circles with the boar bristle brush and cataloging his handsome face once more.

Even with the bruising from his battle, he was the handsomest man she'd ever seen—somehow more so now than before. She'd never imagined watching a man shave would affect her in any way, let alone making her wish she could climb into his lap and get a closer look.

Really Adelaide, the man was unconscious mere hours ago.

She'd found a razor in the table by the washbasin, and he worked it back and forth in a slow, hypnotic rhythm on its leather strop. "What are you thinking?"

She followed the movements, ignoring the way her heart pounded with each slide. Ignoring the way other parts of her pounded.

"Adelaide." Her name was firm on his tongue, and she snapped to attention.

"I was thinking that this . . . It is . . ." She searched for the word.

He found it. "Intimate."

"Yes." Her reply was barely there, more breath than sound.

A growl sounded in the back of his throat. "Christ, that's pretty," he rumbled. "I wonder all the other ways I could make you say that word."

Now she was wondering, too, as he set the blade to his cheek. On the first stroke, he winced, sucking in a sharp breath.

"What is it?" she said. "Did you cut yourself?"

A quick shake of his head. "No. But the angle." He slowly twisted in the seat. "It's strange what one finds one cannot do with a broken rib."

He turned the razor around and offered the handle to her. "Would you—"

She looked to the razor and again to him. "And if I told you I had never shaved a man?"

"Have you?"

"I have." Alfie thought a daughter no more than an expensive servant.

He closed his eyes for a moment—a touch longer than normal, and when he opened them, there was fire there. "I confess, that revelation made me more than a little jealous, Adelaide."

The words tumbled through her. "Oh."

He gave a little laugh. "You like that? That I am suddenly twisted in knots at the idea of you shaving another man?" She didn't have to admit it. He could see her pleasure. "Tell me the blade slipped, and put me out of my misery."

"It did not." She laughed. "And that's a terrible thing to wish."

"Who was he?"

Her gaze met his. "If I said he was my lover?"

"Then I suppose I would say his loss is my gain." He paused, then added, "And resist the urge to get his name from you so I might pay him a visit."

She dipped her head to hide her smile at the words. "He was not my lover," she said, finally. "I am not the kind of woman who attracts lovers."

It was the truth, and also a shameless hunt for a compliment. She would be well served if he agreed with her. *Please don't agree.*

"As I have spent the better part of the last two years imagining all the things I would like to do to you, I must disagree. Vehemently."

She gasped. "You have?"

"In great detail. So much so, that I'm eager to resume my position as your current lover, so can we get on with this?"

It was difficult to think of anything but his frank confession. "What sorts of details?"

"Shave me, and I will show you."

She swallowed. "I—"

"Unless you're through with me?" he prodded.

"No—" she said. "No."

He exhaled, harsher than normal, as though he'd been waiting for just that answer. "Excellent. Then do you mind hurrying up? Because I have plans to get back to kissing you."

He did not have to ask her twice. She set the mirror aside and took the razor from his hand, standing to consider the proper angle for her task.

"You should sit," he said, as though he read her mind, the words a bit rough. "It will give you better access."

She looked to his lap, his trousers tight across his thighs. And across other things . . . Realization coursed through her, chased by desire. He wanted her. "On you?"

A delicious hesitation. Then, on a low rumble, "If you like."

She shouldn't. This wasn't a game. This was a sharp blade to the man's throat, and it wasn't as though she were a trained barber. But the temptation to sit in his lap, to feel the hard press of his muscles against her . . . It was too great. She took her seat, one of his hands coming to her hip to hold her steady, sending heat sizzling through her.

"Is this . . . Are you comfortable?"

He was in no way comfortable. She could feel him, rigid against her—his thighs, his chest, his . . . other bits. She resisted the temptation to explore just how rigid she'd made him when he said, tight and clipped, "Perfectly."

She cut him a disbelieving look, but focused on the

task at hand, setting the razor to his cheek and carefully pulling it along his skin.

She released a breath when she reached the line of his jaw and rinsed the blade in the basin nearby.

He raised a brow. "Are you nervous?"

"No," she lied.

"You seem it."

"If I am, it is because you are making me nervous," she said, taking another line of beard.

"That's interesting, as I am the one with the blade to his throat."

"That's why I'm nervous," she replied, rinsing the blade once more. "No talking, please. As you know, I don't care for dead dukes."

"Until me, I'm not sure you cared for living ones, either."

Another stroke. "Who says I care for living ones now?"

He caught the hand with the razor in it, meeting her gaze firmly. "You care for me."

Why did it matter so much to him? And why did confessing it feel like she was stepping off a cliff, making her heart pound? "I do."

He released her and relaxed, his lips, cloaked in soap, twisting in a little, satisfied smile. "Good."

They were silent for a long moment, his gaze tight on her, watching her every move until she thought she was desperate to hide from the inspection. As she began shaving his neck, she whispered, "Close your eyes."

"Why?"

"The blade at your throat isn't enough of a reason?"

"I confess, Adelaide, I enjoy looking at you enough to take the risk."

Her eyes met his then, that deep cerulean blue, and she shook her head. "I can't concentrate if you're watching me."

His fingers tightened on her waist at the confession and

he grumbled, "Only because I want this to go as quickly as possible." He closed his eyes, and she took the opportunity to steal a look at him. To lock away a memory of this moment, his dark, impossibly long lashes against his cheeks, dots of soap at intervals across his face, the newly formed bump on his bruised nose—hoarded proof that he'd thrown himself into battle for her. That he'd been hers for a heartbeat.

"If I can't look at you, at least let me hear you," he said, the words shaking her from her inspection.

"Shall I tell you a story?" she said, letting herself tease him. Just for now. Just for tonight.

"Yes." He leapt upon the question. "Tell me a hundred of them."

She smiled at this new man—nothing like the duke she'd once thought him—and dragged the razor back and forth in the warm water. "What would you like to hear?"

"Tell me who you were when you were young."

She shook her head before she remembered that he could not see it. Working carefully at the underside of his chin, she said softly, "There are too many stories, and none that make for good storytelling."

"That suggests there are many that make for good storytelling, sweet. Come . . . you can surely find one."

What could she tell him that would not remind him of the differences between them? The story of her learning to pick pockets? The story of always, always feeling alone?

The story of finding a man she wished to be alone with?

Stalling for time, she reminded him, "You owe me a story, too. Your first kiss."

He opened his eyes, reaching up to stroke a thumb over her cheekbone before he said, "I find I cannot remember any kisses before yours, Miss Frampton."

She couldn't help the sound that came, something that

could only be described as a giggle. "I'm sure that's not true. Close your eyes."

"It is," he said, doing as he was told. "I can only hope you are as superior a barber as you are a kisser?"

She smiled, enjoying the tease. Enjoying him, as she checked her work, looking for extra bits of beard that she might have missed. "I would not like you to be dissatisfied."

"Oh, I am dissatisfied," he rumbled, low and soft and so close. "So much so that I think I deserve restitution."

She reached for the towel she'd set next to them, reaching up to wipe soap from his smooth face.

"Beard restitution?"

"Mmm." That sound. That singular, delicious sound. Would she ever be unmoved by it?

Leaning back, she considered her handiwork. "I've done quite well, I'm afraid. No restitution necessary."

"Then I am left with payment. Name your price."

Kiss me.

She would never know if she'd given voice to the thought. It did not matter. Because he did as she asked, pulling her to meet him, licking into her mouth and giving her the kiss she'd been aching for, his hands chasing over her waist to hold her on his lap as her hands tangled in his hair and she kissed him back, matching him move for move, until the kiss ended and they gasped for air.

"My services are more expensive than that," she teased softly, reaching for him again. He met her, kissing her until she felt as though the world had slipped away— everything gone except Henry, smelling like mint and soap and rosemary.

Finally, he pulled back, pressing his brow to hers as they both panted their pleasure and he whispered a wicked curse before asking, "How is it possible that you haven't been won, Adelaide Frampton? How is it that you are here, ripe for me, making me ache and aching for me, in return?"

She placed her hands on top of his, where he held her tight. "No one has ever . . ." She searched for the words. *Wanted me. Come for me. Wooed me. Won me.* She couldn't say any of that, obviously. It would make her seem . . . needing.

She was needing. She needed him.

She pushed the thoughts aside and finished the sentence. ". . . noticed me."

He shook his head, slow and certain. "You've said that before. That you are not noticed. It is not true."

"I prefer not to be noticed."

His brow furrowed. "Why?"

"Because if no one notices me, they won't notice that I don't belong." She gave a little laugh. "Of course that's silly, isn't it? I don't belong. Not in Mayfair. Not at your dinner parties where everyone laughs when husbands insult their wives. Not at your balls where people go out of their way to ignore the outcasts. The ones who aren't beautiful. The ones who are aging. The ones who never quite got the hang of the quadrille." She looked to him, feeling that she ought to confess, "I'm not good at the quadrille."

"I don't care."

"Of course you do. You notice every imperfection. You told me once that I *overstepped* when I was the only person in the room to defend Lady Coleford in her sitting room when her husband was a monster."

His sigh was full of frustration . . . and contrition. "I did."

"I was *furious*."

He nodded, his lips curving in a half smile. "You were. It was magnificent."

"You should not underestimate the power of a woman's fury, Duke."

With his thumbs, he raised her chin, and he pressed a kiss to the soft underside of her jaw. "I have seen you at work, Miss Frampton. I do not for a moment underestimate you."

"Do you know that when I left that evening, I immediately went looking to fill your file?"

Another kiss, this one lingering, made better by the way he finished it by whispering at her ear, "I can respect vengeance."

She clutched his forearms, her words going to breath. "I wanted to destroy you."

Another kiss, lower, where her pulse pounded. The swipe of his tongue, and then he lifted his head and looked her deep in the eyes. "I did it to protect you. To keep you unnoticed. If that man—if any of these men you loathe—with good reason, I would add—ever noticed you . . . Adelaide, don't you see what would happen?"

She'd seen what bad men could do with their lack of conscience. Had spent years fighting them when the world turned away from their behavior. "I can hold my own, Duke."

He nodded. "That much I know. But you shouldn't have to."

"I'd rather speak than be silent. I'd rather fight than be protected. But you forget, Henry, that it's not my speaking that gets me noticed. When a woman speaks too loudly, fights too passionately—that is when she goes unnoticed. They would rather shun me than hear me." She paused. "They'd like me to shut up and dance the quadrille."

"Hang the quadrille."

"I would wager all I have that you are excellent at the quadrille." When he did not answer she said, "Aren't you?"

"Adelaide." He gave a little laugh, as though she was being silly. And maybe she was. Maybe she was irritable.

Or maybe it was frustration, and she was simply reminding herself that there was no future for them. And maybe she needed that. "Aren't you?" she repeated.

"Yes. I am good at the quadrille."

"There, you see?"

"I assure you, I do not. But I also do not care about the quadrille, because it has nothing to do with being noticed. Shall I tell you why?"

She shouldn't care. And still, "Why?"

"Because the only person I noticed at the Beaufetheringstone ball didn't dance the quadrille; she never does."

Her heart started to pound. "What do you mean?"

"She never dances. Though she does pick the occasional pocket."

Her cheeks were burning again. "I sometimes dance."

"When?"

There were parties that didn't have dancing with mincing steps that she simply had not been able to master in the five years since Duchess took her in. Nor did they have mincing people. Duchess loved parties that existed beyond the aristocracy. That welcomed people of all walks. And there, there weren't orchestras, but bands. Fiddles and pipes and drums and wild, raucous reels. And Adelaide adored those dances. But she couldn't tell him about them. They weren't for dukes. "When there is no one around to notice."

He nodded. "Show me."

"Show you what?"

"Dance with me."

Her brow furrowed. "There is no music."

"No?" he said, and moved, tipping her to her feet as he stood. "Are you sure?"

"You're mad. It's an effect of the blood loss."

"Maybe. You ought to take pity on me and dance with me, then, as it might be my last time."

Adelaide didn't mean to step into his arms, but suddenly, there she was, wrapped in his warmth. "This isn't—"

He didn't let her finish. "Where shall I put my hands?"

She reached for him, knowing she shouldn't. Put one of his hands at her waist, took the other in her own.

"This is familiar," he said.

She stepped closer, until they were nearly touching. "Like this?"

"Still familiar," he said softly. "I've danced like this before."

Her brows rose. "Not in Lady Beaufetheringstone's ballroom, I wager."

"Are you jealous?"

"I am not," she said with a smile. "After all—I was your first kiss."

He laughed, a low delicious rumble, and Adelaide stepped closer. His grip tightened, making it impossible for her to move away. "What about this?"

"Mmm." That low rumble that never failed to turn her insides liquid. "This is less familiar."

She couldn't help her little smile. "This?" She stepped closer.

The rumble became a growl as the band of his arm tightened around her. "Miss Frampton . . ."

"Yes, Your Grace?"

"I don't care for the idea that you've danced quite this close to other men."

"Are you jealous?" His words, thrown back at him.

"Burning with it," he said, the words low and clipped. "I know I haven't the right to, but I hate the idea of you in the arms of another."

She shouldn't like that. But oh, my, she did. She liked it very much, and rewarded him for it by pressing even closer. "Does this help?" she whispered. "I've never danced this close to another."

He had so many sounds. This one was pleasure. And

she liked it the best. "So, this is how you would have us dance?"

"If there were music, yes." She paused. "But Mayfair would most certainly notice."

His lips were so close. Was he well enough for this?

"Not me," he said. "They'd notice you, though. Certainly."

He was so warm, and so alive, and so perfect—it was impossible to imagine the wide world letting him go unnoticed for even a moment. He was the opposite of her.

"I notice you, Adelaide."

His touch on her skin, his voice in her ear, his heat . . . all around her.

"I notice this."

She clung to it, that vow. The impossible truth of it.

Knowing that it would not always be true. Knowing that it would end, because there was no other option. Knowing that every moment she stole was just that . . . stolen. Criminal. Smuggled.

And then he kissed her, and he played the thief.

Chapter Seventeen

He had been lost the moment she sat on his lap.

Before that, truthfully. When she'd perched on the edge of the bed, mirror in hand, and he'd noticed the tremble in her fingers as she tried not to look at him. But she'd wanted to. She'd liked looking at him.

Just as he liked looking at her. Just as he liked touching her, testing the curve of her hip on his thigh, the weight of her on his lap, the silk of her skin.

The warmth of her in his arms when he pulled her to her feet and danced with her, teasing her closer until they were pressed against each other, and he was wondering how quickly he could get her back to London, so he might take her to a ball and scandalize the doyennes of the aristocracy by claiming every dance, and scandalize the rest of the aristocracy by tugging her into dark gardens and having his way with her.

And scandalize *her*, because he was coming to see that she liked to be scandalized.

Bandages and rosemary balm be damned, Adelaide was his cure.

The realization was a gift, as though he'd found something for which he'd been searching for years, and now that he'd found it—found her—a new road rolled out before him. He'd spent months watching her and days chasing her and mere hours discovering her, but there, in that house on the hill, with his brother eloped to God knew where and heirs to come, suddenly it was all clear, and Henry was free to watch her and chase her and discover her at his leisure.

She liked it when he watched. And chased. And discovered. She reveled in his notice. And he intended to give her more of all she wished.

All she asked for. All she deserved.

So he did what any intelligent man would do and returned to his chair, tugging her into his lap, so he could give her his undivided attention.

"Like this," he whispered, pulling up her skirts until her knees were on either side of his thighs and she stared down at him like a queen.

His queen.

"Have a care for your ribs," she said, resisting giving him her full weight. "You couldn't shave."

"Could I not?" he asked, his fingers at her hips, holding her on his lap. "I cannot remember anything painful about the experience. Not when you made it so pleasurable." He moved to the ribbons of her skirts, toying with them. "These ribbons—the first time I saw you use them, tossing your skirts away on the docks to run faster—they're brilliant."

Her smile was full of pride. "Not just to run faster. Don't forget the element of surprise."

"How could I? Those grey skirts disappeared and sudden I was chasing this . . ." His hands went to her bottom and squeezed. "Glorious."

She sucked in a breath. "I am very lucky to have a very clever dressmaker."

"Mmm," he said, tugging at the ribbon, just enough for it to hint at untying. "Who is she?"

She hesitated, and he regretted the question. He didn't want to play their information game right now. He didn't want to be reminded that there were countless secrets between them.

Surprising them both, however, she answered. "Her name is Jane Berry."

Even that—the tiny piece of information—felt like triumph. "I assume she does not have a shop on Bond Street."

Adelaide gave a little, secret smile. "No. Her shop is in Croydon."

Far away from the prying eyes of the aristocracy. "And yet, her designs take London by storm."

She leaned in and kissed him, quick and sweet and distracting.

Not distracting enough. When the kiss ended, he stroked a hand over her long body, loving the way she arched into his touch, and said, "You trust me here." He didn't wait for her reply, instead pausing at the place just above her bodice, where her heart pounded. "But not here." Wrapping his fingers around the back of her neck, he pulled her close and pressed a soft kiss to her forehead, whispering there, "And not here, either."

She looked away, over his shoulder, as though searching for the right way to answer. "It isn't specific to you. I trust very few people."

"The Duchess of Trevescan."

She nodded.

"Sesily Calhoun. Lady Imogen Loveless. Maggie O'Tiernen. Lucia."

Another nod.

"Others, I assume," he said. "All women with skill and talent and a wicked sense of justice."

She did not nod then. Instead, she stared down at him and said, "You *have* been noticing me."

The way one noticed a candle in darkness. "Every time you enter a room. And one day, I shall earn the rest."

The words did not tempt her to confide in him, and he did not expect them to, but she rewarded him in other ways, with a flush of awareness across her breast, a flash of desire in her eyes.

He had waited a lifetime for this woman, and he would take the pieces she gave him, every hint of her secrets, and he would put them with his own. And she would trust him one day, because he had earned it from her.

Now was not the time for such a vow, however—not when Adelaide was so quick to hide. Instead, Henry returned to her ribbons, toying with the pretty silk. "When I was with fever . . . unconscious . . . I dreamed of these ribbons."

She watched him. "What did you imagine doing with them?"

"Catching you. Untying you."

She nodded. "Show me."

He did, loosening the ties that held the skirts bunched between them. When he was through, he found the seam of the fabric and tugged.

They fell away, draping over his legs to reveal—
Dear God.

"Why, Miss Frampton," he said, unable to stop his fingers from sliding up her thigh to the bare curve of her bottom. "This is . . . scandalous."

Beneath those skirts that were so easily dispatched, Adelaide was bare. "I did not expect anyone to be interested in what was beneath my skirts today."

"That was your first mistake," he said, the words coming on a low growl he could not control. "I find myself endlessly interested in what is beneath your skirts." His fingers chased over the smooth, warm skin of her bottom, to the seam there, skimming over the sensitive flesh, loving the way she gasped her surprise at the touch.

She rocked against him, the heat of her teasing through the fabric of his trousers. "Henry."

"Take your hair down," he ordered, reaching for those rich, fiery strands. "I've dreamed of this—of your hair down around you as you reign above me."

"I don't want to hurt you." Her fingers stroked over his torso to his bandaged wound, and he sucked in a breath.

"I promise you, love . . . what I feel when you touch me is nothing like pain."

Her hands went to her hair and he stroked over her laced bodice—the only thing left on her body, the fabric straining where her breasts rose and fell in staccato rhythm—a clear sign that she was as wild as he was.

She was so beautiful, rising above him, her long arms up as she worked at her hairpins, her hips canted against him, her lovely strong thighs hugging his own as his fingers found the soft, silken curls between them, stroking over them. "So pretty," he whispered, tracing gently over her folds, teasing her, loving the way she rocked toward him, her body begging for his touch.

"Henry," she said, his name like a plea.

She wanted him to touch her, and he liked that very much. "Mmm. Here?" Another soft stroke. Barely there. Torturing them both. "What was it you said to me on the dock all those days ago? She who finds, keeps?" Another stroke, a temptation. "I have found something . . . tremendous."

He watched her, growing heavy and hard.

"I'm going to keep it."

Her eyes flew open, meeting his. "Me."

"Mine."

She writhed against him, searching for more, and he pulled back, refusing her. Toying with her. She gasped, and the sound, full of desperate need, was the most beautiful thing he'd ever encountered.

"You'll let me, won't you? Keep you?"

"Yes," she panted. "However you'll have me. As long as I might keep you, as well."

And then the hairpins were dealt with, and her rich red curls were down around her shoulders, and he couldn't stop himself from touching them, his free hand immediately tangling in them, and he had a heartbeat to marvel at their softness until she was touching him again, one hand on his shoulder and one—*Ahh.*

She found his wrist, her touch firm, holding him tight as she lowered herself to him, sliding over his fingers once, twice, until he was there, in her silky heat, and they both groaned their pleasure. "This—" he said, hot at her ear, loving the sound of her shattered breaths. "I am going to make you come like this."

He stroked, smooth and slow, and she whimpered, a magnificent little noise that would have unraveled him if he didn't have plans for this woman. For this moment. He licked at her ear, and stroked his thumb over the bud of pleasure at her core, reveling in the way she twitched beneath his touch. "And then I am going to make you come with my mouth."

"Henry . . ." Two syllables turned into a dozen.

"Tell me, love."

"Please."

He grew impossibly harder. That word on her lips. He was ruined for her. He would give her whatever she wanted. She only had to ask for it.

"Look at me, sweetheart." She did, her eyes opening, black centers blown wide in rich brown velvet. He groaned, straining up to kiss her, ignoring the pull at his side. "I have more to tell you."

"Show me instead." She sighed, rocking against his hand. "More."

"Look at you," he whispered, watching her work herself on him, painting little circles over her softness, finding the place where her nerves screamed for him.

Her hands came to his shoulders on a gasp. "Henry."

He turned his head and nipped at her wrist, running his teeth over her skin. "What will you do when you've ridden my fingers and tongue, love? What will you do when you've come against me twice?"

"I'll . . ." She rolled her hips against his fingers. "I'll want more."

The confession nearly did him in. He'd give it to her. Whatever she wanted. "What more?"

"Your—" She stopped.

"You know the word. Use it."

"I shouldn't."

"Yes, love, you absolutely should," he whispered, wanting her to say it.

Those eyes again, full of desire. "Your cock."

He growled and claimed her mouth, licking deep, sucking the profanity off her tongue. "Yes," he breathed, harsh and aching when he released her from the kiss and reached for the laces on her bodice, yanking at the strings until it was loose enough to bare her breasts.

He captured one straining nipple in his mouth, sucking it deep and slow, as his thumb circled the place she needed him most. When she cried out, one hand tangling in his hair, holding him to her breast, he knew he had her, his fingers and mouth and words sending her higher and higher.

When she whispered, "Please . . ." he released her breast, just long enough to say, "I'm going to let you ride my cock."

The words catapulted her into her orgasm, and he leaned back to watch, loving the way her eyes found his, knowing that his watching was part of her pleasure. He was devastatingly hard by then, a fine sheen of sweat across his torso, his body a singular ache, desperate to take her.

Not yet. Not until he'd made good on his promises. "Beautiful girl," he whispered, guiding her back, over his arm, pressing kisses along her torso, sucking at her nipples again. "So sweet here. So stunning."

She had found a source of pleasure strong enough that she was not embarrassed by his compliment, and for the first time since he'd begun telling her how beautiful she was, she did not deny or hide from it.

A flood of triumph coursed through him. If this was

what it took to make her understand how perfect she was, he would give her this every day. Forever.

He lingered on the word—one he rarely considered, as *forever* required a certainty in the future he'd not had since he was a boy.

But somehow, here, with this woman, he did not run from the idea.

Adelaide. By his side. A passel of little girls with fiery curls and curious, all-seeing eyes.

If she knew what he was thinking, she *would* run.

As it was, she was moving in his arms—had he spoken his thoughts aloud? "Where are you going, love?"

She leaned in and pressed a kiss high on his chest, lingering on the muscle there before licking over one of his nipples, forcing a hiss of pleasure from him. She wasn't running. Dear God. She was coming off his lap, lowering herself to her knees between his thighs.

She wasn't running.

"Adelaide." He reached for her, his fingers catching in her hair, guiding her to look at him. "What are you doing?"

Her smile set him aflame as she removed her spectacles and tossed them on a nearby table, instantly forgotten as her hands slid up over his legs, pressing along his thighs on their quest to the buttons of his trousers. She paused there, the touch of her fingers soft and tempting as she looked up to him. "I find your plan for the afternoon extremely appealing, but I wonder if you would mind if I add one additional activity."

She was the most beautiful thing he'd ever seen, on her knees, between his legs, lush and languid from the orgasm he'd given her. Knowing she watched, Henry sucked his fingers into his mouth, tasting her there, sweet and sinful. Her eyes went wide, and he went impossibly harder at the expression, full of surprise and desire. "Delicious," he said, a scrape of sound. "Why not come back and give me another taste?"

He saw her consider it, and held his breath, waiting for her to choose her pleasure. He reveled in that pause, in the knowledge of her desire for him, for his touch and his mouth and his cock. He reached for her hair, like fire. "Come, Adelaide. Let me pleasure you until we are both lost to it."

"No," she said, capturing his hand and pressing a kiss to the palm, licking over it and up one of his fingers. He cursed, foul and full of desire, as she sucked the tip into her mouth, her tongue laving the pad of it, a promise.

She released him with a knowing smile, moving his hands to the arms of the chair and wrapping his fingers around them. "No distractions. I've plans."

He released a punch of breath and leaned back, his heart a riot in his chest as he stared down at her as she took him in, her own hands exploring without hesitation, fingers dancing over the skin of his torso, his muscles tightening beneath her touch as his whole body snapped to perfect attention. He gritted his teeth at the twinge in his side.

No pain. Not now. Only pleasure.

Only Adelaide.

Lower and lower she moved, until she reached his trousers, the hard, straining length of him impossible to ignore. Her hands hovered there, above the bulge in the fabric, for a heartbeat. A lifetime. Her beautiful gaze found his. "May I?"

"Fuck, yes," he breathed.

Another small, secret smile. "What language, Duke. How the world would react if they knew what a filthy mouth you had."

"Let me use it on you," he said, the words harsh, part command. "Let me lick you again and again, until you forget your name." She rewarded him with a sharp inhale. A flicker of her dark lashes. She wanted it.

Good. He intended to give it to her.

But then he couldn't intend anything, because she was

touching him, stroking and exploring the hard straining column of him beneath his trousers. His grip tightened on the arms of the chair, the wood creaking in his hands as she worked his buttons with speed.

Thank God. He couldn't bear slow.

She struggled with one and released a little sound of frustration, and Henry thought he might come from that sound alone—the proof of her desire for him. But no. He wasn't coming without her.

Not even when she spread the fabric wide and revealed the length of him, hard and hot and aching.

"Oh," she said softly. "That is—"

It was rude. A gentleman would apologize for it.

"—beautiful," she finished, delight in her voice.

His eyes slid closed and his heart pounded and the edge of the chair's arms bit into his flesh and he willed himself not to touch her. To let her touch him.

Was she going to touch him?

One finger. One sinful finger, sliding over the tip of him and down the throbbing column. Like fire. Like torture.

"Adelaide." All the years he'd tried so hard to be in control. To be a decent man. To be noble. And with one finger, she turned him into an animal. He cursed, low and wicked.

She gave him what he wanted, gripping him more tightly, rubbing her thumb over the broad head of him.

He hissed out a breath, throwing his head back against the chair, his gaze rapt on her hand as she worked him over with her pretty, tight fist—down, then up again. He wouldn't be able to control himself much longer. She didn't want him touching her as she did this? Thought he could resist her? She'd have to lash him to this chair if she wanted that.

With effort, he tore his gaze from where she touched him to find her waiting for him. She wasn't watching the movements. Wasn't gauging his desire from the iron stiffness in her hand. Instead, she was watching his face. Watching him, watching her.

He found control again. "You like what you see."

"I do." Another stroke, long and lingering. Another breath, punched from his chest.

"You see what you do to me?"

A small smile. A whisper of triumph. "You want me."

Want was too small a word. Four letters where he needed forty thousand. "I do."

"My hand." Those smooth, rich slides would kill him.

"Yes." His hand flexed on the chair. "Adelaide. Let me touch you."

She shook her head. "Not yet."

"Why not?"

"Because . . ." She paused. "If you touch me, I won't be able to concentrate."

"I don't need you to concentrate, love," he said. "I need you to lie down and let me worship you." She needed it, too. He could see it in the way her pretty sable lashes flickered with desire. "God, you're beautiful. Let me show you how much."

She shook her head, leaning in and whispering to the tip of him, "Have you imagined this?"

What was the right answer? Should he tell her how he'd imagined it? A dozen times? A hundred, on her knees just like this? Her hands on him? Her beautiful lips just barely open, waiting for him? How he'd stroked his cock and come in thick ropes, wishing she were there to catch them?

He couldn't tell her that.

He didn't have to. "You have," she said, knowledge and something else in her words. Something breathless. Like pleasure. "I can see it. You've imagined me here, yours."

"How could I not?" he admitted on a growl. "Mine."

She rewarded him for the confession, licking over the hard, aching tip, pulling him inside her perfect mouth, tasting him with little flicks of her tongue. He exhaled, harsh and raw, his hips bucking just barely before he turned all his strength to stopping them. He didn't want to hurt her. Didn't want to shock her.

And then she shocked him, with a long, low hum of . . . *Christ*, she liked it.

He could see it on her face, her eyes sliding closed as she relaxed and took him deep. Pleasure and power and absolute need. No. It couldn't be need. That was what he was feeling. Need and desire and an absolute unhinged frenzy to make her his. And not just here, now, in this room, in this chair, in this bed, but everywhere. Always.

One hand slipped down his cock as she took him deep, her hum becoming a rhythmic sigh as she loved him with her mouth and tongue and hands, and he was lost to the sensation, clinging to the chair and telling her all the ways he'd imagined her taking him. *Deeper. Harder. Yes. Please. Adelaide.*

His hips moving against her, his mouth spewing filthy things, and his cock, heavy and aching, waiting for her to lead him into release as she found the exact rhythm that had them both groaning.

Control snapped, and he reached for her, lifting her beautiful hair from where it fell in silken waves over her face and his thighs, so he could touch her—so he could see her . . . watching him. God, he loved her eyes on him. Loved the way she looked at him. The way she noticed him. Always ahead of him, reading him, his brilliant, beautiful girl.

"Adelaide." He tightened his grip, pulling her back from him, slowing her irresistible pace. "If you continue . . . love . . . I shall spend."

"Yes," she said, her eyes alight with desire that edged into greed. What a goddess she was. "Yes." The word thrummed through him on a current of pleasure. "Yes, I want that."

And then she was back in control, taking him deep,

cloaking him in tight, warm pleasure until he couldn't hold himself back, and he gave himself up to her, shouting his release to the room and the countryside and the sun.

And all the while, she watched him, hot for him, full of power. Of dominion.

He was never letting her go.

He leaned forward, pulling her up to him, taking her mouth with a wicked growl that told her how good she had been, his orgasm having not nearly assuaged the wild desire that consumed him now that he knew what it was to have her. One hand slid over her body to find her breast, her nipple hard and straining.

She whined her pleasure as he toyed with it, and his own flared to life again. He released her and said, "Remember what you told me the other night, love? That I could simply fuck you?" He kissed her again, her hands tangling in the hair at the back of his neck.

Releasing her, he stood, one hand still tangled in her curls, and helped her to her unsteady feet. "Now you see . . . nothing about what we do together is ever going to be simple. If we did this a thousand times . . . it would never be simple." Another kiss, deep and slow. "It will always be earth-shattering," he promised. "Shall I show you?"

"Yes. Please." That word. He would give her whatever she asked for, forever. And he'd make sure she liked it, forever.

Starting that moment.

Chapter Eighteen

Since she'd joined Duchess and her crew, Adelaide had broken forty-three matches, saving as many women from a lifetime of unhappiness with myriad scoundrels, rogues, and monsters. In addition, working with the Hell's Belles, she'd taken down six earls, two marquesses, a duke, and about two dozen rich, entitled gentlemen who had deserved everything they'd received.

And still, that day, in that warm, wonderful room in that quiet house on that quiet hill in the quiet English countryside, as Henry turned his pleasure over to her and lost the control he held so tightly, unable to keep his hands and mouth from her as he found release, she'd never felt more powerful.

Never more cared for, either.

Because somehow, even as she fell to her knees and pleasured him in every way she'd ever imagined she could, it had been Adelaide who had felt worshipped as he'd watched her, his blue eyes riveted to her movements, his chest rising and falling with ragged breath, and finally, when he could no longer resist, his touch firm and careful and full of heat.

And then he'd pulled her up into his arms and returned to the bed where she'd kept vigil for so many days, but instead of leaving her at his bedside, he drew her down with him, his hands warm and sure on her skin, his lips tempting and sweet.

"Come," he whispered, the word soft and sinful. "Like this."

He pulled her to straddle him, and she hesitated. "Your bandages . . ."

He sat up, his hand running up over her back and pulling her down for a kiss. "Don't worry, love. You have tended me well, and now . . . I shall tend to you."

She reached for him, her hands stroking over his chest. "I wanted you well," she confessed. "I wanted you awake and moving. I hated how still you were."

He captured one hand and pulled it to his lips, kissing her fingertips. "I am awake now. I move now." He lifted her, guiding her up his chest. "Let me show you how well I move."

Her eyes went wide as he showed her, moving her up, over his chest, until she was straddling his shoulders. "Henry, what—"

"Shh," he whispered, reaching for her, parting her folds, running a single finger through her wet heat. "Let me look."

"I can't—" She closed her eyes. It was too much. It was too . . . *good.* Another stroke and a wicked circle where she instantly ached for him.

"So beautiful," he whispered. "This is the most beautiful thing I've ever seen. So wet and warm and"—another swirl of a finger, and she sucked in a breath—"wanting," he finished, parting her and lifting his head, licking into her with a long, slow suck. She cried out, and he released her. When he spoke, he was all satisfaction. "You want me, don't you? Here?"

Before she could answer, he was there, against her, and she couldn't contain her moan, her hands coming to hold him, her fingers thrusting into his hair, tightening as she held herself perfectly still, embarrassment threatening even as he sent a thundering pleasure through her.

He stopped, his fingers tightening on her bottom, turning to press a kiss high on the inside of her thigh. "You taste like honey and sin."

Adelaide closed her eyes at the words, at the flood of delight that coursed through her at them.

"Come closer, love," he whispered there, at her core. "Give me more."

And then he pulled her down so he could cover her with his mouth, working her over with his tongue again and again, rumbling against her as she lost control, rocking against him. Just once. Just enough to get . . .

"Closer," he growled, swatting her bottom. She yelped, surprised by the quick bite of pain and the slow lick of pleasure.

She looked down at him to find—dear Lord. He was watching her, his beautiful blue eyes tracking up the long line of her body, a wicked light of discovery there. *You like that.*

He didn't have to speak the words aloud. He could see the truth.

"I—" She bit her lip. Another swat. His hand lingering over the sting. Large and warm. She moaned, rocking into his firm grip. "*Yes. Henry . . .*" His name came on a long, slow sigh.

"What a very good girl you are," he whispered up the length of her body as he pulled her to him, not looking away. "We are going to explore that at length another time. But now . . ." He rewarded her with a long, lush lick, enough to have her bucking against him, her head falling forward as she panted her pleasure. Another growl rumbled from him, the sound nearly too much.

His magnificent mouth ate at her, licking and sucking and stealing her control until she lost herself to his touch, turning herself and her pleasure over to him, her fingers tight in his hair. He released her for a heartbeat, just enough to command, "That's it, love. Take it. Take me."

And she did, unable to stop herself. Unable to resist his pull, closer and closer to the edge. Not wanting to stop as she rocked against him, his tongue tracking over her secret places and his fingers sliding over her bottom, finding another secret place, painting slow, languid circles until she was beyond herself, panting his name and begging him not to stop. He didn't, not until she had taken her climax in a slow, increasing wave that crashed hard and fast through her on a scream.

Even then, he didn't release her, seeming to know what she needed—the flat of his tongue, the weight of his palm. And then a languid slide down his torso, where his cock waited, hard once more. Ready for her.

She hesitated, lifting her weight from him. "Your bandages . . ."

This wasn't—they couldn't—

He moved, lifting her up and over the crisscrossing white linen, until she was seated below, straddling the straining length of him. "I swear to you, Adelaide, there is no pain right now. There is nothing but you."

"It's too much," she whispered, even as she rocked, just barely, just enough to make them both sigh. "It's too soon."

"It's been an eternity," he replied, reaching for her face, running one thumb over her cheek. "You took such good care of me, love." Then that hand fell, fingers finding the scar at her side, tracing it gently. "Now we are a match."

The words rioted through her, the idea that there might be a match for her. The teasing, tempting lie that there might be a partner for Adelaide, born alone, raised alone. That *he* might be that partner.

Impossible.

Tears came, unbidden. Unwelcome. She dashed them

away, but he noticed them. Misunderstood. "No, love. I am well. I'll never make you cry again."

She leaned into the touch, her eyes closing at the words. At the lie in them.

There was no question he would make her cry again. When he left her—whether it was tomorrow or a year from now—she might never stop.

He was not for her. Not forever. But that moment, in that room, in that cottage, on that hill . . . he could be for then.

And that moment, as she straddled him, and his hand slid down over her breasts and belly and up her thighs to the place where she throbbed and ached for him, she did not cry. She reveled in him, in the certainty of him. In the way he took his cock in hand and worked it against her, making her impossibly wetter and more wanton.

"Henry." The word came out on a whine—desperate for him.

"You want this," he said, raw and perfect.

"Yes," she admitted, already lifting herself, already making room for him as he parted her folds, positioning himself at her entrance.

"Adelaide," he said, her name like a prayer.

She met his eyes. "Henry . . ." She lowered herself over him. Barely. Just enough that they both groaned their pleasure.

"Yes, love—"

"That feels—"

"Perfect."

She moved again. An inch. More. Her eyes sliding closed and her hands coming to his thighs behind her. "You're so—"

Warm. Wet. Full. Their words ran together. *Yes. Please.*

His hands were at her hips, holding her tight as she continued, seating herself on him.

"You're a queen," he said softly. "Reigning over me."

He thrust up into her and they both groaned at the sensation, her hands coming to rest on his chest. "Ruining me."

She lifted herself, just barely, just enough to bring his gaze back to hers, full of lust and greed. "Christ," he swore, his hands gripping her. "Do it again."

Full of heady power and triumph, she did. Again, long and slow and languid, her hips rolling against his when she was seated once more.

He cursed, low and dark, and she couldn't help her smile.

"You like that, don't you?" he said, his hand sliding up over her body, between her breasts, to her neck, where his fingers caged her throat. No pressure. Just pleasure. "You like owning me? Controlling me?"

She did, but she did not have to say it. He knew it. He knew it and controlled her in return, his fingers everywhere, on her breasts, playing down her body, seeking out the hard nub of pleasure that strained for him even as she rode him. Working it in tight circles as she rode him, slow and shallow and then in rolling waves, her own hand coming to his, to hold him tight against her and show him exactly how to touch her even as she chased her pleasure, rocking and begging for release.

He teased her with it, slowing when she came too close to the edge, gentling when she started to come, until she opened her eyes and leveled him with a wild, dark-eyed stare. "Enough," she said, setting her palms to his chest. "Give it to me."

The demand, firm and full of desire, summoned a low, lingering growl from deep in his chest, and he did, blessedly, as she asked, playing her body like an instrument, thrusting up into her as she ground upon him, until she was chanting his name and he was whispering hers, fast, then faster, his fingers moving in perfect circles, until she was wound tight as a spring.

"Henry," she panted. "I need you. I need it."

He pinched one nipple with his free hand. "I know,

love. Take it. Take whatever you need. It's yours. I'm
yours."

I'm yours.

Pleasure shot through her—the feel of him, the sound
of the words, the promise in them—and she was there,
and it was like nothing she'd ever experienced.

"Now, love."

As though all she needed was his permission, she
looked down at him, surprise and shock and a wild
amount of fear coursing around her, and he sat up, catching her to him, taking her mouth in a deep, delicious
kiss, thrusting up into her once, twice before ending the
caress and grinding out, "Christ. Yes. You are the most
beautiful thing I've ever seen. Come for me, love. Right
now."

She did as she was told, her gaze fastened to his as the
wave of pleasure washed over her. And only then, when
she was lost to it, wild and wanton on him, did he follow
her into bliss, thrusting and stroking and circling and
groaning, until she collapsed on top of him, their hearts
pounding in rhythmic unison, and he collected her in his
arms like a treasure.

At some point—seconds? minutes? longer?—she
moved, loath to leave him but fearing that if she stayed,
she would hurt him.

Fearing that if she stayed, she would hurt herself.

Still, with the tempting warmth of him and the soft
kiss he placed at her temple, she found she was not
strong enough to leave him. Even though she knew it was
the best course of action to protect her heart. Perhaps she
knew the truth, though. Perhaps she knew that it was too
late, and her heart was no longer hers to protect.

The sun, now high in the sky, painted the walls with
dappled shadows of the trees outside, and they mimicked
the actions inside, on each other's skin. And Adelaide
wondered at the quiet of the room. Of her thoughts.

When was the last time she had simply . . . been?

When was the last time she had felt purely . . . her?

Never.

Another might have heard that word whisper by and imagined a lifetime, cleaved in two—the past and the future. A new beginning, finally understanding what others meant when they said they were content.

Adelaide knew better. There might be a past and a future. A new beginning. A new understanding of what could be. But what *could* be was not what *would* be.

Moments like this . . . they weren't forever.

If her wildest, most private dreams came true, and Henry wanted to keep her—even for a short while, even for stolen nights in her rooms above The Place, for quick moments in the shadows of Westminster, for heated kisses on the docks—here, in the heart of Lancashire, in the middle of nowhere, unwed and secret in a place all their own—it would not last.

It could not. And every time she looked at him, every time he smiled his beautiful smile that softened the stern lines of his perfect, aristocratic face, she would have to remind herself . . . *he is not yours. Not really.*

Not forever.

Could she live with that?

She stiffened at the thought, the way it tightened her chest. The way it stung in her throat, even as he turned his head and kissed her temple again, breathing her in. Stealing more of her. Parts she would never get back.

Already gone, promised to him, like the rest of her.

He might not be hers, but she would always be his.

"Adelaide," he whispered, and she closed her eyes, trying to commit the word to memory. The way it sounded on his breath. On his tongue. In his perfect accent, honed in extravagant schools and the halls of Parliament, where he spoke for those who had no voice.

"Henry," she whispered back, wincing at the way her emotion revealed her truth. The jagged cobblestones of Lambeth. The twisting, uneven steps of the South Bank.

The raw education of the thousands of pockets she'd picked.

The rotten, soiled past reaching its tendrils up to remind her she could never have forever with someone like him. That this—whatever it was, whatever it might become—would mark him if it ever became public. The daughter of the leader of London's largest crime ring, born in the gutter and raised in the streets, her proudest accomplishment her nimble fingers—a South Bank pickpocket. And a *duke*.

It was laughable.

Don't laugh, she willed him. *Not yet.*

Give us a little more time.

She was lost to him and to this, to his rare smiles and his strong arms and his pride and his *goodness*.

After all this time, Adelaide had found a good man. And she would take a moment with him over a lifetime without him, without hesitation. She would be with him for as long as he'd have her, and count herself lucky to inhabit even a small, secret corner of his life. And when the time came, she would let him go, free and clear, and ignore the hole in her chest where her heart used to be.

Her decision made, his hand stroked down her spine, his touch holding her like a breath. And then he asked, "Where is my box?"

Chapter Nineteen

As they lay there, the light shifting through the room, moving from morning to bright noonday sun, Henry marveled at the quiet of the countryside, and breathed in the smells of the autumn in the world beyond the windows, and wondered how much it would cost to buy this little house on this little hill in this little town and live here with Adelaide for as long as it took to convince her to be his.

He would follow her wherever she chose—give her whatever she wished. He would live in her apartments above The Place if she liked—if Maggie O'Tiernen would suffer a duke as a tenant.

Whatever Adelaide wanted, it was hers. He'd make sure of it.

He opened his mouth to offer it. To ask her to be his, to spend her life by his side. But, what would he be asking? He disliked the term *mistress*, and the way it carried ownership and impermanence with it. There was nothing impermanent about what he wanted with this glorious woman.

And as for ownership. He did not fool himself into believing he would own her. Not when he was so thoroughly hers.

He knew how she thought of her life in Lambeth. Knew she considered it a mark against her. And he would never give Adelaide even a moment of believing she was not worthy of all of it. Marriage. The title. A collection of babies—preferably little girls with hair like fire and eyes like velvet and a wicked sense of justice.

With a deep, piercing ache, he knew that he wanted all of that with Adelaide. And he knew that he could not have it.

He couldn't bear for there to be any misunderstanding between them about *why*, however.

So, it was time for her to open the box.

When he asked for it, her eyes went wide with surprise, as though it was the last thing in the world she'd expected him to ask, but she didn't hesitate. Finding her spectacles on the side table, she slid out of bed, leaving him aching for her as she crossed the room to fetch it.

"You could have taken it from me at any point," he said as she returned to him.

"Would you believe I have been distracted by other things?"

He smiled, a thrum of arrogant pleasure coursing through him. "By me." He'd seen the tears in her eyes when he woke, though. Had held her in his arms as she'd shaken with relief. This woman felt something for him. And he was not about to turn it away.

She extended the box to him, and he shook his head. "You do it. I'll teach you."

The wary look in her eyes was unmistakable and he knew she was worried about what truths he might demand in exchange for tips about the cube, but before he could speak, she gave him a little, uncertain smile and said, "As I said when we began it, I am an open book."

Henry was through with the game, despite desperately wanting to play it. He'd been drinking in the little bits of her, tiny moments of revelation, filled with skirts tied with beautiful ribbons and secret passageways behind paintings of shield-maidens and kisses on bridges. She liked Westminster Bridge. He'd buy it for her, dammit.

But the little sips of her were no longer enough. He wanted to bathe in her.

First, he'd show her that he would never ask for more than she was willing to give. That he would be the only person with whom she did not have to perform. He lifted his chin in the direction of the box she held. "Show me what you remember."

She made quick work of the mechanism, remembering each step without hesitation, until she landed where she'd been before, a narrow cylinder in her hand. "It doesn't open," she said, more to herself than to him. "I thought it might be a key."

"It's not so simple," he replied, wanting her to keep talking. Wild about the way she turned the puzzle over in her mind.

And then, his brilliant lady touched the tip of the obsidian cylinder to the exterior of the box. And gasped. "It's a magnet!"

He wanted to kiss the delight from her lips. "It is."

With supreme focus, she ran it across the box. "It sticks in some places, but not others." Her eyes found his, bright with triumph. "It's a maze. The key is *inside*."

It took her no time to find the place where the magnet collected an item on the inside of the cube, nor to trace the large letter C that filled one side of the cube with slow, sure patience, until she reached the bottom of the curve and a little *click* sounded. Her lips twisted into the prettiest smile he'd ever seen, triumphant and sweet and enough to make him want to toss the box across the room and take her back to bed.

She'd found another latch, a seam along the edge of the box popping open, allowing her to slide a piece of wood from its mooring there, releasing what appeared to be the top of the cube.

"Be careful now." He couldn't stop himself from helping.

She looked to him, her gaze tangling with his for a

moment and searching for clues. He didn't give them to her. Instead, he gave her a dozen other things—hoping she would understand them. Pride. Pleasure. Adoration. Desire. A promise that when she was through with the puzzle, if she set the box aside and asked him to make love to her, he would do it without question.

Because in that moment, he belonged to her. She was discovering his secrets just as much as she was discovering the secrets of the box. And for the first time in his life, Henry felt clear to share them. She worked on the box, her touch gentle and seeking and soft—enough to make him wish she was working on him instead. When she lifted the panel, it revealed a second wall inside, a smooth piece of oak painted like a starfield, that looked at first glance as though it was a red herring.

Except it wasn't. There were three small circles inlaid in the painted wood, beautifully decorated: a sun marked with a swirling L, a moon with a C, a planet surrounded by rings with an H. Not just circles. Buttons.

"Careful," he said again, steel in the word.

She understood immediately. "The wrong button will destroy the contents."

His blue eyes found hers and his pride was overpowered with something else. Admiration. *Fire*. She thought for a moment, one fingertip coming to tap at her lower lip, making him want to lean forward and take it between his teeth, to kiss her until she was panting with pleasure. Unaware of the direction of his thoughts, she quickly understood what she faced. "Ink?"

He nodded. "Clever girl."

"The benefit to being a lifelong thief. I've seen traps like this before." Her brow furrowed. "Do you not wish to ask me a question?"

"I wish to ask you a thousand of them." The truth. "But not now."

"And what, I will owe you?"

The question made him want to rage. Who had taught her this? That every moment with another person was a transaction? Who had made her believe that she had to give up pieces of herself for others? "Adelaide," he said, quietly. "You owe me nothing. Do you understand? You saved my life. You healed me and sat vigil as I mended and you still think I will ask you payment for a piece of me. You owe me *nothing*."

She shook her head. "I don't understand."

He did kiss her then, stealing the caress, licking into her mouth, stroking deep before retreating to send a slow, lingering lick along her bottom lip. "You're so close," he whispered. "Finish it."

For a heartbeat, she appeared to consider kissing him again instead of working on the puzzle, and Henry wondered if they might be able to pause her activities to do just that. But before he could suggest they make good on her desires, she spoke, her fingertip barely running over the box. "H is for Henry."

He nodded. "But it is not my box."

"C is for . . . Clayborn?"

"My father. But it's not his box, either."

She tilted her head and studied him, the box nearly forgotten in her hands. "Whose box is it?"

He suddenly felt more sorrow for his father than he had in a decade. In longer. "It was my mother's. He made it for her. To keep what is inside."

"Henry," she said, the puzzle forgotten as she lifted her hand to his face, tracking her thumb across his cheekbones. "I'm so sorry."

"I was ten when she died. Too late to forget her, too early to really remember her. She's shadows and feelings and warmth and beauty in my memories. But I can't quite reach them."

She nodded. "I did not know my mother, but sometimes I think I remember her."

Yes. It was like that. He clung to the words—to the

truth in them and the little piece of her she'd shared. He lifted his chin toward the box. "Press it. L for Laura."

She did, and the top sprang open. "Henry," she said softly. Different than earlier, when she spoke with pity. This one sounded remarkably like awe. "It's *beautiful*."

She was beautiful.

"Every birthday, he'd build us a new one and hide something inside." She turned to face him, her eyes light with interest, setting the unlocked, unopened cube on the bed between them. "Sometimes they would take hours to open. Jack always got frustrated and wandered off."

She smiled. "Not you, though."

He shook his head. "Not me. I loved the mystery of them. The challenge. I loved the way they revealed their secrets only once I'd proven myself." He looked to her. "I still do." He didn't say more. Didn't tell her that he would do whatever was required to prove himself to her.

She knew it. She had to.

"What was inside them?"

"Trinkets. A coin. A length of new fishing twine. A sack of lemon candies." He gave a little laugh. "That's why Jack always gave up. He thought the real gift was whatever was wrapped in paper and string."

"You knew better."

"I've never been interested in what's easy." He indicated the box. "This one is the most complex he ever made. Ours never had security measures."

Because it kept a secret that he'd never wanted revealed. She reached between them and lifted the box, moving it several inches toward him. "Thank you for teaching me."

His brows rose. "You don't want to know what's inside? What's so valuable that a notorious gang of thieves was hired to steal it? What kind of secret might be able to do in the Duke of Clayborn?"

"No," she said. "Some secrets are not for me."

This one was, though. This one, he wanted her to

have—the proof that he would stand with her, at her side, facing whatever came, for as long as she'd have him. Proof, too, that he could not marry her.

She would understand when she saw. He pushed the box toward her. "Open it."

Something flashed in her eyes. Something honest and urgent. "Henry—if I do . . . I need you to know . . . whatever it is . . . I'll never use it."

"I know," he said. "But even if you did—I would not regret giving it to you. I would not regret this moment. This time, here in this place."

"But . . . I deal in secrets."

He caught her cheek in one hand and leaned forward, kissing the whisper from her lips. "This one comes with no charge."

She opened the box just as he had a hundred times before her, marveling at the little tray within, suspended beneath a vial of blue ink that would have snapped in two if she'd pressed the wrong button, rendering the square of paper seated in the tray unreadable.

He watched as she inspected the mechanism, and reveled in her smile as she recognized how it worked. When she pronounced, "This is very clever," Henry found he wanted her to feel the same way about him, and vowed to do his best to impress her every day, as long as she'd have him.

Removing the paper, she lifted the tray to reveal a tiny compartment within, just large enough for a second wooden box, this one filigreed with an elaborate L. She hesitated, and something tightened in Henry's throat at the pause. At her respect. Her understanding that what was within was the most valuable thing he could give her.

"Go on," he said, the words coming ragged.

Her eyes found his, wide with concern, but she did as she was told, lifting the box and opening it, revealing his mother's wedding ring, a thin band of the greenest emeralds Henry had ever seen.

"It's stunning," she said, running her fingers over the jewels.

"Emeralds for her eyes . . . one of the few things I remember about her," he said. "Her green eyes. *Like spring, every minute*, my father would say."

Adelaide smiled at the little story. "When you say you believe in love, it is because of them."

He nodded toward the paper she'd removed, and held his breath as she lifted the square carefully, unfolding the thirty-six-year-old parchment. He knew what she read. Had read it so many times himself that he'd committed it to memory.

Dearest L—

This is likely not the letter you wished to receive, or at least, it is not from the sender from whom you no doubt wished to receive it. And yet, it is imperative I write to say all the things that I wished to say this morning. The things you would not let me offer—in your misguided belief that I was acting too much a gentleman.

What I feel now, in this moment, is nothing like gentle. I am full of anger for how you have been left. Full of rage for how you have been hurt. And full of hope for how you might heal.

I have spent a lifetime knowing you. A lifetime loving you. And now, if you will have me, I wish to spend a lifetime by your side, as father to your children. What I have, I offer to you—a home, a hearth, and a future.

I have never put much stock in the title; I have always believed that how a man lives is far more valuable than what the world calls him. But I find myself willing to make every possible argument in the hope that you will accept my offer. If it is land you wish for the babe, or wealth for him, or title, that is my

*offer. Consider him there, with you, already my heir.
Already with a father who will be filled with pride at
his every accomplishment.*

*Here is all of it: you may have all that is mine if
only you wish it. All I wish is a future that we might
together call ours.*

*Yours, always,
Clayborn*

"Clayborn," she said when she reached the end, tracing one finger over the signature, once bold and passion-
ate and now faded with the years.

"My father," he explained, though he did not have to.
"Well, not my real father. The father who raised me."

"No. *Your real father,*" she insisted, looking up from
the letter, tears in her eyes.

The ache in Henry's chest grew tighter as he reached
for her, wanting to stop the tears, one of which spilled
over, down her cheek, leaving tracks along her beautiful
skin. He brushed it away with his thumb and whispered,
"Love, no . . ."

She shook her head. "I'm sorry—it is so . . . This is
so . . ."

He nodded. "It is beautiful."

"He loved her so much." She looked back down. "And
you—my God, Henry. The way he loved you . . . even
before you were born."

"I didn't know," he said. "There was never a moment
in my childhood when he was not my father. Not even
when Jack, the son of his blood, was born."

"You were every bit as much his as Jack was. This letter is nothing if not proof of that," she said with a smile.
"I imagine he was an insufferable father, crowing about
his lad to all who would listen after you were born."

He let himself laugh. "From what I hear, I was walking at four months. Reading at six."

"Of course you were," she said, looking back to the letter with a wistful look that made him feel the same—longing for a past that he would never know.

For a future he'd never imagined.

Until her.

"She married him. Of course."

He nodded. "She was the daughter of a landed gentleman my father was in business with in a town not far from the country estate. She believed another when he told her he would stay. He did not."

"She was not the first to believe pretty words. Nor will she be the last," Adelaide said.

"My father—he loved her enough for both of them. He made the box for her when I was born," he explained quietly, wanting her to understand. "So she could keep his promise safe. So she would always remember he'd take care of us." He paused. "We should have destroyed it. But . . ."

She shook her head. "I would never be rid of it. It's too beautiful."

"The last I have of them, together." He went quiet for a moment, memories crashing over him. And then, "I do not know who my father is. He could have been anyone."

"Do you wish you did?"

He had considered the possibility before, of course. "Over the years, there have been more than a few times when I've wondered if I could find him. What I would say to him if I did."

"And?"

He shook his head. "I had a father, and I would trade every question I have for the man who sired me for five more minutes with the man who raised me." He paused. "I should like to know I made him proud." He'd never said such a thing to anyone before, not even to Jack. But for some reason, it came easily with Adelaide.

Perhaps because he wished to make her proud, too.

"You did," she said without hesitation. Without doubt.

"You made him so very proud before he died, I'm sure of it. And now . . . if he could see you as the world does . . . as I do . . ." She smiled. "His boy. His family. Not born of blood," she said. "Born of love. Of care."

"I'm not the only one with a family like that," he agreed. "Yours as well. In these past few days, I've seen the kinds of friends you collect. The Duchess, Miss O'Tiernen, Gwen. Lucia."

She nodded. "I am very lucky to have made a family of friends in the years since I left the South Bank. And still . . ."

He waited for her to finish, knowing not to push. Finally, she looked down at the letter in her hands—the one in which his father changed a destiny. "This—she was his sun."

As Adelaide might be to Henry.

As she was, already.

Like that, he understood. He saw his father's life with perfect clarity. Saw, too, how his mother had blessed him. Blessed them all.

How he, too, might be blessed. "What a gift she gave him," he said. "A family to love. To be proud of."

Adelaide nodded. "And the gift he gave to you. His love. His support." She pressed a soft kiss to his lips.

Let me give you the same.

They looked at each other for a long time, and he would have given anything to hear her thoughts before she finally said, "No wonder you are such a man. So vocal in Parliament. Using every bit of your voice to speak for children who have not been so lucky."

"I think any decent person with sense and a shred of humanity would do as I have done if they saw the conditions in which these children live."

She shook her head. "Plenty see it and say nothing. Do nothing."

He cleared the lump in his throat, the relief that someone finally understood. "My mother would have been cast out. From her family. From her community. And me with her. We could just as easily have found ourselves in a workhouse than in an ancestral home. I could have just as easily not have become a duke." A pause. Then, "And there is the fact that I am not a duke. Not really."

"What does that even mean? Not really? You've the name and the title, the letters of patent."

"And another letter. One that tells the truth. That though I was born to married parents, I am not my father's son."

Thunder flashed in her eyes. "Bollocks." She raised the letter. "Trust me, as someone who spent a childhood with a father who thought of me as nothing but money in the coffers, the idea of a father claiming his children with such certainty, with such . . . *devotion* . . . Henry—what could be more legitimate?"

Her enormous brown eyes were on him, full of urgent concern. "This man—he loved you unconditionally. And your mother as well. What a glorious truth to hold close."

"When he told me—" he began, then stopped, the memory of that day coming on a flood of shame. "I was furious." She stilled, watching him without judgment, and he pressed on. "I was fourteen, and home from school. An absolute monster. Entitled and full of bluster and certain that I knew everything there was to know about the world."

"An aristocratic man in the making," she said with a gentle tease.

"My father was nothing like that. He was . . ." He searched for a word.

She lifted the letter in her hand. "I know him."

"You do," he agreed. "That letter—it was the heart of him. And I was too angry to see it. I was so furious with him—I blamed him for lying to us. For telling us at all. For burdening me with the truth—and the knowledge that if anyone found out, it would mark us forever."

"But it wouldn't. They were married when you were born. You were his son." She paused. "Are. You *are* his son."

"He died three years after he told me. And I was still angry. Because his secrets were mine, and they made me a fraud."

"They most certainly did *not*," Adelaide said, the words loud enough to startle him. He met her eyes, flashing with frustration and righteous outrage. "I think they made you more a duke than any of the others who wander the halls of the House of Lords. I think they made you strong and noble and kind and decent." The words were soft, but full of steel, as though if anyone wandered in to disagree, Adelaide would happily hand him his head before seeing him out. "I think you have spent a lifetime trying to prove that you were worthy of a title that is nothing close to worthy of you. And I think the man who wrote this letter would be so very proud of you, Henry Carrington, Duke of Clayborn. Son. And brother. Prince among men."

She was magnificent in her anger, and it occurred to Henry that anyone who had Adelaide on his side—in battle or in life—would be immensely lucky.

"I am sorry that he was not able to see what you would become," she said, reaching for him, tracing over his skin, down his arm to his hand, where she laced her fingers through his, the movement full of all the truth the words carried.

He lifted her hand to his lips, pressing kisses along her knuckles. "Thank you."

She let him linger for a moment, watching him worship her hands, before adding, "The only thing I do not understand is why you will not marry."

"Adelaide, the storm that would come for me in that scenario—I would not lose the title, but I would lose everything else. Reputation. Community. Respect. Any woman would regret loving me when it came."

"Why, because the world might think you less a duke, because your father was more a man?"

"That's not all of it."

"Tell me the rest," she said, fairly vibrating with her affront. He reached for her, drawn to her fury on his behalf, his fingers sliding into the curls that made her an avenging angel.

"When I was ten, Jack was born. He is the image of my father."

She stilled, immediately understanding. "Henry."

"No—" he said. "I know what you will say."

"And you should hear it. *You are Clayborn.* The law says it. Your parents were wed when you were born. Your father claimed you as his. That makes you legitimate." She brandished the letter. "This man—he would have wanted you to claim it."

"You misunderstand," he said softly. "It is not that my father did not wish me for heir. He did. He was the best of men—and I never for a moment doubted his love, which is why I was so angry when he told me the truth. He never cast me out. I cast myself out."

She shook her head. "Why?"

"Because Jack . . ." He sighed, searching for the right words. "I do not pass it to him because of the circumstances of my birth. I pass it because of the circumstances of his." He looked away from her. "He is *theirs.* Born of love. Is that not the best way to continue the line?"

"Henry," she said softly, reaching for him, holding him tight. "He was born of their love, and you were raised in it." She kissed him, soft and sweet. Still there, surrounding him, even now, with his secrets revealed. "And what of that? Do you not deserve children born of love?"

Those babies again. That collection of fire-haired, bespectacled little girls. A serious boy or two in the mix. Something tightened in his chest. "I did not think much of them until recently. Until you."

Something flashed in her enormous brown eyes.

Something soft and quickly shuttered. "I have thought of them recently, too." She pressed her lips to his again, then whispered, "But I cannot promise you children. All I can promise you is myself. For as long as it suits us both."

It was an offer. She'd made it before.

Marriage isn't the only path.

"And what, we hide from the world?"

To his surprise, she laughed. "I have only ever hidden from the world, Henry." He didn't like that, but before he could say so, she pressed on. "Think of it. We would be harming no one, and I cannot think it immoral for two adults who want one another to have one another. I do not need a benefactor: no money need change hands. I have my own income, work I do not wish to part with—a world to change from Covent Garden."

Her girls. Her shield-maidens.

"And you . . ." she continued. "You've a wide world to change from Parliament. And this way—we can taste all of it."

It was meant to tempt him.

Surely, plenty of men had played this game over the years. Had taken partners in secret. Had loved and grown old and had families with them. The world gave men a wide swath of opportunity for it. But Adelaide, who'd spent her life alone in the turret on Westminster Bridge, keeping herself safe, trading bits of herself for fear of being cast aside—it was not enough.

She deserved so much more from the world.

From him.

"I straddle two worlds, Henry, one foot in the muck of Lambeth and one in the ballrooms of Mayfair. Neither fits me." She shrugged one shoulder. "It's a strange half-life that never seemed to have a path that would lead to this. But this path, I can walk it."

There was another path, though. She could find a decent man who could give her a full future. A full heart. All she deserved.

And still, he was greedy for her, wanting to say yes. Wanting to take everything he could have of her. Whatever pieces he could carve off.

Hoard.

Before he could find the words to explain, Adelaide was once again lost to the letter.

"Wait. I *stole* the box. I stole it, and the letter within, from The Bully Boys, who stole it from you—for someone. Alfie Trumbull does not steal puzzles for sport—and I do not imagine he would care one bit if he knew the truth about you, other than to blackmail you with it until you were bled dry. But even that is not my father's preferred sport. Which means someone hired him to get it, and paid him well to burgle it from Mayfair. He knows better than to draw the attention of Scotland Yard."

He nodded. "Havistock." She recoiled at the name as he pressed on. "The Marquess of Havistock was a childhood friend of my father's. *Friend*," he spat. "My father was a decent man who led too much with kindness. Believed too much in others. Thought Havistock the kind of friend he could trust, and showed him the letter. The box. The ring."

"*No*," she said. "A man like Havistock—he would use this to get whatever he wanted. Forever."

She shook her head. "But there isn't a whisper of this in your brother's file. For all Havistock disdained your parents—he never spoke of it."

"I don't think it mattered to him. Until recently."

"Why now?" He didn't have to reply. She divined the answer almost as soon as the question had left her lips. Her turn to be clever. "Child labor. He wished to stop your campaign, which threatens his workhouses."

He shouldn't be surprised, and yet, "How did you know about them?"

"Havistock has a file, too. And it's not full of gambling debts and idiocy. It's thick as my thumb, and filled with a score of activities that, though not illegal, are most certainly immoral."

"Including employing children in his factories," he said.

"Yes, well, *employing* is not the word I would use for the way he treats them, and the little he pays them."

"And there's nothing to be done. It's not illegal. But it will be," he vowed. "Unless Havistock finds a way to turn Parliament against me."

"By making you a scandal."

He nodded. "I wouldn't lose the title, but I would lose all its influence. The cause would be set back years. Longer."

"And the only reason why it hasn't been revealed already . . ."

He met her gaze. ". . . is because you stole it."

She adjusted her spectacles, unable to resist the quip. "You may thank me any time."

They shouldn't joke. And still, he liked her too much not to. And she liked him, too. He flashed her a smile. "I intend to. Thoroughly."

She leaned in and kissed him, long and sweet, like a treasure, drugging him with her softness and the scent of her, thyme and fresh rain. When they parted, he said, "I was afraid of that box, of its contents, for so long. I made to destroy it a thousand times, knowing that it was a risk to let it exist. But I couldn't, because it proved that love existed. That it was good and worthy and true. And so I took the risk."

He kissed her again, unable to stop himself from stealing another moment with her. Another piece of her here, in this magical place. "All that time, I thought the truth of that letter would weigh heavy when it was released. And instead . . . because of you . . . I am free of it."

Staring deep into his eyes she said, "Why did you let me keep the box? Why did you let me open it?" There had been a dozen moments when he could have emptied it, and she knew it. "Why did you leave the letter there?"

He'd asked himself the question a dozen times. Told himself it was because the letter was safer there than it was on his person. But it wasn't the truth. "I wanted you to know," he said, finally. "I wanted to trust someone with it. I wanted that someone to be you."

She shook her head, and he knew what she was going to say before she said it. "I'm a thief."

He reached for her, pulling her to him, willing her to understand all the ways she was a marvel. "You think I don't know that?" He said, "You stole me that first day, on the docks. The first time you kissed me."

She pressed her forehead to his and closed her eyes. "I intended to give you back."

"Impossible. I'll never allow it."

"So imperious." Something flashed in her eyes even as she smiled. Something he wanted to banish from her thoughts. Something he wanted to banish from their time together.

She kissed him then, long and lush, and somehow sad and urgent—a kiss that left his chest tight with fear that it might be the last one. And when it was over, he said the only thing left to say to this woman who had stolen his heart.

"I let you keep the box because I trust you." Another kiss, like a reward. "I let you keep it because I wanted you to have a piece of me that no one else has ever had." And another, like a temptation.

Tempting him to tell her everything. "Adelaide, I let you keep it because I love you."

Chapter Twenty

The confession was raw and beautiful, and Adelaide did not know what to do with such a gift, so she did what she had done for her whole life and escaped it. She left the bed, reminding herself that they required food and drink.

In the kitchens, she filled a plate with ham and cheese and apple and spoonfuls of mustard and pickle that had been left in the stores, trying the whole time to forget what he'd said. How it had sent a current of excitement through her.

How it had made her believe in a future with him.

In her lifetime, Adelaide had never been a coward. But when she returned to the room, plate piled high, to discover Henry up and washed once more, a shirt pulled over his head, hiding bandages and muscles, she found she could not look him in the eye. She was too full of a dozen emotions, none of which was pleasant, and she feared that if he saw them, he would come for them. Vanquish them. Chase them away.

Foolish Adelaide; he came for her anyway. Crossing the room the moment she entered, relieving her of her burden and pulling her to him, tilting her chin up so he could look past her spectacles into her eyes and read her thoughts. And then, without a word, he tugged her into his lap, refusing to let her hide.

Somehow, impossibly, she didn't mind, because Adelaide had never been interested in hiding from him, not from the first moment she'd met him. Not since. It was why she'd gone head-to-head with him the first time they'd ever met. Why she watched him in Mayfair ballrooms, willing him to see her. Why she had kissed him on the dock, why she had challenged him to a race across Britain, why she had stayed there in that house for days, waiting for him to wake. Waiting for him to see her.

Which he'd done from the start.

So she let him pull her into his lap and hold her tight as he ate the food she'd prepared for him. Of course she did. Because of all the strange, uncomfortable, wonderful emotions he evoked, the one she was able to name—willing to name—was desire.

She desired him. This. And not in the way she'd been trained to think of desire. Not in covetous gazes, quick and hot. She desired him in a cool, steady stream, like a balm. And it was a balm when he touched her, soothing aches that she'd never noticed until he was there, that she'd had for a lifetime.

His hunger had returned, and Adelaide delighted in watching him eat, loving the knowledge that she nourished him in some small way—giving this magnificent man a bit of herself, risking it.

This cannot last, she tried to remind herself, again and again, but the words of warning were washed away every time he paused to feed her little tastes, the best morsels from his plate, as though she were a prize to be won. A treasure to be held.

As though it was he who nourished her.

He loved her.

So she looked to that magnificent man who made her feel magnificent, too, and said, "I want to trust you. I want to know what it's like."

He stilled, a piece of cheese in hand, halfway to her mouth. His eyes found hers, serious and searching, and a muscle in his cheek twitched, as though he had a thousand things to say. Finally, he settled on one. "Please."

She took his hand in hers, accepting the food he'd been about to offer her, using the time it took to eat to consider how to tell him all the things she wished him to know, even as she knew her story would end whatever she might have dreamed.

"You asked about information. About why I collect it. Why conversations with me feel like they must be bought and paid for."

He shook his head, passing a hand over her back. "You don't have to explain it."

"I think . . ." She paused. "I think I want to."

Back and forth, his fingers trailed over the thin lawn of her chemise, ignoring the ridge she knew he could feel there, knew he'd found before. He was no fool; he would not be surprised to discover it was part of her story. Indeed, it was Adelaide who was surprised, because she had never imagined she'd speak of it to anyone.

"I do not know where to begin."

His hand was still there, at her back, stroking. "Your father is Alfie Trumbull."

Her gaze shot to his. "How did you—"

"Our visitors at the Hungry Hen."

"You were half dead."

"Excuse me, I was not."

She slid him a look, but did not argue.

"I might have been worse for wear, but my hearing was in pristine order."

He'd known. All this time, he'd known who her father was. And still, he'd made love to her. Still, he'd held her in his arms and fed her and touched her and listened to her. Trusted her.

Loved her.

Impossible. He must not understand. "Alfie doesn't just own a warehouse in Lambeth. He's the leader of The Bully Boys. The gang is literally named for him."

"Two rival gangs, brought together by a fearsome leader." This, too, he knew. "The scourge of South London. Believe it or not, they've come up in Parliament a time or two."

"And you've paid attention?"

He looked positively offended.

"Apologies," she said instantly. "Of course you did. You're you."

"That, and my brother has been in debt to them on more than one occasion."

She shook her head. "Your brother is not very intelligent."

"I am hoping his new bride will sort that out." He fed her a slice of apple. "He is the handsome brother, though, so at least he has that."

She smiled. "What with you being so ghastly looking." Even bruised and bloodied and full of half-healed wounds, he was the handsomest thing she'd ever seen.

"Not anymore."

"No?"

He shook his head and said, "Not now that my nose is broken."

She laughed, and the moment was a gift—a calm before the storm she was about to loose. "My father—he was . . . a king. He has never owned a single thing he did not believe he might one day sell for more than he paid. Everything had a price, and Alfie Trumbull's goal was to demand the highest one. Always. Everything in his possession, everyone in his employ—if they did not hold monetary value, they were not for Alfie." She paused, then added, "And that included me."

His touch stuttered on its path down her spine, just barely. Just enough that she looked to him again, finding his eyes clouded with something she might like if she were willing to think on it.

"My being his daughter wasn't enough. I needed to pull weight."

"So you became a pickpocket."

She nodded. "A nipper. Lots of girls did—when you're small and fast, you've a better chance of cutting a purse and not being caught."

He nodded. "And you were good."

She couldn't stop her proud grin. "Aye," she said, letting the South Bank into the words. "Stickiest fingers in all South London. Mayfair never saw me coming."

He laughed. "They deserved what they got, I assure you."

"Toffs never expect it inside their own circles. And let me tell you," she underscored, "there are a half-dozen people with titles who are cutpurses themselves."

His brows rose. "Really?"

She ticked them off on her fingers. "Oxford. Tillborn. Lady Weatherby."

He was astonished. "They're good?"

"No, they're terrible. They'd be knifed inside of two minutes in Lambeth. But like I said, toffs never expect it inside their own circles. And unlike the rest of us, aristocrats don't get caught."

His grip tightened on her hip. "You've been caught?"

"You don't get to be the best cutpurse on the South Bank without learning what happens if you fail."

"Tell me."

She risked a look at him to find him there, watching her. For a moment, she searched his gaze, sure she'd find judgment. Instead, she found him, open and welcome. A man who'd shared his own secrets, thinking they were dark. Not knowing what a secret might be. "Sunlight is the enemy of most criminals, but it was always my friend. I cut most of my purses early in the morning, when the sun was just peeping over the rooftops, turning the whole filthy place to gold. The pockets were light from nights of drinking, but easier to take. Drunk and tired marks made for stupid ones. And I learned early to take advantage." She paused. "That, and if I made my quota early in the day, I could spend the rest of the day doing as I pleased."

"Exploring London's bridges?"

"Every one of them," she said. "'Course, it was the bridges that got me into trouble." She lifted a bit of food from the plate and nibbled at it, taking the excuse to think. "I mistakenly thought that early morning in Mayfair would be the same as early morning in Lambeth."

He sucked in a breath, even as she gave a little laugh. "The mark caught me the second I sliced his purse."

"How old were you?"

"Eight."

He went hard like stone, every muscle in his body tensing, and she looked at him. "Henry—"

"I want his name." The words came on a scrape, like carriage wheels on cobblestones.

"For what, punishment?"

"Damn right."

She gave a little laugh. "You're so righteous."

"You were a child."

"And you know better than most that such a thing did not matter."

His eyes were dark with fury, his words clipped when he asked, "What happened?"

"The magistrate took pity on me."

"Released you."

She cut him a look. "No. He gave me sixteen days."

"Sixteen—" He stopped, his fists clenching. "Christ, Adelaide. In jail."

She nodded.

"I'm going to find that bastard and destroy him. I'll end him alongside his friend who thought to send an eight-year-old to the magistrate."

She couldn't help the warmth that flooded her at his angry words. "You think to destroy every person who has ever harmed me?"

"Yes." The response was instant and categorical.

What would her life have been if she'd had this man by her side from the start? What a partner he would have made. Would make. What a father.

A vision flashed, a row of dark-haired, blue-eyed moppets, each one so loved. So cared for, with their father the duke watching over them. Their father, and their mother, who would be his match in all things. Pretty and perfect and pristine—born graceful and sweet-tempered. Adelaide's opposite.

"Where was your gang?" he asked, unaware of the riot of thoughts in her head.

She swallowed around the knot in her throat. Focused on the story. "Alfie was outside when I was released."

"Your father came when you were released? Not before?"

"What could he have done?"

"I would have torn the place down, brick by brick, until they released you."

She smiled. "And they might have let you, Duke."

Perhaps he did not deserve the gentle reminder of his position, but Adelaide gave it anyway, to remind him of how distant they were from each other. To remind herself, she finished the story. "Alfie was there to give out my second punishment." He froze, but she kept going. "Punishment for getting caught."

His fingers found the long scar on her back. Settled. "This?"

"No." She shook her head. "*That* was the second time I was caught," she said. "I was greedy. A fur muff. I wanted it for my father's consort—the only one who was ever nice to me—for Christmas. He'd left her for a new girl, and she was heartbroken. I thought a muff would make her happy."

His chest tightened. "And?"

She smiled. "Tough to hide a woman's fur in a girl's skirts." She paused. "Fifteen lashes for the second infraction, and two months inside."

"God, Adelaide . . . Prison is no place for a child."

"Prison is no place for most of the people sent there," she replied. And she'd been in the section of the prison that was reserved for children. "After my second trip, I vowed never to return." She gave him a little smile. "I also vowed that I'd come for Mayfair eventually—the big fish I was determined to catch."

His brows rose. "And look at you now."

"Stealing kisses and secrets from dukes," she whispered, even as he was the one who stole the kiss that followed the words.

"And hearts," he added on a low rumble when he released her.

"Don't give me your heart," she urged him, softly. "I am not virtuous enough to return it."

He had to understand. She had to make him understand. If they could agree that being together would make more trouble than happiness, she could put this beautiful idyll behind her and let the rest of her life begin. He would become a dull ache—the kind that came in a long-broken bone when the weather changed. A distant memory from when she had fallen stupidly in love with a man she could not keep.

She forced herself to add, "So there it is; the worst of it."

Now you know why you shouldn't love me. Why there is no forever for us.

He nodded gravely for a moment and then said, "Now tell me the best of it."

Her brow furrowed. "The . . . best?"

"Tell me your happiest memory."

Had anyone ever asked her that? Worse, why was it so difficult to summon an answer? She thought for a long moment before settling on, "I do not dislike the memory of this morning." Her name on his tongue. His touch on her skin. Her body on his.

He smiled and kissed her temple. "Neither do I. But tell me one from before we knew each other."

"No," she said softly, not wanting to give up another piece of herself. "You don't understand. You can't know more of me."

"Why not? What if I wished to know all of you?"

She shook her head. "You can't. We . . . can't. Don't you see?" She felt frantic, as though she'd lost her way in a dark alley. Or worse, in the bright light of Mayfair. "*I* can't."

He was silent for a long moment, considering the words. *Please, Henry*, she begged silently. *Please understand. I must hold back enough of myself to be able to stand tall when you leave.*

And still, when he repeated his request, she was powerless to resist. "One happy memory. Give me that, at least."

He made it seem like a barely there thing, impossible to refuse even as they both knew the truth. That every time she peeled off a piece of herself and shared it with him . . . it was more difficult to imagine letting him go.

Still, she thought for a moment, looking for the kind of happy memories others discussed. Christmas feasts and birthday presents and holidays at the sea. But she'd had few of those things, and the ones she'd had were transactions—payment from her father for a decent haul or a quiet tongue. So none of them was really happy, because they didn't come free.

So she settled on, "I had a cat."

He tucked her into his chest and set his chin to the crown of her head. "Did it have a name?"

She smiled. "Tail."

"A very ordinary name," he teased.

"He was black, with little white socks and a white bit on the tip of his tail," she explained. "And a pink nose that looked like a heart." He smiled at the description— unnecessary to the story and somehow extremely important for him to know. "Once, my father's boys were hired to steal a shipment of illegal bourbon from a ship on the docks, and when it arrived, a handful of the cases were not bourbon at all. They were books."

He made an encouraging sound.

She waved a hand. "Cavendish and Austen and the Norse myths."

"The shield-maidens."

"Among others." She nodded. "My father wanted nothing to do with books; they held no value for him."

"So he gave them to you?"

"Of course not. He would never gift me with something I might be willing to trade for. Those books—they could have demanded a dozen more purses cut." She paused. "They were the first thing I ever stole from his warehouse."

"Mmm," he said, the sound warming her with its approval. "And that is the happiest memory? Stealing books out from under your father's nose?"

She gave a little laugh. "It wasn't meant to be, honestly, but now that you suggest it . . . I cannot say I did not enjoy it."

"Of course you did. You were free of him then. Of his rules. Free to take pleasure without having to pay for it."

She nodded, looking to him.

"Adelaide," he said, his thumb coming to stroke over her cheek. "Your joy—it should be free. It should come without taxes and tallies."

She put her head back to his chest then, afraid to face the words. Afraid of the truth—that if she asked, Henry would give her anything she wished. Free of charge.

He sighed, the heavy breath the only sign of his disappointment that she did not face him. There was no hint of it when he asked, "And what of Tail?"

Her fingertips stroked along his arm, playing with the crisp hair there. "Tail is the happy memory. I snuck those books into my bedchamber like treasure—lined the underside of my mattress with them. And at night, I would light a small candle and devour them, while Tail lay on my chest and purred." She paused, lost to the memory of those nights, when books had transported her from the real world and its threats and promises.

One of Henry's large hands slid down her spine, warm and heavy and perfect. "A book, a bed, and a cat is all it takes, is it?"

She snuggled closer. "A duke might do in a pinch."

The words were out before she could stop them. Before she could stop him from breathing her in, lips at her temple and nose in her hair. "Thank you," he whispered there. "For sharing it with me."

She wanted to share more with him. All the rest. Every tiny moment of joy. Every time she'd been the first into a snowfall. The taste of the lemon buns in the bakeshop by Lambeth Palace. The thrill of a successful pickpocketing. Instead, she said, "Those nights with book and cat and bed were the happiest I had. Before I became a . . ." She paused, the rest of the sentence surprising her.

His hand stilled low on her back. "A . . . ?"

She fiddled with a threadbare spot on the chemise she wore and considered the repercussions of her next words. He had trusted her with his secret, had he not? "A Belle."

He exhaled, the sound less surprised and more relieved. "So it's true what the papers say—that this gang of women exists."

"It's true. And can you blame us?"

"I suppose that explains the dossiers."

"The Matchbreaker serves several purposes."

"Let me guess."

She stayed quiet as he thought, eager for him to guess. Wanting him to be one of the few who understood.

"There's the obvious bit. Your group of women, bringing down the worst of men—those with unchecked power and nonexistent morals."

"We would not have to if Westminster would do it for us," she replied.

"Instead, you are called to service. And you put your-selves in harm's way." His brow furrowed. "You realize that if you are ever caught . . . if you are ever named as the Hell's Belles . . ." He pushed a lock of her hair back from her face. "Christ, Adelaide, I shall have to rethink Parliament. You need a body man."

She smiled at the words. "You've proven yourself a sound bruiser."

Frustration flashed on his handsome face. "Don't joke. What you play at—"

She leaned in and kissed him, slow and sweet as he deserved, this prince among men. "I know what we play at, Henry. Even if we were not exceedingly good at the game, I've played it for a lifetime, on my own."

"Not any longer."

Irritation flared. "You expect me to, what, wait for those in power to police themselves? To change the rules? That's a pretty suggestion, Duke, but while you make your speeches, the real world turns. And real peo-ple are caught in the balance."

She made to move off his lap, but he caught her. Kept her. "No, Adelaide. I don't mean that at all." She looked back to him, his beautiful blue eyes clear and honest. "I mean, not on your own any longer. Now you have me."

Adelaide caught her breath.

"I pledge you my sword, shield-maiden. Let me fight with you. For you. Beside you."

Oh.

This man. He would break her if she was not careful. He would destroy her with his vows and his promises and his beautiful eyes and his warm touch and the way he noticed her.

She almost believed him and the promise he delivered. God knew she wanted to. But she knew the truth—she was lucky enough to have had him here, now, for a time. Like a dream.

She ought to send Danny a note of thanks.

"Henry—" she began, but he cut her off, as though he knew what she was going to say.

"Tell me the rest. To tear these men down, to pull them from their pedestals . . . You need access to their information. Some of that comes from your friends, to be sure. But dinner parties don't bring access to secrets. Not the important ones."

She nodded, allowing him the change of topic. "No one has looser lips than a woman attempting to escape a bad match."

"So you build the dossiers about the poorly chosen bridegrooms . . . like Jack . . . and collect the real secrets in the balance?"

"There are secrets and there are secrets," she said, wanting him to understand that the circumstances of his birth were not what the Belles were after. "We're after the secrets that should bring a man down. The ones that should spell ruin. Building a file on Jack was easy enough—and it gave us access to Helene, who . . . has a secret of her own."

His attention sharpened on her. "What kind of secret?"

She shook her head. She could not tell him everything. Not without knowing Helene was safe. "The kind that sends peers to prison."

He went to steel at the words, immediately identifying the villain. "Adelaide, you cannot go head-to-head with Havistock. He's a monster. What he used to hide—what he hid from my father—now, he shows in full light. He sees the world changing and knows his time is borrowed. He's against a wall . . . and will destroy you if he has the chance."

She nodded. "That is precisely why we must go head-to-head with him, don't you see? No one else comes for these men. No one else brings them to justice."

He knew she was right. She could see it in his eyes. In the shadow of frustration there.

"Havistock built a fortune on the backs of the worst

of our sins—every one of them legal and every one of them corrupt," she said. He knew that. He saw the way the world twisted in knots to keep Havistock and his ilk out of trouble.

She went on. "But men like that . . . they don't stop at what's legal. And our work is to meet them there, when they overstep. At least when our justice is meted out, we are able to protect the innocent bystanders."

"Wives and children," he clarified.

"Children, often. Like Helene. Wives . . ." She inclined her head. "They're trickier."

"Proximity to power is a heady drug."

"Too many of them cannot see the truth." She nodded. "It is not unheard of that a wife might work in tandem with a wretched husband. Against her best interests."

"The long run will never hold sway the way the short run does," he said. "You're talking to a parliamentary reformer."

"I read a speech of yours once. In the *News*. About Newgate."

"About closing it. For good." He paused, lost in thought. And then he said, "I would take it all away if I could; I would spend my life erasing the memories, if you would let me."

She shook her head. "I don't want them erased."

"No?"

"No. Henry. Don't you see? They are fuel."

He hadn't seen, but in that moment, as she spoke the words, he seemed to.

"They forged me," she said softly. "A girl from Lambeth who should have married a brute and raised a generation of them. And instead . . ."

"A new path."

"A strange one," she said. "Without country—half on one side of the river, half on the other. And because of it, always untethered from both. No longer a South London nipper, not yet a North London darling."

"You're my North London darling," he said softly, stealing a kiss.

She grinned, and allowed it. "It's odd. Logically, I know that I have a place with the Belles. They're my crew, my family. And yet sometimes in my heart I fear that at any moment, they might decide I am not worth their time or energy. As though they might remember I do not belong."

Just as you will notice someday. She hated the thought—the way it paced through her, like a wild beast.

Silence fell between them—long enough that she finally looked to him.

Henry looked thunderous.

"Not worth their time? Adelaide—" He bit back whatever he was about to say. "You are a marvel in a dozen ways. A hundred of them. Your worth—it cannot be quantified. Not in time. Not in energy. The sheer enormity of it . . . My God, Adelaide, that you cannot see it makes me want to raze the whole of your father's empire to punish him for not showing it to you every day."

"I've heard worse ideas," came a voice from the doorway. "And it can certainly be arranged. But we've a larger, more pressing problem."

Adelaide and Henry snapped to attention, turning to the doorway to find the Duchess of Trevescan there, tall and blond and beautiful, her lush mauve skirts showing barely any sign of the days-long travel she must have endured to find them here.

Shocked, Adelaide made to stand, but Henry held her close and did not move. "I'm not sure you don't deserve a bit of punishment, too, Duchess."

The other woman looked to him, surprise in her eyes. "I confess, I am pleasantly surprised by your ferocity. I did not think you had it in you." Her cool blue gaze tracked over his bruises and bandages. "Though you have looked better, Clayborn."

She swept into the room, revealing that she was not alone. Imogen and Sesily followed her inside.

"Oh!" Imogen's brows rose and Adelaide imagined what her friends saw—her clad only in a chemise and spectacles, on Henry's lap.

"Ooh!" Sesily tossed her a delighted grin. "Well done, friend!"

Ignoring the excited pronouncement and her own flaming cheeks, Adelaide spoke directly to the unflappable Duchess. "What pressing problem?"

Duchess crossed the room and lifted the now open puzzle box, inspecting the mechanism within. "Lord Carrington and Lady Helene."

"I expect they are returning as Lord and Lady Carrington now," Henry said. "As I've been abed for five days."

"I imagine you have been," Sesily retorted from her place by the door.

Duchess slid a look at Sesily before saying, "They are not, in fact, returning."

Adelaide stilled, concern rioting through her. "What happened?"

"They are missing." She clapped her hands together once, firmly. "I think you ought to be properly dressed for this."

Chapter Twenty-One

The last time Henry had been in the kitchens of the house, Adelaide had knocked him out. Standing there again, surrounded by a collection of women he'd always thought fearless and now knew also to be fearsome, he was not certain unconsciousness was not a possibility once more.

It did not escape him that Adelaide had been ready to run from the room on numerous occasions since opening the puzzle box, and he knew without question that the trio of women who'd arrived would not hesitate for a moment to help her leave him if she asked.

Indeed, in the ten minutes it had taken him to dress and make his way down the stairs to the kitchens, her crew had situated themselves to protect her—she was at the far end of the room, by the stove, with the Duchess. Between there and the door, Lady Imogen and Lady Sesily sat at the large table. At his entrance, the women turned like a battalion of warriors protecting a prize. Shield-maidens, ready to thin the battlefield.

Adelaide might not understand the message they sent, might not believe it was on her behalf, but Henry did: If he wanted anywhere near her, he would have to go through them.

Which he would.

But first, he would be grateful that she had them by her side.

That, and he had questions that needed answers.

Addressing the foursome, he said, "Where is my brother?"

"It is not the first time you have misplaced him, is it?" the Duchess of Trevescan said, her icy blue gaze on his. "Nor is it the first time he's gone missing with Lady Helene in tow."

"Duchess—" Adelaide said, her tone sharp with warning. "Need I remind you that Henry was unconscious for the last four days and does not deserve your censure?"

"What of you then, Adelaide?" Duchess retorted. "Do you deserve my censure? After all, it was you who let the girl go to stay behind and protect *Henry* . . ."

Adelaide narrowed her gaze on the other woman. "I thought they were safe. It was an error in judgment."

Well. Henry didn't like that.

"You do not make errors in judgment," the Duchess replied, her cool words setting Henry on edge.

"Don't speak to her that way," he said.

Silence fell, and all four women looked to him, a range of emotions in their gazes.

Finally, the Duchess said, "Do not mistake me, Duke. Adelaide chose to stay back and keep you alive. My question is this: Are you worth it?"

"Likely not," he said, raising a brow in the direction of the woman all of London worshipped. "And yet, here I am."

"So we return to Adelaide's error in judgment." She paused, then added, "Dammit, this is what happens when we let men in."

He should have been annoyed. Instead, Henry rather imagined he was being initiated. And that wasn't annoying at all.

"That's enough, Duchess," Adelaide said, sending a searing look at her friend, who did not flinch.

"My brother is many things," Henry said, unable to keep the frustration from his tone. "He's a halfway decent fighter, absolutely terrible at cards, and far too trusting of the world at large. Lord knows he's made a fair number of mistakes, but he lacks artifice, and if he was headed to Gretna with the lady, he was headed to Gretna for marriage. Are you saying that they never arrived?"

"They arrived," Duchess said. "We've a half-dozen witnesses that say so, including the blacksmith who married them himself. Your brother and his bride spent the night at the inn there, only to begin their return journey the following morning, three days ago. They changed horses and had luncheon not five miles from here, and then . . . disappeared."

Henry's heart began to pound. Jack had been five miles away, under threat, and Henry had not been able to help. He'd failed to protect him.

"I should have been there." Adelaide's words echoed those in his heart, and he turned his attention to her, meeting her brown gaze across the room. There was sadness there, in her eyes. "I made a calculation that they'd be safe once they were married. I stayed here, when I should have followed her."

"And what," he replied. "Been taken with them?"

The anger and frustration he felt at his brother's disappearance would have become panicked rage. Already threatened to become so at the very thought that she might be gone, and he might not know where she was.

"No one would have taken me. Even if I were worth taking—I've a blade and I know how to use it."

There it was again. *Even if I were worth taking.* As though she weren't worth everything.

"Goddammit, Adelaide—"

"As much as I would enjoy watching whatever this show is about to become," Duchess interjected, "we must find Lady Carrington. And her lord, I suppose."

Around the room, the women got to work, their words coming in quick rhythm, as though they had played this particular game a hundred times before. Adelaide began. "Who's got them? The Bully Boys?"

"That is our guess, yes," Sesily replied, turning away to search the cupboards. "Is there food?"

Henry shot Adelaide a look at the question, and she waved a hand. "Ignore it. She's always hungry," she said before returning to the discussion. "Danny was here."

"So we heard," Duchess replied. "He was delivered quite delightfully to Alfie's warehouse, tied up like a prized hog, alongside a very large brute who Mary asked us to handle."

"That's Billy," Adelaide said. "He stabbed Henry."

"Ah," Imogen said, looking to Henry. "Well, he won't be a problem. He's on his way to Australia, as I understand it."

Henry blinked. "Excellent."

"Danny did report something quite interesting before Alfie gave him a public dressing down, though. Aha!" Sesily spun back to the group, triumphantly holding a tin of sardines aloft. "Apparently, you're the duke's mistress."

Henry shifted at the word, reported from the outside world. From London, via that weasel of a man he should have sent to his maker. He didn't like the way it sounded, salacious, like what they had done was to be whispered about and traded like gossip, as though she were a stop on the way to something else, that the world considered more valuable.

And he did not like that he had done that to her—put her name and what they had done in the mouths of criminals who made it seem they were in the darkness, when being with Adelaide only ever made him feel like he was in full sun.

Like she was his equal in all ways.

He was about to tell her that. To apologize for the mess he had made, when she spoke. "I'm not."

"You're not his mistress?" Imogen clarified.

"I'm not," Adelaide repeated. "It's not—"

As a group, the women's brows rose.

"It certainly looked as though you were . . ." Imogen waved a hand to indicate the bedroom abovestairs.

"We were," Adelaide said, the words slightly panicked. "But . . . we're not . . ."

Whatever she was about to say, they absolutely *were*, and he didn't like the suggestion that whatever was happening between them was not forever. If there was not a word for it, they would invent one. Partner. Companion. Love.

He was never letting her go, did she not see that? *Shit.* He didn't want it this way. Didn't want all of London knowing about them before he'd had his chance to convince her to live in the light with him. He didn't want secrets. Or a mistress, or a secret lover, or whatever half-light she'd offered him. He wanted *her*. With him. Now. Forever.

And he would do whatever it took to get it.

The words from his father's letter whispered through him—*You may have all that is mine if only you wish it. All I wish is a future that we might together call ours.*

Whatever she wanted. He would give it to her.

Before he could send her friends from the room and tell her as much, Adelaide said, "I've no need for a sponsor or a benefactor. I am not his mistress."

"Then what," the Duchess asked from her place at the far end of the room. "Is he yours?"

Adelaide gave a little laugh. "I can't afford him."

Sesily had also found a box of hard biscuits and was munching on one. "Do you require a loan?"

"No!"

Sesily looked to Imogen. "Maybe the kiss on the dock has inspired her to . . . do a bit of sampling."

It was Henry's turn for raised eyebrows, and he couldn't resist a firm look at Adelaide, whose pretty ears were turning scarlet. "There will be no sampling."

"Hang on!" Sesily announced, as though she'd just invented the wheel. "You were the man on the docks! I didn't recognize you without your beard—that's a very nice shave, by the way. So. You're not sampling, and she's not your mistress . . . are you planning to make an honest woman of our Adelaide?"

A little groan escaped Adelaide. "Sesily."

"Someone has to play the older brother, Adelaide."

"And you think you're the one for the role?" Imogen interrupted. "You? Sexily Talbot?" Henry's brows rose. He had heard the name bandied about in men's clubs and smoking rooms, but was shocked to hear it aloud with the woman in question.

"Are you lot always like this?"

"Always," Imogen replied.

"You'll get used to it when you make an honest woman of our Adelaide," Sesily said with a grin.

"No one is making an honest woman out of me!" Everyone in the room stilled, turning to look at her. "I've no intention of marrying, and neither does he."

A fact from earlier that suddenly did not feel so true. He filed the realization away.

"Fair enough, but it does beg the question, Adelaide—" Lady Sesily began, teasing delight in her tone.

"It does not, in fact, beg any questions," Adelaide interrupted.

"Is the duke taking advantage of you?" Imogen finished the question.

There it was. The opening he required. "I am."

Everyone in the kitchens looked to him, each with a different expression. Admiration. Delight. Surprise . . . and on the face of the only woman who mattered . . . the only one who would ever matter . . .

Abject horror.

"You are *not*."

"I am," he said. "There's only one solution."

"There is no solution!" she insisted.

"Then you admit there is a problem."

"With your senses? Yes. You've taken leave of them." She turned to her friends. "There is no problem. He is not taking advantage of me. If anything, I am taking advantage of him."

What? He didn't like that. "Hang on."

"I am. It's clear to the whole world." She adjusted her spectacles. "I am me and you are . . . you. And you look . . . like you . . . and I look . . . like me . . . and you were good for a . . ."

"Brisk walk?" Imogen suggested.

"Yes. Fine. Yes. Whatever." Adelaide waved a hand at Imogen. "A *brisk walk*. So yes, I'm taking advantage of him."

Everyone went silent at the words, and if he'd been able to look away from the infuriating woman he loved, he would have noticed that they were all staring at him, watching wide-eyed as he crossed the room, ignoring them all, to stand in front of Adelaide.

Tall and beautiful, she lifted her chin defiantly, a challenge in the velvet eyes behind her spectacles when she said, "Someone ought to free you from my clutches."

"Hear this Adelaide Frampton," he said, quiet steel in his words. "You are the most remarkable person I have ever known. Strong and brilliant and with more courage than I've ever seen in another. And more beautiful than any one person has cause to be. I've no interest in being freed from your clutches."

And then, in full view of these women who were her partners and friends, who clearly loved her as much as he did, Clayborn pulled Adelaide close and kissed her, fast and lush, until she was clinging to him and there was no question as to his intentions.

When he lifted his head, he met her gaze and whispered, "You may clutch me anytime you like, love."

"Oh, that's very romantic," Sesily said happily.

The words unlocked Adelaide, who stared at him with a dazed look that made him feel big as a house. "Don't encourage him. It's nonsensical," she said, stepping out of his embrace. "And *irrelevant* to our current situation."

He bit his tongue, tempted to put the whole conversation on hold and take her back to bed for a bit, even knowing that Jack and Helene were more pressing.

But the moment they were found . . . he was taking her for a brisk walk until she was too weak with pleasure to deny him what he asked.

Which would be forever.

She looked to Duchess. "So, The Bully Boys have them."

"We believe so. But they haven't sent word to Havistock," Duchess said. "Which is . . . odd."

"Why not?"

Henry looked from woman to woman. "Are you suggesting The Bully Boys are expected to ransom Helene and my brother to her father?"

Duchess turned to Adelaide. "You didn't tell him."

She gave a quick shake of the head. "It's not my secret to tell."

"What secret?" he demanded. In the silence that fell, things began to sort into place. "Havistock. You said he had a file."

Adelaide nodded.

"Thick as your thumb, you said. I thought you meant the factories."

"As if that isn't enough," Imogen interrupted. "But we'll take care of them."

He ignored the words. "Adelaide?"

"There's something else."

"What?" He paused, his mind racing. "You were in the house as the Matchbreaker. Not there to end Helene's marriage to Jack. You don't care about that."

"No. Jack is imperfect, but he is not a monster. I was

there to learn more about the whereabouts of Lady Helene."

He came forward, irritation flaring. She'd kept something from him. Something important. Something that impacted her safety. That of his brother. "Why? Why does she matter? What do you have? The children in the factories . . . It's none of it illegal."

"Not until you make it so, no."

He would. He would do whatever he could to make it so. To make her proud of him. But that didn't mean he wasn't growing increasingly frustrated with her.

"It won't matter soon enough," Imogen interjected, which Henry wanted very much to discuss, but the Duchess spoke, then, and everything changed.

"Lady Helene witnessed Lord Draven's murder."

Draven. Henry's brow furrowed at the name. The earl had been pushed off a balcony at a ball weeks earlier. A woman had been seen fleeing the crime. A group of them. "They thought it was you lot."

"Really, Duke," Sesily said. "We've a name now."

"We've also more finesse than to toss an earl off a balcony during a ball," Duchess added.

"Didn't you blow up Scotland Yard, as well?" Henry asked.

"No one can prove that," Lady Imogen replied happily.

Pride filled Adelaide's gaze, as though she'd been hoping he would put it all together. "Lady Helene came directly to us to request help, knowing that if she went anywhere else, she might not be believed. Of course, we agreed. She needed to escape her father's house and find hiding as quickly as possible, for a long enough time that we could sort out his capture."

"Not easy with a peer," he said.

"Precisely, so we concocted an elaborate plan—Lady Havistock's meeting with the Matchbreaker was intended to be a distraction for Lady Helene's escape. But she and your brother eloped, without apprising us of the plans.

"It wasn't what we'd intended, but we decided it could be turned to our advantage. Her father might believe it was the reason she'd disappeared, and she'd be protected by Jack. All we had to do was follow her to the border and collect her. She'd be married and safely out from under her father's thumb." Adelaide paused. "We didn't expect . . ."

"You didn't expect me unconscious in your hideout for five days." He cursed, guilt crashing down around him. "You should have told me." He was furious. They'd all been in danger. Adelaide, Jack, Lady Helene. "You should have told me why we were headed north. Why it was important that we find them."

"I didn't have to," Adelaide said, stepping forward, sensing his frustration. "We knew where they were every step of the way . . . until you were hurt. And then . . ." She trailed off.

She'd stayed for him. Because she cared for him.

Because she ached for him as much as he ached for her.

"We were watching them," Duchess interjected. "We knew where they were. Every overnight. Every horse change. Every stop for food or weather. You did not disappear them, Adelaide. Something went wrong."

"Are they dead?" Henry finally voiced the question that had been knocking around in his head since the beginning of the conversation. Had his brother been so caught up in this mess that he'd died for it?

"We don't believe so," Duchess said. "First, any person willing to take money to kill not one, but two aristocrats isn't smart enough to do it quietly. We are talking about men who cannot cut a purse without regaling half the world with the tales of their great adventure."

"And the second?"

She reached into the pocket of her skirts and extracted a small card. "This."

Adelaide's gaze locked on the ecru square. "What is that?"

"It was delivered to the Hungry Hen not two hours ago." She paused. "Addressed to one Adelaide Trumbull."

Adelaide went cold in the wake of Duchess's words.

Trumbull.

Not Frampton. Not the name she'd used for years as she'd rebuilt herself.

She reached for it. "What does it say?"

"I don't know," Duchess said.

Adelaide trembled as she slid her finger beneath the blood red seal there, her heart pounding as she realized the gravity of the moment. As she realized what this small missive meant. How, even before she read it, it returned her, without argument, to the world she'd escaped years earlier.

How this cold reminder of her past—of where she'd come from and who she had once been—highlighted all the reasons she would never settle into this new world. This new life. How she had spent the past five years living half a life. For fear of this—of becoming too tied to the world north of the river, and still, being nothing but a girl from the South Bank.

Opening the parchment, she read, recognizing the jagged writing on the paper. The creative spelling of a man with a head for numbers who had taught himself to read and write.

Received yer package. Well done, Addie.
I've the boy and his gel.
Time to come home. Bring that duke yer tupping.

Adelaide went cold at the words, refolding the paper into a crisp square. Hating it, she looked to Clayborn, already pulling her into his arms, warm and firm and safe. For a heartbeat, Adelaide let him do it. Even as she knew the truth. That this was the end.

He tilted her face up to his. Searching her gaze. "Tell me."

"Jack and Helene are alive. For now."

He exhaled, and she could hear the relief there. He didn't realize there was no cause for relief. "Where?"

Oh, no. She shook her head. She could not tell him. Couldn't bear the idea of him with her in Lambeth, his tall frame ducking through narrow, dark alleyways, his shining boots on the filthy cobblestones where she'd grown up.

"Adelaide," he said firmly, the words pulling her gaze to his as though she were tethered to him. "Whatever it is," he began, reaching for her, his touch sure and true, and she barely stopped herself from leaning into his warm palm and turning herself over to him, "we shall face it together. You and I. And your league of terrifying women."

Her attention flickered to the women in question at that. Not terrifying. Wonderful. Dear. And strong as steel, a line of warriors watching, waiting, ready to do whatever it took to keep Adelaide safe. But at what cost? Too much.

Not the Belles, who had a bolder, broader battle at hand.

And not Henry; beautiful, strong Henry, honorable and good and powerful enough to bend so much of the world to his will.

Not this world, though.

This world abided by different rules. Different power.

And if Henry walked into it . . . if any of them did—it would destroy them.

But Adelaide had been forged in its fire, and so, this fight was hers.

It was time for her to go home.

Together, they made a plan. Spent most of the evening sorting out what was to come and how they were going to fight. They decided to leave at first light, so they could move as fast as possible in the carriages they had.

They worked out the places for food and safety and fast horses on a nonstop ride to London, using a map spread wide on the scarred kitchen table where she and Lucia had saved Henry's life.

And the whole time, as the people she loved planned to go to war for her, Adelaide made her own plan . . . to keep them all safe.

Because if she allowed this magnificent crew into her father's lair and surrounded them with her father's men, they'd never leave alive.

That night, they took to their beds, and Henry tugged her into his own, making slow, quiet love to her, whispering his love at her ear, to the tip of her breast, to the swell of her stomach and the hot, aching core of her. He gave her one final night of imagining they were possible. Of loving her.

Of letting her love him, even as she did all she could not to speak it, fearing that if she let it out, she might never be able to put it back.

When he slept, Adelaide slid from his arms, ignoring the ache that came at the loss of him. Snatching up her bag, she stepped into the hallway beyond, making quick work of dressing before creeping down the stairs, planning to be miles away before anyone in the house noticed she was gone.

Slipping out the back door and into the cool night, she made for the stables, hitching the horses and tossing her bag into the carriage—nearly making it before Duchess spoke from the darkness. "Stealing off in the dead of night is something of a cliché, don't you think?"

Adelaide stopped, somehow not at all surprised that she'd been found out.

Duchess had found her once before, had she not? On her wedding day, as street gangs in Lambeth fought for position and power. She'd offered Adelaide a new life, and hadn't blinked for a moment when Adelaide had threatened her with a Bible. She was the kind of woman who would always find what she was looking for.

Adelaide turned and closed the door to face Duchess, leaning against the door of the carriage, arms folded tight to ward off the chill.

"Why did you choose me?" Adelaide said, finally. "It wasn't my age or my station."

"No," the other woman agreed.

"Not who I was, nor where I came from."

Blue eyes glittered in the lanternlight. "It had nothing to do with where you came from, no . . . but, Adelaide, it had everything to do with who you were."

"Alfie Trumbull's daughter." She paused. "But you never asked me to go back. In five years, the only time you sent me to Lambeth was this time."

Duchess nodded. "A mistake."

No. It was perfect. "It wasn't."

The other woman's lips curved. "Because of Clayborn."

Because of Henry. She'd have returned to Lambeth. Spent the rest of her life on the South Bank if it meant a day with him. An hour.

She was to do just that.

Duchess nodded and moved toward the horses at the front of the carriage, checking harnesses and bridles. "I did not invite you to join me because you were Alfie Trumbull's daughter. Alfie could have had a dozen daughters, and I wouldn't have invited them to join me." She paused. "Or, rather, I might have, but only if they'd had your taste for justice."

Adelaide gave a little laugh. "I was many things, but a servant to justice was not one of them."

"Were you not?" Duchess asked casually.

"I was a nipper from Lambeth; I saw the inside of more than one London jail."

"Well, there's justice and there's *justice*, don't you think? The kind of justice that makes a man build a jail, and the kind that lands a girl inside it." Duchess was quiet for a moment, her blond hair gleaming in the light of the single lantern. "You do yourself a disservice, Adelaide. You weren't simply a cutpurse; you were a genius. You could see coin in a pocket at twenty yards. But more than that, you could read the marks. And in the two years that I watched you there, on the South Bank, I never saw you take a purse from anyone who didn't hold power north of the river." She stroked a hand down the side of one grey's neck. "I am not wrong."

"You are not."

"So tell me, Adelaide Trumbull"—the old name shattered through her—"why is it that the one time you've a duke offering up his fortune freely, you're too afraid to take it?"

The words, softer and gentler than Duchess ever appeared, summoned Adelaide's tears. She shook her head. "He'll regret it. In the end."

"Why, because you were born one thing and became another?" The Duchess shook her head. "My friend—is that not the story of everyone worth loving?"

Adelaide shrugged. "He's a duke and I'm a thief."

"All that tells me is that one of you has had to work for what you have, and the other was born with the world in his grasp."

Adelaide refrained from pointing out that her work wasn't exactly honest. Or that Henry had lived his life knowing he didn't deserve what he'd been given at birth. Though she suspected that Duchess would happily tell her that no aristocrat deserved what they were given at birth.

"He was worth it," she confessed on a whisper. "Staying with him. Mending him. It was worth it."

There was no censure in Duchess's eyes when she nodded. "Inside, you said you could not afford him."

"I am not what he requires."

"Why not?"

For a while, she had thought she might have a chance at it. At being partner and perhaps even love. A quiet, secret affair beyond the edges of society or family or friends.

Private.

But now, as her past caught up with her, Adelaide realized that life—the one conceived here in the middle of nowhere—would never be theirs. He would always be a duke, education and money and power, and she would always be . . . "I'm a girl summoned home to Lambeth."

It had been a beautiful dream, the two of them together sharing bits of their lives and their selves and pretending they had a future with no name.

But the dream was over now.

It was time for her to wake.

Duchess watched her for a long moment before sighing, and approaching. "Adelaide, don't you see? You're not a girl summoned home. You're a hero headed to battle. And someday, you will learn that you never have to fight alone."

They were pretty words. But that night, as she climbed onto the driving block, she knew the truth. This was her battle. And alone was the only way to win it.

Chapter Twenty-Two

"I told you to bring your duke."

Adelaide didn't flinch when her father addressed her, club in hand, from the doorway of St. Stephen's Chapel, still a stronghold of The Bully Boys, five years after her life had changed course forever inside its walls.

She'd ridden through the night, paying handsomely for a driver at the first place she'd changed horses, which had given her the opportunity to stop only for new mounts on the way back to London. She'd had to ride fast, as she knew that the moment Henry discovered her gone, he would follow—and he'd have the Belles in tow.

Sleep had come in fitful starts and stops on the journey, until they'd entered the city at dusk on the second night, and she'd let the driver off with enough coin to get him to wherever he'd like to be. She knew better than to bring a stranger to her father's turf, and didn't want anyone tangled up in whatever mess she was about to walk into.

Adelaide lifted her chin and met her father's brown eyes as he stared down at her, his craggy face made craggier by the late-day shadows. He wouldn't like it—the defiance in her look. He wouldn't like that she'd come alone. His gaze narrowed on her, scanning her pinned hair and her lined cloak and deep purple skirts and the leather boots she wore that hadn't been stolen from another.

"You look like one of them."

It was the worst of insults. The kind that would come before a good pounding on the streets—a disdain for anyone who thought to get above themselves and this place. And if she'd been twelve or sixteen or even twenty, the words might have struck like a blow.

Cor, if it had been three weeks earlier, they might have.

But things had changed, and Adelaide Frampton, née Trumbull, had no plans to be intimidated by her father that day. "Where are they?"

Alfie Trumbull didn't like insolence, and he didn't like being treated like just anyone—self-made kings rarely did. He narrowed his gaze on the only child he'd ever claimed and said, "Yer duke, Addie. I specifically told you to bring 'im."

Not her duke.

It was a lie, of course. He'd always be her duke. Even when he married a lovely highborn woman and had a passel of lovely highborn children . . . to Adelaide, he'd always be hers.

"Why? This isn't about him." This was young Addie, come home to the turf that had raised her, to fight.

"Jaysus, Addie. Every time I have a plan, you turn up to send it south." He paused. "'Salright. We'll go get the man." He shouted up the street. "Find me that feckin' toff." He looked back at Adelaide. "Danny tells me he's after you like a hound in heat, so it won't be difficult."

Fear whispered through her, and she pushed it out of the way. "Where are Jack and Helene?"

"Inside," Alfie said, pointing over his shoulder at the chapel. "Thought it was time to let the place have some newlyweds who can stomach each other."

Pushing past him, she stepped into the chapel, half expecting to find it upended—untouched since the day her wedding had devolved into a turf war with however many men dead, including the groom. Of course, there was no evidence of the past—that night, the chapel was tidy. A handful of candles burning in the sacristy on one side of the room, the sting of incense in her nose, a light dim enough that she had trouble adjusting to it. She stood for a moment, letting the space wash over her. And then, "Where?"

"Now, now, Addie, is that any way for you to treat your old da? We haven't seen each other in years!"

"I would be lying if I said I wasn't disappointed that we've ended our streak," she retorted, moving swiftly into the space—empty except for them. She marched down the center aisle, searching the floors, the pews. All empty. "Risky, being here alone, Alfie."

He smirked. "You think you'd get three paces beyond this church if you harmed me?"

She watched him for a moment. "I think I'd do alright. People 'round here always thought I was the best of you."

A beat. Something in his eyes that she'd never seen before. Something strangely like . . . nerves? Before she could be sure, he laughed, big and brash. "Ah, I like that. Mayfair 'asn't cleared me out of you, 'as it, girl?"

She didn't reply as she approached the front pew.

"But you don't live in Mayfair, do you?" her father continued from his place at the back of the church. "You've never been welcome there, 'ave you? Och, you've got your ladies, and now that American brute who put poor Timmy Crouch into retirement—"

"Caleb Calhoun," Adelaide said. Caleb had come for the high-ranking Bully Boy a year earlier for laying hands on Sesily.

"Yeah, that one. Timmy was one of my best boys, you know. Now 'e's got a wonky shoulder and likes to whinge about it. I'm still piqued about that one."

"I'll let him know," Adelaide replied, dryly.

"—this ain't about that, though, Addie. This is about you not really being one of them, and you know it. They do too, girl. I see you, livin' in rooms above that place in Covent Garden and attendin' balls like they're fancy dress parties, pretendin' all the time that you weren't christened here, in my dirt."

"I know exactly where I came from," she said, lifting one end of the pew and pulling it forward, revealing the panel cut into the floor beneath it, a lock inlaid in the wood. "It's impossible to forget it."

"Good," he said. "You shouldn't forget it. I give you the world, and you run the first chance you get? Where's my gratitude?"

She looked up from fiddling with the pendant of her necklace, to attach one of her skeleton keys. "Gratitude! For what? For making me work for food, for clothes, for—" *Love.* She held back the last word. "For selling me to John Scully as a bride?"

"Come now, Addie. Ye can't be angry at that. That's 'ow it works! I was consolidatin' power!"

"You went to war on my wedding day!"

"Turned out he thought *he* was the one consolidatin' power," Alfie said with a shrug. "And what are you complainin' about? You cut and run that day. Left your poor da all alone. How do you think I felt?"

Adelaide rolled her eyes and rounded the pew. "I think you were grateful for the newly free room in the house."

Alfie shoved his hands into his pockets and rocked back on his heels. "Well, now. A man does like his space. But the important bit is this—I didn't bring you home then. I could've done. I could've made you a proper example—shown people wot they get when they leave me wivvout permission. But I didn't. I let you join that Duchess who don't act like any lady toff I've ever met, and her feckin' army."

How did he know about Duchess?

"You surprised? You think I wouldn't keep tabs on you? My own blood?"

"I am, as a matter of fact," she said, turning to crouch over the hatch. "You never showed any interest in me when I lived here."

"That's coz when you lived 'ere, you weren't a fucking legend." He waved a hand toward the doors to the chapel. "Half my turf is filled with little girls dreamin' of bein' just like Addie Trumbull."

"Gone from here."

"Do you know how much work I 'ad to do to make it so it sounded like I willed your toff Mayfair life into bein' for you? Christ, Addie. You owe me. And we was fine, but I can't have you comin' back here and makin' trouble."

"Let's consider my lesson learned, then, Alfie," she said searching for the proper key to open the hatch.

He paused, watching her work the necklace. "You're still the best thief in Lambeth, Addie Trumbull."

"I have better tools now," she said, ignoring the pride in her father's tone. Knowing it for what it always had been—manipulation. She inserted the key into the lock and pulled open the hatch. Looking into the small room below the sanctuary, she noted a half-dozen crates marked *Explosives*, and another stack that were likely weapons.

And there, sitting on the packed-dirt floor along with the munitions, was a young white woman, pretty as a picture in a lovely pink dress, matching bonnet on her wrist. And next to her, a handsome, blond man with a wicked black eye and a swollen cheek. The two of them looked up, eyes wide and worried.

She looked to Alfie. "Why does this man have a shiner, Alfie?"

"I can't be held responsible for what happens when my packages are . . . disagreeable."

With a disgusted look to her father, she returned her attention to the hole. "Jack and Helene?"

The couple nodded, and Jack pushed Helene behind him, or, as much as he could. "Who are you?"

Protecting her. Just like his brother would.

"I'm . . ." There were a dozen ways to introduce herself,

so why did she choose, "An acquaintance of the Duke of Clayborn's."

His brow furrowed. "Henry?"

"Trumbull!" The shout came from a distance outside the church, and Adelaide closed her eyes, recognizing Henry's voice, deep and loud and angry, reverberating off the stones of the narrow lane at the end of which sat St. Stephen's Chapel.

She closed her eyes. *No.* He couldn't be there. Once he was here, Alfie had all the power.

"Sounds like he's here!" Jack said, looking to Helene, who smiled for the first time since Adelaide had opened the hatch. "I told you he'd come. And if I were to wager, he's furious."

"I would not take that wager," Adelaide said, adjusting her spectacles, willing her heart to cease its pounding. *He was there.*

Infuriating man.

Wonderful man.

Keeping her attention on the newlyweds, she said, "Are you hurt? More than the . . ." She waved a hand at her eye. When they shook their heads, she said, "Stay there; Trumbull has guards everywhere. You'll be safe soon enough."

"Alfred Trumbull!" Another shout from outside, sounding like an elocution professor from Oxford had arrived.

She straightened and turned toward it, as her father raised his brows. "Oho! *Alfred* he calls me! Just like a toff."

Making a show of checking his pistol in its holster, Alfie tugged the waist of his trousers up and made for the doorway of the church, leaving Adelaide no choice but to follow, but not before she slipped her own blade from where it was strapped at her thigh.

Had Henry come alone? Into this place? Onto enemy turf?

Of course he had. Because for Henry, Duke of Clayborn, there was no such thing as enemy turf. He'd been born into a world where he could walk wherever he liked, without repercussions.

Not here, though. Here, there were repercussions. "Let's have a look at your boy, shall we?"

"He's not a boy," she said, regretting the words even as they escaped her lips and made her sound like a petulant child.

"'Course he is. He's never had cause to grow up and be a man, 'as he? He's had everything given to him, along with that silver spoon that was down 'is gullet when 'e was born." He stood in the door, looking down the lane, and Adelaide joined him, her heart beating in a chaotic rhythm as she stared down the empty alleyway. Of course, it wasn't empty. It was full to the brim with bystanders and onlookers and a half-dozen brutes who were paid to linger near Alfie and keep him safe. The only reason that Adelaide got close—the only reason that Henry would—was that they had been requested. Otherwise, they would have been knocked cold long before they reached this place.

Alfie hefted his club, making a show of adjusting his grip. Reminding her that Henry might still be knocked cold if he didn't behave.

She tightened her grip on the hilt of the blade she had hidden in her skirts, and held her breath, hating that she couldn't be certain her father and his thugs wouldn't take him in hand and rough him up. Or worse. Maybe this was all a ruse for Havistock to get everything he wished. His daughter, her groom, and his nemesis all gone in one fell swoop.

But she couldn't ask her father to keep him safe. Revealing that she cared about Henry's safety would ensure that her father mistreated him, simply to toy with Adelaide. So instead of begging for his safety, she willed him safe, watching him without moving—barely even breathing.

A shield-maiden, watching her warrior.

And he looked like a warrior, dusk having fallen over the city, casting long shadows down the alleyway, turning it into a battlefield. Ready to fight, with his broken nose and bruised face and bandaged knuckles, straight shoulders and strong, bearded jaw—he hadn't shaved on the journey—and stiff hat and the billow of his greatcoat behind him.

He saw her immediately, the moment she appeared in the doorway, his gaze sharpening on her as his stride lengthened and his pace increased. The rest of the world was beyond his focus, and Adelaide held her breath, hating that he did not look to the rooftops where a sniper would be stationed. To the stairways and upper walkways, where others watched, weapons out.

He didn't care about any of that.

Her heart thundered in her chest.

He only cared for her.

He'd come for her.

The realization shattered through her, sending pain and frustration and pleasure and a thread of foolish hope through her even as she knew she did not deserve to feel the last two. Even as she knew this might be the last she ever saw of him.

She ached with gratitude for this—one last moment, like fresh water.

And then she reminded herself that he did not belong here.

She hated him in Lambeth.

Yes, she'd seen him there before, on the South Bank the day she'd stolen his box, but that had somehow been different, perhaps because she hadn't expected him there, and perhaps because she hadn't known him and how good and decent and *wrong* he was in this place, so when he'd turned up, it had felt less horrific and more like . . . a gift of some kind. Like finding a blade of bright green grass growing between alleyway cobblestones.

Except blades of grass didn't belong in London alleyways, and the Duke of Clayborn didn't belong in Lambeth, and that night, as he stalked his way through the cobblestone streets toward St. Stephen's, he did not feel like a gift. He felt like a liability.

The memories of her youth there, in the night, when nippers and pickpockets and cutpurses and thieves came out of the woodwork to fill their coffers, shouted through her, and even as she told herself there was nothing shameful about where she'd come from, she knew it wasn't true.

Her father put voice to her thoughts. "You think he'll have you? A nipper from Lambeth? Aw, Addie. Ye never could stop dreamin' of Mayfair. Remember—thievin' from toffs never won you anyfin' but trouble." He shoved his hands in his pockets and rocked back and forth on his heels before adding, "Well, let's see, shall we?"

A chill ran though Adelaide at the casual curiosity in the words, as though this were a game and not her whole life approaching. But that was how Alfie had made his fortune and built this sooty kingdom full of criminals—by treating every moment like a game. Nothing important. Nothing that couldn't be cut loose or tossed out or traded.

Which made playing the game impossible for someone who cared.

Like Henry.

I love you, he'd whispered to her the other night. *Be with me. Stay with me.*

Adelaide swallowed the memory as he approached, strong and furious, knowing that whatever was to come—whatever test her father had devised—it would trade on Henry's emotions. His decency. His goodness. His honor. And because of that, he would not pass. She drew tight as a string, preparing for it. To save Jack and Helene. To save him.

This was the only way she could love him, this man

who deserved the wide world. This was what she could give him.

"Why didn't you ever come after me?" she asked, not taking her eyes off Henry.

"You chose North over South. What was I to do? Fetch you from those rooms you let above O'Tiernen's place? Bring you back? A traitor to your home? To your da?"

She narrowed her gaze on him at his reference to The Place, the tavern that gave safe haven to any women who needed it. "You've sent your thugs to knock over The Place a dozen times since I've lived there." She'd fought Bully Boys herself inside the taproom on more than one occasion.

"Och. 'Tweren't personal, gel. I take the job when it comes."

"I'm to believe you didn't enjoy taking those jobs?"

"Enjoyin' it ain't the same as orderin' it. You ought to thank me, honestly, for not taking the lot of you out. There's more than enough money in that job."

"Then why not do it?"

He sniffed and looked over her shoulder, down the fast-darkening alleyway. "Don't feel right, offin' your own."

"That, and we're better fighters than you expected."

He tilted his head, his lips turning down in silent acknowledgement that she might be right. Another day, she might have enjoyed the revelation. "So I'm not here to be punished or made an example of." She turned to face her father. "Then why summon me? Why summon him?"

"Because, Addie, there's more to life than punishment. Why not trust your ol' da?" The words struck fear deep inside her, but she could not ask for clarification. Alfie was already shouting over her shoulder to the street below. "Your Grace, my boy! Good of you to come!"

Sucking in a breath, she turned around to face Henry, to look down upon him from where she stood on the steps of the church. For a wild moment, her mind played a trick on her, and she imagined another scenario, another lifetime, when she might be on church steps looking down at him with hope and happiness and joy at their future, spread out before them.

The vision disappeared like smoke before she could toy with it, and she caught her breath at the ferocity of his gaze and the steel set of his jaw. At the way he didn't look at her. Didn't meet her eyes. Didn't look anywhere but at her father. "You won't think it's good when I put you into the dirt, Trumbull."

Behind him, the shadows shifted. Alfie's guards.

"Now, now. Is that 'ow they teach you to treat your elders in Mayfair?" Alfie held his hands out. "We've never even met! How is it you think me deservin' of a brawl today?"

"Not only today," Henry said, his hand flexing at his side. "You were deserving of a brawl when you took my brother and his wife from their wedding holiday to use them as bait."

"Can't blame me for that, Duke. It's no' as though you and Addie would have come round for tea. They're perfectly fine and just inside." He waved at the church.

"That's true," Adelaide added, wanting him to look at her. Aching for it.

He didn't, that muscle in his cheek twitching with anger at her father. And maybe, just a bit, for her. "You're deserving of a brawl for the lifetime of crimes you've committed. The weapons you've run. The fathers you've taken from children. The husbands from wives. The scores of terrible men you've lent muscle to."

"A man's got to eat, Duke. We ain't all born rich and titled."

"And tell me, do men who have to eat often land their eight-year-old daughters in prison?" Adelaide went cold, then hot with recognition at the words, at the fury in them. At the way his fist curled, ready to fly.

"Oh, it's that, is it?" Disdain crept into Alfie's tone.

"You're horrified by my treatment of my daughter? I taught her how to survive. You lightweight toffs teach your girls nuffin', then throw them to the fuckin' wolves, and I know it, because then you hire my boys to do the dirty work of coverin' up your mistakes.

"I taught my girl the truth about the world. And look at her. Now she tells you lot the truth. And you pay her for the privilege of hearin' it." He paused and looked to Adelaide, a gleam some might think was pride in his eye. "What do they call you, Addie? The Matchbreaker?" She didn't nod, but he carried on. "A whole lot of 'em want your head, gel. But you've forgotten the most important bit of truth. That world, over the river? It ain't yours. And this"—he looked at Henry with disgust—"*duke* ain't for you on the best day, is he?"

She shook her head. "No."

"Adelaide . . ." Henry said, and it was her turn not to look at him.

"'Course he ain't. But what's the first rule I taught you? Everyone has a price. And this one—his is mighty high. He and his brother know things they shouldn't. And the young lady inside? She's *seen* things she shouldn't. Pity, that, as that filth, Havistock, is willing to pay good money to see 'er dispatched." He looked to Henry. "And *I'm* the bad father."

Duchess had been right from the start. Havistock didn't just want Helene returned, he wanted her dead. And he'd asked The Bully Boys to do it.

Alfie was still talking. "Now. While I think that's some dirty business that will send the man straight to hell when he finally meets his maker, that ain't my problem, and money is money."

"So it's to be a double cross," Adelaide said. Alfie Trumbull didn't waste time if there wasn't a trade in the offing. "You'll let Helene and Jack go free."

"You see?" He spread his arms wide and looked to

Henry. "There's my smart girl. Brain in her head direct from her da."

Henry did not move. "You said there's a price."

Alfie showed his full grin. "'Course there is, duke. As there should be. Addie knows. Anything done out of the goodness of the heart is dangerous expensive."

He had taught her that. That everything in life was a transaction. A good or service to be bought and sold. But it wasn't true. She'd seen goodness of heart a thousand times over the last five years. She'd seen what the Belles could do out of the goodness of their hearts. She'd seen what Henry could do. What Jack had done to protect Helene. What his father had done—loving his wife. His sons. Raising decent honorable men, who did decent honorable things . . . out of the goodness of their hearts.

But maybe Adelaide didn't get the luxury of such things. There wasn't room for it on the South Bank, where the poor scraped and fought for everything they had, and to rise . . . to win . . . there wasn't space for good.

"Get on with it, Alfie. Name it. The price to free them all?" She'd pay it. Whatever it was. Even as she knew, without question, that it would be outrageous. That it would take more from her than she'd ever given before.

"Addie, my girl, we're consolidatin' power." A cold thread whipped through her, and she instantly saw it. The whole plan. The enormous price.

"No." She shook her head, turning an agonized look at Henry. *No. Not like this.*

The words were already out of her father's mouth. "You're finally gettin' your wedding."

Frustration and anger and absolute panic flooded through her as she rounded on her father, who looked like a fox who'd found a henhouse. She cursed, harsh and angry and turned to Henry, ready to tell him that she'd had nothing to do with this. That he could—no . . .

he *must*—refuse. That they would find another way out, a way that wouldn't mean tarnishing the legacy of his loving family and his own future with her father's unbearable greed.

But he was back to not looking at her. Back to looking only at Alfie, his blue eyes glittering in the waning sunlight.

He would regret it. Instantly. Adelaide knew in her soul that this man would instantly regret marrying her. Tying himself to her. To this place. To her father, who would immediately wield every tool in his arsenal to manipulate and control them.

And what of his work? What of his future? What of his legacy?

This wasn't the plan. It was never what she wanted.

For him. The words whispered through her, and she hated the truth of them. It didn't matter that she might have wanted this. He was all that mattered. "No. Don't . . ."

Don't make it so you regret loving me.

Don't make it so you forget loving me.

And then Henry gave his answer. "Yes."

A wide grin split Alfie's face. "Say it again, boy."

"Yes," Henry repeated, the word firm and cool and without any doubt. "Yes. I accept the offer, on one condition."

"Oho! A condition!" Alfie rocked back on his heels. "Go on, then, I find I'm in a givin' mood."

Only then did Henry turn to her, and she caught her breath at what she saw in his beautiful blue eyes. *Triumph.* "We do it tonight."

Chapter Twenty-Three

Henry had never known fear the way he'd known it when he'd been jostled awake two mornings earlier by Sesily Calhoun, standing at his bedside like some kind of specter. "No time to stand on ceremony, Duke. Get up. Our girl is already gone."

He'd been out of bed instantly, dressed within minutes, fear and fury battling his control. She'd left him. Headed into battle without him. Without her sisters in arms.

She'd taken matters into her own hands, never realizing that this wasn't how it ended. Not like this, her against the world.

If she was going up against the world, he would be with her, dammit.

In the two days it had taken for them to return to London and for him to find his way here, to this church deep in the labyrinth of Lambeth, he'd been consumed with two goals:

1. Find Adelaide.
2. Make her his. Forever.

He'd been able to breathe again when he'd turned down the street to find her standing on the steps of the church, tall and beautiful, red hair gleaming in the lantern light. She was found. And she was unharmed. And the world, which had been spinning out of control, had righted itself.

Yes, he was furious with her for leaving him. For putting herself in danger. For forgetting that she belonged to him, dammit, just as he belonged to her—and they were going to have a long and serious conversation about that . . . just as soon as he convinced her to marry him.

Granted, this was not the way he'd planned to marry her, but it would get the job done, and he could spend the rest of his life making it up to her with flowers and wedding brunches and string quartets and new frocks. Whatever she wanted would be hers, and he would make a lifetime of giving it to her.

Why had he ever doubted that they could have it all— the time together, the children, the future . . . the love? Whatever it was that was left between them, they'd sort it out, just as soon as he could pack her into a carriage and take her home and get on with the business of loving her, hang Alfie Trumbull's wild plans for the future.

Whatever they were, Henry and Adelaide would face them. And fight them. And triumph.

Together.

After all, Henry came with a dukedom, and Adelaide came with a battalion of women warriors. Alfie wouldn't stand a chance once they were joined.

And so, standing on the sooty steps of St. Stephen's Chapel at dusk on that particular Thursday evening, after two days of racing across Britain, furious that the woman he loved would walk herself directly into danger rather than letting him stand beside her . . . things were looking up.

Right up until she refused him. "No."

He turned to look at her. To explain. To coax. "Adelaide."

It was as though he was not present. She did not look away from her father as she delivered her blow. "I'm not marrying him. You'll have to choose something else. I won't do it."

"Why in hell not?" Henry asked. Did she not see what they might have? What this could be?

"You ain't got a choice, gel," Alfie replied. "That's the price."

"Let there be another one, then. How much are they paying you to kidnap the girl? How much is the price on her head? On his brother's? On Clayborn's? I've wealthy friends now, Alfie, and whatever they will pay you, I am able to pay you more."

"I'll pay my own damn debts, thank you—" Henry bit out, feeling like the whole thing was spinning out of his control.

"Fine," she said, still not looking at him, but at least acknowledging his presence. "The duke will pay his own way. And I will double whatever it is. Is that enough?"

"Now that's a lot of money, girl. You'd be puttin' yourself deep in debt to pay it."

It would be exorbitant. Alfred Trumbull was nothing if not a shrewd businessman, and he knew the price of silence. Knew, too, that such a price increased with danger, and crime, and a threat to a family and a future. Whatever Havistock was offering, it would be an enormous amount. And with no guarantee for Adelaide's future.

But if she married him, Henry would guarantee her future. Immediately. Forever.

Hell, even if she didn't marry him, he would guarantee it. But given the choice between spending his life with the woman he loved and spending his life alone, stinging from her rejection—it was no choice at all.

"Adelaide, we're marrying," he said, the words like steel.

"No, we're not." She rounded on him. "We're going in there and we're getting your brother and his bride out of the *hole* my father has put them in, and you are taking them far away from here."

"*And you*," he said, suddenly furious. "Dammit, Adelaide, some day you will stop leaving yourself out of the equation. I'm taking *you* away from here, too."

She shook her head. "Why won't you see?"

Henry took a deep breath. "I do see, love. I see you."

See me. Trust me.

For a heartbeat, he thought she might, her brown eyes glittering behind her spectacles, riveted to his. And then she looked away, to her father. To the rooftops. Up the grimy lane. And instead of replying, she turned and made for the church door, leaving Henry standing on the steps, frustrated and furious.

He looked to her father. "I hope you have a team of brutes in there, Trumbull."

"I've one or two," Trumbull said. "Why?"

Henry clenched a fist at his side. "Because I'm spoiling for a fight."

Alfie watched him for a long moment, then said, "All this time, I thought she'd fallen for you, Duke . . . and here we are . . . you're absolutely sick for her, ain't you?"

"I am, in fact. Sick enough to welcome you into the family."

Alfie grinned wide. "That's a priceless value, that. Ain't enough money in the Havistock coffers to compete. Think of it! Alfie Trumbull's blood in a ducal line!"

And standing there, as one of London's most hardened criminals crowed his delight at his daughter marrying a duke, it occurred to Henry that his own father, a duke who never thought twice about choosing love over the bloodline, would have found this entire afternoon thoroughly entertaining.

And he would have been very proud of his son for following in his footsteps.

Climbing the steps, Henry followed the woman he loved into the church where he fully intended to marry her, dispatch a few of Alfie's bruisers, extract his brother and sister-in-law from a hole, apparently, and take his new bride home to bed for a solid week—or however long it would take to convince her that he'd married her because he loved her, despite her superior skill at driving him mad.

A week might not be enough, but Henry was nothing if not persevering, and his plan was flexible.

Inside the church, Jack and Helene were no longer in a hole. Instead, they were seated on the steps leading to the altar, Lady Helene—Lady Carrington, Henry corrected himself—tucked beneath his brother's arm as Jack fussed over her adoringly. Relief at seeing his brother well was quickly replaced with a pang of envy. Jack, at least, had found a woman willing to marry him.

The pair was guarded by two Bully Boys, each one big and broad and with fists the size of hams. Jack looked up as Henry entered and stood. "Henry!"

Henry scowled down the aisle at Jack's black eye. "Are you hurt?"

"I'm grand!" Jack said with a bright smile. "Barely feel it!" He pointed to the pretty girl next to him. "My wife!"

Lady Helene offered him a little wave and a curtsy. "Hello, Your Grace!"

It was an odd sequence of events, but Henry's training took over, and he offered the young woman a little bow. "Congratulations, my lady," he said before returning his attention to his brother. "Jack, we're not quite out of the woods yet, so . . ."

"That's fine!" Jack pronounced, turning to settle Helene back on the steps before he fisted his hands at his sides.

That sorted, Henry turned his attention to the rest of the church. To Adelaide, paused halfway up the aisle, again refusing to look at him. And to the rest of those assembled—the women who refused to let him come for her alone.

Distributed quite casually throughout the small chapel were the Duchess of Trevescan, Imogen Loveless, and Sesily Calhoun, each seated in a different pew, bright, jewel-tone skirts shining in the candlelight, as though they were at a musicale and not lingering with villains on the South Bank.

"Oy!" Alfie said, from behind him, marching up the aisle. "Where did you lot come from?"

"I'm curious about that, too, honestly," Adelaide said. "Why can't you people stay where I leave you?"

"We've no intention of leaving you on your own, Adelaide. I do believe I made that clear. Where one of us goes, the others follow. So . . ." Duchess picked at an invisible piece of lint on her skirts and turned to Trumbull. "Here we are. There's a back entrance to this church, Alfred. Surely you know of it."

"'Course I know about it! But how'd you get through it? There was a guard posted there."

"I'm sure that he is ordinarily a very good guard," Her Grace continued. "But the truth is, men often become flummoxed when women turn up."

Trumbull turned on her. "Are you telling me that you got the better of my bruiser?"

"Not me, in fact," The Duchess said, pointing to Imogen Loveless. "Lady Imogen."

"Oh, I wouldn't worry about him," the woman in question reported. "He'll only be unconscious for an hour or so."

Trumbull was flummoxed for a beat, until he seemed to remember why they were all there. "Alright. While I would ordinarily be proper unhappy about somethin' like this, it's my Addie's wedding day, so I'm willing to let this slide."

"Wedding!" Sesily Calhoun exclaimed.

"I daresay we did not expect *that*," Imogen replied. "Think of what we can do with two duchesses!"

"That's grand!" Jack said, seeming not to fully grasp the danger of his situation. "About time you settle down, Henry, if you ask me!"

Henry wasn't at all certain he'd call marriage to Adelaide *settling down*, but he'd take whatever she'd give him.

The Duchess of Trevescan remained silent, her eyes on Adelaide.

"I'm afraid there won't be any wedding, Jack," Adelaide said. "Duchess, I require a loan."

A single blond brow rose, but the other woman answered unequivocally. "Of course."

"It will likely be a great deal of money, and I may not be able to pay it back."

Her friend nodded. "Nevertheless, if you need it, it is yours."

The three women stood then, coming to flank Adelaide like a team of well-trained lieutenants, facing Henry, as though he were the enemy and not Alfie Trumbull, the actual hardened criminal in the place.

Each of them looked as though they would protect her with their life. And Adelaide somehow believed the world did not value her.

"Thank you." She nodded and turned to her father. "Name your price, Alfie. And I'll sweeten the pot."

Trumbull cut Henry a look. "I'm listening."

"You get your money—whatever Havistock's price is—" Adelaide said.

"Not sweet enough, girl," Alfie said.

"—which is why I am not finished," she said, irritation sliding into her tone as she repeated herself. "*You get your price* . . . and me. Returned."

Gasps went up around the room, and heat exploded through Henry. He'd burn Lambeth to the ground before he allowed that. "Absolutely fucking not."

Somewhere, the Duchess said, "What in hell?"

Alfie's brows rose. "Returned."

"I'm still the best cutpurse you've got," she said, eyes only on her father. "And now I've ties to Mayfair and the aristocracy. I'm a proper thief—one of the best in

London—which you know, as I've stolen from you in broad daylight. You won't get better." She paused, taking a deep breath. "That's the offer. The money, and me. For the newlyweds. And for Clayborn."

"And for my promise never again to work for Havistock," Alfie guessed shrewdly.

"Once you let Lady Helene go with Duchess, you'll never have a chance to work with him again," Adelaide said. "But I want a promise that you'll never come for any of them again."

"Fucking hell, Adelaide." Henry had had enough. Without waiting for Trumbull's decision, he headed for her, ready to toss her over his shoulder and carry her out of this church, and sort out his brother only after he'd tied Adelaide Frampton to a damn chair. "You absolute madwoman." He didn't look to Trumbull as he added, "Alfie, I will personally use every tool at my disposal to destroy you and your gang if you accept that offer. What I cannot do myself, I'll bring in the goddamned Royal Guard to finish."

"Adelaide. This is—Listen to him." Sesily Calhoun agreed with him, but Henry didn't have time to think on the opinions of her friends, each one likely preparing to do battle.

Henry reached Adelaide, pulling her into his arms, resisting the urge to shake some sense into her. "I will tear this place apart before I let you stay here, do you understand?"

She pulled away from him. "Dammit, Henry! This is the only way through! The only way to keep you all safe. Your brother. Helene. *You*."

"Keep me safe from what?"

"You want to be tied to me? To this place?" She waved a hand at it. "This will ruin you!"

"And what of *you*?"

"It's different for me. I was born here. I know it. I can't

bear having you here. Knowing what you will sacrifice for me."

"What sacrifice? You think your past is hidden from me? I've been here before, Adelaide. *With you!* I knocked out half a dozen of your father's men and chased you through the fucking place!"

"That's not the same! *I didn't love you then!*"

The shout reverberated through the chapel, and relief burst in his chest, mixing with fury.

"You love me?" he repeated.

"Yes!" There was nothing soft in the reply.

Good. He wasn't feeling soft, either. "Not enough."

Her eyes went wide and she fairly vibrated with anger. "What did you say?"

"You clearly don't love me enough if you're willing to toss it away."

"Toss it away?" Her words were loud. Furious. "Can't you see what I am trying to do? To give you?"

"I don't want it." He closed the distance between them. "Do you hear me, Adelaide Frampton, Addie Trumbull, Matchbreaker, fucking chaos—I don't want any of it if it ends with me loving you from afar. Me, wild with need for you, tearing Lambeth apart to get to you. To hold you. To keep you safe." He rubbed a hand over his chest at the ache that came with the memory of waking to discover her gone.

"I am not a damsel in distress!"

"But I am?!" Henry fairly roared the question. "Christ, Adelaide, you really do think yourself one of your pretty shield-maidens, left alone to choose who lives and dies on the battlefield. You don't get to choose this. You don't get to stand in front of me like a shield. I am here, and I have the means to fight all on my own. And dammit, I intend to save the fucking day!"

Silence fell, and behind him, someone said softly, "My goodness! Did you hear that?" Lady Sesily, perhaps.

"I like him. With that scruffy beard, I'd consider marrying him myself." Lady Imogen.

Henry didn't much care who liked him at the moment, as he was busy coming unhinged. "You think I'll leave you here? Marry me, or don't. Love me, or don't. Spend the rest of your life with me, or don't. But don't for one second think that I'm leaving you here. Alone."

"Argh!" Adelaide shouted, her frustration palpable. Good. Let her be furious. He was, as well. "That is the problem! You're too noble! You think love is enough. You can't see that this won't be a real marriage; it shall be a transaction. You think you can beat Alfie Trumbull at his own game. You think you want me. But you don't. You want to save your brother and his wife—and you should! That is good and decent, and you should want to do everything you can to save them. But trust me when I tell you that marrying me is not the way. Marrying me makes it all worse. It brings you here. To Lambeth. To the crime and the muck and to my *father*"—she spat the word—"who has never in his life been noble or good or decent."

"Oy!" Alfie interjected.

Adelaide continued, "He's a criminal. A thief. Just as—" Her voice cracked, and Henry reached for her, aching for her. Wanting to hold her. To make it right. She pulled away from him, denying him. Taking a step back and finishing. "Just as I am." She shook her head. "You once told me you'd never marry for love, because you were afraid of what your secrets would do to your wife."

"You freed me from that," he said. "I want to marry. I intend to marry. I intend to marry *you*, dammit."

She shook her head. "Your secret . . . It is the best of us. It is honor and hope and love. It is what we all aspire to. But mine . . ." Adelaide spread her arms wide. "You think you won't one day look up and see that marrying me is the worst of us? Greed and lies and crime. I shall ruin you, Henry. And I—"

She stopped herself.

"Say it." Her beautiful eyes found his, velvet and full of tears, and he knew what she was going to say. Knew, too, that it was all he wanted. "Say it, Adelaide."

"How will I survive the man I love . . . turning from me? How will I survive being the person who ruins you?" The words were a blow, threatening to knock him back.

"Ruin me? Christ, Adelaide, you *made* me. Again and again, in every way that matters. Without you, I'm nothing. A man who learned too late what his father tried so hard to teach him—that love is all there is. All that matters. What do I have to do to show you that marrying you would be a gift! That I have spent the last two weeks—even the time I was unconscious, I might add—imagining what it would be like to follow you into battle with these madwomen who love you just as much as I do?"

"They're not madwomen."

"Oh, don't worry about us, we don't take offense to that at all," Sesily said from a distance.

"To be fair, we are a bit mad," Imogen said.

"Speak for yourself." The Duchess.

"It's a good thing they love you, too," Henry doggedly continued, "because if they didn't, I'd be terrified of them, as they know everything and seem to be in all places at once, inescapably."

Adelaide gave a little laugh. "They're definitely not going to take offense to *that*."

Henry tilted her chin up, marveling in her impossibly soft skin, the high bones of her cheeks, the velvet of her eyes behind her spectacles. The little furrow in her brow, which he intended to spend the rest of his life smoothing. "Adelaide. You want me."

"Yes. Obviously."

He smiled at the terse reply. "You love me."

She shook her head. "I shouldn't have said it. It doesn't matter."

"Of course it matters, love. It's all that matters. You love me."

"Yes," she confessed. "But it's not enough."

"Love . . . It's enough." He pulled her close. "Of course it's enough. You, this wild world you live in, these wild women who come with you, all of it . . . it's so much more than I imagined. It's everything." He paused, pressing kisses to her knuckles until she let out a little sigh. "Now. You love me and I love you and we're in a perfectly nice church."

"There are so many explosives hidden beneath the pews of this place, we're one dropped match away from razing the South Bank," she retorted.

His brows rose. "Are there? Then let's get married quickly and leave it." He was bent toward her, his thumb stroking over the soft skin of her cheek, the scent of fresh rain surrounding them even here, in this ancient church. "Marry me. Not because your father wants it. Not because you made a bargain. Marry me because I love you. Because you love me. Because here, like this, we win."

She clasped his hand, pressing her cheek to his palm, and he would have given all he had in that moment to know what she was thinking. But she turned her unreadable gaze on her father and said, "I marry him, and you release Lord and Lady Carrington. Immediately."

Henry exhaled, harsh and hopeful. This was it. She was going to be his.

Alfie's smile went wide. "Of course!"

She narrowed her gaze on her father. "Immediately, Alfie."

"Absolutely." He turned to the guards near Jack and Helene. "Linus—go fetch the vicar." His will done, he turned back to them. "There's just one more thing."

Of course there was. "Go on."

"A small thing, really. Just enough to ensure that this"—he waved a hand between them—"new partnership don't go sideways the moment you leave the South

Bank." Henry waited, wondering what Alfie's final request would be. "I want what was in the box."

Adelaide stiffened next to Henry even as he said, "What box?"

"Nah, don't play the fool with me. I know too well that you've a head on your shoulders. Addie stole something from me that belongs to you. Something Havistock was willing to pay a pretty penny for. And I want it. You know, for insurance. In case you start thinkin' 'bout annulments."

Irritation flared at the suggestion that Henry wouldn't honor his marriage vows—vows he intended to honor every moment of every day for the rest of his life.

"No," Adelaide said to her father, the word clipped and cold. "That's not for you."

"In fact it is, as you stole it from me."

"You stole it from him first."

"And he who finds, keeps," Alfie said.

"I think you mean *she* who finds, keeps."

"It doesn't matter," Henry said, reaching into his pocket and extracting his father's long-ago letter, which he'd tucked into his pocket before coming to fight for this woman he loved. Just as his father had done. "Not anymore."

She reached out a hand to stop him. "Henry. No. That's not for him. It's not for anyone but you." Her brow furrowed in concern. "The memory of it. The reminder of it. It is yours."

It proved that love existed, he'd said to her about the letter and why he'd never destroyed it. *That it was good and worthy and true.*

Except he did not need it now. Now, his proof was Adelaide, and the way she had freed him from the fear he'd had of what was in that letter.

He lifted her hand in his and pressed a kiss to her knuckles. "You may have all that is mine, if only you wish it."

Tears welled in her beautiful eyes as she recognized his father's words to his mother. As she answered, softly, "All I wish is a future that we might together call ours."

"Yes," he said, leaning down and kissing her thoroughly, until Alfie grumbled and Jack and Helene clapped happily, and Sesily Calhoun gave out an enthusiastic hoot.

When he finished the kiss, Henry handed the letter to her father despite her sound of protest. Trumbull opened it, his gaze tracking slowly over the words, his expression unchanged when he refolded the parchment and tucked it into his coat pocket. "You toffs spend more time than any of the rest of us concerned with where you come from. Better to pay attention to where you're goin', eh?"

Before he could answer, the guard Alfie had sent to get the vicar returned with the man in tow. "Right!" Alfie clapped his hands, approaching Jack and Helene and the altar. "I'd like to note that this halfwit agreed to two dozen fights, and he still owes me. I expect to be paid. I'll consider it my dowry."

Adelaide cut him a look. "Dowries typically work in the opposite direction, Alfie."

Alfie's eyes went wide. "Wot? *I'm* to pay *him* to take you off me hands?"

"Well, it's not as though I've been *on* your hands for several years, but yes."

"Cor!" he said. "I ain't doin' that."

"Imagine my surprise," she said dryly, as those assembled joined them at the front of the church, creating a small half circle around the vicar.

"I do love a wedding," Sesily said.

Duchess sighed. "Another man added to the mix, I suppose. Such a great deal of work. So emotional."

"Best to have a husband on an island in the sea, is it?" Adelaide tossed over her shoulder at the Duchess.

"Best to have no husband at all," Duchess said. "But

needs must, and if you must have one, this duke appears to be not the worst of the options."

Henry inclined his head in the Duchess's direction. "High praise, Your Grace."

"Congratulations on your nuptials, Your Grace," came her reply.

Henry grabbed his bride's hand, turning her to him, putting his hands to her face and tilting her up to look at him. "I love you. My South London nipper. My North London darling."

Something fresh flashed in her eyes, something new and perfect. What he'd been aching for from the start. Something honest and clear and full of hope of a future. And she reached up to wrap a hand around his neck and pull him down for a kiss.

When it was through, she opened her eyes and smiled, spreading warmth through him until all he wanted was to get her married and get her home. To their bed.

Behind him, the door to the church opened, loud and ominous, and her gaze flickered past his shoulder, and everything changed.

"Is it too early for me to speak now, else forever hold my peace?"

The entire assembly turned to the back of the church, where Danny stood, looking as though he'd just won at the races. And by his side, pistol in hand, was the Marquess of Havistock.

Chapter Twenty-Four

The last time she'd been in this church, Adelaide had been wearing a too-small stolen frock, and she'd been without a weapon. This time, she was prepared, joined by the women who had stood by her side from the moment she'd left the South Bank.

And the man who had vowed to love her forever. To share a future with her.

Except now, just as she had Henry in her grasp, Danny and the Marquess of Havistock had arrived to ruin another one of her weddings.

Adelaide had had quite enough of that, and she was not alone. In the wake of Havistock's words, those assembled turned and shifted, each one reaching for the closest weapon. Hands slid into hidden skirt pockets, inside coats, and—in Adelaide's case—to the blade strapped to her thigh. She gripped the ivory handle of her blade and waited as her father palmed his club and stared Danny down.

Henry spoke first. "I should've taken your head when I had the chance, Danny."

"Double crossed by a damn traitor," Alfie added. "And after I treated you like a son."

Danny spread his arms wide and smiled at the assembly. "It ain't personal, Alfie. I got with the man most worth my time. Just like you did." He paused. "Except you made a mistake, because this story don't end with your precious girl gettin' married to a duke."

"That's quite enough, Daniel," the Marquess of Havistock said, obviously annoyed that Danny was receiving more attention than he was. "I shall handle it from here."

He raised his voice to be heard throughout the church. "It is true what they say, is it not? That if you want something done, you've got to do it yourself."

"Father!" The horror and disdain in Lady Helene's voice were undeniable.

"Oh, shut up, Helene. We wouldn't be here if not for you, you little bitch."

Her eyes went wide and Jack stepped in front of her, suddenly looking much older than his twenty-six years. "You don't speak to her that way!"

"I'll speak to her however I like, boy. And you'll do well to know your betters."

With Helene in Havistock's sights, Jack made a full change, voice lowering, fists clenching, and charming affect turning to full menace. "We are to think you better? You, who happily murders his business partner in full view of London?"

Havistock's gaze narrowed on his daughter behind Jack's outstretched arm.

She lifted her chin. "I heard everything. Heard Lord Draven was concerned about the state of the factories. The way you treated the children who worked there."

"Draven made hundreds of thousands of pounds off of those factories," Havistock scoffed. "And then he found that a fresh conscience doesn't keep you from an early grave. And to think, if you'd kept your mouth shut, you might have avoided one, too." He lifted the pistol and pointed it toward the newlyweds.

At the far side of the church, Imogen searched the hidden pockets of her evergreen skirts.

"Remarkable. It is not every day a man confesses to murder in front of a dozen people," Henry said in his coolest, most aristocratic voice. "Though I never found your logic sound during debate, so I should not be surprised."

Havistock's weapon swung to aim directly at Henry's chest, and Adelaide began searching the space for ways to end the man. How dare he threaten her nearly husband!

"Clayborn." The marquess's words dripped with disdain. "Always so high and mighty. Just like your father. Good and noble and aristocratic perfection." He spat. "But not really, are you? There isn't a drop of aristocratic blood in you. And you, pontificating on what is just and right in the House of Lords. What a hypocrite, now you've thrown your lot in with *women*," he spat. "You're an embarrassment, and you should thank God I'm going to end you all." He swung the pistol around wildly, pointing it in turn at Duchess and Sesily.

No. Not one person Adelaide loved was dying that day.

"It's a bold thing to threaten a roomful of people with only Danny for muscle, I'll say that," Adelaide said, injecting all the bravado she could muster into the tone.

Henry stiffened next to her as Havistock's pistol found her. "Perhaps I'll start with you. The one nobody cares about. No money, no name, no connections—no value. Return you to the muck you came from."

A low growl sounded, and Havistock looked to Henry. "Oh, Clayborn doesn't like that."

"Best aim true, my lord," Adelaide said, lifting her chin. "Because if you miss, I can assure you, you will learn just what it feels like to be in the muck. I shall enjoy regaling all London with the story of how the odious Marquess of Havistock was ended by a coalition of powerful women and a crime lord from the South Bank."

"You've made your money on the backs of the poor and the weak." Henry took a step forward, toward the gun. "The tide is turning, and look at you." His voice dripped with disdain. "Quaking with fear."

He was baiting Havistock. And if the man's wild-eyed look was any indication, the bait would work. The marquess was red with anger at her words, at the challenge in them. Adelaide knew she took a risk. He'd come unhinged, knowing, in that wild way that men against the ropes do, that there was no exit for him here. He could not kill them all. He could not survive this. But he would try very hard to take some of them with him.

Havistock narrowed his gaze on Henry. "I heard that you climbed down into the gutter with the girl. Tell me, how do you think the aristocracy would respond to discover that the Duchess of Trevescan's precious cousin is nothing more than a baseborn whelp from Lambeth?" He looked to The Duchess. "You think anyone would come to your parties once they discover your lies?"

Duchess did not hesitate. "I think that half of London only exists because of lies. One only need look at you, Havistock. The idea that birth makes us noble is the biggest lie of all."

Hatred seethed in him. "I shall enjoy putting bullets in all of you."

"Is that your idiot plan?" Helene spoke up, clearly having had enough of the man. "To kill everyone here?"

"I'll do what I have to do."

"Not without my muscle, you won't," Alfie said, nodding to a man standing by the door to the church. "You're on my turf now, Marquess, and I've thrown my lot in with another."

"Of course you have. It's no more than I would expect—an utter lack of honor," Havistock said. "But you see, I'm using my own muscle—you've a problem, Alfie. There's a new generation, ready to take over."

Danny grinned and pulled a wicked-looking knife from his waist. "Time for new leadership in The Bully Boys. Some that don't choose themselves over the job."

Alfie scoffed. "Nah, boy. If you're aimin' to be king, tell me you want my throne. But don't tell me it ain't because you like the look of my crown." He nodded in the direction of a guard at the door, who immediately left, no doubt to summon more muscle. "The boys won't stand with you if they don't trust you, and they'll never trust you if they think you're sellin' them lies. Then you're no better than the toff you've thrown your lot in with." He tilted his head. "Though sidin' with rich titles ain't the best way to earn the boys' trust, either."

Danny scowled at the words—delivered with the calm certainty of a man who'd lived a thousand lives and knew the score. Just as it looked as though the two would clash and the brawl would begin, Imogen found what she was looking for.

"Warm in here, isn't it?" she called from her spot.

The Belles, knowing what was to come, turned their backs to her. A bright flash of light accompanied a loud bang at the far side of the pews, leaving Havistock and Danny distracted for a barely there moment.

Long enough.

"Come!" Sesily grabbed Helene's hand and pulled her into the cloud of smoke that lingered, toward the back door to the church—the one Adelaide knew well would make for quick escape, as she'd used it herself, years earlier.

"After this, Lady Helene, we shall have to discuss your father," Sesily said.

"After this," Lady Helene said, unexpected steel in her tone as she followed Sesily from the church, "I shall very happily discuss my father."

Meanwhile, Jack ran straight for the marquess, pushing the weapon out of the way and bringing him to the ground. His pistol discharged as they fell, reverberating throughout the dark, now smoky church.

"Adelaide!" Henry turned to her instantly, the moment he heard the pistol's retort, pressing her firmly to his chest, shielding her from the violence. When silence fell, he loosened his grip, and they reached for each other, their concern matching. "Are you—"

"—hurt?"

Their hands raced over each other, searching for blood, for fresh wounds. "Christ . . ." Henry leaned down and kissed her, quick and hard. "Stay here."

And then he disappeared, back into the fray, where Alfie's half-dozen brutes had descended from outside, summoned by the explosion along with a handful of others—who presumably banked on Danny's triumph. Henry threw a punch and dodged a fist aimed for his broken rib.

Adelaide was filled with indignation that someone would think to harm him. Her duke. "I absolutely am not staying here!" she pronounced, palming her blade and following him.

"Dammit, Adelaide!" he shouted, knocking another one out with one punch. "There are weapons everywhere and your friend has exploded the church!"

"Not really *exploded*," Imogen called happily from a distance. "It's not *harmful*. It's just a little one that"—the smoke cleared and she brushed a thin layer of dust off her dress—"made quite a delightful mess!"

"I look forward to debating the particulars of your explosives at another time, my lady," Henry said, tossing a pew aside to get to another fight. "But at some point, these brutes are going to remember that, though this skirmish is between them, the war involves the Hell's Belles."

That much was clear, and Imogen nodded. "They're already going to be quite put out when they discover . . ."

Henry's attention snapped to her. "Discover what?"

Adelaide was distracted from the answer by movement in her periphery—Alfie, using the melee to make his way toward the door. She met his eyes, as brown as hers, but far less honest, and said, "Plan for the fight, prepare for the flight, is it, Da?"

He didn't even look chagrined. "Not worth dyin' for. That boy won't stop till he marries you, so I get what I want, either way."

Two bruisers barreled into Adelaide from behind, pushing her into Alfie's chest. Grabbing onto his coat, she righted herself. "Not if your bruisers take him out."

"Bah." He waved a hand. "They're on your side tonight."

Her brows rose. "Bully Boys, fighting for my girls?"

"I said *tonight*, Adelaide. Call it a weddin' gift."

A shout came from over her shoulder, and she turned to see Henry knock one of Danny's men back. When she looked back . . . her father was gone. Of course.

"Imogen!" They all turned toward Duchess's sharp summons, to discover her crouched over Havistock, aiding Jack in binding the murdering marquess, who continued to bluster. Duchess looked down at her captive and said, "Any chance you brought some of that lovely concoction you use to stop men from talking?"

"Oh, I don't leave the house without it!" Imogen pronounced, and off she went to render the odious man unconscious.

Henry raised a brow in Adelaide's direction. "Should I worry?"

"Only if you ever cross us," she replied happily as he gave a little nod and returned to his fight.

"Why would I cross you?" he asked. "I'm part of the crew now, aren't I?"

In that moment, as chaos reigned around her, and Henry's words settled, lovely and honest, Adelaide realized that, brawl or no, she was really very happy with the way things were going. Lady Helene was safe, Lord Havistock was about to be quite captured, and somehow, impossibly, the Duke of Clayborn was by her side. A partner.

And perhaps she could be a South Bank cutpurse and a duchess, all in one.

Family was what you made it, she'd told Henry when he'd revealed the truth about his father. He'd chosen love, so why shouldn't she? Why shouldn't she claim it as hers and hang the consequences?

She'd found it, after all. Perhaps it would not be terrible to keep it.

Odd to find peace like this in the midst of a melee, but somehow it seemed appropriate to a girl raised a princess among thieves.

"Could do with another tie here!" Imogen said, and Adelaide started for her friends, already working to pull a ribbon from her skirts. She looked down, losing the room for a split second, no longer noticing the crowd or the location of everyone within it.

A split second was all it took.

A heavy arm banded across her stomach, pulling her tight to a tall, foul-smelling body.

Danny.

"Not so fast," he said. "You should have stayed gone."

"Adelaide!" Henry's shout came from across the room, and he was approaching, a newfound pistol in hand. "Let her go, Danny."

"Nah," Danny said, "I don't think I will. Do you know how long I had to listen to Alfie whinge about how he'd lost his best thief? His best cutpurse? How Addie was the only one who could pick a lock fast and clean? Do you know how many times some starry-eyed girl asks me if I knew Addie Trumbull?" His breath was hot and acrid in her ear, the blade of his knife at her throat. "I'm going to enjoy making sure that this time you're gone for good."

Henry was approaching, eyes glittering with anger, and Danny didn't care for it, pulling her tighter to him. "Lay down your weapon, Duke."

The blade tightened, biting into her skin, and Adelaide squeezed her eyes shut, bearing the sting. When she opened them, Henry was crouching several feet in front of them, his blue eyes on hers, lowering the firearm to the ground. "Lady Imogen?"

"Yes, Your Grace?" Ever casual under pressure.

"It is warm in here, don't you think?"

Adelaide's breath caught in her chest.

A wide grin passed over Imogen's face. "Terribly so."

Adelaide turned her head, as Imogen punctuated the words with another brilliant flash and a smoky bang. Unable to see, Danny loosened his grip, and Adelaide pulled free, moving out of the way before—

A gunshot rang out.

"He shot me!" Danny cried from the floor as the smoke cleared, revealing Henry, pistol in hand. "The bastard shot me!"

"It's about time, if you ask me," Duchess said, as though she were at a croquet match and not a church brawl.

Henry caught Adelaide in his arms, a hand coming to her cheek. "Are you hurt?"

"No." She shook her head. "Not now that I am with you."

He kissed her, quick and firm. "I don't believe you." Worry furrowed his brow as his fingers traced down her neck to the spot where Danny's blade had been tight to her skin. He scowled at whatever he saw there, a muscle ticking in his cheek as he made to set her aside. To go after him. To finish the job.

Adelaide reached for him, holding him back. "No."

Henry didn't like that—of course he didn't, her warrior, pledging his sword. Instead, he looked to Danny, who writhed on the ground, hand to his thigh. "Give me a reason to let him live."

"Because the South Bank don't like traitors, do it, Danno?" And then she pulled a long ribbon from her skirts, and offered it to Henry. "Instead, I suggest we leave my father a gift."

Danny was the last of the fights, and while Henry dealt with him, Adelaide considered the chaos they'd left in the chapel that day, pews upended, a candelabrum on its side, smoke still dissipating from Imogen's explosion, a dozen men either knocked out cold or headed for a night wishing they had been.

In the midst of it all, Duchess and Imogen were assuring the vicar that not only would they pay for the damage to the alcoves and pews, they would make a generous donation to repairing the stained-glass window that had been cracked for as long as Adelaide could remember.

The vicar assuaged by this, and the promise that he could use the Duke of Trevescan's finest carriage to visit his sister in the country that very day, Duchess turned to the rest of the group from her place at the end of the aisle, by the door, and said, "Considering Imogen has caused two rather loud noises, I think we ought to do our best to escape notice while we still can?"

"I beg your pardon," Imogen pointed out. "Those loud noises saved the day."

"So they did," Henry said, softly, tucking Adelaide beneath his arm and pressing a kiss to her temple as they made their way up the aisle. "I'm very grateful to you for that, Lady Imogen. Would you allow me to purchase you a gift of some kind?"

Imogen stepped over a fallen pew into the aisle herself. "I enjoy chemicals."

His brows shot up and Adelaide laughed, feeling light, her heart full of joy.

Henry stopped at the sound, turning toward her and kissing her until she sighed and gave herself up to him. When the kiss broke, he pressed his forehead to hers and said, low and perfect, "I'm going to marry you, Adelaide Frampton. And I'm going to spend the rest of my life loving you."

She closed her eyes and whispered, "Tell me that last bit again."

Another soft kiss to her lips. "The bit where I love you for the rest of our lives?"

She nodded, tears glistening. His breath caught. Would he ever grow used to those beautiful eyes? He'd have a lifetime to try.

"I love you, Adelaide Trumbull." He kissed her, quick and sweet. "Frampton." Another kiss. "Carrington." A final one. "Duchess of Clayborn."

She shook her head and gave him a small smile, her heart impossibly full. "Not those yet."

It wasn't true. She bore the names already in his heart. In hers, as well.

Henry took Adelaide's hand, leading her from the church to find Imogen and Duchess piled into the carriage Sesily had summoned for them. Henry had other plans—a walk through the labyrinthine streets of Lambeth, slower than usual, for all the long lingering kisses he delivered as they made their way past the docklands and over Westminster Bridge, to the fourth turret from the Westminster side.

"It's not the morning," he said, softly. "But I hope it will do."

The moon had risen and the river gleamed silver—a different kind of beauty to be wrapped in.

"Tell me again what you would wish for," he said, pulling her close.

"You," she said, lifting her face to his. "I wished for you." He captured her face in his big, warm hands and tilted her up to stare into her eyes. "I wished for you, strong and noble and kind and standing by my side. Protecting me. Loving me."

He nodded, serious and stern in the moonlight. "What else?"

She shook her head. "Nothing else. He would have loved me. That's all I wanted then."

"And now? Now what do you want, Adelaide?"

"Now . . ." She met his eyes, so blue. So honest. And gave him honesty in return. "Now, I just want you. However you come." She shook her head. "But it seems impossible. That you might love me like this. Even knowing all my secrets. My past. What happens when the wide world knows you've married a thief from Lambeth? What would you get done then? What laws would you pass then?"

He shook his head with a little smile. "Hang the wide world. If they won't let me pass the laws, I'll fight alongside you to change the world another way. You glorious, brilliant, strong woman—I will spend the rest of my life trying to be worthy of standing at your side."

A single tear spilled down her cheek at the words, at the feeling of finally, finally believing him. She lifted herself up to his lips, kissing him thoroughly, and whispered her love.

Catching her close, he spoke, the words rough in her ear. "You nearly destroyed me when you left me. No more leaving me."

"No more leaving you. I promise."

He nodded and slipped a hand into his pocket, extracting a small box—and Adelaide sucked in a breath when she recognized it, beautiful filigreed oak. The ring inside gleamed in the moonlight when he removed it and took her hand in his.

"Marry me?"

"Yes," she whispered.

He slipped the ring onto her finger. "When?"

She smiled. "Now. Forever."

"Now," he repeated. "Forever." Another kiss. And then, "You once said my mother was my father's sun." He paused. "I think you were right. Until you—I did not know what light was."

It didn't seem possible that this was her man. That they would marry and live and love and have a houseful of children and animals. That they would argue and laugh and love . . . and make a future together.

Full hearts.

"Take me home, Adelaide Frampton."

She shook her head. "My apartments—they're not for dukes."

"As they belong to a future duchess, I must disagree."

She winced at the words. "I shall be a terrible duchess."

"I don't think so. I think you shall be the kind of duchess who uses her power to hold a mirror to the world. I think you shall be the kind of duchess who changes what duchesses might be."

She looked down the bridge. "I would like that."

He pressed a kiss to her temple. "I *shall* like that."

Her eyes found his. "I like you."

The kiss he gave her was rich and dark and sinful. Like a stolen treasure. And when it ended, and he pressed his forehead to her and whispered her name, Adelaide could barely catch her breath.

When she finally did, it was to say, "About my apartments . . . you should know . . . I've only one bed."

"Excellent. I'm considering throwing out all the extra beds in my house, too." She laughed as he pulled her closer, a wicked gleam in his eye. "Chairs, as well, as we've demonstrated we only need one of those." He pressed a kiss on her jaw, right below her ear, sending a shiver through her as he whispered, "And the carriage. There's only one of those, now that you wrecked the other with your distracting beauty."

She laughed, wrapping her arms around his neck as he promised her the world—whatever she wished. As long as she married him. As soon as possible.

And as she was no fool, she happily agreed.

Chapter Twenty-Five

Detective Inspector Thomas Peck was having a bad day. It would not even be considered a full day at that point, but Tommy had experienced more than his fair share of bad days and knew, without question, when a morning began with a constable knocking at his rooms in Holborn, waking his landlady and setting her off on her favorite sermon—*Why Decent People Do Not Call Before Breakfast*—he was in for a bad day.

It was confirmed when he walked into St. Stephen's Chapel in Lambeth, where there had been multiple reports of a battle the night before. The only evidence of such a thing a few overturned pews, two of which revealed empty bunkers beneath, as though someone had cleared out storage below while in a hurry.

The vicar assigned to the chapel was visiting his sister in Nottinghamshire, apparently, so Tommy had been left to inspect the place alone, only to find what looked to be a third hatch in the floor beneath a front pew, which had been left askew.

He'd just leaned down to open it when someone called through the church, "Detective Inspector! Hello!"

He knew before he turned what he would find: Lady Imogen Loveless—daughter to some earl, sister to far too many lords, and friend to several of the most powerful women in the aristocracy. Barely five feet tall, plump, pretty, and absolute pandemonium.

He bit his tongue. Not this woman. Not today. He shook his head and pointed to the door, indicating she should leave.

"No. Out."

Thoroughly ignoring him, she continued her approach, casting a curious look at the door in the floor at his feet. "Now that is a nice, well-hidden hole. Did you make it?"

He gritted his teeth. "I did not."

"Ah. What is in it?"

"Nothing."

"Can you be sure if you haven't opened it?"

"Lady Imogen, isn't there someone else you could call upon this morning?"

A beat, and then, "In fact there is not."

He'd feared as much. "And I suppose it is too much to wonder how it is you knew precisely where to call upon me?"

"Not too much at all, as a matter of fact," she retorted. "I usually know where you are."

He did not like that. "And why is that?"

"Why, so I might call upon you in a pinch, clearly." She set her carpetbag on a nearby untouched pew and unzipped it. "Would you like to know what I did last week?"

Absolutely not. "What did you do last week?"

"I invented a new kind of explosive."

What on earth was this woman on about? And why was he unable to ignore her when she was around? "It occurs to me, Lady Imogen, that such a pronouncement might be taken as a confession."

"Oh, don't worry. I haven't done anything with it yet."

He waited for a moment, then, "Yet."

"Well, unless you count covering my laboratory with unexpected shiny projectiles."

He blinked and tilted his head. "Unexpected projectiles."

"No, the projectiles were expected. Obviously, what with it being an explosive," she said, waving one hand, gloved in intricate white lace. "It was unexpected that they were so shiny. I knew they would be very small, but this—it was a lovely surprise. Exceedingly difficult to clean up, but beautiful, really. More irritating than dangerous."

"I cannot imagine what it must be like to encounter such a thing."

She smiled at him, and he absolutely refused to be dazzled. "I'm very flattered that you would think so."

"I—" He was about to tell her he hadn't meant to call her beautiful. Except she was beautiful. In the wild, terrifying way unpredictable storms and lionesses on the hunt were beautiful.

Before he could find the words, she said, "However, you are incorrect. I am *far* more dangerous than I am irritating," she said happily, supremely out of place here, in Lambeth, on Bully Boys turf.

Why did this woman regularly make him feel as though he'd taken a blow to the head? She was close now, near enough that if he reached for her, he might touch her. Not that he would ever touch her. She might have doused her clothing in poison during some mad experiment. "Lady Imogen . . . what are you doing here?"

She stopped and looked up at him, her pretty round face framed in a halo of black curls. "I've brought you a gift!"

"No." The last time he'd received a gift from this woman, he'd been standing in the rubble of his jail.

"Really, Detective Inspector," she chided him. "If I didn't know better, I would think you were being deliberately rude. I should think you would like my gifts by now. Last time, I made you one of London's most eligible bachelors! Is that not what they called you in the *News*?"

"I wouldn't know," he lied.

"I'm certain it is," she said. "I read that the unmarried

women of Mayfair dearly love summoning Scotland Yard to their homes in the hopes a certain detective inspector might wander in. It's a game of some sort. It has a name."

He looked to the ceiling. *Don't say it.*

"A Peek of Peck!"

He clenched his teeth. "I don't pay attention to the papers."

"Really," she asked, a dangerous gleam in her eye. "That *is* a surprise, considering how you've been quoted in more than a few interviews about . . ." She paused, no doubt for mad effect. "What is it you're calling those ladies? The Hell's Belles?"

Tommy would wager a year's salary that this wild woman was one of *those ladies*. "I have given no such interview, Lady Imogen. In fact, I think the name is ridiculous."

"Oh, I don't," she said. "It's rather perfect. Makes me wish I had a fiery sword."

"Lucky for you, it's difficult to set steel aflame."

"Well, with that attitude, it most certainly is." Before he could beg the woman not to set fire to the South Bank, she dug into the nonsense carpetbag that she carried everywhere she went, as though she might have to make camp for the night at any moment.

He watched her bend over and rummage through the thing because she might at any point destroy something. Not because he enjoyed watching her ample bottom beneath her skirts. Certainly not because he wondered what that ample bottom would look like without skirts.

The woman was bedlam; he was not interested in her bottom.

When she straightened and turned to face him, brandishing a small wrapped parcel, it was not disappointment that coursed through him. At all.

"Never fear, despite your ungratefulness, I shall still give you your gift."

He didn't mean to take it, but he seemed unable *not* to accept it, small and round and warm through the paper wrapped around it. "What is this?"

"A bacon sandwich," she said simply. As though it were a perfectly ordinary thing to deliver to a policeman in the middle of a church.

Flummoxed, he said, "You came all the way to Lambeth to bring me a bacon sandwich."

She smiled, and there it was again, that feeling that he'd taken a facer. "I understand you were summoned here before you were able to eat breakfast. One should never catch villains on an empty stomach."

"How did you—" he started, then stopped. "Lady Imogen, you should not be here. It is not a place for decent people."

"Really, Detective Inspector. It is a house of worship." She returned to rummaging about in her bag.

"I'm fairly certain that it is a house of worship that was recently stocked to the gills with munitions." He cast a glance at the unopened hatch in the floor. Possibly still stocked with them. She had to leave.

She turned a bright smile on him. "Aren't you clever. But someone has taken good care to solve that problem for you, haven't they?"

"I would rather know where they have been moved."

"Oh, I wouldn't worry," she said. "I'm sure they shall be put to good use."

He narrowed his gaze on her as a wild, impossible thought occurred. "Lady Imogen?"

"Yes?"

"It was not you who removed the weapons, was it?"

"Oh, goodness no," she said, with a look of wide-eyed innocence. "Can you imagine *me* carrying crates of explosives about the city? I would most certainly ruin my dress."

He shouldn't have looked to the dress in question, fine velvet the color of an evergreen forest. Her cloak was open, revealing the line of her bodice, tight enough to reveal her ample breasts, which he most *definitely* should not have looked at. "Of course."

"I have people for things like that."

What?

"Very large, strapping men," she added, and Tommy found he didn't like the image those words evoked. Before he could reply, she brandished a blue folder marked with an indigo bell high above her head. "Aha! Would you like your proper gift?"

He knew that folder. He'd seen one before, left in the rubble when someone had exploded one of the cells in the jail beneath Scotland Yard. Unsurprisingly, this woman had been in the building immediately before it happened.

She held it to her chest and he forced himself to keep his focus on her eyes.

And that's when he heard it. A sound, muffled and urgent. And human.

Lady Imogen Loveless heard it too, turning wide eyes on the closed hatch at his feet. "Detective Inspector, do you think you ought to open that thing?"

He pointed to the far end of the church. "Go stand back there."

She followed his indication. "Whatever for?"

This woman would be the absolute end of him. "In case."

"In case of what?" she asked, but still backed away, up the aisle of the church. "This is very thoughtful of you, but I'm perfectly capable of defending myself, should it be required."

No doubt the woman had a garrote at hand. Turning his back on her, he crouched, extracting a knife from his boot. "Oh, excellent idea, that," she said encouragingly.

"Thank you," he replied like a proper idiot before opening the hatch in one smooth movement.

There, in the hole, tied and gagged with colorful silk ribbons, was—

"My goodness. Is that the Marquess of Havistock?" She was back, standing at his shoulder—or more like his elbow—peering down into the stores. "What a surprise."

"It's strange, Lady Imogen, as you don't sound at all surprised." In fact, the ribbon binding the marquess's hands was the exact color of Lady Imogen's gown.

"Yes, well, I'll be honest, I've always thought the man *belonged* in a hole. But didn't you say this store was for munitions? He doesn't look like a munition." She paused. "Is it possible to have one munition? In the singular?"

Tommy looked to her. "What?"

"Anyway. I recommend reading the file before you free him." She patted him on the arm. "And as for the missing munitions, never fear. They will most likely turn up sooner or later, one way or another."

"Mmm," Tommy said, opening the file to discover a signed witness statement of one Lady Helene Carrington, née Granwell, only daughter of the Marquess of Havistock. Apparently the marquess was not only wrapped up in whatever went on here the night prior, but he'd also murdered Earl Draven, and his daughter had witnessed the crime. The lady had left her direction for further questions. Beneath the witness statement, a collection of additional data—questionable treatment of employees at the man's factories, strange ledgers, missing children and more.

He closed the file and ran his fingers over the blue bell. Another file full of evidence, another aristocratic felon left for his discovery.

The Belles again.

And only then, in the midst of his surprise, did Lady Imogen's words echo through him.

The munitions will be put to good use.

He looked up. "What did you say?"

She was gone, the file in his hand the only evidence that she'd been there at all.

He looked back to the aristocrat bound at his feet and cursed, the foul language punctuated by the door to the church, a heavy echo that drew his attention to the young constable who entered, wide-eyed and breathless, pulling up short as soon as he saw Tommy. "Detective Inspector, sir."

Tommy waved at him. "Come."

He did, already fishing a missive out of his pocket.

Opening it, the detective inspector scanned the text there.

Early morning explosions reported at all five Havistock factories. No casualties or witnesses. Return to Whitehall for debrief.

And like that, Thomas Peck's day went from bad to worse.

Epilogue

The Duke of Clayborn woke to the morning sun, next to the woman he loved, just as he had every morning since they'd stood together in Lambeth and fought shoulder to shoulder for their future. As the light streamed through their bedchamber window, casting the room in a golden glow, the world beyond still heavy with the quiet of dawn, he lingered over her, just as he had countless times in the past year. Just as he would countless times for the rest of his life.

Taking a deep breath, he rubbed a hand over the familiar ache in his chest—part relief that he had found her, part joy that she was his, part disbelief that he had been so blessed as to call this magnificent woman his own.

Unable to resist her a moment longer, he leaned down and pressed a kiss to her cheek, warm and soft and pink with sleep. When she sighed, he could not help the little rumble of pleasure in his chest as he kissed her again, at the line of her jaw, beneath her ear, at the place where her neck met her shoulder, soft and sweet and smelling of thyme and fresh rain. His hand stroked down her side, finding the round swell of her belly, full with the child she would soon bear.

With a lazy stretch and a self-satisfied smile, she turned into his embrace, winding her arms around his neck and pressing herself to him, long and warm and perfectly soft, before saying, eyes still closed, "Happy anniversary, husband."

He thieved the words from her lips. "And to you, wife."

While Alfie Trumbull's plans had gone sideways and he had not overseen the wedding of his daughter to a duke on that night at St. Stephen's, Henry and Adelaide had found their way back to Lambeth the following day, where the Duke of Clayborn had used every inch of his power to secure a meeting with the Archbishop himself . . . and they'd been married by special license in the chapel at Lambeth Palace. Jack and Helene had been in attendance, along with Adelaide's crew—the Duchess of Trevescan, Lady Imogen Loveless, Lady Sesily and Mr. Calhoun, and Maggie O'Tiernan, who'd opened The Place immediately following for a raucous wedding celebration. The morning had turned into an afternoon and an evening filled to the brim with celebration and well-wishes and so much dancing.

And no one in Mayfair would have believed that the Duke of Clayborn, known for his cool control, a man who showed passion only on the floor of the House of Lords, spent the evening with his wife in his arms, holding her scandalously close as they reveled in each other and the promise of their future.

That night, exhausted and happy, they'd tumbled up the stairs to Adelaide's apartments—to her single bed in her rooms, full of books and devoid of most everything else—and made slow, lingering love to mark the beginning of the rest of their lives.

Since then, the two divided their time between Covent Garden, where the rooms they let above The Place were filled with lush fabrics and lusher memories and the laughter of friends and family, and their home in the country, where they spent their days exploring the estate, far from the prying eyes of the aristocracy, and their nights abed, exploring each other.

And Henry could not believe his luck—this beautiful,

brilliant, magnificent woman . . . his. Forever. With another kiss, he whispered, "I am sorry. I did not mean to wake you."

Adelaide arched up to him. "I am not sorry you woke me." Tangling her fingers in his hair, she met his gaze and said, "What were you doing?"

"I was . . ." He paused, running a fingertip down her cheek. Down her neck. Down her chest to where a fiery red curl circled the tip of one breast. "Noticing you."

She smiled. "You always notice me."

"I do," he agreed, softly, sinking into her velvet gaze. "When you laugh with your friends, in your carriage like a charioteer, as we do battle together . . ." Because they did do battle together. When they wrote his speeches and stood her ground, though for the moment they were doing slightly more of the first and less of the latter, until the babe came. "And today . . . as you slept, wrapped in the beauty of the morning. My wife."

She pulled him close, hesitating just before she kissed him. "My husband."

Rolling her over, rising up from the caress, Henry stared down at her, so full of her . . . of his love for her, that he could barely make sense of it—this feeling that he had never expected. This partnership he'd never dreamed of.

"How lucky I am," he said softly. "To love you so well."

"How lucky *I* am," she replied, her hand coming to his cheek. "To be loved so well."

Another kiss, long and lingering. She broke it this time, sliding from the bed to the sound of his protest as she pulled on her pristine, white silk dressing gown and crossed the room.

"It's early, my love. Come back," he called, even as he leaned back against the pillows and watched her, the light casting golden stripes across her lovely, long body. Teasing him with what was hidden beneath the garment.

Ignoring him, she opened a drawer and retrieved a box

from within, turning to bring it to the bed. "Do you not want your gift?"

His eyes lit with delight. "A gift?"

She laughed. "You look like a boy, desperate for a new toy."

"You are the only toy I require," he retorted, reaching for her as she neared, pulling her down over his lap and reveling in her little shout before adding, "but I would not like to be considered rude."

When she set the mahogany box on the bed next to him, he stilled. It was flat—perhaps ten inches long and only two deep, decorated in beautiful filigree. Two letters, gilded among a stunning amount of woodwork: A and H.

"Adelaide and Henry," he said, running his fingers over the design before realizing what he held. He met her eyes with another smile. "It's a puzzle."

She nodded. "Not nearly as complicated as the one that brought us together, but I thought you would—"

He was already working at it, finding buttons and levers and false bottoms and magnets, and within ten minutes he'd slid a hidden drawer from within to discover a familiar blue file, marked in indigo ink with an intricately detailed bell. And there, across the bottom, a clear label that read: *Clayborn, Duke of.*

His brows rose in recognition. It was a dossier from the Hell's Belles, one that might have been collected and prepared by the Matchbreaker herself. He slid Adelaide a sly look. "How long have you had this?"

She met his gaze briefly before returning her attention to the folder in his hands. Were her ears turning red?

"Adelaide?"

She spoke to the dossier in his hands. "I compiled it as I returned to . . . my father. I intended to give it to you that night. To have it delivered to your home, once I had dealt with him. With everything."

"Once *we* dealt with everything, you mean." After that

night, Havistock had been tried and convicted of murdering a peer, Danny had been delivered to a surgeon and then to the docks, where he was given the choice to stay in Lambeth and battle Alfie or head to Australia and try a new life. And Alfie—he remained the head of The Bully Boys—a thorn in the side of Adelaide and Henry, but easier to manage now that he was looking for respectability . . . and heirs.

"Once we dealt with everything," she allowed. "But it never seemed the right time to reveal . . . what is inside."

He watched her with a curious gaze. "And today is?"

She smiled. "It is. It feels . . . appropriate."

"Fair enough." With no hesitation, he opened the file, discovering two pieces of paper within. The first he recognized instantly, a small gasp catching in his throat as he lifted his father's letter to his mother from within, running his fingers over the years-old writing. "How did you—" he started, then stopped. "Alfie Trumbull had this. I gave it to him that night."

She smiled, a cat with a bowl of cream. "And I picked his pocket."

His brow furrowed. "When?"

"Not ten minutes after he put it there for safe keeping."

He laughed at that, big and delighted. "I imagine he didn't like that."

"I imagine he didn't," she said. "But he did not raise a cutpurse queen for nothing."

He opened the letter, reading it . . . remembering it. Reminding himself that he'd lived up to his father's expectations for him. That Jack had, too—happily married to Lady Helene, and already a father.

Adelaide reached for him, setting her fingers on his arm as he stared down at the paper.

"Happy anniversary, my love," she whispered. "Here is to the future that we might together call ours."

"Yes," he said, looking up at her. "Together."

"Together," she whispered, before nodding at the

folder. "You've another thing to find." He followed her instructions, lifting the second slip of paper from within. "That one is yours to keep."

Henry looked down and read the text, his heart pounding wildly in his chest:

The Duke of Clayborn makes a perfect match.
Signed, The Matchbreaker

Henry looked up, pleasure flooding him even as year-old frustration thrummed through him. He found her watching him, searching his gaze. In hers, he found a collection of emotions. "You intended to give me this . . . and leave?"

She nodded. "I thought you might decide to seek out love if you knew how . . . perfect you were."

"Adelaide." He pulled her close, pressing his forehead to hers. "Don't you see, I never would have sought love beyond you. There was no one else. There never would be. Love . . . I am not perfect. I am only perfect *with you*." He kissed her again. "Christ, I love you . . . beyond reason." He shook his head. "No, that's not true. There are a dozen reasons. A hundred of them."

She smiled, pure happiness. "Are there?"

"Shall I enumerate them?" He returned his attention to her neck, pressing kisses down her throat as he pulled her into his lap and began his list . . . a list that could have gone on for another year . . . another fifty. "Your brilliant mind . . . your quick wit . . . the way you pick a lock, drive a carriage, wield a dossier . . . The way you terrify the men of Mayfair and make the girls of Lambeth proud . . . Your beautiful eyes . . . your stunning hair . . ."

"Mmm," she said, her arms twining around his neck. "All excellent reasons."

"You're mine, Adelaide Frampton," he whispered at her ear, low and dark like a gift. "As someone once said to me, he who finds, keeps."

"Mmm," she said, threading her fingers through his soft, lovely hair. "But *I* found *you*, if you'll remember."

He kissed the smile from her lips until she sighed her pleasure and said, "Alright then. You found me . . . but *I'm* keeping you . . ."

Any argument she might have had was lost in another kiss. And another. And another . . .

Acknowledgments

Two years into a global pandemic, it's not too much to say that romance novels have kept me going. It's no surprise to anyone who knows me outside of my books that the lion's share of my joy comes from this genre I adore. Reading romance gives me a daily reminder that the world runs on hope, and writing romance—especially the Hell's Belles—over the last two years, has given me a constant, hopeful escape to a world where beautiful, brilliant, deeply extra people are able to live beautiful, brilliant, deeply extra lives.

But the wild thing is this: in all the years I've been writing historicals, I've never once had an idea that I could not find at least a glimmer of evidence for in history, and the Hell's Belles are no different. Several years ago, I discovered The Forty Elephants, an all-woman crime ring and the largest shoplifting ring the United Kingdom would ever see. The Forties were born into a world that taught them early to steal to survive—and those who rose through their ranks not only survived, but *thrived* for nearly a century.

Without the wild, wonderful stories of The Forty Elephants, I would never have imagined the Hell's Belles, with their far-reaching network of scouts and spies and partners who know their way around highwaymen (and women), church brawls, and pickpockets. The Bully Boys are inspired by the men's half of The Forty Elephants—

the Elephant and Castle gang—which predated the Forties but didn't come with furs and fashion and a queen of their own. For more on both gangs, do not miss Brian McDonald's *Alice Diamond and the Forty* and *Gangs of London*.

Adelaide herself was inspired by the gorgeous collection of Horace Warner's photographs of Spitalfields Nippers, collected and published by Spitalfields Life Books. The puzzle box Henry's father designed was inspired by the beautiful boxes crafted by Craig Thibodeau, to whom I am so grateful for hours of videos and explanations.

As always, I owe a tremendous debt to the Museum of London, the British Library, and the New York Public library for endless rabbit holes of research . . . even during a global pandemic. Hug your closest research librarian.

2021 made me more and more grateful for dear friends, whom I would happily fight alongside any time they need it. First, thank you to Kate Clayborn and Megan Frampton for generous use of their names—you are the best of the absolute best, and I hope I did you proud. This book would not exist without Louisa Edwards, Sophie Jordan, Jen Prokop, Adriana Herrera, Joanna Shupe, Christina Lauren, Meghan Tierney, and Erin Leafe—each one of whom believed in it before I did. Special thanks to Kennedy Ryan, who dragged me over the finish line . . . *again*.

Thank you to the amazing team at Avon Books, which continues to make books happen despite paper shortages and printing delays and pandemics. Thank you to Carrie Feron, Asanté Simons, Brittani DiMare, Brittani Hilles, DJ DeSmyter, Jennifer Hart, Eleanor Mickuki, Jeanne Reina, Liate Stehlik, Bridget Kearney, Christine Edwards, Carla Parker, Andy LeCount, Kristine Macrides, Fritz Servatius, Rachel Levenberg, Stefanie Lindner, and Jessica Montany.

Rounding out this truly excellent gang are Holly Root,

Kristin Dwyer, Alice Lawson, and Linda Watson—I'm so grateful for each of you.

Thank you to my loves, V and Kahlo, who are sweet and funny and never fail to cheer me on when I need it, and Eric, who always tolerates my chaos and sometimes finds it charming. To my sister, Chiara, who is on my couch right now, as I write this, the most patient of houseguests—you can finally read it!

And this is all before I get to you, Dear Reader! The books are just words until you read them . . . thank you for bringing Adelaide and Clayborn to life. I can't wait for you to see Imogen and Tommy burn up the pages next year!